I Knew I Loved You

Desiree DuBois

Author's Note

Hello lovely reader!

Thank you so much for continuing to follow my spicy Why Choose Romance duology. By this point, I hope you love these three as much as I do. A few content warnings: exhibitionism, DPiV, past child abuse mentioned, child protective services (no children taken from their parents), knife play, CNC, and a lot of alcohol use. Other than that, I hope you enjoy reading a lot of sex, because there's a lot of it!

One last thing: I'm Canadian! I chose to use American spellings for the most part, but I kept the Canadian spelling of pyjama. I hope you don't mind my eccentricities.

Love you all! Mwah!

Desiree DuBois

Part One:

The Letter

Chapter One

Tony

There was only one letter in their mailbox, and Tony's heart rate sped up when he saw the return address; it was from San Francisco Child Protective Services. He'd been waiting semi-patiently for news about the work exchange program for months, and now the excitement turned to nervousness.

Tony fumbled with his keys as he unlocked the door. He kicked his shoes off onto the little mat just inside, and hung his coat on his usual hook before taking the stairs two at a time up to the main level of the home he shared with his two best friends, trying not to panic.

A thin letter could be good news, right? If it was good news, there were other considerations. *It's only for a month. Adam and Sophia said I could stay with them. I'll get more time with little Cody and baby Travis. But I'll be away from Amanda and James...* There it was. The big one: *And they don't even know I applied for this.*

Tony winced as he thought about the last time he and James had butted heads over his lack of communication. They hadn't spoken for two days and James had slept in the spare room instead of in their room with him and Amanda. *Why can't he see that I'm trying?* Tony grumbled to himself, weaving through the dining room and kitchen on his way to the living room. *I didn't want them to worry until I knew for sure one way or the other.*

He dropped his backpack before sinking into the couch with his letter. With shaking hands, he slit it open and began to read.

> *Dear Mr. Anthony Carlson,*
> *We are pleased to invite you to our exchange program...*

Tony heaved a sigh of relief, then checked the start date. "Three days! They don't give much time!" He fished his phone out of his pocket and tapped on the icon with his brother's face.

"Hey, man," Tony said when Adam answered the call.

"Hey! What's up?" Adam's relaxed tone instantly calmed Tony down.

"I got into the exchange program."

Adam chuckled. "Which one?"

"The one in San Francisco. With CPS."

"Oh yeah?" Tony could hear the surprise in his brother's voice.

"So... Is that offer from you and Sophia still good? To stay with you for a month?" Tony crossed his fingers.

"On one condition."

"What's that?"

"Sophia and I want you to babysit at least once a week so that we can go on dates."

Tony laughed. "Done! I look forward to spending a lot of time with my nephews while I'm there. I have no idea what my schedule will be like, though, so don't plan those dates just yet."

"Of course. When will you get here?"

"A couple of days. They want me to start on Monday."

"Jeez, that's not a lot of time."

"Yeah. I guess they make us hustle," Tony said with a chuckle. "I wonder why they didn't email instead of snail mail. I'll have to email my boss to let him know that I finally got the response I was waiting for."

"What were you going to do if you didn't hear from them?"

"Continue at my job as it is now."

"Hmm. But this will give you an edge for a promotion."

"And I'll get to see how cases are handled differently in other states. The DCF is great, but there's always room for improvement."

"True. Well, I should get back to work."

"Good luck with that."

"It's actually going pretty well today, but thanks."

Adam hung up and Tony put his phone on the coffee table. He got to his feet and stretched. "Guess I should start packing. And book a flight."

An hour later, acceptance of the exchange program confirmed with a quick call to the west coast, his flights booked for the next day, boss emailed, and suitcase mostly packed, Tony was out of ways to keep his mind distracted. His best friends would be home soon and he still hadn't figured out how to tell them.

The front door creaked open. "Honey, we're home!" Amanda sang out cheerfully. "Tony?"

"I'm here." Tony strode out of the office to loom over the half-wall at the top of the flight of stairs to the front door. "How did your presentation go, darlin'?"

Amanda beamed at him as she bounced up the stairs. "Very well, thanks to you letting me practice all week. They didn't ask a single question that stumped me."

"That's great!" Tony wrapped her up in a hug. "And your day?" he asked James, who was following at a slower pace.

James bit his lip nervously. "Well enough. I set up my classroom today. I'm looking forward to meeting the kids next Tuesday."

"What grades have you got?" Tony asked. "Have they finally told you?" He relished in the press of her body against him and buried his nose in her hair. He was going to miss this.

"A third grade inclusion class. They gave word this afternoon." James rolled his eyes. "Talk about last minute."

"That sounds complicated. What exactly does that mean?" Tony asked, fully confused. He didn't remember any of his classes sounding like that.

"A class of mixed ability levels. I'll have to learn different students' abilities and disabilities to ensure everyone can learn to the best of their, for the lack of a better word, abilities," James finished with a chuckle.

"Sounds complicated, but I know you can handle it." Amanda pulled back from the hug to gaze into Tony's face. "What have you got on your plate next week? Arranging schedules still?"

Tony rubbed a hand through the shaved hair on the side of his head and stepped away, his heart squeezing painfully. "Yeah, about that... I got a letter today. An exchange program I applied to wants me for a month. I start on Monday."

"What exchange program?" Amanda asked, hurt flickering behind her eyes. "Why haven't you mentioned it before?"

"Where?" James asked.

"San Francisco." Tony dropped his gaze to his friends' knees. He winced as he heard a sharp intake of breath from James.

"Why didn't you tell us about it?" Amanda asked. She sounded like she was swallowing back tears.

"It wasn't a sure thing." Tony shrugged. "And it seemed wise to avoid any conflict that might arise over it."

"We would have supported you," James growled. "Instead, we're fighting about you not *talking* to us. Again!"

Tony finally raised his eyes. "I'm *trying*," he spat. "I'm not exactly used to dealing with people who care about what I do."

"How do you think your parents would feel, hearing that? Or Adam?" James glared.

"You know what I mean."

"No, I don't. Because you don't *talk* to us about the important stuff!"

Tony scoffed. "Sure I do."

"Then why is this the first we're hearing about this exchange program that'll send you all the way across the country?" James stomped down the stairs.

"Where are you going?" gasped Amanda. "We only have a couple more days together!"

"My flight's tomorrow at one," Tony put in.

"I'm going to the library. Don't wait up," James snarled, stuffing his feet back into his shoes. He ripped open the door before they could say anything else, letting it slam behind him.

Amanda wrapped her arms around herself. A sob escaped her throat. She lifted tear-filled eyes to Tony. "You need to learn to share more," she said softly. "We want to be with you for the good *and* the bad. Please don't push us away."

Tony swallowed the lump in his throat. "I'll try harder," he said fiercely, trying to reassure both of them.

"Your flight's tomorrow?" Amanda asked, her lower lip quivering. "They really didn't give you much time."

"They didn't." Tony sighed.

"Rude." Amanda sniffed wetly. "How are we supposed to cram a month's worth of sex into one night?"

Tony huffed a laugh and wrapped his arms around his girlfriend. "I don't think they take that into consideration."

"They *should*." Amanda tilted her head up. "You should consider therapy when you get home. Maybe we can do couple's therapy?"

"I'll think about it." Tony kissed her lips lightly. "I'm sorry I got so into my head about this stuff."

Amanda shivered. "Didn't your psych classes cover this? How to communicate with the important people in your life?"

"The important people? Who might those be?" Tony asked playfully.

"Oh, you know, your parents," Amanda said with a smirk.

"Very important," Tony said solemnly.

Amanda poked his chest. "James and I are the most important people in your life and you know it."

Tony grinned. "You are."

"I'm going to miss you so much."

Tony cupped her face in his hand. "I won't be gone long, just a month. And you'll have James with you."

"You'll be all alone on the other side of the country!" Tears gathered in her eyes.

"I won't be alone. I'll be spending a lot of quality time with my nephews. Good practice for the future," Tony said gently.

Amanda's breath hitched. "Make love to me, Tony," she whispered. "Make me forget about your impending departure."

"That I can most definitely do." He kissed her again, deeper this time, breathing in her scent and reveling in the feel of her body pressed against his own. "Amanda," he groaned. "I love you so much."

"I love you too," she gasped. Her fingers clenched in the fabric of his shirt, hiking it up. "I want you."

"I need you like a parched man needs water," Tony said, trailing his lips along her jaw.

"Good thing I'm soaked," Amanda said, laughing.

Tony chuckled. "Fuck, Amanda."

"We can do that later tonight."

"Yeah, we will." Tony's fingers slipped under the hem of her plaid sweater vest. She always dressed warmly because her office was freezing with the AC on. "May I undress you?"

"Yes, please."

Reverently, Tony peeled her vest up and off her body, dropping it somewhere behind him. Starting on the buttons, he pressed kisses to each new inch of skin he revealed, skipping over the lace of her bra to continue down her stomach. When he got to the last button, Amanda moved to shrug it off, but Tony stopped her with a hand on her shoulder. "You said I could undress you."

Amanda smiled. "I did."

"Then let me do it my way." His fingers slipped under a bra strap and glided down to where it met the cup. "Alright?"

"Yeah," she agreed, pupils wide with desire. "Okay."

"Good." She was wearing a black demi-cup bra today, Tony noted with delight. The edge of her nipple, a slightly darker pink than her skin, could be seen peeking over the top of the cups. He traced the edge of the cups, the rough pads of his fingers catching on the softer texture of the areolas. He did it again, more firmly the second time, watching, fascinated, while the smooth nipples wrinkled as they tightened. One last pass, pulling lightly on the skin of her breasts until her nipples popped over the edge of the bra. "Nice," he breathed.

"Tony," whined Amanda, her hands flying up to grip his wrists tightly. "Stop teasing!"

His mouth quivered with a half smile. "I fully intend to follow through on every tease." Tony grazed his thumbs over the nubs of her nipples, making her arch into his touch. He felt his cock twitch in his jeans, begging to be released. With a growl, he dragged her tight skirt up her thighs and picked her up by her ass, pressing her against the narrow wall behind them.

Amanda wrapped her legs around his hips and ground against him.

"Fuck yes," Tony groaned. He latched onto one breast, flicking over the nipple with his tongue. Amanda's hands clenched in his hair, holding his head tightly against her. Her gasps and moans filled the air around them, egging him on. Tony switched sides, using his teeth to scrape lightly over the tight bud.

"Yes, God, yes!" Amanda cried out. Her hips thrust again, seeking relief. "Tony, please!"

"I love hearing you beg," Tony murmured against her skin. "Best high in the world."

"Tony, I need you, please!" Amanda begged, writhing in his grip. "Come on, fuck me against this wall."

Drawing in a sharp breath, Tony tried to regain control over himself. "I thought you wanted slow lovemaking?"

Amanda's head fell back against the wall with a thud. "Can't we do both?"

"Darlin', we can do whatever you want," Tony said. "You want me to take you to our bed and make love slow and sweet, I can do that. You want me to take my cock out right now and fuck you against the wall just like this, I'm game. You want me to bend you over the dining room chair over there and eat you until you scream to be filled, you know I'm always down to go down. So tell me, how do you want this to go?"

"Fuck, Tony," Amanda gasped, eyes wide. "Wall first, then chair, then bed."

Tony chuckled. "I thought you might say that." He leaned his weight against her, pressing her more firmly against the wall. "Hang on, gotta get my pants down," he grunted, fumbling with the belt and enclosure of his jeans, tight over his hard cock. Once freed, he focused his attention on Amanda's underwear, slipping them to the side and pushing two fingers into her easily. "Damn, you're dripping. Ready?"

"Fuck me until I can't walk straight," Amanda demanded.

"Your wish is my command," Tony murmured, sliding her down his body until his cock caught on her opening. More slowly now, he lowered her over his length, clenching his jaw at her warmth. "Every time we do this, I am grateful that you took the initiative with us. I know it's been over two years, but feeling you around me like this still blows my mind."

"You feel incredible to me, too," Amanda gasped. "I love you so much. Now fuck me!"

"As you wish," Tony said with a smirk. He sank in fully, and before she had a chance to recover, he was pistoning his hips into her depths again and again, slamming her body against the wall with the force of his thrusts.

"Oh, fuck *yes*!" Amanda shouted, her fingers digging into Tony's shoulders through his t-shirt. "Yes yes, Tony, oh my *God*!"

Tony loved it when she got loud. He sent mental apologies to the downstairs tenant, but then remembered it was just before dinner, they wouldn't be asleep, and he *really* didn't care. "This feel good? You like this?" he growled.

"More! I'm going to come like this. Fuck, Tony, *yes*!"

She ended on a shriek that he felt in his nervous system, her body clamping down on him so tightly that he didn't register that he was coming too. "Damn, love," he panted, pressing his forehead to hers. "That felt amazing." He locked his knees to keep them from wobbling. "Ready to have that beautiful pussy eaten?"

"You really don't mind eating your own cum?" Amanda asked, running a hand through his hair.

He wanted to purr like a cat, his scalp tingling from her delicate petting. "Why would I mind? Not like I haven't done it before. And it's going to taste delicious mixed with yours."

Amanda blushed. "I overheard some girls in the office today at lunch, and they were rather negative about the whole thing."

Tony frowned, putting her down on her feet. "What whole thing?" He continued removing her clothing as she talked.

"Swallowing, giving head, getting eaten out, oral in general, really. It's silly."

Tony dropped her skirt to puddle at Amanda's feet. "That *is* silly. Ignore them. Do *you* enjoy it when one of us eats you out?" At her enthusiastic nod, he grinned. "And do you enjoy giving head?" Once again, she nodded. "Then ignore them. They don't know what they're missing." He slid her underwear down her legs to join her skirt. "Go to that chair and bend over. Let me see how much I wrecked you."

As Amanda walked over to the chair, Tony removed his clothing. His mouth watered as she bent over, exposing her sex. "Spread your lips for me, darlin'. Make a mess on the floor."

"Fuck," Amanda gasped, shuddering. She reached between her legs, fingers separating her folds.

Tony watched as his cum gathered at her entrance before gravity pulled on it, stretching it until it dripped onto the hardwood flooring in a puddle. "Oh fuck yes," Tony whispered reverently, getting to his knees. "Look at you, all pink and swollen, gushing with my cum. I love it when James and I stuff you full, pushing more and more inside you until you overflow with it, making a mess everywhere. I love fucking you until you're gaping, your little pussy stretched to take me." He slid a finger inside her, pulling out more cum. "Taste us," he ordered, bringing his finger to her lips. "We're so good together."

While she sucked on his finger, Tony pressed a sloppy kiss to her lower lips, tongue delving inside her to get at their combined juices. He hummed, greedily taking all she gave him before dropping lower and sucking on her clit.

Amanda's thighs shook on either side of his torso and Tony huffed a laugh. "Enjoying yourself?" he murmured.

"Don't stop!" she wailed. "I'm so close!"

Tony chuckled. "So impatient," he said against the thin skin of her inner thigh. "Bend over more. Put your hands on the ground. Show me how flexible you are."

"Good thing I keep up with stretching," Amanda grumbled, pushing the chair away and putting her hands flat on the floor, either side of the puddle of cum.

"You stretch because you like riding us in the splits," Tony scoffed. "You like that we can manipulate your body in any way we choose."

Amanda smirked at him from between her legs. "You like it, too."

"Never said I didn't." Tony smacked her vulva lightly with the tips of his fingers, making her yelp. "Now be a good girl for me." He got up on his knees and sucked her clit into his mouth again. He didn't have to wait long to see if she got his hint. She gripped his cock, still soft from coming inside her, and licked it like a popsicle. "Yeah, Amanda, feels good," he breathed, pulling back just far enough to encourage her.

Tony held her thighs to keep her steady, feasting on her juices and swollen clit until she came, shaking and with a muffled cry that echoed through his cock.

She let him slip from her slack lips and braced herself on the floor with her hands, panting heavily. "Damn, Tony!"

"You like that?" He felt like the cat who got the cream. "Need help getting up?"

"Yeah."

Tony got to his feet and helped Amanda stand upright again. "Are you hungry?"

"Oh, but..." Amanda pouted. "I don't really want to get dressed."

"You never do," Tony said with a laugh. "We can order in. Or I can run down to the deli on the corner and pick up subs. What are you in the mood for?"

"Not letting you out of my sight and subs."

"Then I guess we're both getting dressed." Tony picked up his boxer briefs. "I don't want to let you out of my sight either."

Chapter Two

Flashback: Moving Day

The drive from their hometown to Boston felt like a parade.

It had been a frantic last couple days after Adam and Sophia's wedding to pack and make sure they had everything they would need, on top of working at the sports complex.

But now everything was packed in the U-haul or one of the three cars that flanked it on the road.

"If you've forgotten anything important, we can drive it up," Julie said, twisting slightly to see her daughter, squished in the back seat of their sedan along with several boxes that hadn't fit on the truck.

"Don't be ridiculous," Paul chimed in. "We'll just toss it."

Amanda laughed at her dad. "I don't think we've forgotten anything, but I'll let you know when we're ready for visitors."

"This house has three bedrooms, doesn't it?" Julie asked. "Are you sure you'll have the space?"

"Actually, it has four bedrooms, but we're turning one into an office space and one into a home gym. The second bedroom upstairs will be our spare room since we're all going to sleep together," Amanda replied, confused. "Did you forget that we're in a relationship?"

"No, no," Julie said, flustered. "I just thought each of you might want your own space too."

"We'll have the extra bed if one of us needs to stretch out, but it's going to be mainly for visitors."

"You're happy, right, dearest?" Julie asked.

"Incandescent," Amanda said gravely.

Paul coughed uncomfortably. "You're not being pressured into anything?"

"God, no!" Amanda was horrified. "You practically raised those boys. How can you even *think* that about them?"

"We're not," Julie rushed to reassure her. "We're just checking in on you. You're our daughter, our only child."

Amanda shook her head. "You could have phrased it differently, instead of making it sound like I was being forced into becoming their sex slave or something."

The back of her dad's neck turned scarlet.

"I know you were thinking it," Amanda snarked. "Don't get all modest on me now."

"Dearest, that's not appropriate," Julie scolded. "We were trying to be caring parents."

"No! Seriously, I can't believe you two. If you'd said this kind of thing about Crystal, that would make sense. You didn't know her at all. But you changed James's diapers. You bandaged Tony's scraped knees when he fell off his bike when he was trying to learn a trick. You helped all three of us with projects all through middle and high school. More importantly, you've seen how they behave around me. Have they ever done *anything* to make you think that they don't respect me?"

Frustrated and angry, Amanda brushed tears away from her cheeks. "You'd better not treat those *men* any differently than you ever have before. I chose them, both of them, and I'd rather you didn't drive them away with your insinuations."

"You're acting like a teenager throwing a temper tantrum because you got grounded," Julie snapped. "We were checking on you!"

Amanda threw her hands in the air. "Are you going to tell me to go to my room? Order me not to live with my boyfriends? Drive me back to your house so I miss the beginning of my Master's semester? I'm an adult, and I'm making adult decisions about what to do with my life."

"We weren't casting aspersions on the boys," Paul said placatingly. "I don't know how else we could have phrased our concern."

"You could have left it at asking if I was happy! You don't have to like how I'm handling my life, but I'm asking you to respect our decision." She seethed in silence for a minute. "I thought you were on our side."

"You're right," Julie said. "I didn't think of it from that perspective. I'm sorry."

"I'll give you grace by not telling them about this conversation, but only if you actively put in the work to change your attitude regarding our relationship," Amanda said.

They finally reached the outskirts of Boston, the sound of traffic almost oppressive in the silent car.

"We're behind you one hundred percent, dearest," Julie said at last. "I'm glad the boys are too. It makes me feel so much better knowing how loved you are."

"Thank you."

"Turn left in five hundred feet," chirped the GPS, drawing Amanda's attention.

She squinted at it from the back seat. "We're almost there," she said, trying to dredge up the enthusiasm she had felt when getting into the car. Thinking about the house that she and her boyfriends, her best friends in the world, were going to make into their home did the trick. "I can't wait to see it!"

"Do you regret not coming up when the Lavallee's bought the place?" her mother asked.

"A little. I saw the pictures online, but it's not the same as in person. I would have just been in the way for the inspection, though."

"Turn right in five hundred feet," the GPS instructed.

"You'll get to see it in about five minutes," her dad said.

He turned down the one-way street lined with stately brick houses.

Amanda stared out the window, trying to spot the house numbers to see which one was hers. "Twenty-one!" she exclaimed. "We're close!"

"You have arrived at your destination."

Paul turned down the street beside the house, parking in the shade of the two-storey building. "James will have to fight with the neighbors for parking," he remarked, grunting as he got out of the car and stretched his back.

"The street parking is my least favorite thing about the house," Amanda admitted, joining her dad in the road. "But there seems to be plenty of it. We're just hoping that the tenant we inherited downstairs won't have a car as well."

"There you are, you beautiful sight for sore eyes!"

"Glenn!" Amanda shrieked, turning and running towards the front of the house where the young man was leaning against the fence. Their high school friend hadn't been sure he would make it to help them move in. Privately, the trio assumed he didn't want to put in the manual labor required. "I didn't see you when we drove up, I was so focused on the house!"

"Yeah yeah, I know where I rate," he teased her, holding his arms open for her hug.

"Thanks for helping us today," she said, pulling back a little. "You only moved here earlier this week, didn't you?"

"Yeah, I needed to get out of my parent's house ASAP," Glenn said, leaning against the white picket fence again. "They were harshing my vibe. It was a matter of throwing a little money at the movers to shift my date, and I was in the city."

"Was your house ready early?" Amanda asked.

"Oh yeah. I just had the cleaners hurry it up after the renovations were done. All that's left is the outdoor area. I can live without a pool for a few weeks, and I'll be up early for classes anyways." Glenn grinned.

"What did your parents catch you doing that you had to leave early?"

"They didn't appreciate my natural state of existence in the living room."

"Ah. Parents." Amanda rolled her eyes, but it was more *at* him than *with* him. Glenn's parents had given him everything on a silver platter, and while he wasn't cruel, he didn't seem to realize he was a brat. "Your movers did all the heavy lifting for your move, so you came to help us with ours?"

"Can't leave my best friends hanging! Besides, I skipped my workout this morning. Need to put in the time somehow, and I haven't met any of the ladies on campus yet." He waggled his eyebrows suggestively. "Come on! Show me the place! Your *casa* away from *casa*."

Amanda dug into the pocket of her shorts for the keys. "Let's get some boxes. I don't want to waste a trip." She led him to her parent's car and chose the one with her favorite lamp carefully swaddled in blankets.

"All of this is going to the top floor," she said. "So grab whatever."

"Aye aye, *mon capitaine*," Glenn said, saluting her before picking up a sealed box that read "Upstairs Bathroom" in blocky lettering. "How much soap do you guys have?" he grunted.

Amanda laughed. "There's a giant linen closet in that bathroom, so we're putting all the cleaning supplies and stuff in there, as well as towels and sheets."

"Which box do I need to accidentally drop in order to catch a glimpse of your toy collection?" Glenn asked with a wink.

"We kept her old toys at our house," Julie said, overhearing his comment. "They're not needed *yet*." She shot her daughter a glare.

"Of course they're not needed. I'm in school, I don't have time for a baby," Amanda said with a sigh. "Mothers," she muttered out of the corner of her mouth to Glenn. "Come on, I'll give you the five-cent tour before the U-haul gets here."

She shifted the box to her left hip and leaned it against the railing as she fitted the key into the lock. She pushed the door open for him to pass. "Shoes off, please."

"Course." Glenn kicked his shoes off in the narrow entryway and trotted up the stairs immediately inside the door. "Tight fit," he called over his shoulder. Then a low whistle left his lips as he reached the main floor. "This is *nice*!"

"Hang on," Amanda said, leaving her sandals behind and the door open for her parents as she made her way up the stairs. "Oh wow! There's so much space!"

Immediately at the top of the stairs, there was a large open room, with the kitchen beyond it. Taking two steps into the room, she could see another one beside the kitchen with a fireplace. Two more rooms with doors opened off the space, one much larger than the other. She spun to look behind her, spotting the laundry room at the bottom of the next set of stairs.

"I need to see the upstairs!" she squeaked, running up two at a time. The lamp rattled in her box and she slowed at the top.

The hall was small but bright, thanks to the window in the stairwell. She tried the door to the left of the stairs, which led to a small bedroom. The door beside it was the bathroom, and the final door opened to a large bedroom at the front of the house.

"My new room!" she announced loudly, gently placing her box near the closet door. She spun in a circle, her arms outstretched.

"Where do you want this?" Glenn called from the hallway.

"Be right there!" Amanda darted across the hall and into the bathroom, sliding open the pocket door of the closet. "Find a shelf that it'll fit on."

"I'm kinda in love with this bathroom," Glenn said admiringly. "Look at that tub!"

The tub in question was claw-foot and took up a large portion of the floor space beside the toilet.

"I don't usually take baths," she hedged.

"Then I'm going to get you bath bombs as your housewarming present. You haven't lived until you can soak in a tub like that at the end of a long day."

"If you say so."

The shower didn't look like it would be able to fit both her and the two guys, and she bit back her disappointment.

"The truck's here!" her dad's voice echoed up the stairs.

"There isn't much space out there," Amanda said. "We need to hurry to unload it and get it out of the way."

"Roger that."

They thundered down the stairs and swerved to the side to avoid a large mattress being carried in by James and Tony.

"Hi! Love you!" Amanda said to each one as they passed her.

"We need a better system," James's father, Xavier, said leaning against the front door frame. "Taking off our shoes while carrying heavy objects is not going to work."

"Not to mention the tripping hazard," Debra, Tony's mother, remarked, peering over his shoulder.

"We've got a shoe rack in my parent's car," Amanda said. "I'll go grab it—"

"I've got it," Paul said. "If I can just get to the door..."

Space was made for him and shoes put away.

"As I was saying," Xavier continued, "We need a better system. Half of us out here, emptying the truck and passing items to the people inside should work."

"Great plan. We'll start with one person in the truck and see what happens from there," Paul said.

"*I* was going to suggest a chain of people," Tony's father, Michael, said.

"You're right. We definitely need a better system. I think a chain would work really well," Amanda put in. "Less than half of us outside, because we need more people inside the house to distribute boxes. We'll alternate who climbs all these stairs."

"Great idea."

They organized themselves quickly, systematically unloading the truck into the house. They made light work of the heavy items, passing them from person to person with jokes and laughter.

"You know what would make this move even better?" Tony asked, his eyes twinkling. "Music!"

"Yes!" James said enthusiastically.

"The sound system was in your car, right?"

"Yeah, front seat. I parked on the side street behind the Beyer's." James tossed him the keys, which he caught easily.

"Excellent." Tony left his place in the outdoor lineup. "Shouldn't take long to set up."

When he came back, he squeezed by the people on the stairs.

"You're just doing this to get out of work," Glenn teased.

"It'll take me less than two minutes to plug in the speakers. I'd let you do it, but you'd probably plug the aux cable into the wall instead of the sound system," Tony retorted.

"I should be offended, but you're right," Glenn replied cheerfully. "Timer started."

"Hey! I'm not even upstairs yet!" Tony yelped, taking them two at a time.

In the room at the top of the stairs, which they'd decided would make a good dining room, he placed the sound system on the ground next to the half-wall and plugged it in. He connected the speakers, set them on the wall, and popped the disc drive open. "Any preference?" he asked.

"Something peppy," Amanda suggested. "Give us energy."

"Alright, how about some classic *DDR* sound mixes?" He flipped through the CD binder they'd had ever since they were kids, easily finding the disc he'd suggested.

"Thirty seconds," Glenn warned.

The heavy beat of the first song thumped out of the speaker.

"Nicely done," James said, passing by with a box.

"I knew it wouldn't take long." Tony grinned at his best friend before trotting down the stairs. "It was just a quick set-up, not the full thing. That's going to take us a while."

"Us? You'll let us help?" Amanda teased.

Tony stuck his tongue out at her, wiggling his feet back into his shoes and returning to his position outside.

"Careful, your face might get stuck that way," Michael teased, handing him one end of a bookcase.

"What, happy?" Tony said, beaming.

Xavier took the other end of the bookcase and they started towards the house. "It looks good on you."

"Thanks."

They passed the bookcase to the people inside, and returned for the next item.

"I'm glad you came into the kids' lives," Xavier continued, clapping him on the shoulder. "You've been good for them."

Tony flushed. "They've been good for me too."

"I'm glad it's a two-way street."

The truck was emptied in record time, and Xavier drove it to the drop-off location, his wife Ava following in their car to bring him back to the house. The rest of the group unloaded the three cars. By the time the Lavallee's returned, they had started unpacking the kitchen boxes and washing the dishes.

"Hey, I've been meaning to ask you guys," Glenn said, flipping his drying cloth over in his hands. "Are you planning on going to the high school reunion thing at Thanksgiving?"

Amanda, James, and Tony exchanged glances.

"We were planning on heading home to visit the parents, so we can swing by," James said.

"I hadn't really thought about it," Amanda added. "It feels so far away."

"Halloween comes first," Tony said firmly. "We're having a party, and you, my man, are top of the invite list."

"I better be." Glenn grinned. "Looking forward to it."

James

The slam of the front door echoing in his ears, James thundered down the porch stairs. By the time he'd reached the corner, the burning anger in his chest had turned into fear.

How can we make this work if he refuses to communicate? How can our relationship survive?

He took a breath to center himself before he continued, not wanting to scare anyone with his anger.

James reached the local library in a very short time, welcoming the air conditioning of the entryway after the harsh Boston heat. He scraped his feet on the mat to clear any dirt from his shoes and moved further into the library.

"Hello, can I help you with anything?" asked a middle-aged librarian, her hair graying at her temples.

James gripped the straps of his backpack tightly. "Hello. I start teaching next week, a third grade inclusion class. I was hoping to get some more ideas for my lesson plans?"

The woman, who had greeted him with a stern disposition, had brightened considerably during their brief exchange. "Of course! You've come to the right place." She led James to a far corner of the library and gestured at a bank of shelves. "These should have everything you'll need. I recommend starting with this one." She pulled out one of the books. "If you need any more assistance, please let me know."

"Thank you," James said, taking the book. "How late are you open tonight?"

"Until eleven." The librarian studied his face. "No big parties tonight?"

James shook his head. "I'm not really up for partying."

The librarian checked her watch. "My dinner break is in an hour. Did you want to share a pizza and talk about it?"

James ran his fingers along the spine of the book he was holding. "I don't know…"

"You'll need to eat. We don't have to talk if you don't want to." The librarian turned to leave. "Think about it. I'll come check on you before I leave."

"Thanks." James flicked his fingers in a wave and sat at a nearby independent work station, pulling his laptop from his backpack and flipping through the book to the table of contents.

He had managed to take a couple notes when his cell phone vibrated. He checked it and found a message from Amanda reminding him to eat and that she missed him. He grimaced. He couldn't fault her for staying with

Tony; as much as he wanted her comfort right then, she needed to be with Tony tonight.

James sighed. Maybe talking with a stranger would help him feel better.

The hour passed quickly, and by the time the librarian returned, James was feeling much more confident about his lessons, though not his love life.

"Have you made up your mind?" The woman asked him.

"You sure you want me hanging around on your break?" James asked.

The librarian smiled. "I wouldn't have asked if I wanted you to say no."

James couldn't fault her logic and told her so.

She laughed. "I'm Theresa, by the way."

"James."

"There's a local pizzeria around the corner that I like to spoil myself at. Shall we?"

Once they were seated and waiting for their order, Theresa folded her hands under her chin and stared at James. "So. Talk or not talk?"

"Maybe talk a bit?"

Theresa smiled. "Why are you not up for a party tonight?"

"My best friend is leaving for San Francisco tomorrow. He only found out today."

"How long will he be gone?"

"A month."

"Why did you fight?"

"How did you know we fought?" Their pizza arrived and James thanked the server.

"You're not with him on his last night in town. Was it a girl?" Theresa selected a piece of pizza.

James chuckled. "Yeah, that's really not a problem."

"Oh? Not interested in the same type?"

"Not relevant." James sighed and rubbed his forehead before picking up a slice. "Or maybe it is. We're in a relationship with the same girl."

"A Vee poly relationship?"

"You know the terminology?" James asked, surprised.

"I work in a library. We have seminars and workshops and guest speakers on all sorts of topics, including different types of relationships."

"That makes sense."

"But you want to be a triad."

"Yeah," James whispered. "How did you know?"

"Typically, people aren't this upset and angry when their best friend moves away for only a month. Why haven't you told him? You don't know if he's open to that?"

"That's it in a nutshell."

"Isn't the cornerstone of a poly relationship good communication?" Theresa asked sternly.

James laughed bitterly. "And therein lies the crux of our fight. He didn't tell us that he'd even applied for this exchange. What else is he keeping from us?"

"Mmhmm." Theresa raised an eyebrow.

"You think I should tell them about my feelings."

"I do."

"Before he goes away?" James felt like he was whining.

"Do you want this secret festering in your heart while he's gone?" Theresa asked mildly. "Do you want to wait even longer to tell him?"

"But what if he doesn't feel the same way?" James asked softly.

"He obviously cares for you a great deal. You'll work through it if that happens."

James nodded. "It's scary."

"Of course it is! You're putting your heart out there! How did it feel when you two first got together with your girl?"

James coughed sheepishly. "Amanda did most of the hard work on that one. She put her heart on the line, and Tony and I reciprocated."

"Ah. No wonder you're nervous now." Theresa sat silently for a minute. "You could write him a letter if you're worried that talking wouldn't go well."

"That's a great idea. Thanks."

"Are you still angry?"

"Mostly just anxious. For multiple reasons now."

Theresa patted his hand. "That's life."

"That's not really comforting."

For the rest of the evening, James alternated between working on his lesson plans and writing a letter to Tony to give him before he got on the plane.

At closing time, Theresa came to see him. "Are you going to be alright?"

"Yeah, I think so." James gave her a small smile. "Enough that I can go home tonight. Would you... Would you like to read it?"

"Sure."

James watched her eyes flick across the page as she read. He practically had it memorized.

> *Dear Tony,*
>
> *This probably isn't the best time to tell you this, with you leaving for San Francisco, but it's been almost a decade since I realized my feelings for you were more than just platonic.*
>
> *Those feelings have only grown since we started dating Amanda. Possibly it's our shared connection with her or even just the intensity of, well, everything, but I can definitely say that I am in love with you.*
>
> *And I'm terrified.*
>
> *Do you think you could feel the same way for me, given time?*
>
> *Will our relationship survive if you can't?*
>
> *These past two years have been the happiest of my life, and that's saying something, considering how amazing our childhood was.*

> *I know writing this letter and giving it to you at the airport labels me as a coward, but I couldn't handle it if you don't feel the same. This way, you have the flight to consider my words, and your feelings, and how you'd like to respond without the pressure of being face-to-face.*
>
> *It also gives me time to tell Amanda. I don't know how she'll take it either, finding out that she's not the only one I love. I'm about 90% sure she'll be thrilled.*
>
> *It's the other 10% that scares me.*
>
> *I needed to tell you now because you're leaving for a month. And it was pointed out to me that if I want you to be better at communicating, then I probably should work on my own skills too.*
>
> *I hope you remember me, us, when you're in doubt.*
>
> *I love you, Tony.*
>
> *Will you be my boyfriend?*
>
> *James*

"That's beautiful," Theresa said, giving him the paper. "Now make sure he gets it."

"Right." James flushed darkly.

"Let me know how it goes."

"I will. And thanks for the resources. I'll be back later this weekend, I think."

"I look forward to it." Theresa walked him to the front door and locked it behind him.

James tucked his hands into his pockets and headed for home through the dark night. His walk was pleasant, if chilly; unexpectedly so for the heat of the late August day. The house was silent when he entered, all the lights off but one.

James tried to keep his noises quiet as he removed his shoes and climbed the stairs. He slipped the letter for Tony out of his backpack, momentarily stumped about where to put it so that he'd remember to bring it to the airport the next day.

Tony's suitcase had been left near the bottom of the stairs, his passport and flight information resting on top of it. James briefly considered tucking it in the suitcase, but ultimately decided to fold it and put it in his back pocket.

He turned off the light in the kitchen before continuing upstairs.

Their bedroom was softly illuminated by the nightlight that Amanda insisted upon having. James crossed to his usual side of the bed, stripping off his clothes as he moved through the room. Amanda was hugging his pillow, the full expanse of her bare side visible over the sheet, Tony's arm wrapped around her and disappearing underneath the pillow. James knew from experience that he'd be holding her breast, Amanda's preferred way to fall asleep.

James brushed the back of his fingers along her arm, waking her gently. "Hey, I'm home," he whispered.

"Come to bed?" she murmured sleepily, reaching for him.

"If you want me to."

"Please?" Amanda yawned. "Missed you tonight."

James huffed a laugh, slipping under the sheet in place of the pillow. "I'm sure you found ways to occupy yourselves."

"Worried 'bout you," Amanda said around a yawn, burying her nose in his collarbone once he was settled. "Mmmm, you smell like pizza."

"Went to a pizza place for dinner with a librarian."

"A sexy librarian?"

"No, a middle-aged busybody librarian." James bit back a laugh.

"Ah. Do you feel better now?"

"I'm not angry, if that's what you mean. I'm still scared things will change." James stroked the hand she placed on his chest.

"Change could be good. All the best plots happen because of a change."

"The best what?" James asked, but only soft breathing met his ears. "Love you," he whispered to his best friends and drifted off to sleep.

The next morning came too quickly. James's eyes fluttered open, something feeling off in their room. Amanda's soft snores met his ears.

But Tony wasn't on the other side of her.

James's heart sank. *Is he that eager to get away from us?* He got out of bed and searched for his pants on the floor. They were draped over the bench at the foot of the bed. The paper in his pocket crinkled a reminder of what he had to do.

He left the bedroom and trotted down the stairs, heart pounding. Was Tony's suitcase still there?

It was, and he breathed a sigh of relief. But before he could unzip it to put the letter in it, the front door opened.

James rounded the top of the stairs and looked down into the foyer. Tony had just entered, and he was holding a bag from the bakery around the corner.

"Hey," Tony called up, his voice a little above a whisper. "How long have you been up?" He joined James on the main floor.

"Not long." James shook his head. "You weren't in bed, and I thought maybe you'd taken off early."

Tony's face fell, his emotions shuttered behind a stony expression. "You really think I'd leave without saying goodbye to you? To *her*?" He jerked his thumb over his head to indicate the top floor.

"How am I supposed to know what you'd do?" James hissed. "You don't *talk* to us!"

"That's not fair," Tony said with a frown. "I promised Amanda last night that I'd work on it. I'm going to promise you the same thing. But *you* have to promise me something too." He got in James's face, their breath mingling. "You can't jump to conclusions about what I'm thinking. You have to communicate better with me too."

James swallowed hard. Tony was so close that James could see the flecks of hazel and green in his golden-brown eyes. It would be *so easy* to close the distance between them, join their lips, press him against the silly extra wall that separated their dining room from the extra rooms on this floor, forget that he was holding their breakfast, forget that he was flying across the country in a few hours... "Deal," James said, barely stopping his whimper when Tony nodded shortly and stalked over to the kitchen.

"I called Adam yesterday. I'm going to be staying in their guest room and babysitting as payment," Tony said, turning on the stove's front right element.

"You're getting a raw deal," James said, pulling one of the bar stools out to sit on. It was on the opposite side of the island, meaning he wasn't as likely to leap across to grab Tony and throw him down against it. He clenched his teeth and willed his erection away.

"Nah. I'm looking forward to hanging out with the munchkins. They know I'm there to work." Tony pulled out plates and set a croissant on each, cutting them open with practiced slices of their bread knife. Next, he cut a chunk of butter and dropped it onto the frying pan, setting it on the pre-heated element. Eggs were cracked and went into the pan once the butter had melted. "What else do you want on your sandwich?"

"Tomato, lettuce, and cheese," James said.

"No bacon?"

"We don't have any left."

"Shit, you're right. I guess I should've bought some when I was out."

"The bakery doesn't sell bacon," James pointed out.

"I could have gone to the butcher's."

"Amanda and I'll go after dropping you at the airport."

"There might be some you could scavenge from our dinners last night," Tony suggested, flipping the eggs. "We had subs, and both of us had bacon."

"You didn't finish your dinner?" James asked incredulously. "Either of you?"

"We didn't want to stay out any longer," Tony said. "And when we got home, we were too busy fucking to think about eating."

"Ah, that makes more sense." James rounded the island on the opposite side from the stove and opened the fridge to hunt for the leftovers. He put everything on the counter and grabbed a knife to prepare the ingredients. He popped the bacon into the microwave on a paper towel.

"Something smells good," Amanda said, wandering into the kitchen wearing the shirt Tony had been wearing the day before. "Oooh, fresh croissants? Thank you." She beamed at them both.

"Tony got up early," James said.

"You'll have to find a good bakery in San Francisco," she told Tony, wrapping her arms around his waist from behind.

"I'm sure Adam and Sophia have already explored their neighborhood," Tony replied, bringing one of her hands to his mouth and pressing a kiss to the palm.

"Then you'll have to bring back some samples for us to decide what's better, East or West Coast bakeries," Amanda said decidedly.

"I think they get their flour from the same kind of store," James said with a chuckle.

She shrugged. "You never know."

"You just want more baked goods," Tony teased.

"Guilty as charged." Amanda smiled. "Are you going to deliver?" She dropped to a sultry, suggestive tone.

"Darlin', I'll deliver any package you might want." Tony clicked off the stovetop and brought the pan over to the waiting croissants, flipping the eggs onto the cheese James had set out on the bottom half. "Starting with your breakfast." He slapped her lightly on the ass when he passed behind her to put the pan in the sink.

Amanda pouted. "But what if I'm not hungry for food?"

James chuckled. "You need to eat, sunshine, especially since you didn't finish your dinner last night."

"My tummy woke me with a growl," she admitted. "But how can I eat when you're leaving so soon?" she asked, raising sad eyes to Tony's. "I need to feel connected to you more than I need food."

"I think your digestion might disagree with that," James chuckled.

"I've got an idea." Tony gathered up their plates and brought them into the dining room. "Come here, darlin'." He held out his hand for her, spinning her into his arms when she took it.

Amanda tipped her head back and Tony joined their lips lightly, barely grazing over them, his fingers tugging the shirt she was wearing up her body.

Her curves were revealed to James's greedy eyes, not a stitch covering them. He wasn't surprised, but his cock still twitched in appreciation.

Tony broke the kiss to pull the shirt over her head. "Do you trust me?"

"Of course I do," she scoffed. "Silly question."

"Bend over and eat your breakfast while I strip," he ordered. "You're going to get fucked nice and slow while we eat, but as soon as the last bite is swallowed, I'm going to plow you until you scream."

"Okay!" Her eyes sparkling, Amanda obeyed him, presenting her ass to the two men.

"Only if you behave, though." Tony made quick work of his clothing, leaving them in a pile on the floor.

James was glad Tony was entirely focused on Amanda because he was sure his desire for his best friend was written clearly across his face as each inch of sexy tattooed skin was revealed.

Oblivious, Tony slid inside her with a grunt, taking his plate and resting it on her flat back. "You can't wiggle, or else it might fall off and break, and then you're not going to get thoroughly fucked."

"Cruel," Amanda mumbled around her bite of sandwich.

"Yep, that's me. Cruel and sadistic," Tony said sarcastically, pulling out slowly and sliding back in. "Do you need any lube, darlin'?"

"Maybe a little."

Before Tony could ask him to get it, James headed for one of their many stashes of lube. He slicked up his fingers on the return trip, sliding them around Tony's cock and into her without waiting for him to pull all the way out.

Tony's breath hissed out between his teeth, his cock getting impossibly harder under James's touch. "Fuck, dude, warn a guy."

James shrugged. "This way you won't get lube on your breakfast. Good, Amanda?"

"Feels great," she moaned. "Love when you're inside me together." She shifted her sandwich to one hand so she could clench the other into a fist. "Fuck me, Tony, I'm not going to break!"

"Alright, alright." Once James pulled his fingers away, Tony pushed slowly into her, making them both groan. "Now eat your breakfasts, both of you." He mock-glared at James, the effect somewhat ruined by the glaze of arousal in his eyes and the twin spots of red on his cheeks.

Clenching his jaw to prevent himself from reaching out and fusing his mouth to Tony's, James stalked into the kitchen to wash his hands and grab his plate. The slick sounds of Amanda's pussy clinging to Tony's cock echoed through the house like it had many times before, serving to make him harder than a rock.

He shucked off his jeans beside the already discarded clothing, the crinkle of paper in his back pocket reminding him of the letter. Now wasn't the best time to tell Tony his feelings.

James breathed a laugh. *It would be funny if I just laid one on him right this second. I wonder what he'd do.* To avoid the temptation, he sat beside them at the table.

"Eat your breakfast, Amanda," Tony teased her.

"Are you serious right now?" she demanded, about to try to twist around to see him.

James put a hand on her shoulder. "Ah ah ah. Don't break our plate."

Amanda huffed indignantly and eyed her breakfast. "Thank you for the croissant, Tony."

"My pleasure." He pumped slowly into her again. "Fuck, if you keep doing that, I'm not going to last."

"What's she doing?" James asked.

Tony grunted. "She's clenching around me like a vise with her Kegel muscles." He met James's eyes. "It's fucking distracting."

"I bet it is," James said with a chuckle. He ran a hand over Amanda's body from her ass to her swinging breasts, and tweaked a nipple. "Are you being a brat on purpose?"

"I need him to go harder," she whined.

James chuckled. "He'll fuck you soon enough. He's halfway done with his breakfast."

Amanda groaned, her croissant hanging from her fingers. "I'm not really hungry."

"Would you rather eat while I take my time sliding in and out of you, or do you want me to stop?" Tony asked. "I don't want you to choke on your food."

"Fine." Amanda took a big bite and chewed viciously. "But only because we're on a time crunch," she added after swallowing.

The men laughed.

Tony popped the last of his breakfast into his mouth before removing the plate from Amanda's back. James watched avidly as Tony traced the nicely toned muscles all the way down to the three little dots that made a 'V' at the base of her spine before curling possessively around her hip bones. "Have you finished eating?" he asked, his voice such a low growl that James almost didn't recognize it.

"Not quite," Amanda whimpered.

Tony smirked and pulled out slowly until just his tip was inside her. Then, just as slowly, he started back in.

"Tony, fuck!" Amanda almost sobbed. "Please, I'll finish eating after!"

"I told you the rules," Tony said smugly. "This feels amazing to me. I could most definitely come like this. But *you* won't unless I speed up. Finish your breakfast, darlin'." He reached the deepest part of her and started pulling out again.

"I can't! I need you, Tony! Please, please, *please*!"

"You're wasting time, sunshine," James said with a smirk. "Eat."

She glared at him over her arm.

Tony chuckled. "Just two more bites. Come on." He slid back inside her with a squelch indicating a fresh flow of juices.

Amanda growled but took another bite.

"I'm done," James announced. "Maybe we should have let you eat *before* trying to fuck you."

"I'm seriously almost done," Amanda whined before stuffing the last bite into her mouth and wiggling her ass.

Tony smacked it. "Chew first. I don't want to have to heimlich you." He continued his slow pace, muscles rippling under the dark Monstera leaves inked into his skin.

James was impressed by Tony's patience. Having Amanda's warmth around him was one of the best feelings in the world and the quickest way to make him lose control.

"Okay, I'm done!" Amanda announced, wiggling her hips again. "Ready!"

Tony pulled almost all the way out and smacked her ass with the other hand, leaving matching red prints on both cheeks. "Hold still for me and let me use your body for my pleasure," he growled, and she shivered at his words. He grasped her hips firmly and started a brutally fast rhythm that had her crying out in ecstasy within seconds.

James gripped his cock with his hand, giving a few lazy strokes as he watched his best friends.

"Yes, yes, Tony! Right there! Fuck!" Amanda screamed, her short fingernails scratching at the surface of the table. "Oh my *God*!"

"That's it, come for him. Let the neighbors hear how much he rocks your world." James could feel himself nearing the edge and bit his lip, hanging onto his control. He wanted to come inside her. "Come on, Amanda."

"*Tony!*" she shouted as she clenched her hands into fists.

Tony groaned and jerked, yanking her hips against his to come deep within her. He collapsed across her back, breathing heavily for a minute before pulling out. "She's all yours," he said.

James turned his chair to the side, pulling gently on her wrist until Amanda shakily straddled him. He held his cock for her to impale herself as she sank down over his thighs. "That's it, sunshine," he groaned, cupping her face. "Take your fill of us."

"Until you paint the chair white with my cum," Tony teased, half-collapsing into another seat, sprawled out like an indecent lord. "Fuck, you two are hot together."

Amanda peeked over her shoulder at him. "You like watching someone else's cock fuck into your girlfriend?"

"He isn't 'someone else'," Tony scoffed.

James gripped her chin to draw her attention back to him. "If you can make smart remarks, you're not working hard enough," he growled. "Bounce on me. I want to hear your thighs slap against mine."

Amanda tossed her head, throwing her hair over her shoulders. "Maybe I should make *you* work harder for it."

Tony hummed and lazily stroked over his cock. "If neither of you start moving, I might have to take matters into my own hands and fuck you again."

"Ohhh, yes please," Amanda said, rocking her hips. "One last time before you leave?"

"I'm only going to be gone for a month," Tony said with a chuckle. "You'll barely notice I'm not here." He swiped the lube off the table and liberally coated his fingers. "I'm gonna take your ass, darlin'. Give me some room."

James was only slightly disappointed that he wouldn't feel Tony's cock snug up against his, but Amanda would need a lot more prep for that stretch. He scooted to the very edge of the chair and leaned back, giving her enough room to present her ass for Tony.

"God, yes," Tony murmured appreciatively.

Amanda sucked in a breath and her body went pliant. The press of Tony's fingers on his cock through the thin membrane made James's head spin.

"You're opening up beautifully for me," Tony said. "You like this?"

"Yessss," Amanda drawled. "Feels great."

"Give her an orgasm," Tony ordered, his eyes meeting James's over her shoulder.

From anyone else, that demand would make him bristle, but this was Tony. James's hand quested between their bodies to find Amanda's clit, the little nub of flesh pressed hard against his pubic bone. He grazed his thumb just above it, and her internal muscles clenched hard.

"Fuck," she hissed, pressing her forehead into his shoulder.

He rolled the hard nerves back and forth, his cock twitching in anticipation. "Come on, sunshine. Come on my cock."

Her hips moving in tiny stilted rolls, Amanda whined, "It's too much!"

"Let go," James whispered in her ear. He pressed a kiss to her temple. "Let yourself feel good." He felt her teeth dig into his shoulder, and then her muscles shook and squeezed hard on his cock. "Fuck," he hissed. "Tony, get inside her. I'm not going to last."

"Ready?" Tony asked her, brushing her hair to the side with his clean hand.

She turned her head, eyes closed. "Please."

"Never skip leg day," Tony muttered as he squatted behind her, straddling James. "Just so you know, this is the last condom down here. You'll have to replenish for when I get home."

"You think I won't take her ass just because you're not here?" James asked, his voice strained.

Tony shrugged. "Possibly. But when I get home, we're not going to make it up to the bedroom."

James huffed a laugh to distract himself from feeling his best friend's cock rubbing along his as he entered their girlfriend. The thin membrane between them was negligible; it was all about the weight and pressure, and it felt too good. The drag of Tony's balls against his signaled that he was all the way in, and it was time to move. With the other two bodies pinning him down, James couldn't.

They paused for a beat, their breath mingling in the small space.

Amanda tilted her head slightly, her lips lightly grazing first Tony's, and then James's. Tony chased her mouth, pressing hard against her and in turn, James.

His head spinning at the intimate contact from the other man, James begged for entrance into Amanda's mouth with his tongue. It turned into a three-way tango. His fingers tightened convulsively on Amanda's hips, dying for more than just the slight taste of Tony that he was getting.

"Gotta move," Tony muttered.

"Yes," Amanda whimpered.

Tony's phone alarm went off. He met their eyes. "Ten minutes before we have to leave to get me to the airport on time," he said.

"That's plenty," James said. "Get us off, Tony."

He drew in a sharp breath before nodding once. "You got it." He gripped the back of the chair beside James's head, his name on Tony's skin close enough to lick.

It took all of his willpower to resist the urge. James couldn't bring himself to care that it only took three pumps of Tony's hips before he came, his eyes locked with the other man's up until pleasure forced them closed.

Amanda was close behind him, her muscles milking him, and then Tony grunted, his cock twitching as it pulsed with his orgasm.

"I hate to hurry us, but we've gotta get going, and Amanda needs a thorough cleaning," Tony said at last, not lifting his head from where he'd pressed it against her shoulder blade.

"I'll just wear period underwear," Amanda said with a slight shrug. "I'll clean up after we get back."

"Okay." Tony shivered and finally pulled out, then helped her stand, cum dripping down her thighs. "Oh darlin', we've made a mess of you," he said admiringly.

"Don't start things you can't finish," she said, tapping his nose. "I need to pee."

"And get dressed," James added, clenching the seat of the chair until his knuckles creaked to keep from reaching out to either of them.

"I suppose," she teased, swaying her hips as she walked to the stairs.

In less than half an hour, they were at the terminal.

"I am going to miss having you around," James told Tony. It felt like the letter was burning a hole in his back pocket, but his heart clenched in fear.

"You can reach me on video chat, text, and email. I'll be back before you know it," Tony replied.

"Good luck," said Amanda quietly. She threaded her fingers through his short hair to pull his mouth down to hers.

Tony held her head between his hands and moved his lips over hers for long moments, bodies pressed together with no space between them. They slowly separated, breathing hard.

"I will miss you so much," whispered Amanda. "I love you." She backed away so that James could move forwards.

The guys hugged for a long moment. Tony pressed his forehead against James's, one hand behind his neck. "Don't forget me."

"How could I?" James teased. "You're only leaving for a month."

Tony huffed a laugh, his breath ghosting over James's lips in the semblance of a kiss, before releasing him to heft his duffel over his shoulder and head for security.

Guilt welled in James's throat as he watched his best friend walk away from him, deeper into the airport. Tony turned at the last minute to wave at them, and then he was gone.

"I just want to curl up with you on the bed and cry," Amanda said with a sniff.

"I can think of much more enjoyable things to do on a bed," James said playfully, leading Amanda back to the car. "And even more in a long, luxurious bubble bath?"

"I like how your mind works. Stupid San Francisco." She pouted. "I hate that he'll be so far away."

They listened to music in silence as they drove home, the ungiven letter in his pocket branding him as a coward.

The door was unlocked when Amanda got home from her lecture. Wearily, she closed it behind her, robotically kicking off her boots and hanging her coat on her usual hook.

She could hear the boys talking in the kitchen, the low rhythm of their voices soothing her after the frustrating day.

"You won't *believe* the day I had," Amanda stomped up the stairs as she complained to the guys, dropping her bag at the top. She whipped her sweater off over her head and unsnapped her bra. "That annoying dude was in fine form in class today." She threw her bra onto her sweater. "Is there time for one or both of you to relieve some of my stress before dinner?"

Both guys turned away from the counter to gape at her.

"Shit, Amanda, grab your—"

"No, wait, stop—"

The cacophony of their responses overlapped, but her attention was caught by movement from the living room entry.

"Mom!" Amanda exclaimed, clapping her hands over her breasts and spinning around. "What are you doing here?" She grabbed her sweater and yanked it on.

"Your father surprised me with tickets for the theater," Julie said. "Is this how you come home every day?"

Amanda rolled her eyes. "Only when I'm wearing an underwire and Jonathan is annoying."

Julie raised an eyebrow.

"Do you really want to know the answer to that?" Amanda asked with a sigh. She crossed the dining room to the kitchen, reaching Tony, who had returned to chopping the peppers, and rested her head on his shoulder.

He gave her a slice of green pepper, which she accepted after a quick kiss before moving on to James, who was stirring a pot of red sauce on the stove. He gave her a tasting spoon to test the sauce.

"Needs more cinnamon," she said after licking it clean.

"You always say that," he said, a twinkle in his eye.

"And am I wrong?" she said coyly.

"Probably not," he said agreeably. He tapped his lips and she pecked them lightly.

"Hello, jelly bean," her dad said, getting up from the living room couch.

"Hi Daddy," Amanda said, kissing his cheek. "What's the occasion for the theater?"

"There's a production of Chicago in town. It's your mother's favorite musical," Paul said gruffly. "Early Christmas present."

"That's sweet. Christmas is more than two months away."

"The show run ends next week."

"Ah. I see."

"Do I get a hug?" Julie said, arms outstretched.

Amanda only spared half a glance for her bra at the top of the stairs before giving her mother a squeeze.

"Run along and get changed for dinner, dear."

Amanda crossed her arms. "I'm not a child."

"Then stop acting like it."

Resisting the urges to both stamp her foot and demand that her boys follow her up to their room, Amanda gritted her teeth and did as her mother said, scooping up her bra on the way.

She decided it was a bad idea to strip in the laundry room, as was her usual habit, and simply tossed her bra at the basket, silently cheering when it landed inside.

See? I'm not stomping up the stairs like a little kid, she thought to herself, taking them two at a time. Her defiance reared again at the top of the stairs, and she wiggled out of her clothing, leaving them in the middle of the hallway on the way into the bathroom.

A quick splash in the sink to clean her face and armpits, and a stop at the toilet before she crossed the hall to the primary bedroom.

"Amanda, dear," her mother said.

She yelped in surprise, not having noticed her sitting on the foot of the bed. "Don't you know not to enter someone's room without permission?" she grumbled, yanking out the dresser drawer harder than necessary. "What do you want?" She stepped into a pair of black cotton briefs and picked out the matching demi-cup bra.

"I miss my daughter. Isn't that enough?"

Amanda bit her tongue to refrain from snapping at her. "I was coming right downstairs."

"I know, dear, but we're hardly alone down there."

She faced her mother, her hands on her hips. "What did you need to talk about that you didn't want the guys to hear?"

Julie picked at the comforter on the bed. "Is it everything you'd hoped it would be? Living with them?"

"And more," Amanda said decisively. "I love it."

"That's good."

"Is that all?" Amanda opened the closet door and walked in, rifling through her clothes.

"How are your classes going?"

"We didn't need to be alone for that!" She chose a pink sweater dress and black leggings and carried them back out to the main room.

Her mother twisted her fingers in her lap. "No. I guess I just wanted to see you with my own two eyes. See that you're okay."

"Not this again," Amanda said with a groan. "Are you seriously still worried about those men? They treat me like a princess. They haven't harmed a hair on my head." She smirked. "Well, unless you count the bruises on my hips." She pulled the side of her underwear down and twisted to show her mother the fingertip bruises. "They only happen occasionally, but last night was extra passionate for some reason."

Her mother turned scarlet. "I don't— Dear, that's hardly—" She flapped her hands in the air, flustered.

Amanda adjusted her underwear. "You asked." She sat on the edge of the bed and started pulling on her leggings.

"That wasn't what I was expecting you to say!"

Shrugging, Amanda got to her feet and hopped on the spot, tugging on the waistband. "You were circuitously asking if they were abusive, which I take extreme offense to. The only time they hurt me is when I ask them to."

"Why would you ask them to?" her mother asked, horrified.

Amanda chuckled and pulled her dress over her head. "It's called pain play, Mom. Google it. I don't like much, but a little spanking, some hard gripping, a bit of a pinch... That's enough for me." Her head popped out the neck hole, her hair in disarray. "Maybe you shouldn't google it unless you're wearing your pearls. Then you'll have something to clutch."

"Sometimes I don't understand you."

"You don't have to. But Mom, this has got to stop. I promise I'll tell you if I want to leave, but the boys are going to start picking up on your prejudices if you don't actively work on them."

"I'm not prejudiced!"

Amanda raised an eyebrow, aware that she looked even more like her mother when she did so. "What was this really about then?" She shook her head and started brushing her hair. "Don't answer that. *Think* about it. We'll be home for Thanksgiving and Christmas."

Her mother was silent until Amanda put the brush down on the dresser.

"Do you always... you know?"

Amanda chuckled. "Do I always what, Mom?"

"Walk around naked?" her mother whispered.

"No, not always. It's getting a little chilly." Amanda shrugged. "If we sit on furniture, we clean it afterwards, if that's what you're worried about."

"I wasn't worried," she replied too quickly.

Amanda laughed. "Come on, we should go rescue Daddy. Who knows what those boys might be doing to him." She didn't wait for her mom, walking barefoot out into the hall and scooping up her scattered clothing before trotting down the stairs and shoving them into the laundry room.

Her father was now sitting at the kitchen island, a glass of red wine in front of him.

"Dinner's almost ready," James said over his shoulder as he poured the pasta into a colander in the sink.

"I'll set the table," Amanda said, squeezing past Tony to get to the cutlery drawer.

He smacked her lightly on the ass on the way by, and she winked at him.

"In front of your parents?" James murmured out of the corner of his mouth.

"I was looking forward to a thorough dicking down before dinner," Amanda whispered back.

The pot hit the side of the sink with a loud *clang*, drawing the attention of the others.

"Sorry," James apologized to the room.

Amanda bit her lip to hold in her giggles.

"Brat," James said affectionately. "You'll pay for that after your parents leave for the theater."

"Looking forward to it," Amanda replied, sticking her tongue out at him on her way back to the dining room.

Tony and James exchanged glances and shook their heads as one, their eyes twinkling with suppressed mirth. They quickly served the spaghetti, filling each plate with pasta and sauce, working seamlessly as a team.

"It's fascinating to watch you two work together," Paul said, waving a finger around between the stove and counter. "You don't even have to talk to each other, it's like a predetermined choreography."

"We *did* take ballroom classes together," Tony pointed out.

"I'll lead, you follow," James said with a chuckle, dropping the pasta scoop in the pot and grabbing Tony around the waist, pulling him into a box-step around the island.

"Dude, I'm going to drip tomato sauce onto either you or the floor," Tony said urgently.

James neatly plucked the spoon out of his hand and dropped it into the sink. "We're done anyways."

"I think the point he was trying to make was that we're in sync with each other," Tony said, gripping James's shoulder so hard his shirt wrinkled. "They have to eat to get to the theater on time."

James paused their dance, his eyes skimming over Tony's face. "You okay?"

"I'm fine." Tony knew a muscle was jumping in his jaw from how tightly he was clenching it. "Hungry, though."

"Let's eat," James said, spinning Tony around and walking him back over to where the plates were cooling.

Tony shrugged him off. "I can walk."

"Wow, we really need to get some food in you, Mister Grumpypants," Amanda teased, bumping her hip against his as she grabbed her plate. She took his free hand in hers and pulled him into the dining room ahead of the others. "And if that doesn't help raise your spirits, I'm sure I can come up with something once my parents leave."

"You always make me feel better," Tony replied, squeezing her hand and trying not to think about how right it had felt to be held by James. He hadn't meant anything by it, and Tony had to stop reading too much into every interaction he had with his best friend. The line between friendship and more was blurring, and every day it was harder to see where it lay. Ever since that party at Glenn's at the beginning of summer, when James had cockwarmed him on a dare, he couldn't stop thinking about what it would be like if James *wanted* to go down on him, his jaw stretched wide to accommodate his girth... Tony gave himself a shake and willed his erection away. He couldn't let his feelings ruin the best thing that had ever happened to him.

He brought Amanda's hand to his mouth and gently kissed her palm. "For later," he whispered.

"Love you," she replied with a grin.

James watched his best friends interacting, an ache in his chest.

"Are you alright, son?" Paul asked.

James gave himself a shake. "Just thinking."

"Not jealous?"

He shook his head and moved into the dining room. He wasn't jealous in the way Amanda's father meant; there was no animosity in his regard for Tony. Instead, he wished he had the freedom to hold his hand, drag him into a kiss, or even just dance with him without feeling like he was pushing the limits of their friendship past the boundary that Tony set between them.

The two of them could fuck the same girl at the same time, cocks pressed against each other in the sheath of her body, but a fully clothed hug had Tony breaking away from him after only a few seconds.

James's jaw muscles clenched, and he had to forcibly relax as he sat beside Amanda, mirroring Tony.

Amanda's slender hand rested on his thigh, giving a light squeeze.

His frustration simmered and cooled in the wake of her unspoken affection. His hand found hers under the table and he returned the squeeze before letting go so he could eat.

James couldn't wait until her parents left so that they could spoil her with orgasms. If he couldn't be with Tony alone, he would accept the next best thing. He almost groaned out loud, disgusted with himself for even thinking that way. He loved Amanda with all his heart. The thing was, he felt the same way for Tony, and it was killing him that he couldn't tell him so.

It was unlike James to be so quiet. Tony's lack of communication must have hit him harder than she realized. But the car was not the place to try to make James feel better, so she held her tongue until they got home and parked.

"I'd like to take a bath with you," James said, but his smile didn't reach his eyes.

"I would love that." Mentally, she added, *And then I can pry out what's bugging you.*

The house felt too silent without Tony's presence. She missed him already and he wasn't even on his flight yet. "How will we survive a month without him?" she mused, not expecting an answer.

"With plenty of distractions. That presentation you did at work yesterday is going to lead to a big project, isn't it?" James tapped her ass lightly as she climbed the stairs ahead of him.

"It'll take some time to set up the analysis, but I'm in charge of that as well as the new marketing plan." She spun to face him once she reached the main level.

"Turning the company on its head already," James said admiringly. "I'm proud of you."

"Thanks." She beamed at him, wrapping her arms around his neck.

"Put your clothes in the laundry," he said, walking her backward into the laundry room. "We'll put on a load and then go relax in the tub."

"You get the water ready, I'll do the laundry."

"Deal." He sealed it with a kiss that quickly turned heated, her whimpered gasps puffing air directly into his mouth. He pulled back slightly, teasingly, running his nose along her cheekbone to her ear. He tongued at the lobe before gently biting down.

Amanda's knees buckled and James caught her, holding her between him and the washer, one knee between her thighs. Deft fingers pulled her shirt up and over her head, his mouth only separating from the skin of her neck for the briefest moment.

"Undo my belt," he ordered, gripping his shirt by the collar at the back of his neck and yanking it over his head.

Her brain spinning, her fingers fumbled over the familiar clasp of his belt, tugging the leather aside to get the bit of metal out of the way. She didn't even notice that he'd undone the clasp of her bra until he ran his thumbs over her sensitive nipples. "Didn't you have to get the bathwater ready?" she asked, remembering the tasks they had set for each other.

"My clothes need to be washed too," James said, now focused on pushing her skirt over her ass, her panties following its trajectory down her legs to pool at her feet. "Haven't you finished yet?" he asked, obviously amused at her attempts to rid him of his belt. "You're naked, and all I've lost is my shirt. Why don't you start filling the machine while I finish stripping?"

Amanda pouted. "I could've finished if you hadn't been distracting me."

James chuckled. "What you're telling me is that I didn't give you enough incentive."

"That's not what I said," she replied, shaking her head.

"Turn around," James said, twirling his finger in the air. "Stick your pretty little ass in the air while you fill the machine, and you might be filled as well."

She snapped her mouth shut, eyes wide as she stared at him for a second.

He raised one eyebrow, waiting patiently, and she whipped around, opening the front load door of the washing machine.

"Good girl," James purred, his voice almost better than a caress.

While she filled the machine, the sounds of him undressing filled her ears. The metal of his belt clinked together, the swish of the leather against the jean material as he pulled it through the loops, the buzz of the zipper, the soft flump of material hitting the floor...

His hands brushed against the skin of her hips, curling around to the front of her thighs at the same time as he pressed his cock against the seam of her ass. "You're still a mess from this morning," he murmured in her ear, pressing kisses to her shoulder blades.

The skating of his fingertips through the sticky cum on her thighs made her shiver. "I am."

James pressed one finger between her lower lips, sliding easily through her arousal. "And yet you're still dripping for me."

"How do you know that's not your leftovers?" she sassed, trying not to sound too affected by him.

"You think I don't know the difference between my cum and your arousal?" he replied, grinding his cock against her ass and spearing deep with his finger. "This is new and it's just for me."

"What's the difference?" she asked, clenching on his finger.

"Yours is slick and slippery," James whispered hotly in her ear, circling her clit until she whined. "But I can see I'm distracting you from your job. I'll see you upstairs."

Before she registered his intent, his hands and warmth had left her, and footsteps echoed on the stairs. Amanda gripped the top of the washing machine to stay on her feet, her clit throbbing from her denied orgasm. "God *dammit*, James!" she shouted up at him.

His only reply was laughter and the distant sound of the water turning on.

She stuffed the rest of the clothes from the basket into the washing machine and turned it on before running up the stairs and into the bathroom. "You are a horrible human being," she informed him, poking his chest on his heart-shaped tattoo, a copy of the one on both her and Tony's bodies.

"So horrible," James agreed readily. "The water isn't quite ready yet."

"That's fine." She sat on the toilet seat and watched him move around the bathroom, collecting her favorite body wash and a loofah from the shower across the room. Her gaze lingered on his powerful thighs and the obliques arrowing down his hips to his bobbing cock.

He noticed her distraction when he headed back in her direction. "Something you want?" he teased.

"I was trying to decide which bath salt I wanted," Amanda said. "Lavender?"

"And vanilla?" James suggested.

"Naturally."

"Can you get them from the closet, please?"

"Sure thing." She crossed the room to their closet, which was a massive walk-in with a sloped ceiling. The bath salts were easy to access, right inside the door, but she had to hunt through them to find the right ones. "We're almost out of—" She ran into James's hard body, blocking the door. "Vanilla," she finished breathlessly. "Is the water ready?"

"No idea," James answered, cupping her cheek with one big hand.

Her eyes fluttered closed and she leaned into his touch.

He slid his hand through her hair to the base of her skull, pressing her back against the shelves holding their spare towels. "I needed to hold you," he whispered into her neck, his loose hair tickling her cheek.

Amanda clenched the two vials of bath salts in her fists, wanting to grab onto him. "You have me."

He groaned, pressing his lips to her skin, goosebumps erupting from his touch. "I need to be inside you."

"Yesssss," she hissed, arching into his grip. His cock twitched against her lower belly, in agreement with her words. The wooden shelving dug into her back and ass, preventing her from moving too much. "In the water?"

James bit her shoulder lightly, his tongue soothing the sparks of pain a moment later. "Okay," he rasped.

Rather than let her go, he scooped her up by her thighs and carried her out, leaving the closet door open behind him.

"I can walk," Amanda reminded him, wrapping her legs around his waist and grinding her clit against his cock.

"You say one thing, but your body is telling me another."

"You keep teasing me, and I'll have to pin you down and ride you," Amanda countered. She tried to get the angle right to get his cock inside of her, but she couldn't get the grip she needed on his shoulders with her hands full.

"That's not the threat you seem to think it is," James replied with a chuckle. He put her down, much to her disappointment, and took the two bottles from her.

He made quick work of pouring the correct amounts into the steaming bath water, their scents filling the air and immediately soothing her.

The wide stand-alone bathtub was one of her favorite things about this house. All three of them could fit, with some creativity, and the faucet didn't dig into anyone's head because it was on the long side of the tub.

James sat at his usual end and held his hand out for her to use as support.

Amanda joined him, straddling his lap and sinking down on his cock at last. The water added levels of complexity, the buoyancy making it difficult to get him as deep as she wanted, as well as preventing her from thrusting down on him.

James leaned back, resting his head on the lip of the tub in a pillow of hair, and closed his eyes.

She plastered herself against his chest, resting her chin on her hands. "This is nice," she murmured, not wanting to disturb the quiet.

He traced nonsense patterns on her back with his fingertips, giving her goosebumps despite the warmth of the water.

"Relaxing in the bath, lovely scents surrounding us, me warming your cock." Amanda clenched her Kegel muscles and James hummed in pleasure. "Are you going to tell me what's been bothering you now?"

His eyes snapped open, staring up at the ceiling.

"Don't try to tell me everything's fine. I've known you my whole life. I know when something's wrong." Amanda studied his panicked expression before kissing his chin, stubble scraping over her lips. "It's not just Tony going away. What is it?"

"I'm such a coward," James whispered the words to the ceiling so quietly she wasn't sure she heard him.

It was also the last thing she expected to hear him say. "I don't understand," she said.

His throat bobbed as he swallowed. "I love you."

"And that makes you a coward?" She was fully confused now.

James huffed a laugh. "No. I just wanted to make sure you knew that. I'm in love with you. That won't change."

"Why would it?"

He swallowed hard again. "I love Tony."

She nodded her agreement. "So you've said, many times."

"I'm *in love* with Tony," James clarified, his voice thick.

"Ohhhhh." She laid her cheek against James's chest, listening to his heart beat, waiting for him to continue.

"I wrote him a letter last night. I was going to give it to him, or put it in his suitcase or *something*, and I didn't. It's downstairs on the table in the hall. Because I was too much of a coward. I couldn't tell him to his face. I couldn't even let him read it in a letter on the other side of the country. I'm such a fucking *hypocrite*!" He let out a bitter chuckle. "I told him he needed to be a better communicator, but look at me!"

Amanda didn't reply, letting his heart and breathing calm down after his outburst. "You're allowed to be afraid," she said at last. "It's scary to tell your best friend that you're in love with him."

"How did you manage it?"

She chuckled. "By being impatient, remember?"

"I wasn't there at the beginning. Tell me." James closed his eyes again.

"Oh my God! I forgot you weren't there!" Amanda propped her chin on her hands again. "Tony was a little more flirty than usual, letting his eyes linger on my body. Then came the sunscreen test!"

James's lips quirked up. "Sunscreen test?"

She nodded vehemently, rocking her body in the water and making both of them hiss in pleasure. "Yeah. You know how, when we were kids, we'd put sunscreen on each other and it was super platonic? No lingering touches, just briskly rubbing it in?"

"Vaguely," he teased.

"Well, he lingered. And he didn't brush me off when I suggested some risky spots." She shrugged. "Enough that I knew he wanted me. As for love…" She hesitated. "I wasn't sure whether you guys would love me. Friends-with-bennies wasn't what I wanted. I guess I just hoped that you two felt the same way, and were okay with sharing me."

"I don't think of our relationship as sharing you," James said slowly. "Possibly because of my feelings for Tony as well, but…" he trailed off, biting the inside of his cheek as he thought. "You know, when we first met him, back when we were all twelve, I was jealous that you wanted to include him in our group for all of ten seconds."

"Ten seconds," Amanda repeated, amazed. "What happened?"

James shrugged, the water sloshing. "He fit. It was like he belonged with us. His dry sarcasm, his slight roughness… It was a perfect fit. And he didn't treat either of us any different because you were a girl, or I was Black."

"Wait, you're Black?" Amanda teased.

He tickled her ribs, making her squirm on his cock. He sat up, hugging her close. "I want to feel you come."

"We're not done talking about this. Why were you so scared to tell him?" She nudged their noses together, breath mingling.

"I've been keeping it a secret for so long. It's hard to get out of the habit."

Her eyebrows rose. "How long?"

"Long enough."

"*How long?*" she pressed.

He captured her lower lip between his teeth, releasing it a breath later. "My love for both of you has felt eternal."

"Poetic," she said sarcastically.

"Truth." He met her eyes, the rich brown of them almost hypnotizing. "I have a hard time untangling my emotions. When did a hug become more than comforting? When did I crave your, plural, presence because I enjoyed hanging out with you compared to missing the other pieces of my soul?"

Amanda blinked in surprise. "Really poetic."

James blushed, his cheeks darkening. "I've been thinking about this a lot since we moved in together."

"And in the *two years* we've been living together, have you come to any conclusions?" She wanted to snuggle in, press kisses to his neck, and bite down on his shoulder. She couldn't do any of that until he finished talking because it would distract them both.

"I'm in love with him." James shrugged helplessly. "And I guess," he added sheepishly, "him leaving without much notice was the kick in the pants that I needed."

"Except you didn't tell him," Amanda pointed out.

He groaned and rubbed his hands down his face, leaving trails of water behind. "Don't remind me. Now I have to wait a whole month, terrified out of my wits that he doesn't return my affections and it'll tear our lives apart."

"I think you're being a little dramatic. You know that Tony wouldn't do that." She grabbed his wrists and pulled them down. He let her; there was no way she could move him otherwise.

"Suppose he isn't interested in me like that," James said. "You don't think he'd be weirded out by the fact that I'll still be seeing him naked, lusting after him in our bed?"

"Lusting," Amanda repeated with a snort.

"Yes," James replied seriously. "It took everything in me this morning not to reach for him, kiss him, suck his cock, bend him over, *fuck*, even bend over for *him*!" His eyes widened. "I've never done that, never felt the deep-seated need to have my lover inside me."

Amanda swallowed hard. "That's hot. I would love to see that." She gave herself a shake, banishing the mental image of her best friends fucking each other. "Nico never fucked you?"

"No. He never even asked." James shrugged. "I didn't mind. It wasn't his thing."

"I can see why. You're a really good lover," Amanda said with a wink. "I love having you inside me."

"I'm shocked. This is my shocked face." He sobered. "Will you be alright if Tony *is* into me as well? You wouldn't be the center of attention at all times."

"Hmm." Amanda sat back and held out her hands, palms up, as if she were weighing her options. "Always being the center of attention from two men, or watching the hottest guys I know delight in their own intimacy?" She clapped her hands together, a little water splashing them in the face. "I really can't see the downside."

James laughed. "What did I do to deserve you?"

She gave in to the urge to snuggle him. "You said yes. You met my enthusiasm with your own." She bit down the muscle of his shoulder and he grabbed her ass in response. "You give me heaps of orgasms whenever I demand them," she said with a giggle.

"You *are* demanding," James growled. "I suppose you want one now?"

"I'm desperate for one," she replied breathlessly.

"Hmmm," James said, rocking her on his cock. "I'm not sure you're desperate enough just yet."

"You are so mean to me," Amanda whimpered. "Please make me come. Don't you want to feel me clenching around you?"

"I do," James said agreeably. "I also know how to practice patience."

Amanda huffed. "How long?"

"I can make you come when we call Tony tonight, how's that?"

"Fuck," she gasped, shuddering. "Maybe I should get off you now, then."

"If you insist."

Amanda rose on her knees, until only his head rested inside her, ready to call his bluff. But he only supported her ass in his hands, not urging her one way or the other. "What do you want me to do?"

"Whatever you want." James leaned forwards and sucked one nipple into his mouth. "I'm not stopping you."

"Where do you want me?"

"Wherever you're happiest."

She huffed again, impatiently blowing damp hair out of her face. "Right now, I want you inside me."

"That would feel fan-fucking-tastic."

"And I want to come."

"You're more than welcome to get yourself off," James said.

Amanda slowly sank back down his rock-hard cock, so turned on that she could barely think straight. "What about you?"

"If you come, I'll probably paint your insides white," James readily admitted.

"*God*," Amanda groaned. "I want that."

"Then do it." James held her hips down in the water, keeping himself seated deep within her. "Make yourself come."

She cuddled back into his neck, nuzzling his ear and sucking the lobe into her mouth. Amanda started a slow grind of her clit in a figure-eight over his pubic bone, the hair a pleasurable tickle that she welcomed. It didn't take long for her breathing to start coming in gasps and pants.

"That's it, sunshine," James murmured encouragingly. "Use my body for your pleasure. Make yourself come."

"Oh God," she muttered, all her senses on high alert. A deep breath in filled her nose with the scent of his skin mixed with lavender and vanilla.

The rasp of his stubble against her temple was bordering on irritating, but the little pleasure zings it was sending directly to her clit were outweighing the pain. She sucked at his earlobe again, needing something in her mouth to ground her, only to release it around her next whimper.

"Fuck," James groaned, his fingers dimpling her skin. "You're really testing my control, love."

"Wait for me," Amanda gasped. "Want to come together."

"You have no idea how much I want to reach between us to rub over your clit."

"I'm not stopping you."

He shook his head. "It'll be my turn later. Come on, Amanda. You can do it."

She closed her eyes, visualizing where they were joined, where she was stretched around his girth. Her breathing hitched, her pleasure mounting higher with each roll of her hips. "Hold me," she begged. "Wrap me up in you."

Amanda was so relieved she didn't need to explain what she meant; James released her hips and banded his arms around her body, one hand holding her head and the other on her ass. "Yesssss," she hissed, rocking down into him. "Oh God, yes, James," she moaned, chasing her orgasm now.

The water splashed against the sides of the tub from her efforts.

She tipped over the edge of ecstacy unexpectedly, her nerves singing with pleasure as she shook apart.

James buried his forehead in her shoulder, hot pants of air feathering down her chest.

Amanda could feel his cock pulse within her, his release mirroring her own.

"Do you feel any better about Tony?" she asked, her words sounding loud after the stillness. She ran her fingers down his back, finding the muscle groups that were tense and rubbing them.

"I feel better now that it's out in the open with you, now that I know you're not upset about my feelings. But I don't think I'll feel one hundred percent better until Tony's back home and I can talk to him." James lifted his head to look her in the eyes. "I love you."

Amanda slid her lips over his, the plushness of his bottom lip giving under the pressure. "Love you too." She rested her forehead against his tiredly. "I'm starting to feel like a prune."

James chuckled. "We haven't been in here that long. You're out of practice at being in the pool for hours on end."

She shuddered. "You have no idea how glad I am to have an underwear job now. Wet spandex is just..." She trailed off with another shiver of disgust.

"I've got a pretty good idea." James pushed up on the sides of the tub, his biceps bulging as he lifted them both out of the water, Amanda still wrapped around him.

"Show off," she teased him.

"I don't want you to get off me just yet." He carefully stepped out onto the tile. "There's a lot of water on the floor. We'll have to clean it up."

"We can use our towels," Amanda suggested, letting him slip from her body and putting her feet on the floor. "They could probably use a wash."

"Good plan." James made sure she was stable before letting go of her. "I'm tempted to let you drip all over the floor," he murmured, running gentle fingers between her legs. "Just to see my cum leaking out of you."

Amanda gripped his shoulders and chuckled. "Tony had me do that last night."

"Great minds think alike." He sank one finger inside her and drew in a sharp breath. "Tasting his cum as it gushes out between your legs is one of my favorite treats."

She shivered. "I swear I'm in a constant state of arousal around the two of you. That's so hot."

James ran his nose along her cheekbone. "Let's get you cleaned up before I make you dirty again."

"I'd believe that more if you didn't have your finger inside me," she teased.

"Maybe I'll tie you to the bed and leave you with a vibe attached to your clit while I head back to the library," James threatened playfully, pulling his hand away and smacking her ass.

"You're going out?" She hated that a lump formed in her throat at the thought. She wasn't the type of person who needed to be around her partners twenty-four-seven. Usually.

James must have sensed her emotional turmoil, because he wrapped her up in a hug. "I still have some work to do. Want to bring your laptop and come with me?"

"I wouldn't be a bother?"

"Never. A distraction, perhaps." He grinned when she poked him in the ribs. "A very nice distraction."

"I know how to behave myself."

"That's true. I'll have to think up some form of reward if you behave." He tapped his lips in thought.

"And if I don't?"

His voice deepened in a drawl, "Oh, so many possibilities."

"I want you to be able to tell Tony I was your good girl," Amanda said, giving him her best puppy dog eyes.

"You know how to be good for me."

"Blow job?" Amanda asked innocently.

James chuckled. "Maybe later. Do what you're told."

"Yes, sir."

Amanda feasted her eyes on Tony's tired face late that night. "How was your flight?" she asked.

"Not too bad," he replied, reclining in his chair and stretching his arms overhead. "Not enough leg room, but what else is new?"

"Unca!" shrieked a tiny voice. "Hi!"

"Of course, kiddo," Tony said easily, gesturing off-screen. He bent out of frame, only the top of his head visible for a moment, and then a small child's face was filling the screen.

The child stared at her, suddenly shy, and stuck two fingers in his mouth.

Amanda chuckled. "Hello, Cody! Nice to see you. Did you do anything fun today?"

He nodded silently.

Tony tickled his ribs. "You interrupt my time with my beautiful girl-friend to say hi, and then you say nothing? You little monster!" He made nomming noises and pretended to eat Cody's neck, making the toddler shriek with laughter.

"Oh, *there* you are, Cody," came a woman's voice from off screen. She briefly appeared. "Sorry, Amanda. I'll get him out of your hair, Tony."

"No worries, Sophia," Amanda said.

"I'll make sure to lock my door if I want privacy," Tony added.

"Good idea. He can't pick locks yet." Sophia scooped up the toddler and balanced him on her hip. "Say bye to Aunt Amanda."

Cody tucked his head under his mother's chin and waved at the screen.

"Time for your bath."

"Nononononono!" the toddler shrieked, the sound getting quieter as he was taken from the room.

"I'll get the door," Tony said, standing up and giving Amanda an eyeful of the crotch of his jeans.

"What did I miss?" James asked, coming into the room and dropping a kiss on the top of her head.

"Cody being adorable," Amanda said. "Tony's just locking the door."

"I just put the laundry in again. You forgot to add the detergent."

Amanda gaped at him for a moment. "Ohmigosh, seriously? That's so funny. You distracted me that much."

"Yeah, I did." His eyes twinkled with mischief. "We're alone?" James said, once Tony was sitting back down.

"Yeah. The door isn't super sound-proofed, but as alone as I'll get," Tony replied. "You got something in mind?"

"I needed to tell you that Amanda was a *very* good girl today," James said.

"Oh *really*?" Tony leaned forwards, elbows on his knees. "What reward did you have in mind?"

"Strip," James ordered her.

Amanda obeyed while James filled Tony in on the plan. She finished quickly and waited naked in front of them.

"Come here, sunshine," James said, taking her by the hand. "Sit on my lap. Spread your legs and show Tony that beautiful little pussy. Are you dripping yet?"

"I'm naked, of course I'm wet," Amanda said with a chuckle.

Tony echoed her laugh. "So well trained for us."

"Show us," James urged, grabbing a toy off the desk.

His clothes rasped against her sensitive skin as he shifted, heightening her awareness of him. She speared her fingers inside herself, collecting her wetness. She showed the camera, twisting her hand under the overhead lighting to highlight the glistening.

"Beautiful," Tony murmured.

"Is the app ready?" James asked. The toy buzzed to life in his hand. "Nice. Let me clean your fingers, sunshine."

Amanda held her hand to his mouth at the same time as he slid the bulbous end of the J-shaped toy into her. The dual sensations of James's tongue and the vibrations controlled by Tony were setting her nerves alight. "Feels amazing. God, yes, Tony, that level is perfect."

"This is brilliant, James," Tony said, fumbling with his belt buckle. "Amanda, you look so good, spread out for us, taking all the pleasure we can give you."

"I'm glad you're still able to connect with us," Amanda said breathlessly, the roughness of James's jeans scraping against her thighs and ass. His cock was swelling to attention behind her and she reveled in her power over her two men. "Tony, I have a question."

"What's up, darlin'?" he asked when she was silent for a moment.

"When did you fall in love with me?"

"I loved you from that first summer we were together."

"Yeah, but that's not the same thing," Amanda said, her free hand grabbing James's and squeezing tightly. "Fuck, so close."

"I see your point," Tony said slowly. He stroked his cock, only the tip visible at the bottom of the screen. "Sometime in high school. There wasn't exactly a *bam* that's it, I'm in love,' moment. But definitely well before that video, if that's what you're asking."

Amanda shuddered at the thought of the video of her topless that had been circulated around their class in their junior year. "I'm glad that wasn't a deciding factor."

"You know that we wouldn't have watched it at all without your permission," Tony said seriously. "No matter how many fantasies I'd had about you by then, watching that video would have felt gross without your go-ahead."

"You fantasized about me, Tony?" Amanda gasped, grinding back hard against James's cock when the toy inside her increased in intensity. "Tell me about one of them?"

Tony grimaced. "Trust me, the reality *far* surpassed the teenage fantasies," he said wryly.

"I still want to hear them."

"My favorite recurring fantasy was you crawling into my bed with me, fully naked, and sucking me off to wake me up," Tony said, a light flush on his cheeks. "You also joined me in the shower fairly often."

"Those sound like fun. I'll make your fantasies a reality when you come home." The vibrations increased again, feeling like they were throughout her body. "If you knew you were in love with me in high school, why didn't you say something?"

"I didn't want to lose your friendship," Tony said, shrugging up one shoulder. "And there was James to consider, too."

"What do you mean?" Amanda pulled her fingers out of James's mouth so he could participate in the conversation.

"In my teenage brain, there were two reactions to my declaration; either you returned my affections, or you didn't. But no matter what, things would change between the three of us. Would things get weird if you didn't love me back? How would James feel if you did? And then I found out he loved you too, and it got even more complicated."

Amanda turned her head to kiss James's jaw. "Why didn't you say anything?"

"I was scared things would change," he said quietly.

Amanda recognized the same reasoning that James had used to put off telling Tony his true feelings. "I'm sorry I didn't recognize my feelings earlier. I knew I loved you both, and I was constantly horny around you guys. I just didn't understand what being in love felt like."

"We got here in the end," James said, adjusting his grip on the toy. "Now come for us like the good girl you are."

Chapter Six

Flashback: Dance Class

"*Why* are we doing these classes?" Tony complained to James under his breath.

The two sixteen-year-olds were leaning against the ballet bars opposite a wall of mirrors, where their parents were chatting in a small circle.

"Because it's something that the parents always wanted to do as a group," James whispered back. "And Amanda was excited about it."

Tony inclined his head in acknowledgement of that fact.

"It'll be fun!" James added bracingly.

"I hope you're right," Tony muttered.

The Beyer family arrived, Amanda a little breathless as she hurried over to her friends. She fidgeted with her skirt, turning it so that the tag was in the back. "Sorry we're late. Volleyball practice ran late, so dinner was late, so *we're* late." She heaved a sigh and beamed at them. "Ready to have some fun?"

"I am!" Tony enthused, avoiding James's eyes. James would know why he was acting more excited than he felt, and he wouldn't blame him. James felt the same way about Amanda; butterflies in his stomach, always wanting to impress her, the swooping feeling when she laughed or smiled because of something he said.

Amanda beamed at them. "Who would like to be my partner first? I can't promise I won't step on your toes. I'll probably have trouble following your lead, and I might get frustrated with you."

"Why would we want to partner you then?" James teased, smirking at her.

"Just for that, I choose Tony," Amanda said, sticking her tongue out at James while simultaneously tucking her hand around Tony's arm. "We'll have more fun than you, partnered with the teacher."

"Yeah, but I'll probably learn more and won't have sore feet by the end of the lesson," James pointed out, a twinkle in his eye.

Amanda pouted and glanced up at Tony. "I'll do my best not to step on you."

"Should I have worn steel-toe boots?" Tony asked, cringing playfully away from her.

"Hello everyone, and welcome to Ballroom 101! My name is Vivian." Their teacher greeted them with a wide smile. She gestured to a young girl behind her, who stepped forward. "As there was an uneven number, I asked my daughter Isabelle to round us out."

James bowed to the young girl and she drifted towards him.

"I've won *several* junior ballroom competitions," she informed them.

"I took a hip hop class one year when I was younger," James replied with a grin.

"Then I'll have a lot of work ahead of me," Isabelle said with a sigh.

"How old are you?" Tony asked.

"Eleven." Isabelle eyed him curiously. "Do *you* have a dance background?"

"Zero," Tony replied cheerfully.

"I've done ballet and gymnastics, and that one hip hop class," Amanda volunteered.

"The ballet might help you," Isabelle conceded. She looked back at her mother and sighed, rolling her eyes.

James and Tony smothered a chuckle behind their hands. Amanda elbowed Tony, who was closest to her, in the ribs.

"We will start with a simple waltz." Vivian helped them adjust their arms so that they were holding each other properly and then demonstrated the step. "Listen to the music and it's ONE, two, three, ONE, two, three." She clapped her hands to the beat as she moved her feet. "Don't anticipate, ladies, follow the movement of your partners. Men, you show your partner where you're going by applying pressure on their waist."

Tony's brow furrowed as he tried to concentrate on the steps and directing Amanda. "Who knew that dancing could be so complicated?" he mumbled.

Amanda giggled. "I assume we'll get used to it if we practice. I'm enjoying spending time with you."

"Yeah?" Tony was surprised and flushed lightly. "Good," he said gruffly. He looked back down at his feet.

"Look at your partner's face, not at your feet," admonished Vivian.

"When do we learn to spin, do you think?" Amanda asked Tony.

He grinned. "No time like the present!" He gave her waist a little push, sending her spinning out under his arm, her skirt billowing around her legs.

He tugged on their joined hands and she spun back into him, colliding with his chest with an "oof!" from both of them.

Amanda laughed. "Great first attempt."

"We'll get to more complicated steps like spins *after* you've mastered the basics," Vivian said firmly. Then she smiled. "I'm glad you're having fun."

They moved on from the waltz to a salsa, and it was amusing to watch everyone try to wiggle their hips in the proper movements.

Surprisingly, James's dad got it first.

"Very good!" Vivian praised him. "Just think of your pelvis as a cradle and you're rocking a baby to sleep."

Amanda giggled. "I don't think I'm very maternal then."

Tony and James both had furrowed brows as they watched their hips in the mirror across from them.

"I thought I almost had it, but then I didn't," James muttered.

"I feel like a robot," Tony said, frustrated.

"Everyone should practice at home," Vivian said. "See you all same time next week. We'll do a quick refresher of the waltz and salsa before moving on to the foxtrot and rumba."

"Shall we get together to practice tomorrow after school?" Amanda said, skipping between Tony and James.

"I don't know..." Tony hedged playfully.

She pouted up at him. "Please?"

"Those puppy dog eyes are dangerous, sunshine," James said, tugging on her hand. "Better be careful what you use them for."

"After practicing, we can do whatever you want," Amanda suggested. "Go for a run, watch a movie—"

"Whatever I want?" Tony's eyes twinkled with mischief. "I'll come up with something."

James chuckled. "And what's *my* incentive?"

"Isn't spending time with your best friends enough?" Amanda said. "What do you want?"

"Your grandmother's shortbread recipe," James said.

She gaped at him. "That isn't mine to give! I don't even know where Mom hides it! It's only for family members."

"Aren't we practically family?"

"I can try asking Mom, but since we're not married…" She shrugged.

"I think you're a little young to get married," Tony said wryly.

"At least in this state," James added.

"Wow, you must really want that recipe," Amanda teased. "I'll let Mom know we're on the way to the altar, and maybe she'll allow you to peek at the recipe."

"Why don't we start this relationship by learning how to dance?" James said.

"Great idea!" Amanda said enthusiastically.

"Wow, he gets marriage *and* the family recipe? I'll have to think up something really good," Tony said thoughtfully. "How about a date?"

"A date?" Amanda asked, stopping abruptly and staring at him.

"Yeah, like the three of us order pizza and binge-watch something on a streaming service?"

"Normally there aren't three people on a date," James said.

Tony scoffed. "Since when are we normal?"

"That's what you want to do?" Amanda asked.

He shrugged. "I always want to hang out with you guys. I was just teasing about not wanting to dance. If you want to work on our hip movements, I'm game." Tony wiggled his eyebrows suggestively.

She laughed. "Actually, that's not a bad suggestion. We've been practicing separately. Maybe together would make it easier."

"I was joking!" Tony gasped.

"I know." She patted his arm. "I know you two don't think of me *that* way. It'll be fine."

Tony and James exchanged glances over her head as they continued their walk home. *What exactly did she mean?*

None of them had after-school activities on Friday: a rare case. They walked home from the nearby high school, changed at their separate houses, and then met on Amanda's back porch.

"What's the plan?" Tony said, rubbing his hands together. The fall weather hadn't yet turned too chilly, but the breeze had a bite to it.

"I want to use the kitchen doors like the mirrors of the dance studio," Amanda said, gesturing at them. "I practiced a bit this morning, and I think I got the hang of it. So instead of us lining up, you'll each practice with me to guide you!"

"Guide us?" James echoed questioningly.

"Yeah!" Amanda chirped. She took her place in front of the door and pointed to the spot behind her. "Your front to my back, and we'll do the steps together. Try to match your hip motions to mine."

"How close?" James asked, hovering behind her.

She grabbed his hand and tugged, pulling him right up against her. "Like this. Your hands on my hips. We'll start with the right leg going forward, roll the hips with it. And to the center, now the left leg goes back. You're still really stiff. Relax, it's just us here. Forward and roll, backward and roll—What's wrong?"

James had broken away from her, turning to face the yard. "I just need a break."

"I felt like you were getting better, though," Amanda said with a frown. "Was it not working for you?"

"No, it was working fine." James drew in a long breath. "I just got a little too into it."

"What do you mean?"

He sighed, exasperated, and turned back around. "I got a little *excited*," he said meaningfully, his eyes dropping down.

Amanda avoided following his gaze and waved a hand. "That's not a big deal. I know you don't like me like that. You'd get a little hard if you were dancing like this with Tony, too. Now, can we continue?"

James gaped at her. "Uh, I guess?"

"Good. Right leg, roll. Left leg, roll." Amanda glanced over at Tony, who was imitating them. "We could make an Amanda sandwich! Come here, Tony. You'll be doing the steps backwards compared to us, is that okay?"

"It would be like actually dancing with you, wouldn't it?" Tony moved to face her.

"That's true. But we're not going to focus on arms, just the hips for now." She wasn't going to say anything to them, but being surrounded by her best friends was doing something to her head. She felt slightly dizzy, and more than a little aroused. Possibly because she could feel James brushing against her ass every time his hip movements didn't fully match hers. Or because Tony's gaze was intense in a different kind of way. One that made her think that perhaps there was something more than just friendship between them.

Her breath caught in her throat, and she stumbled.

Instantly, both guys tightened their grip on her hips, supporting her.

"You okay?" Tony asked.

"Yeah. Clumsy, sorry," Amanda said, trying to disguise her flustered reaction. "Let's switch up. James, are you ready to try dancing? Tony, you can work on the rolls of your hips."

"Sure."

She spun between them, putting Tony and his intense eyes at her back. Now she was facing James, who gave her a similar look. Maybe it wasn't feelings, but their dancing together that caused the reaction. She tried to swallow her disappointment. She glanced up at James as they continued to practice. She wondered if James was attracted to her too. She hoped not because she could never choose between the two of them if they were *both* into her. She gave herself a mental shake. She was being ridiculous. She didn't have to worry about romantic feelings with her best friends.

After a few more rounds of them alternating who was leading, they all felt more comfortable with the hip movements, and even left a little more space between their bodies.

"I've got to be honest," James said, rubbing the back of his neck with one hand as they headed inside. "I enjoyed this practice a lot more than dancing with Isabelle. It's too bad we can't learn the dances as the three of us."

Amanda tilted her head. "I mean, we could. We're the ones paying for the lessons."

"You mean our parents are paying," Tony interjected.

"Right." Amanda beamed at them. "So why don't we ask them if we can be taught to dance as a trio? I think that would be infinitely more fun."

"I hadn't thought of that," James said. "Do you think they'll go for it?"

"I think the only person who might be hesitant is Miss Vivian, but if we practice this week, dancing together, I mean, I think we might be able to sway her." Amanda spotted her dad in the office near the kitchen. "Daddy! We have a request!"

It was fairly easy to convince their parents, after they saw what the teens had been practicing that afternoon. Amanda's mom called the teacher and explained the change of plans.

"You know what movie we should watch?" Amanda said, bouncing a little on the couch with her slice of pizza.

"I thought this was anything that *I* wanted?" Tony said.

"It is. But I can make suggestions, can't I?" Amanda hurried on before Tony could disagree. "We should watch *Take the Lead*, because it has that ballroom dancing competition and there's a trio of dancers who compete in it!"

Tony deflated against the couch. "It's hard to argue with that logic. At least there are pretty people in it."

"We could change your name to Antonio," James teased.

"No way." Tony shuddered. "I don't even like 'Anthony'."

Amanda cuddled into his side. "Why not?"

Tony hesitated for a long moment. "Maybe some other time."

She and James exchanged glances. Whenever Tony shut down, it was because something from his past, before he'd been adopted by the Carlsons, was bothering him.

"Okay," Amanda said simply, and relaxed further into his side. He wrapped his arm behind her head, letting it drape down to her hip.

"Thanks guys," Tony said quietly.

Part Two:

Together
Again

Chapter Seven

Tony

Tony ended the last sentence, saved, and closed the file. He pushed his chair back and stretched his arms over his head, pulling first on one tricep and then the other.

It had been a long month.

Long, and lonely.

Sure, he'd been surrounded by family. His nephews were adorable. He'd taken Cody to the park nearly every evening and chased him around the play structure, caught him at the bottom of slides, and pushed him on the swings. Then he'd brought the toddler home for his bath and bedtime routine, and Tony got to cuddle Travis and usually ended up taking a nap with the tiny bundle curled up on his chest.

He'd freaked out the first time that had happened, but Sophia had reassured him that he was in the safest possible position, stretched out on the lounge, the baby cradled in one hand.

The slight weight on his chest was super comforting. The trust the tiny infant showed in drifting off to sleep in his arms was incredible, and he was going to miss their daily naps the most when he left.

Tony didn't want to tell anyone, but Travis was giving him baby fever.

He tried not to think about it too often because the thought of Amanda pregnant gave him erections at inopportune moments.

Adam knocked on the doorframe. "How's it going?"

Tony's eyes snapped open. "I think I drifted off for a second there. Just finished the last report."

"Sweet. Beer and the game?"

"Yeah." Tony heaved himself to his feet, twisting his torso to rid himself of the crick in his back. It still felt weird to look down at his older brother. He'd shot up at the end of high school, and when Adam had come home from college, Tony suddenly towered over him. "I'm thinking of bumping my flight up."

"Sick of us already?" Adam teased.

"Sick of *you*," Tony replied without any heat, following his brother to the family room. "Nah, I'm missing home. Nightly calls just aren't the same. And James has a swim meet on Monday. I'd like to be there for him. A red-eye on Sunday night would get me there in time to drive over to the pool with them."

"Amanda's taking the day off work?"

"The morning. She has an important meeting in the afternoon that she can't miss." Tony flopped onto the couch and stretched out.

"Leave me *some* room, you behemoth," Adam said, nudging Tony's knee. "How is there any room for Amanda on your couches at home? James is as big as you are!"

"She's usually on top of one of us," Tony said nonchalantly. "And James and I don't mind touching."

Adam's eyebrows rose as he handed Tony his beer. "Oh, really?"

Tony took a swig. "Not like that," he said quietly.

"That's not as defensive as I was expecting you to be."

"Yeah? Then you haven't been paying attention." If possible, Tony sank deeper into the couch.

"Little bro, I *have* been paying attention. You started getting defensive about your relationship with James around age, what was it, seventeen? Sixteen?"

"About then, I suppose."

"It was a little later than when you discovered girls. Makes sense, I suppose, since you didn't have many gay role models."

"I'm not gay," Tony said with a sigh.

"Didn't say you were," Adam replied easily. "Especially based on how you react to Amanda."

"Like a dog in heat?"

Adam winced. "I'm trying my best *not* to think of your sex life, thanks."

"Dude, you've got two mini-me's running around as evidence of yours," Tony pointed out.

"You want to play that game? Fine. You know it takes more than twice to get pregnant, right?"

"Sure." Tony shrugged. "You really think you're capable of making me cringe by talking about your vanilla sex life?"

"Hey, I like vanilla," Adam said.

"Now look who's defensive."

"Rude. Get out of my house."

Tony drank from his beer. "How about tomorrow night?"

"If that's the earliest you can manage." They were silent for a minute before Adam spoke again. "You know I don't care what queer box you fit in, right, bro? I just want you to be happy."

"So you've said. And I *am* happy." Tony chewed the inside of his cheek. "But sometimes I wonder…"

Adam raised an eyebrow. "If you could be even happier?"

"Selfish, aren't I?"

"A bit," Adam teased. "But not for this."

Tony let out a long breath. "Really?" He hadn't realized how much he cared about his brother's opinion on this.

"Dude, you three have been attached at the hip since the moment you met. To be honest, I'm a little jealous of the bond you share. The fact that you grew from friendship into this—" Adam waved a hand in the air, "—is amazing. You've been living together for two years. What are you waiting for?"

Taking a drink only prolonged the wait. "Don't want to fuck with the status quo." Tony shrugged. "At least if I stay silent, nothing changes."

"Nothing changing isn't a good way to live," Adam pointed out. "You're scared."

"Yeah, obviously. I could lose them both if I speak up."

Adam snorted. "As if."

"You don't know that."

"I know *them*. Not as well as you do, of course, but since your head's so far up your own ass that you can't see that they worship the ground you walk on, I guess it's up to me to point it out to you."

"Graphic," Tony said around a chuckle.

"Did it work?"

Tony wrinkled his nose. "You really think they'd be okay with me telling James I'm in love with him?"

"*That's* what you want to say?" Adam gaped at him long enough for Tony's insides to twist into a knot. Adam broke into a laugh a moment later. "Yes, you clown!"

"I'll think about it," Tony grumbled.

"Good." Adam clinked the neck of his bottle against Tony's. "I think you'll be pleasantly surprised."

Tony thought about how he'd bring up the subject of love the whole flight home. Different scenarios danced through his brain, even invading his dreams. He hadn't warned his—friends? Lovers?—that he was coming home early, so he wasn't disappointed when he wasn't met at the airport. Instead, he found a taxi and directed the driver to his home.

When he saw that James's car wasn't parked in its usual spot, he asked the driver to wait while he dropped his luggage in the front entry, and then took the taxi to the sports arena.

He walked into the sweltering heat of the Olympic-size aquatic facility at Boston University. Hundreds of people were already in the stands, athletes were warming up on the pool deck, and a heat was racing freestyle in the pool.

This was not exactly familiar stomping grounds for him, not in the same way as it was for James and Amanda, who had lifeguarded or taught swimming since they'd been old enough to do so. But he'd attended all the swim meets they'd participated in, and he knew where they liked to sit.

He spotted Amanda at the front near the finish line quite easily.

There was no point in calling out to her; the cacophony of noise from the racers, athletes, and audience would drown him out. Instead, he made his way along the edge of the pool deck.

The heat finished and the racers climbed out of the pool. They were all broad shoulders, tiny waists, and even smaller speedos. His gaze lingered on a tall Black man before he realized he was ogling James.

James, who was heading over to Amanda. She was on her feet, jumping up and down. He leapt up the two stairs to her level, scooped her up in his arms, and planted a heated kiss on her lips.

When he pulled away, she was laughing, her shirt plastered to her body from the water on his.

Tony's heart thumped in his chest, his stomach twisting up uncomfortably. *How am I not the third wheel? Look at how well they fit together without me. What do I bring to the relationship that they don't already have?*

He took a calming breath and watched James head over to his teammates. A turn to wave and blow a kiss to Amanda, and then he was completely focused on his coach.

Tony finished his trek along the pool deck, pausing at the rail below Amanda. "Hello, darlin'. Do you reckon I can sit with you?"

"Ohmigod *Tony*!" she shrieked, practically launching herself out of her seat and down the stairs.

He caught her when she tripped over her feet trying to get to him, and held her tightly, although not as hard as she was squeezing him.

"I thought you weren't arriving until tonight?" she asked. "I've missed you so much!" She buried her face in his neck, planting little kisses on his collarbone, ear, and everywhere in between.

"I caught a red-eye to get here in time for James's meet," Tony explained. "That extra twelve hours apart felt like torture."

Amanda stopped what she was doing, pulling back to look in his face. "I missed you every second of every day," she said, and then she was kissing him, opening her mouth to accept his tongue, clinging to his shoulders, and molding her body to his.

Tony took his time reacquainting himself with her kisses, stroking his tongue along hers and reveling in her taste. He forgot for a moment that they were in public, his ears buzzing with static as desire for her overwhelmed him. Loud cheering broke into their little bubble, and he tore himself away from her mouth only to press their foreheads together. "I was only gone for a month," he rasped, their breath mingling between them.

"Felt like an eternity," Amanda murmured. Then she groaned. "Ugh! And I have to go to work? Not fair." She lightly slapped his chest. "If I didn't have this project, I would take you home after James's meet and have my way with you until neither of us could move."

"Do you want me to leave?" Tony teased, pretending to walk away.

"Don't you dare!" Amanda ordered, grabbing his arm. "Come sit with me. We can cheer James on in his next race."

He obediently followed her back to her seat, where the others on the bench had scooted down to make room for them both. "When do you have to go to work?" he asked.

She glanced at the clock. "Too soon. I'm going to call for an Uber at nine. It should get me to work only about fifteen minutes late, which means I'll miss the pointless all-staff meeting."

"In other words, perfect timing," Tony said with a chuckle. "I'm not expected back in the office until Wednesday."

"I'm going to see if I can take the day off tomorrow then. I know James can't. He was lucky to get today."

Tony scanned the pool deck for James. He was leaning against a wall on the far side of the pool, too far away to make out his expression. Swallowing nervously, Tony turned back to Amanda. "When is he done?"

"Sometime before lunch, unless he makes it to the finals. Are you going to be able to stay?"

"This is the whole reason I'm home early."

She laughed. "I'm just an afterthought?"

"Never, and you know it," he replied fervently.

"I do." She leaned against his shoulder. "God, I've missed you."

"And here I thought you'd enjoy the extra space on the bed."

"No." Amanda shook her head. "I don't know if you've noticed, but I prefer to be swaddled."

"Swaddled?" Tony chuckled. "That's one word for it."

"Oooh, he's moving!" she said excitedly, batting at his arm. "I think it's the relay now. Yes, see, the backstroke people are getting in the water."

"Let's see if I can remember the order," he said, watching as they prepared, holding onto the underside of the starting block. "Backstroke, breaststroke, fly, front crawl?"

"The last one is actually freestyle, but crawl is used the most often because it's the fastest."

"James will be ending the relay then."

The starting beep sounded, and the racers were off, moving powerfully through the water.

Tony rubbed his chest, his heart pounding despite sitting in the stands. "Why do I feel like *I'm* the one racing?" he said.

Amanda chuckled. "Because you care about what happens. I feel the same way. Look, James's team is doing well. They hit the wall third."

"Third is good?"

She wavered her hand. "It's decent. I'm a little worried about the second racer. He's not having a good morning; he lost his first solo heat. Hopefully his coach helped turn his attitude around. Here we go..."

They watched with bated breath as first lane five, then lane three, and finally lane four hit the wall. The instant lane four's hands touched, James's teammate launched into a shallow dive.

"Good start," Amanda said breathlessly. "Keep it up!"

"Racing breaststroke always looks so frantic," Tony murmured. "It's supposed to be a relaxing stroke."

She patted his knee absentmindedly, eyes fixed on the racers. "He's keeping pace, but not really closing the gap," she said. "Come on... Nice flip."

"Is it just me, or is he gaining on the others under water?" Tony asked.

"I think it might be our angle. We'll see better once they get back to the starting point."

The third racers were getting on the starting block, focused on preparing for their turn. Once again, five, three, and then four touched the wall, their third teammates launching into the water.

"Here's where we'll make up some time," Amanda said eagerly, pulling on Tony's arm. "Look at her go!"

Smooth gliding gave way to powerful strokes as the racers cut easily through the water, arching their bodies out to take a breath before plunging back in, arms and legs never stopping. The three front-runners reached the end of the lane far ahead of their competitors, touching the wall cleanly with both hands before pushing off again. James's teammate had closed the gap, but on the second length, her power was flagging.

"Oh no," Amanda gasped. "Something must have happened. Come on, you can do it," she muttered.

It was disheartening to watch the swimmers in lanes six, seven, and two catch up and pass lane four before she finally touched the wall. James was off like a shot, vaulting into the water. He came up for air, his arms and legs pushing him through the water like a rocket. He passed two, then seven and six. He touched the far wall a full length ahead of them, flipping and pushing off underwater for the last lap.

Tony found himself on his feet without knowing how he got there, holding onto the bar in front of him as he shouted encouragement that James couldn't hear.

He crept up on lane three's racer, passing them by the halfway mark, and then it was him and lane five, neck and neck, until a last burst of speed by James got him to the wall a split second before lane five.

"*Yes, James!*" Tony and Amanda screamed.

James rested his arms on the lane rope, yanked his goggles up, and waved a limp hand at the stands. Then he did a double take, looking straight at Tony. A beaming grin crossed his face, and he ducked under the lane ropes, heading for the ladder at the side of the pool.

"Oh my God, what do I say?" Tony muttered, his gaze fixed on the man pulling himself out of the pool, water sluicing off of his powerful muscles.

"Congratulations?" Amanda suggested, a laugh in her tone.

James crossed his arms when he got to the foot of the stairs. "What do you think you're doing here?"

"Congratulations," Tony said weakly, and then belatedly realized that he hadn't answered the question. "Surprise?"

"Get your ass down here," James ordered before beaming, "and give me a hug!"

Tony thought he was going to trip over his feet like Amanda had, he moved so fast. Then he was wrapped up in James's arms, and it felt like home. He squeezed back hard, reveling in the strength of him, and giving as good as he got. "I missed you," he said, his voice choking on the words.

"'Missed you' doesn't even begin to cover it." James pulled back. "Can you stay?" he asked hopefully.

"Yeah. I'm here until you leave."

"Thanks."

Tony thought he saw a flare of heat in his eyes, but an audience member tapped James on the shoulder and distracted him.

"Excuse me, but I thought you might want to know that he kissed your girlfriend, and not in a friendly greeting kind of way."

James raised an eyebrow at Tony. "Is that true?"

"Oh, I kissed her all right," Tony replied easily. "I needed to remind her of my talented tongue. Don't worry, you'll get a repeat performance tonight."

James grinned. "Looking forward to it."

"I'm serious—" the guy started to say.

"So am I," James replied, cutting him off. "This man is my best friend in the world, and he just got back from a month-long work trip. If he wants to kiss *our* girlfriend, there is no way I would even want to try to stop him."

"Boys, I need to run," Amanda said, squeezing between them. "James, that last race was incredible." She kissed him. "I'm so glad you made it in time, Tony." It was his turn for a kiss.

"I hope you have dry clothing," Tony said, holding her hand lightly.

Amanda scoffed. "Do you even know me?" She squeezed his fingers before letting go as far away as possible. "Love you both!"

The audience member who had interrupted them had vanished during Amanda's goodbyes. Tony shrugged. Not his problem. He focused on James instead. "You look good, man."

To his surprise, James flushed. "You do too."

Tony chuckled. "You like the 'fresh from the airport, barely slept' look?"

"I do if it's you."

Now it was Tony's turn to blush. "You flirting with me, Jamie?"

James opened his mouth to reply, but his coach shouted for him before he could. "I gotta run. Talk later."

Jaw agape, Tony watched James walk across the slick pool deck, his ass barely covered by the scrap of spandex. "What?" he whispered. His heart leapt in hope. Rubbing his sternum, Tony returned to his seat. *Is 'no' too hard to say? That's a pretty quick brush off. But if it's a yes...*

Hardly daring to hope, Tony watched avidly as James competed in the quarter finals, and then the semi finals for his events.

Lunchtime came and went, but he wasn't hungry and didn't want to miss the finals.

The individual events were first. The freestyle was last, and he waited impatiently, watching James stretching on the other side of the pool to keep his muscles loose.

When it was finally James's turn, Tony got his phone ready to take video so Amanda could watch it later. He rested his wrists on the bar in front of him to keep the camera steady and tried to remember to breathe.

The beep sounded and the racers dove into the water. James took an early lead, making it look easy. Heart pounding, Tony couldn't keep his eyes off his—best friend? lover? crush?—as he plowed through the water to a first place finish.

He stopped the video before joining in the shouts, so proud of James that he could burst.

James didn't have time to come over for a hug; the medley was next. He waved at Tony, and took his place behind the starting block, shaking his arms and legs out.

The race looked much the same as the previous ones. Backstroke gained them a solid third position, breaststroke lost one spot, fly maintained, and then James dominated, pulling them into first place with a photo finish.

James climbed out of the pool, heading for the stands. His focus on him nearly made Tony's knees weak, but he managed to greet him with a crushing hug.

"Dude, you're getting me wet," Tony complained half-heartedly.

"That's Amanda's line."

"Yeah it is."

James took Tony's head between his hands, bringing their foreheads together. His chest was still heaving from the race. "I want to kiss you," he whispered, so quiet that Tony barely heard it, and even then, he couldn't believe his ears.

"What's stopping you?" he replied, issuing the challenge.

Eyes widening, James sucked in a sharp breath. "We still really need to talk." And then their lips met, just briefly, a light brush of skin and a heady exhale of air.

Tony breathed in shakily, the scent of chlorine and James filling his nostrils. "You're done, right?"

"Done?" James frowned and pulled back.

Tony gestured at the pool. "Your races. You're done? We can leave?"

Expression clearing, James nodded. "Yeah, I'm good to go."

"Good. Get your shit. Because the way I want to kiss you, that little speedo won't contain you."

James laughed. "Reading you loud and clear. Give me five minutes."

"You have two."

Chapter Eight

Flashback:
The Day After Prom

After dancing the night away at prom, the trio returned home and cuddled up in their pyjamas on the king-sized mattress hammock in the Beyer's backyard.

Early in the morning, Amanda was called into the pool to work, so James and Tony were left to fend for themselves.

They started by mowing the lawns of all three houses, working up a sweat until they could jump in the pool. After a quick cooldown, they started taking down the sheer white netting in the Carlson's backyard. It had been the perfect backdrop for the prom pictures the evening before, even though it hadn't been dark yet. Tony's mom had requested that they leave up the fairy lights, something about them looking like fireflies.

"She looked beautiful," Tony said, folding one end of the sheet he'd taken down. He didn't need to clarify who.

"Carolina? I suppose," James teased from the top of a ladder.

"Don't you dare," Tony replied with a glare.

James chuckled. "I thought I was going to trip over my feet when I first saw Amanda in that pink dress."

"I think I forgot how to breathe when I saw how low the back dipped," Tony added. "You could see her spine dimples. I knew she had them. I've put sunscreen on them enough times when she's been wearing a bikini. But seeing them in that dress..." He blew out a breath, shaking his head.

"And that slit in the skirt that went nearly up to her hip?" James climbed down the ladder, carrying another sheet. "What is it about that pink dress that made me lose my mind? I've seen her in much less. Those bikinis she wears..."

"I don't know, but I was ready to drop to my knees and beg her to do whatever she wanted to me."

"Hot."

"You know what I mean."

James sighed. "I do. But we've got two months—slightly less, actually—and then we're leaving for different universities across the country. College is going to change all of us."

Tony made a face. "I don't know. It feels kinda like we're keeping a secret from her."

"We have for two years. What's the difference?"

"Three."

James chuckled. "Fine, three years. Are you absolutely sure that you're in love with her, enough to potentially change our friendship forever, to get two months with her before you have to separate? Because I'm not."

Tony gaped at him. "You're not sure if you love her?"

"I love her." James rubbed his sternum absentmindedly. "I'm just not one-hundred percent sure it's the forever kind of love. The kind my parents have. I want that, and I don't want to hurt her, or you, if I'm wrong."

Tony bit his lip. "Okay, I see where you're coming from. I'd rather have her friendship for four years than lose her completely if I got it wrong."

"I need to be in a relationship. I want to see if I can find out who I am on my own too. And a little separation will help with that."

"Are you saying you regret our friendship?" Tony demanded.

James rolled his eyes. "Don't put words in my mouth. I can't imagine my life without you two in it. That's the problem. I need to see if I *can* imagine it. You know?"

"I already know what my life is like without you two, and I don't like it," Tony grumbled.

"You're an adult now. It'll be different," James said encouragingly. "And we won't be *completely* gone. I couldn't cut all contact with you."

They put the folded material in a pile on the outdoor table and James moved the ladder to the next trellis.

"Her legs, huh?" Tony said suddenly.

James paused halfway up the ladder. "What about them?"

"Your favorite body part."

"It's hard to pick just one, but yeah, I think it's her legs. They're long, powerful, and sexy." He continued up the ladder and started unhooking the next piece of netting. "Her ass for you?"

Tony flushed. "It's just so grabbable."

James laughed. "I can't deny that."

"When we're cuddling to sleep, her ass is pressed against me... It's torture."

"We don't have to cuddle," James teased.

"It might be torture, but I wouldn't give it up for the world."

"I know what you mean. Sometimes her leg hikes up over my crotch in her sleep."

Tony groaned dramatically. "Fuck, that's hot. Are you sure we shouldn't tell her today?"

"I'm not sure of much, but telling her now seems like a bad idea when we're not certain of our feelings."

"I suppose." Tony sighed. "I don't think I'll find anyone more perfect for me than her, though. And it's a really good thing that I'm going to be several states away from her when she brings home her first boyfriend. The jealousy is going to be real."

James clenched his jaw. "Someone's going to be her first, it won't be one of us, and I'm not sure I'll be able to handle that." He blew out a long breath.

"You and me both."

"I just hope he's deserving."

"Forget that, I hope he's good enough that she doesn't regret it, but bad enough that she doesn't keep him around."

James laughed. "You're jealous of a future potential sex partner?"

"Yes."

"Do you think she'd feel the same way about your partners? Our partners?" James asked thoughtfully.

"I guess it depends on if she feels the same way about us as we do about her." Tony shrugged. "I'm not going to pick up a one night stand or anything, but I'd like to, you know, learn how to have sex."

James nodded. "That's a good idea."

"Is it weird that we're all virgins?"

"Virginity is a construct."

"You know what I mean. None of us have had sex."

"You want to have sex with Carolina? I'm sure she'd be up for it," James teased.

Tony shuddered violently. "No, thank you very much. Especially not after her treatment of Amanda last night."

"She handled it beautifully, though," James said. "I was really impressed."

"So was I."

"No, I don't think it's weird, to get back to your question. We spend all our free time together. If either of us had been serious about a girl, she'd have had to fit in with our group. She'd have to compete with Amanda, and I don't know anyone who could possibly win."

"Yeah, the only girl who has ever gotten my attention is Amanda." Tony was silent for a moment, focusing on folding the netting James passed down to him. Then he snorted. "It's funny."

"What is?"

"There have been rumors about the three of us fucking since we were twelve, which, yikes, honestly, and yet we're some of the few who haven't had sex in our graduating class."

James huffed a laugh. "That *is* funny. And none of those assholes would believe us even if we tried to tell them."

"Truth."

Chapter Nine

James

They silently headed for James's car after the meet. Each brush of Tony's arm against his as they walked made his nerve endings stand on edge. He wanted to press him against every car along the way and kiss him senseless, but they needed to talk first.

He didn't know how they managed to make it, but they did. He tossed his swim bag onto the floor in the back, and started the car with laser-like focus.

"Hey," Tony said.

"Not now," James replied, his jaw tight.

"Are you angry with me?"

James wanted to kick himself. "The opposite. Let me get home so I can focus properly."

"Yeah, alright."

Tony's knee bounced in his peripheral vision, distracting him. He wanted to put his hand on it to get him to stop, but once he touched him, he'd want to slide it higher to palm over Tony's crotch, and that would ruin him.

James just barely made it to their house with his patience intact. He was out of the door and on the sidewalk, ready to take the two steps up into the house when Tony grabbed him and slammed him against the car, not an inch of space between them.

"Explain," Tony growled.

"What?" James wheezed a little from the force.

"You kiss me, then you barely speak to me on the way home. We're here, now talk."

"If I'd talked to you in the car, I might have had an accident. I don't want to have this conversation out here." James tried to push off the car, but he couldn't move Tony's weight. The other man's strength was such a turn-on.

"Why?" Tony looked like he wasn't even struggling.

"Because I'm in love with you!" James exploded. "I want to fuck you!" He lowered his voice, his cheeks hot. "I want you to fuck me. And I've really missed you this past month. I didn't realize how often we touched until it was gone." He rested his forehead against Tony's, one hand creeping up to cup the back of his head. "Having you so close in the car and not being able to touch was the most exquisite torture."

"And now?" Tony breathed.

"Now you know how I feel." James shrugged. "You going to run?"

"Fuck no. Not unless I'm running to you. I've been in love with you for years."

Heart feeling like it was about to burst, James changed his grip on Tony's head, threading his fingers through thick waves of hair. "I love that you've let this grow out," he murmured.

"Shut up and kiss me," Tony growled, tilting his head just right and crushing their lips together with almost bruising force.

James groaned and opened to Tony's tongue, matching his enthusiasm with deft strokes that made his head spin. The scent of the other man filled his nostrils, and he was desperate for more. He couldn't get close enough, despite being pinned full-body against each other.

They made out against the car until Tony pulled back, pupils dilated with desire. "I could come at a stiff breeze. I need you naked, and I need it now."

"That's why I was trying to get into the house," James retorted, giving a little shove to Tony's shoulders.

"I couldn't wait that long."

"Get inside," James ordered.

"Sir, yes sir," Tony mocked.

"You're as much of a brat as Amanda, aren't you?"

James remembered his swim bag when he spotted Tony's travel duffel in the entry, but Tony was taking off his shirt before the door closed, so he decided he could get it later. "I need to lick your tattoos," James said.

Tony huffed a surprised laugh. "That'll take some time."

"We've got the rest of our lives."

"Oh, so you don't mean right away?" Tony teased.

"Maybe just one," James said, eyeing his name on Tony's forearm. He gave into temptation, pressing Tony against the wall. "You're so fucking hot," he murmured, grinding their clothed groins together. "Getting my name inked on your body as if I had a claim on you."

"You did. You do," Tony panted, dropping his head back to collide with the wall. "You always have."

"Fuck," James groaned and bit lightly over the exposed column of Tony's throat. The answering response of unintelligible sounds shot straight to his cock. Maintaining eye contact, he brought Tony's arm to his lips, the rasp of arm hair making his stomach swoop in the best way, kissing over the J, licking the curl of the a, biting the m—

Tony's knees buckled and he slid down the wall a little.

"Sexy as fuck," James muttered, finishing off his name with a flourish of his tongue.

"Not sure I'll make it to the bedroom," Tony gasped, fumbling with his belt once James released his arm. "Take off your clothes."

"We should at least try to get out of the entryway," James said with a chuckle, ripping his shirt over his head anyways. He expected to feel a tug on his hair, forgetting that he'd had braids put in the day before.

They kicked off their shoes and then, as if drawn by magnets, their lips collided in yet another passionate kiss.

James slid his hands under Tony's loosened pants, squeezing his ass and pressing their hips together. "Goddammit, we have to make it upstairs," he panted, pulling away from the kiss. "The only condoms are in the bedside table. I forgot to get more for the main floor."

"Fuck," Tony groaned. "Okay. If we run, it'll be like...five seconds."

"Too long," James said, reeling him back in by his belt.

Tony laughed. "God, it feels good to be able to say this shit to you. Come on, let's go. I've been waiting this long to touch you properly, I can wait another five seconds."

"First person to touch the bed gets to fuck the other," James suggested, his heart pounding.

"Jamie," Tony breathed, the hazel in his eyes almost completely eaten by his pupil. "I'm already higher on the stairs than you."

"Yeah," James replied, heat filling his cheeks. He felt shy all of a sudden, not able to meet Tony's gaze. "I know."

Strong fingers raised his head by his chin.

"Hey, you having second thoughts?" Tony asked gently.

"No!" James answered quickly. "I'm just nervous. I've never—" He cut himself off with a shaky breath. "It'll be my first time."

"I'm honored," Tony said seriously. "I'll take good care of you." He brought their mouths together, licking over the seam of James's lips until he opened with a moan. Tony delved inside his mouth, tongues dancing until they were both panting for air.

Breath mingling, James nudged their noses together. "I trust you."

"And I, you." Tony released James's chin with what looked like great reluctance, fingers lingering. Then he grinned. "Race you."

He took off up the stairs, leaving James feeling dizzy at the front door of their house.

He shook his head to clear it before chasing Tony to the top floor, fighting to undo his pants, leaving his shirt behind.

Tony was down to his boxer briefs when James tackled him onto the bed, the frame creaking ominously. "You are such a brute," Tony gasped, winded.

"Then fight back," James challenged him, pinning Tony's wrists over his head and straddling his waist. "Come on."

"Hell yes," Tony grunted, muscles straining. He thrust his hips up, knocking James off-balance, and rolled them over, nearly falling off the bed in the process. "Yikes."

"Don't care," James muttered, pushing up against Tony's grip.

"You need to get your pants off," Tony said, grinding their cocks together through way too many layers.

"Maybe you should take them off," James retorted.

"With pleasure."

Before James knew what was happening, Tony had turned around to straddle his chest, his cock in front of his face. James nuzzled into the hanging material, inhaling Tony's musky scent and wanting more.

Tony made quick work of James's pants, yanking them down as far as he could. "Lift your hips," he ordered.

"Wouldn't that make things too easy for you?" James taunted.

"You are such a brat," Tony grumbled.

"We'll see who's calling who a brat when—Oof!" His world spun around him as Tony manhandled him onto his stomach, pulling his pants down over his hips.

"*Fuck*, this ass," Tony marveled, grabbing at the round globes. "I have wanted to bury my cock in you for far too long."

"Then *do it*," James growled, pressing himself up onto his forearms. "What are you waiting for?"

"Pardon me if I want to take my time," Tony replied, pulling the elastic of James's boxer briefs down as well. "Goddamn," he breathed, his hands smoothing over the bare skin. "This is even better than my wettest dreams."

James huffed a laugh, his head hanging low. "Glad you're having fun. But my cock is trapped and you'll get better access if you take off my pants."

"Are you trying to tell me how to do my job?" Tony teased. "Impatient, much?"

"Very. This has been a long time coming."

"Well, you'll be coming sooner than that." Tony wrestled the material off of James's hips, rolling him onto his back to free his cock, which sprang free. "Your cock is beautiful."

James flushed, heat filling his cheeks. "I really had nothing to do with that."

Tony laughed. "No shit." He licked up the underside, following the thick vein up to the tip, and sucked on the head, tongue undulating around the crown.

James's cock pulsed, eager to be inside Tony's mouth. When Tony pulled back with a smirk, a little bit of pre-cum oozed from the tip. "*Fuck*, Tony," James gasped, his hands flying to grab Tony's hair. "Your tongue!"

"I am a huge fan of going down," Tony said, licking his lips. "If we had a dental dam, I'd rim you."

James's cock jumped again at the thought and his mouth went dry. "You really like that?"

Tony stood up and pulled his underwear down, kicking them off. "I am so hard for you, Jamie. Getting my mouth on you and bringing you pleasure is a dream come true. Yes, I love rimming, but I'm always safe about it."

"How has this never come up?" James demanded, propping himself up on his elbows. "The three of us have been together for two years at this point."

Tony grinned and stretched his arms over his head. "Well, as much as I love to rim, eating pussy is much more satisfying for both Amanda and I. Now that your body isn't off limits, I expect it'll come up a lot more often."

James shivered. "How am I still learning new things about you after knowing you for half our lives?"

"Hidden depths," Tony said, climbing on top of James and crawling up his body to join their mouths.

James indulged in the kiss, burying his fingers in Tony's dark hair and keeping him there, tongues stroking and bringing their desire even higher. Gravity pulled Tony's cock down, dragging it over his own and making it sticky from leaking pre-cum. "*God*, I need you," James panted. "Please, *please*."

"Since you asked so nicely," Tony said, the skin of his chest completely flushed with desire behind the dark ink. "I'll prep you on all fours, but I want to see your face when we're fu—" He cut himself off. "No, when we're making love."

"You're such a romantic," James teased.

"Like you aren't," Tony replied without bite. "On your knees."

James obeyed, feeling extremely exposed.

Tony spread him wider, holding him open with his hands. "You're sure about this?"

"Why, you having second thoughts?" James squirmed a little.

"Hold still." Tony ran a thumb over James's rim. "I want this more than I want to breathe."

James shuddered. "Please keep breathing. The lube's in the drawer, same as always."

"I know where it is." Tony kept playing with James's opening, running his thumbs over the pucker again and again before dropping down to the smooth space between it and his balls.

James jolted forwards when Tony spat directly over his hole. "*Fuck,*" he groaned, his head dropping down onto his forearms.

"We'll get there," Tony promised, rubbing his saliva into the skin. "But first, I'm going to wreck you."

Oh God, James thought, his thighs quivering. *I'm not sure I'll survive this.*

"I *really* wish we had a dam," Tony whispered, fingers digging into James's ass cheeks, thumbs spreading him wide. "You look fucking delicious."

"Anyone ever tell you that your mouth is filthy?" James said admiringly.

"Is that okay?"

"I'm leaking all over the comforter because of your dirty talk. Don't stop."

Tony chuckled. "I can get you a towel?" he offered.

"Don't you dare leave me," James growled.

"Alright, alright." Still chuckling slightly, Tony slipped the tip of his thumb inside James and let gravity pull down. "You're so relaxed. I could finger-fuck you easily right now."

James shuddered. "Please."

"Well, with lube," Tony amended. "Hang on."

The bed dipped as he got off, and then again when he got back on.

"I'm going to warm this up for you. I just grabbed the basic one," Tony said conversationally, as if he wasn't rocking James's world without even touching him. "We can work up to the specialty ones."

"Okay."

"Don't get nervous on me now," Tony said.

James could practically picture the teasing glint in his eyes. "I'm not." And then he jumped when Tony's lubed fingers circled his rim. "Okay, maybe a little."

"I've got you, Jamie," Tony murmured. "Relax."

James closed his eyes, his focus narrowing on Tony's fingers and the awkwardness he felt. But this was Tony, his best friend in the world. Slowly, he felt his tension leave his body, and was rewarded by a finger slipping inside.

"Good boy," Tony said, kissing the base of his spine.

A shiver ran through his body. "I didn't know how much I'd like that," he muttered.

Tony chuckled. "Everyone likes being told they're good. Going to try for two."

James took shallow breaths through the intrusion. Then Tony twisted his fingers and pressed down, and James shouted at the spark of pleasure that shot across him.

"That's it," Tony said, amused.

There was a slight tickle from Tony's hair at the base of James's spine, followed by a huff of hot air over his ass.

"I *need* to get my mouth on you," Tony gasped, pressing biting kisses over the muscle. "Flip over."

James didn't know where he summoned the strength, he was so aroused, but with Tony's help, he managed to roll onto his back, knees splayed. He barely noticed the wet stickiness that he was lying on before it was completely banished from his thoughts by Tony's shoulders spreading his legs even further.

"I can't believe I managed to stop myself from sucking your cock before today," Tony whispered, nuzzling the base and inhaling deeply. He chuckled. "The scent of chlorine didn't used to do it for me."

"I can go shower," James offered.

"You're not going anywhere until I've come so hard inside you that you'll feel it in your tonsils," Tony growled, punctuating his words with short, sharp thrusts of his fingers.

James arched on the bed, pleasure zinging through him. "Big words," he gasped when he could. "Prove it."

"Gotta finish prepping you first," Tony said, mouthing up the length of James's cock. "Third finger, you ready for it?"

"I'm not going to break," James retorted.

"Not yet," Tony said with a smirk before engulfing the head and breaching James's body with three fingers.

"Holy *fuck*," James shouted to the ceiling, his hands coming up to grip his own hair. There was nothing but braids flat to his skull, so he reached overhead to grab onto the comforter. Tony's hot, wet mouth worked him over, his talented tongue undulating against the underside. Thick fingers were stretching him wide, hitting his sensitive prostate on each thrust and making sparks shoot across his skin. His balls were drawing up, ready to let go. "Tony," James said weakly, trying to warn his lover.

"I want your cum," Tony rasped, his throat raw from taking James so deep. "But maybe later, when Amanda's home."

James nodded. "I want you inside me when I come this time."

"I think you're ready for me," Tony said, looking down at his fingers disappearing into James. His cock jumped. "I'm not going to last long."

"Neither am I."

Tony grabbed a condom from beside his leg and opened it, rolling it on with shaking fingers.

"Hey," James said, furrowing his brow in concern. "You okay?" he asked when Tony met his gaze.

"I'm so turned on I can barely stand it," Tony said with a crooked smile, coating the condom in lube. "I'm about to make love with my best friend for the first time, and I don't want to fuck it up."

"You won't fuck it up," James said, shaking his head.

"How do you know that?"

"Because I know you."

Tony blew out a long breath, closing his eyes. "Thanks." He got into position, hovering over James on the bed, one strong arm supporting him, the other going to his latex-covered cock. "Relax."

James chuckled. "I couldn't get more relaxed."

"Okay."

Tony had done a fantastic job stretching him. One second, the head of his cock was pressing against the rim, and then it slipped in. Tony's eyes flew to his, pupils blown so wide he could barely see the hazel of the iris.

"Okay?" Tony whispered.

James bit his lip, concentrating on how he felt. "Big, but good," he replied.

"Gonna push in," Tony said. "Tell me the second it stops feeling good."

When James nodded, Tony continued his slow progress inside him. He'd never felt so full, both of cock and love. He huffed a laugh, but the motion made Tony shift inside him, catching on his prostate and making his breath hitch. "Oh fuck," James moaned, arching his back.

"Good?"

"So fucking good." James took shallow breaths until Tony was fully seated in him, balls tucked up against his ass. "*God.*"

"Tony," Tony corrected impishly.

"Fuck you."

Tony shook his head, an eyebrow rising. "I'm the one doing the fucking." He withdrew and entered in a smooth stroke that had James's eyes rolling back in his head.

"Do that again," he begged.

"Going to adjust a bit," Tony mumbled, widening his knees, and gripping James's shoulders from underneath. He pulled down on his next thrust, hitting even deeper.

"*Tony!*" James groaned.

"You saying my name like that is going to make me come," Tony gasped. "Fuck, Jamie." He managed two more thrusts before his cock started pulsing.

"So close," James whined.

"I've got you," Tony panted, reaching his hand between them, jerking James off with a pre-cum-slicked hand.

His orgasm ricocheted through him, tensing his body like a bow-string before release. Tony's lips on his upper chest made his heart swell with love. He cupped Tony's head in his hands, bringing their mouths together for sloppy post-coital kisses. "You have no idea how long I've wanted this with you," James said, licking into Tony's mouth.

Tony hummed in response.

"I knew I loved you when I was a teenager."

"I guess we both need to work on our communication," Tony said in reply.

"It's less scary now," James said softly. "Now that I know how you feel about me. About us."

"Just to be clear," Tony said, pulling back a little to look James in the eye. "I love Amanda just as much as I love you, and I'm not leaving her. I hope you feel the same way."

"Same. I think we probably should have clarified that before my brains leaked out my ears," James said, running a hand down Tony's muscled back. "We're a true triad now."

"I'm glad we're on the same page." Tony pressed their lips together again. "I think," he said, trailing kisses along James's jaw, "we forgot to bring it up because before this, if one of us was alone with her, there were no issues with initiating sex. Do you think she'll be okay that we had sex without her without asking first?"

Head spinning pleasantly from the tingles Tony's kisses were sending to his brain, James tried to gather his thoughts. "I think she'll be a little disappointed she didn't get to watch, but as long as she's included in the discussion about future sexy times, she'll be fine. This was between us, and I think she'll get that."

Tony nodded, licking James's clavicle. "So me texting to ask her to grab dental dams would be alright?"

James laughed, and then moaned at the feeling of Tony hardening within him once more. "Or we can go get pizza and buy some ourselves."

"What? You don't want to go again?" Tony teased.

"I'm a little sore."

"Dude, don't worry. I get it. I should have dealt with the condom before this, but it feels so good to be inside you." Tony pulled out and they both groaned at the loss. "Pizza sounds great."

"I need a shower," Amanda said, sniffing her armpit and wrinkling her nose.

"After you," Tony said graciously.

James had to run over to the university to meet with his thesis professor, and their parents and Glenn had left, leaving the two alone in their new house. James had given them a wink and told them not to wait for him.

"I want you in with me," Amanda said with a pout.

Tony raised an eyebrow. "I'm not sure we'll both fit."

"Then we'll use the main floor shower," Amanda said with a shrug. "Come on, we'll strip here and then run naked across the length of the house."

Tony chuckled. "I'll get the shower things from upstairs."

"Towels too," Amanda said, whipping her shirt over her head. Her bra followed the shirt to puddle on a box in the dining room, then her shorts and underwear.

"You've suddenly made it very difficult to leave this room," he groaned, eyes fixed on her body.

"You've seen me naked before," Amanda teased, cupping her breasts in her hands. "What's different this time?"

"It's our house," Tony rasped. "Fuck the soap and towels, I need you now." He tore his clothes off and scooped her up, carrying her to the bathroom next to the kitchen.

She wrapped her legs around his waist, grinding down against his hard cock trapped between them. The sweaty skin of their chests stuck together.

"Looks like someone had the forethought to put soap in here," Tony said, placing her on her feet on the bathroom tile.

"Hand soap," Amanda corrected, grabbing it from the sink. "But it'll do." She stepped into the shower stall and turned on the water, which came out ice cold. She shrieked and backed up to the far corner.

Tony chuckled and followed her in, unconcerned by the frigid temperature pouring from the overhead rain shower. He fiddled with the tap until the water warmed, and then pulled Amanda under the shower with him. One hand ghosted down her back to her ass, hooking under her thigh to drag her against his body. "Have I mentioned how much I love that you're tall?" he asked, licking water droplets as they beaded on her skin. The taste of salt from sweat danced across his tongue.

"I like that you don't have to fold in half to kiss me," Amanda said, tilting her head to the side to grant him access to her throat. "But is that all?"

"No way," Tony said, his fingers dimpling her thighs. "There's more of you to touch. We fit together standing or lying down. James would add something about your legs being killer."

"You don't like my legs?" Amanda said with a chuckle, pushing his cock down from between them to slip between her thighs..

"I love them, but my favorite spot on you is your ass. I can grab it so nicely when we stand like this." He squeezed her with both hands, making her squeak.

"Is that why you like doing me doggy style so much?" Amanda asked.

Tony gaped at her. "Have my positions gotten stagnant? You can pinpoint that we do one position in particular more than any other?"

Amanda cupped his jaw. "I was teasing. I love doggy too. You hit me beautifully without even trying. Can we do it now?"

"We should probably install grab bars on the far end." Tony hesitated. "I don't want you to fall."

"You'll catch me." She ground against him, her slick lower lips sliding over his hard cock. "Please, Tony?" She gave him her best puppy eyes.

He groaned. "How do I say no to that? Turn around then." He lined up and slid inside her without any trouble. "Fuck, you're so turned on."

"My body was made for yours," Amanda said, her hands pressed against the tile wall. "Fuck me hard, Tony!"

He picked up the pace, their skin slapping echoing in the stall. "I also love eating you out. Will you let me do that too?"

"Whenever you like," Amanda moaned.

"I'm gonna hold you to that," he teased. "You'll be studying for midterms and I'll slide between your legs to fuck you with my tongue until you're crying from oversensitivity."

Her legs shook and hands slid an inch down the wall. "Oh fuck," she cried.

Tony reached underneath her, fingers finding her clit with the ease of familiarity, and rubbed. "Come on my cock. Milk me," he whispered.

Her fingers clenched on nothing, back arching, as she shook from her orgasm, her insides fluttering from the release. She sagged, and Tony caught her around the waist.

"We can't stay in the shower," he murmured into her shoulder. "Come on, we'll go upstairs and cover the bed with towels."

"We didn't even use the soap," Amanda said weakly.

Tony shrugged. "James will join us in the shower later. Maybe we'll actually manage to get clean."

"You haven't come!" she exclaimed, shocked, when he pulled out of her.

"With James not here, I need to keep you satisfied somehow," Tony teased.

"You satisfy me plenty," Amanda protested.

He crowded her against the wall of the shower, the hot water pounding down on his back nearly matching the heat of her. He nuzzled their noses together and breathed, "I didn't want to end my pleasure so soon. Don't worry, I'll come deep inside you later."

She shivered at his words, swallowing hard. "I want that too." Her hand quested between them, wrapping around his length and stroking it gently. "But I want it sooner rather than later."

His head dropped against her shoulder, his hips stuttering and bumping his cock against her belly, leaving a streak of cum on her skin. "Fuck, darlin', if you keep that up, I'll come before I get back inside you."

Amanda hooked her thigh around his, angling his cock to rub over her clit and then down to where it caught on her opening. She shifted the angle of her hips and his head slipped inside her.

"Yesssss," Tony hissed, closing his eyes. He cupped her ass and pumped his hips, dragging her over his cock. "I was going to eat you out until you begged for my cock, you know."

"You can do that after you come in me," she panted, her short nails digging sharp crescents in his shoulders.

"You gonna come again? Milk my cock for my cum?"

She shuddered in his hold and slid a hand between them, rubbing over her clit. "Yes, almost there."

Tony gripped her ass more firmly, one long finger reaching her back opening, and massaged the outer rim.

Amanda's head dropped to his shoulder, hot breath fanning over his chest. She pushed back against his finger, and he pressed it just inside, stretching her.

"Oh fuck," she moaned, clamping down on him and drawing him into ecstasy alongside her.

He slammed a hand against the wall, his legs shaking from the effort of keeping them both upright. "I'm getting too old for this," he groaned.

Amanda laughed weakly. "You're just tired from moving."

"That does make me feel better," he said, nodding in agreement.

Somehow, they managed to make it upstairs to their new bedroom.

Amanda's mom had made their bed before she left, saying, "You're going to want to unpack fifty million things at once, but at least you won't have to worry about where you're sleeping tonight."

"I love your mother," Tony said while spreading an extra large towel over the comforter. "Although I'm sure this isn't what she had in mind."

Amanda chuckled. "No, probably not." She bit her lip, still annoyed with her mother over her comments in the car about the boys. But she'd promised not to say anything to them if her mother promised to work on her attitude. Based on her making only the primary bed, and not doing the same in the spare room, she was trying.

"What is it?" Tony asked, wrapping her up in his arms. He kissed her temple. "Everything okay?"

She took a deep breath and let it out, melting into his hold. "Just, you know. Mothers."

Tony chuckled. "Sorry to have brought her up."

"No, it's fine. Can you distract me?" She tilted her chin up a bit to accept his kiss.

"Consider yourself thoroughly distracted," he said, before ducking down and scooping her up by her thighs, dropping her onto the bed with a bounce.

Amanda laughed and made grabby hands at him. "Come here," she encouraged.

"I'm not going anywhere," he promised, picking up her left foot and rubbing his thumbs into the arch.

"That feels amazing," Amanda groaned, her foot twitching when he hit a ticklish spot.

He kissed the top of her foot and placed it on the bed, repeating the process with her right foot.

Tingles raced over her skin as he took his time working his way up her body. The bed jostled when he crawled onto it. "Make room for me, darlin'," he murmured between kisses to her hip bones. "Or did you want me to move you myself?" He grinned up at her.

Her heart fluttered when she met his mischievous eyes. "I'm in the mood for a bit rough," she said breathlessly.

"Hot," Tony said reverently, placing his hands high on her thighs. "Fighting back, or just manhandled?"

"Oh God," Amanda whined, thrusting her hips up. "I want you too badly to fight back."

"Gotcha," he replied, pushing her legs apart until she was spread wide open for him. "You're glistening for me, love."

"I think that's the water," she teased. "Or maybe your cum leaking out of me."

"Hmm." Tony dipped down, swiping his tongue over her folds. He traced her opening, tasting both of their releases on his tongue, before moving up to latch onto the hard bud of her clit.

"*Tony!*" she cried out, her fingers gripping his hair tightly.

"Verdict says all of the above," he said, his lips still brushing over her skin. "Let's see how wet you get for me if I don't let you come until James gets home."

"That could be *hours*!" Amanda gasped.

"I might give in and let you come once or twice," he relented. "You'll have to beg real pretty." Tony settled between her legs, pinning her thighs down with his forearms, and delicately suckled on her clit. His tongue swiped over the bundle of nerves between his lips, tracing the alphabet.

Her muscles tensed under him, a sign that she was close, but she held off. Her breath came in short pants, her head was beginning to feel dizzy from the intensity of the orgasm that was building inside her.

"You're doing so well for me," Tony praised her. "You taste amazing. I could lie here all day, just fucking you slowly with my tongue, my drool and your arousal dripping down my chin."

"Fuck," Amanda muttered, gripping the towels so hard that her knuckles turned white. "Tony, fuck."

His cock twitched at how wrecked she sounded. He'd barely even started. "You want to come?" he asked.

"Yeah," she whined. "Please, Tony. Can I please come?"

"I'll make you a deal," Tony offered, pausing to dip his tongue inside her again. "You can ride my face until you come, and then we'll come back to this position. What do you think?"

"Yes, please," she agreed eagerly.

Tony rolled them until she was kneeling over his face, and guided her hips down over his mouth.

She fell forward onto her hands, rocking her pelvis down over his mouth. "Oh my God," she gasped. "Feels so good, but I feel so empty."

Instead of answering, he delved his tongue into her slick channel as far as it could go. Her muscles rippled around it, a sure sign that she was close.

His cock was fully hard again, and he regretted rolling onto his back, because he lost the friction of the towels. He resisted the urge to thrust up against nothing.

"Well, isn't this a sight for sore eyes," James's deep voice penetrated the haze of lust surrounding the two.

"James, you're home!" Amanda cried. "Tony said I could come when you got back."

"And did you hold off?" he asked.

"Barely. Only because I feel empty."

Tony could practically *hear* her pout. He redoubled his efforts, and she came with a muffled shout.

"That was beautiful," James murmured appreciatively. "You should suck his cock to thank him while I fill you up."

"Yesss," she hissed, crawling backward down Tony's body. She paused when their faces aligned, to dance her tongue along his for a long moment.

"Still want to be manhandled?" Tony asked when they parted for air.

"Yeah," she said eagerly.

Tony met James's heated gaze over her shoulder, and he nodded in understanding. Amanda yelped as James yanked her down the bed by her hips, impaling her in the next second.

"Fuck, yes!" she screamed.

Tony grinned, shaking his head. "Your mouth is supposed to be busy." He grabbed her hair in one fist and pulled her head down on his cock, groaning at the wet heat. "Oh yeah darlin', just like that." He used her carefully, keeping an eye on her comfort levels and staying at the pace that

James set. "Fuck," he muttered. "I've already come in her once," he told James. "And I want to do it again."

"Sunshine?" James asked, rubbing her hip to get her attention.

"Hmmm?" she hummed.

"Back when we first got together, we stretched you open enough to take both of us."

Tony groaned. "Is this a special occasion, darlin'?"

She nodded as much as she could with her mouth full of his cock. He pulled her off, and she licked her lips before replying, "Yes, please, oh God, I want you both in me so bad!"

"We're going to do it slightly differently this time," James said. "You're going to do the splits over Tony, so I can get my thighs under yours. Got it?"

"Yes!" Amanda nodded enthusiastically.

Between the three of them, they managed to get into the required positioning, James straddling Tony, their cocks nestled against each other. Amanda splayed herself over Tony's body, legs to either side.

"I'm not going to be able to move much," she warned.

"Me neither," Tony said, his head spinning from the intimacy of the position.

"If you're not into it, we can change things up," James promised. "This view..." He whistled. "Sunshine, you're so wet." He pushed two fingers inside her and scissored them.

Amanda dropped her head to Tony's shoulder and rocked back into the pleasure.

"Patience," James murmured, putting a hand on her hip to keep her still. "It'll be hard for you to relax in this position. You're going to be stretched very full."

"I want more," Amanda whined.

"Brat," James said affectionately, lightly slapping her ass.

"Tony?" she pleaded, nuzzling into his neck before nipping at his ear. "Don't you want to be inside me?"

"Darlin', you need to listen to James. He's going to take care of you. You don't want to be so sore that you can't have sex tomorrow, do you?" Tony cupped the back of her neck in one hand, the tangle of wet hair getting caught on his fingers. "You'll be stuffed full of us soon enough."

She pouted. "I'm ready for you *now*. Oh *fuck*, James!"

"What did you do?" Tony asked, amusement in his voice.

"I fisted her," James replied nonchalantly. "She's clenching around my hand like she's going to come."

"Do you think she's ready to take us?" Tony asked conversationally, taking his cue from James.

A wet sound filled the air as James pulled his hand out of her body. "Yeah, I would say so. She's gaping and absolutely dripping."

"I'm right here, don't talk about me like I'm not!" she cried, her hips pulsing in tiny thrusts, feeling empty.

James drizzled lube over their cocks and slicked them up efficiently. "Ready, Tony?" he asked, fisting both and rubbing their heads over her opening.

"Ready," Tony rasped.

Amanda's jaw fell open on a silent scream as James fed both their cocks to her hungry pussy.

"*Jesus*," Tony bit out through clenched teeth. "Feels like heaven."

"Not going to last long," James groaned. "Love feeling this close to you." He kissed Amanda's shoulder blade.

She shuddered between them. "I love you," she gasped. "Please move."

"Your wish is my command," James vowed, slowly thrusting his hips, his cock gliding over Tony's. "You know, next time we do this, we might want to flip you so that I can hit your G-spot."

"Can we do that now?"

James shuddered to a halt at her words. "Of course we can."

It took some creative reconfiguring, and then they were inside her again, James hitting her G-spot on each thrust.

Tony cupped her breasts in his hands. "As much as I love having you face me, this position has some great benefits." He pinched her nipples, making her shout with pleasure.

James pressed her thighs down, his fingers dimpling her muscles. "And gives me a better position to make you come."

"Oh my God," Amanda moaned, throwing her arms over her head, barely missing Tony's face, and bracing herself against the mattress. "I think I haven't stopped coming since you two entered me."

"The way you're hugging my cock makes me think you're right," Tony panted. "You're going to make me come."

"Come for us," James gritted out. "Make a mess of our girl."

The guys made eye contact over her shoulder, and Tony lost control, his cock pulsing as he filled her up.

"Over sensitive!" he gasped.

"Gonna pull you out, but we'll keep fucking on top of you," James said, raising an eyebrow in question.

Tony nodded his agreement.

"Fuck, Amanda, you feel amazing," James said, sliding Tony out and punching his hips into her. "This feel good for you?"

"Yes, right there!" she cried, her toes curling. "It's so intense. Almost... Oh fuck, hang on, I think I—" Her face flamed as liquid gushed from her, the pleasure overwhelming her embarrassment. "I think I peed," she admitted once she caught her breath.

James sniffed the air. "That's not urine, sweetheart."

"You squirted, darlin'," Tony murmured in her ear. "Fuck, that was hot."

"Can I keep going, or do you want me to pull out?" James asked.

"Come inside me, please," Amanda begged. "I can't believe I squirted. I've never done that before— Oh fuck yes, James, that's the spot."

Adjusting his grip on her thighs to spread her even wider, James leaned down to join their mouths.

She moaned into his mouth, her pussy clamping down on his cock as she came, and then he was falling over the edge with her. His cum mingled with Tony's, overflowing and dripping onto Tony.

"We really need to have a shower now," Tony murmured.

"I'm a mess," Amanda agreed.

"But you're *our* mess," James said, nuzzling into her neck. "In *our* house."

"I'm not so sure that we'll get clean in the shower," Amanda said with a chuckle. "Is there even a point to getting dressed this weekend? I feel like it'll only waste time in stripping each other."

"You said it, not me," Tony teased.

"How was your meeting, James?" Amanda asked after he pulled out of her, a gush of cum following. "You got back pretty quickly."

"He wanted to go over TA scheduling and his expectations regarding my thesis. Should be interesting." James ran a hand over his hair. "Seems like a decent prof at least. He apologized for dragging me there on my moving day, but with classes starting on Monday, he wanted to get everything sorted ASAP."

"Good."

After her project meeting for the analysis report ended, Amanda couldn't concentrate on work. She'd received texts from Tony after each of James's races, but they'd stopped about an hour ago when the meet had ended. Her jittery energy sent her to the bathroom five times in half an hour before she finally gave up.

She knocked on her boss's door. "Hey, I'm going to head home for the day," she said.

Her boss looked up from her computer with a frown. "Are you okay?"

"I'm just not focusing well. My boyfriend just got home from a month-long work trip."

"Ah. Say no more. Mental health day approved. You have tomorrow off as well?"

"I promise I'll work extra hard on Wednesday to make up for it."

Her boss waved a perfectly manicured hand. "Of course you will. Go and be with him."

"Thanks!"

Amanda couldn't get home fast enough. Rather than walk, her usual method, she called for an Uber. By the time she got down to the lobby, the car was waiting for her.

In less than fifteen minutes, she was home. The scent of pizza tickled her nose as soon as she opened the front door. She kicked off her shoes and walked up the stairs, eager to be wrapped in Tony's arms again.

The sight that met her eyes made her simultaneously want to squeal with joy and melt into a puddle.

The guys had been eating at the island in the kitchen, but had gotten distracted, their half-eaten pizza slices on plates while they made out against the solid surface.

She must have made a noise because Tony wrenched himself away from the kiss to look at her. "You're home early. Everything okay?"

"I missed you," she said shyly, her gaze fixed on James's mouth, which had moved on to nip and kiss along Tony's jaw and down his neck. "I couldn't focus."

"I missed you too," Tony said, eyes raking over her. "You look stunning. Take off your shirt for me."

Nearly breathless, she obeyed, undoing the buttons of her translucent blouse one at a time. She had to tug it out of the high waistband of her navy skirt before it slid from her shoulders onto the floor.

"I love that you match your underthings to your clothes," Tony rasped, his hips jolting forwards at something James did to his collarbone. "Come here."

There was nowhere she'd rather be.

"I see you two finally talked," she said, swaying her hips as she walked over to them. "Anything I don't already know?"

"I'm in love with him," Tony said.

Amanda smiled, shaking her head. "I said anything I *don't* know."

Tony groaned and closed his eyes for a second. "Jamie, fuck," he breathed before he refocused on her. "Darlin', I don't know what you don't know. We told each other we're in love, we're both in love with you, I fucked him into our mattress, and we're refueling before round two."

Her eyes widened. "Ohhh, I would have loved to see you fuck him!"

"You'll get plenty of other opportunities," Tony reassured her. "You're not upset?"

"Why would I be?"

"You weren't here."

Amanda pursed her lips in thought. "You're not always here when James and I have sex, and vice versa. I think it's healthy that you two can have sex when I'm not here. If it was *only* when I'm not here, then we'd have a problem."

"I crave you too," Tony said. "It's not going to be an issue."

"James?" Amanda asked, amused because his mouth hadn't left Tony's skin for longer than a second.

"If I could have my mouth on both of you at once, I would be thrilled," he murmured. "Feeling a little clingy right now, hope you don't mind, sunshine."

"I don't mind at all," Amanda said, avidly watching his mouth leave Tony's neck to travel back up to his ear. "It's turning me on. Can I suggest something?"

"Anything," Tony gasped, grinding his clothed hips against James.

"Can we move this up to the bedroom and everyone get naked?"

"I love that suggestion," Tony said. "But I want you naked now."

Amanda chuckled and backed away from them. "If I get naked here, we're not going to make it to the bedroom. If you want to be the meat in our sandwich, we should take this to the bed."

Tony huffed a laugh. "Meat," he said, shaking his head. "Yeah, I'd like that." He ran his hand up James's back to cup his neck. "Jamie, want to fuck me into Amanda?"

"More than I want to breathe," James said fervently.

Tony peeled himself away from his new lover, grabbing his hand and pulling him along after Amanda. "I want to undress you," he said when they reached their room.

"Go ahead," Amanda replied, dropping her arms from trying to undo the clasp of her bra.

He reached around and undid it with one hand, rolling her nipple through the fabric with the other. "I love you in dark lace," he murmured, pinching lightly to draw a gasp from her lips.

Another hand brushed over her pelvis, and she peeked down to see James fondling the thick ridge of Tony's cock through his sweatpants. "Take them off," she breathed. "Jerk him bare."

The men chuckled at her eagerness.

Tony slid her bra down her arms and tossed it to the side. "You need to learn patience." He massaged both her breasts in his hands, rubbing his thumbs over the hardening tips before bending and drawing first one and then the other into his mouth.

"You've been away for a month!" she complained, her fingers gripping his hair tightly, trying to keep him against her.

"And I'm back now. We have all the time in the world to explore each other," he said, standing upright again. Tony cupped her face and drew her into a deep kiss, one that left her breathless and forgetting what she was protesting for. They came up for air, and he drew the zipper down at the back of her skirt. "Shimmy those hips until your skirt falls off," he ordered.

Amanda flushed, but obeyed, her breasts bouncing freely until the tight skirt puddled on the floor.

Tony let out a low whistle. "I'm almost tempted to make you put your bra back on, just so I can get the full effect. Damn, that is a sexy thong."

She smiled. "James helped me pick this out. I bought two, thankfully, because I happened to be wearing this one today. I was going to wear the other one tomorrow to welcome you home."

"Is it navy blue too?" he asked, fingers caressing the single strap at the side.

"No." She could see the dilemma warring behind his eyes.

Finally, he blew out a sharp breath. "Go put it on. I want to see you in my surprise lingerie."

"What will you do while you wait?" Amanda teased.

"I'll think of something," James replied, his voice a low growl.

She kissed them both before entering their large walk-in closet. Muffled moans met her ears as she shimmied the navy blue thong down her legs before dropping it in the laundry basket. She pulled out the forest green set and pulled it on. It had more straps and was completely sheer with a tasteful monstera leaf pattern embroidered on it.

Posing in the doorway, she watched James suck Tony's cock down to the root, his cheeks hollowing as he worked their best friend over. *Private porn indeed,* she thought. "What do you think?" she said, drawing Tony's attention.

"Holy shit," he gasped. "You look so fucking good in my favorite color, I need you to know that right now. Also, I might tear it to shreds to get at what's underneath it."

Amanda chuckled. "Don't you dare. I'll take it off myself." She reached behind herself to undo the bra, but again, Tony stopped her.

"Please leave it on for a little while," he begged. "It fits you like a glove."

"Whatever you want," she said, winking at him.

"I want you to kiss me," he breathed.

"Granted," she said, coming up beside him and bending to capture his lips with hers.

His hand ran up her leg to her ass, gripping her tightly to him with a groan. "Fuck, I love your ass," he breathed between languid kisses. "Oh *God*, James, you're going to kill me."

"Can't have that," Amanda murmured. "Do you need a break?"

"A short one," Tony said.

"I have an idea," James rasped. "Amanda, why don't you show him the best part of those panties you're wearing."

She lifted one knee onto the bed, spreading herself wide, and took his hand, running it down the outside of her underwear until his fingers breached the split in the crotch.

"You two are going to kill me," Tony amended. "Sit on my face, darlin', please?"

James chuckled. "Maybe later. I have a better idea. Is she wet enough to take your cock without lube?"

Tony plunged two fingers inside her, scissoring her open. He grinned up at her. "If I say no, you'll have to sit on my face first."

Amanda's knee wobbled and she gripped his shoulder. "I'm not sure I could get much wetter."

"You'll get your chance, cowboy. Amanda, take his cock, just once, and then I'll suck your juices off of him," James ordered.

Tony fell back on the bed. "This is better than the best wet dream I've ever had," he said. "I'm not going to last long."

"You'll last long enough to take my cock while you pound into Amanda," James ordered mildly.

"God, yes," Tony groaned.

Amanda straddled his lap and James guided Tony's cock into her. She sank down fully, gasping at the feeling of being joined to him once more. Sure, James more than filled her, but Tony hit differently. "I love you," she whispered, barely loud enough to be heard over the harsh breathing of both men.

She didn't worry about them not saying it back. It was obvious they returned her affections. She pulled off and shifted sideways to watch James lick Tony's cock like a popsicle.

"Exquisite torture," Tony gritted out between his teeth. "I'm going to explode."

"You can take one more round," James said, helping Amanda center herself again.

"I've missed this," she said, holding herself up on his ribcage.

"You have no idea," Tony agreed. "At least you had James."

"It's not the same," she protested.

"Of course it isn't," Tony agreed easily. "But you two were together, and I was alone. I really missed you both."

"You can sit on his face now," James urged. "Move higher up on the bed and spread your legs. I need to stretch you to take me."

While they repositioned themselves, James circled the bed to grab the lube. "Need a towel?"

Tony made a face. "I've already smeared the mess you made earlier today down my back."

James snorted. "Elegant."

"We'll put the comforter in the wash after we've made even more of a mess of it," Amanda suggested.

"Then come here," Tony nearly begged, hauling on her thighs until she was over his mouth.

"You don't want me to strip first?" she asked.

"Can't wait that long," he said as he pulled her down. He started with delicate little licks around her clit, careful to avoid the place she wanted him most, before thrusting deep inside her with a groan that echoed in the room.

"Yes, Tony," James murmured. "Relax and I'll take care of you."

Amanda threaded her fingers through Tony's hair, less to guide him, since he was amazing at eating her out, and more to just be able to touch him again. It had been too long.

His hazel eyes twinkled up at her between her thighs as he whipped his tongue over her clit in a rhythm that she couldn't quite make out.

"*Tony*," she gasped, curling over him. "Oh God, oh God, fuck, *Tony!*" She cried out his name as she shattered, her nerves singing his praises.

He let her ride her orgasm out on his face, her hips rocking and smearing her juices over him.

"I need to lie down," she whispered, and suddenly James was there, holding her, helping her off her knees and onto her back beside Tony.

"You've got a little something," James said to Tony, gripping his jaw. "Let me get it for you." He licked over Tony's chin and up to his nose, making him gasp. James took advantage of his open mouth and delved in, tongues tangling messily.

"James," Tony panted. "*Jamie.* I need you."

"I've got you," James breathed, rubbing their noses together. He shifted his weight to one arm and brought the other down between Tony's still-spread thighs. "I've got you, cowboy."

Tony groaned and arched his back. "Why, when I'm definitely *not* a cowboy, does that get me so hot?"

"We can workshop nicknames later. Right now, let me make you feel good." James bit Tony's exposed throat.

"Fuck," Tony whined. "Jamie!"

"You're opening beautifully for me," James murmured. "Amanda, how're you doing?"

"This is better than porn," she said dreamily. "I'm doing great."

Tony half groaned and threw one arm over his eyes. His hips started rocking up in the air. "I've gone past great and am closing in on heavenly."

James snorted a laugh. "Let's get you inside Amanda before I finish. It's easier for your first time with your ass in the air."

"This time, I'm going to be naked," Amanda said, wiggling out of her lingerie and throwing it towards the closet door.

"If you must," Tony replied with a heavy sigh and a teasing grin. "Now get your ass over here and spread your legs for me, won't you?"

"So romantic," Amanda met his tone, but she hurried to position herself on her back. "What are you thinking? Splits or knees up?"

"Knees up," Tony said, tucking her against his body. "I need to be able to spread for James, and splits will get in the way."

"Yes sir," she said cheekily.

Tony huffed, shaking his head fondly. "I love you," he whispered as he sank into her.

Amanda arched her back and wrapped her arms around his shoulders. "I love you too," she said, tilting her chin up to accept his kiss. The combination of her arousal plus the saliva of both guys was heady. She melted into the slow rhythm Tony started, breathing their shared air when he pressed their foreheads together.

"Feel so good," Tony gasped. "I'm going to lose my mind between the two of you."

Amanda understood what he meant. Being the focus of two partners was intense. She reached down and grabbed his ass with both hands, pulling his cheeks apart for James.

Both of them groaned at that.

"Jamie," Tony choked out, begging. "Please."

"Yeah, you're ready for me," James said, grabbing the condom he'd thrown beside them. "Tell me immediately if it hurts. I'll add more lube."

Tony hissed, and Amanda wondered if James had already breached him.

"That's fucking cold! Warn a guy next time, will you?" Tony snarked.

James chuckled. "Sorry." He leaned over, bracing himself on one arm, and met Amanda's eyes over Tony's shoulder. "Ready to love our man?" he asked.

"Ready," she said eagerly.

Tony moaned and stilled within her, his head dropping to her collarbone. "Fuck," he whispered.

"Good?" James asked, chest heaving for breath.

"More," Tony ground out. "Give me more of you."

Arousal leapt inside her at his words, and her pussy clenched down on his cock.

"Damn, Amanda, hang on, darlin'."

"I know," she whimpered. "I know. I'm not trying to rush you. This is just so hot."

James grinned at her. "Isn't it?"

Tony let out a long groan. "God, James, I didn't realize you had such a monster in your pants. How do you take him *and* me, Amanda?"

"Well, usually I'm *really* turned on," she replied with a chuckle that James echoed.

"You're doing fantastically," James said encouragingly. "I'm going to pull out a bit and add more lube. It's going to be cold," he added as an afterthought.

"No shit," Tony bit out. His eyes rolled back when James thrust in again. "Oh my God." James thrust again. "Fucking hell." Once more. "Holy shit!" Tony shouted.

"There's the spot," James said playfully. "You can move too now."

"Yeah, I'll just put my muscles back together after that," Tony joked. He pulled back along with James, and together they thrust in.

Amanda's teeth clacked together. "Oh God," she moaned, gasping for breath. "That was good."

"Again," James ordered, and they repeated the motion. "Faster."

"Harder," Amanda encouraged them. "Oh my God. Oh fuck yes!"

Their hammering into her made the bed squeak and groan, barely noticeable over their three voices crying out in pleasure.

"Tony, James, you're going to make me come," Amanda gasped.

"Yes, come for us," Tony begged. "I'm barely hanging on here."

"Same," James ground out. "Come, sunshine."

One last thrust in, and four things happened at once.

Amanda screamed as her nerves finally exploded in ecstasy.

Tony gave into the pleasure and followed her over the edge.

Once they came, James allowed himself to join their orgasm.

And the bedframe collapsed out from underneath them in a spectacular crash and jarring thud.

Chapter Twelve

Flashback: Rocky Horror Picture Show

Amanda carefully filled in Tony's lower lip with bright red lipstick, her face inches from his. He was sitting on a dining room chair in their bedroom, Amanda straddling his lap.

"Stretch your lips like you're saying 'eeee'," she instructed, and he obeyed, molding his face to her specifications. "Perfect, now relax," she said.

Tony wiggled his jaw, making her chuckle.

"Not quite. Like this." She opened her mouth, her jaw loose.

He copied her, and she applied the final touches.

"There," she said, putting the cap on the lipstick.

"Who knew it would take," he glanced at the clock on their bedroom wall, "an hour to put make-up on me."

"Doctor Frank-N-Furter make-up," Amanda clarified. "And I thought it would take longer, but that was before we decided not to do the white base coat. I'm glad. I don't think you'd be able to control yourself."

Tony raised an exaggeratedly-painted eyebrow and looked down between them. "You're sitting on my lap, not my cock."

She shook her head, a smile on her face. "If I'd been on your cock, you'd still be bare-faced and you know it."

"You're half-dressed. I could've let my hands wander."

"Yes, you could have, which was my point." Amanda tapped the tip of his nose with her finger. "You were a very good boy," she added cheekily. "How would you like your reward?"

Tony closed his eyes and groaned, multiple scenarios playing through his mind, but was interrupted by the doorbell, which had been ringing near-constantly for the past half-hour.

James was on candy bowl duty while they'd been getting Tony ready for their party, which he loved. To be honest, the people bringing kids door-to-door who liked looking at half-naked men probably enjoyed it as well. James was dressed as Rocky, wearing only a tiny gold speedo and a white silk robe.

But instead of the high-pitched voices of trick-or-treaters, deeper tones echoed up the stairs.

"Guests have arrived," Tony said with a sigh. "My reward will have to wait."

"If you insist," she said, standing up.

This put her breasts in front of his face, which was too much for him to resist. "This innocent little white bra is going to get covered with lipstick," Tony murmured, "unless you give me a *very* good reason not to."

"I'm not going to be wearing a shirt."

Tony leaned back in order to see her face. "Come again?"

"I haven't come at all yet," Amanda teased.

He tickled her ribs, making her squirm. "You're not wearing a shirt over this? Also, I thought you were wearing a corset."

"That's my second costume," she informed him.

"Hmm." His fingers skated over the cup of the bra. "That explains why I haven't seen this one before. It's a little more subdued than your usual ones."

"Subdued," Amanda repeated with a snort. "You mean you can't see through this one and it isn't made of lace?"

"You have bras that aren't transparent," Tony said, raising an eyebrow. "But your white ones are usually more on the side of lingerie."

"You know my wardrobe pretty well for only having lived together for two months."

"I've known *you* since we were twelve and you weren't even in training bras," he retorted. "But you haven't given me a good reason yet."

"I did!" she protested.

"You told me you weren't wearing a shirt. That sounds like I should stake my claim, not a reason to avoid it." He nuzzled her cleavage.

"I... I can't think of any," Amanda said. "Mark me, Tony."

"That's Doctor Frank-N-Furter to you, Janet," Tony growled, gripping her hair in a fist and pulling gently until she was arching into his face. He didn't want to waste the best lip-print, so he examined her body carefully before puckering his lips in what he hoped would give a good impression. He pressed his lips directly over her nipple through the cup, and pulled away to reveal a perfect "Rocky Horror"-worthy stain behind.

"Is that it?" she gasped, her head still tipped back to the ceiling.

"Never." He peppered kisses across the top of her breasts, not caring where he smeared the lipstick on both her skin and bra. He bit lightly through the cup on the other side, and she bucked in his hold with a whine.

"Touch me, touch me, touch me," she gasped.

"Wrong character to say that to," Tony replied, releasing her. He had to steady her for a moment. Once she stopped wobbling, he slapped her satin slip-covered ass. "You don't want Rocky to miss out on his lines."

Amanda looked thoroughly debauched, red lipstick smeared across her chest, and her hair a tangled mess. In other words, a perfect Janet.

"Next time, you should let me blot your lipstick first," she informed him.

He raised an eyebrow. "Where would be the fun in that? Scoot along downstairs."

She blushed, the color filling her cheeks and spreading down her chest.

"Problem?" he teased. He knew that she would take the question seriously, and that if she really was uncomfortable, he'd help her in whatever way she needed. Not that he expected her to have an issue.

"Not at all." She squared her shoulders, turned around, and strutted out of the bedroom.

Tony listened to the whistles and catcalls echoing up the stairs as he pulled on his lab coat. Next were the simple blue gloves from the pharmacy. He snapped the latex around his wrist and grinned, thinking about how much fun he'd have playing with Amanda with them on.

He almost didn't recognize himself in the mirror on the landing when he stepped out the door. Amanda had done a fantastic job making him look like Tim Curry. He raised an eyebrow and licked his teeth, his lips curling up in a nasty smile. *Perfection,* he thought, taking the stairs slowly.

The noise on the main floor slowly dissipated as his feet came into view. He wasn't wearing heels because he hadn't wanted to spend the money on them, but he was wearing motorcycle boots over fishnet stockings.

They'd been a pain to get into, but the reaction seemed like it was going to be worth it.

He paused three stairs up, looking out over the party, every head turned towards him. He only recognized about a third of them, probably because they were all in heavy make-up. "Well," he said, doing his best to imitate Tim Curry. "Now that the fun has arrived, this party can get started."

A few people started clapping, and he bowed theatrically to them. "I've been teaching some *private lessons*, if you know what I mean. Have you seen my wayward student?"

Some people shook their heads, but others pointed towards the kitchen with grins.

"Thank you," Tony said, taking the last few steps in one. He glided through the party, not dropping his persona, greeting people with loud kisses near their cheeks.

Only Amanda got to wear his brand tonight.

And James, he thought suddenly. *Do I dare? Since he's dressed as Rocky, would he let me kiss him?*

The temptation almost took him out at the knees. His gaze arrowed in on James standing in the kitchen, talking to Glenn. The lighting was incredible, shining off his skin and making it glow. Amanda joined them, and James tipped her chin up to accept a peck on her lips. Then he looked her up and down, a grin playing at the corners of his mouth when he saw the additions Tony had made.

Their eyes met across the room, the heat practically tangible.

As if he were a moth and James the flame, Tony joined them. "Hello darlin'," he drawled, slinging an arm across Glenn's shoulders so that he wouldn't reach out for James. "Having fun?"

"You certainly were," James teased.

Tony licked over his teeth. "And I could have some more, if you'd care to join me."

James's eyebrows rose.

"Rocky," Tony added quickly, in case James was uncomfortable with real flirting. "I *did* create you to play with, afterall."

"Ooh la la," Glenn murmured. "Is the vibe getting hotter in here, or is it just me?" He fanned himself jokingly.

"On *that* note, I think it's time to put the movie in," Amanda said, brushing past Tony. "Come along Brad," she said to Glenn.

"Are you going to cuddle with me, Janet?" he teased her.

"Brad!" she said, pretending to be shocked. "I am not that kind of girl!"

"What kind of girl are you?" Tony asked, leering at her. "I think you're the kind that likes the antici—" He leaned in close, lightly brushing his nose over her cheekbone to her ear. "—pation."

Glenn stared at them, his jaw hanging open. "Warn a guy," he muttered before heading over to the couch in their living room. He sat down and grabbed a pillow, putting it over his lap. "I'm *anticipating* needing this," he said with a chuckle.

"Does Tim Curry do it for you?" one of the girls in Amanda's program asked, leaning provocatively through the half-wall into the living room. Tony didn't have a good view of her front, but she had to be practically spilling out of her corset in that position.

Glenn's eyes dropped to her cleavage before returning to her face. "Baby, sexiness does it for me, and Tim Curry is nothing if not sexy. Tony's channeling him quite well," he added dryly.

"I'm going to take that as a compliment," Tony said cheerfully.

"Have a seat, Patty," Amanda said to her friend. "He won't bite."

"Pity," Patty said, winking at Tony when she stood upright again. To Glenn she added, "I don't mind it a little rough."

Glenn put his arm behind her on the couch, and she leaned against him.

"Well, that was fast," James murmured in Tony's ear, nearly making him jump out of his skin. "How long do you think it'll last?"

"I didn't even know her name until two seconds ago," Tony replied. "There's no way I could judge."

"Bet."

Tony met James's eyes, spotting a twinkle of mischief in them that made his heart flutter. "Wager?"

"A date."

Tony's breath caught in his throat, and he started coughing.

James clapped him on the back a few times, rubbing gently after each one. "You okay?" he asked once the coughs had subsided.

"Yeah." Tony cleared his throat a couple times and James handed him the glass he was holding.

"It's just water," James said, and Tony nodded before gulping half the glass. "So, a date with Amanda on the line, are you willing to bet?"

Disappointed that James hadn't meant a date with *him*, Tony nodded. "I'll give it until Christmas."

"Oooh, that's what I was going to say." James chewed his lower lip, making Tony want to soothe it with his tongue.

Living with his best friends was incredible. He loved it. But he was going to lose his mind. Every day, he fell deeper in love with both of them, digging himself into a hole of his own making, because James? He didn't love Tony the same way.

They cleaned, studied, worked out, slept, and fucked Amanda together, but nothing had changed since the first time.

Because I'm too chicken-shit to say anything.

Tony thought back to Glenn's party at the beginning of summer, when James had cock-warmed him on a dare. It had felt so right, but he guessed James didn't agree.

"Thanksgiving," James said at last.

"And if they last longer than Christmas?"

James grinned. "We both lose."

"No interference," Tony added, holding out his pinky finger.

"Naturally." James sealed the bet by linking their fingers.

"What are you two up to?" Amanda asked, rejoining them now that the movie had started.

"Just a bet on Glenn," James said, looping his arms around her waist and nuzzling into her neck.

"Ah," Amanda said, tilting her head to give him more room.

"You should say your line to Rocky now," Tony prompted, noting that their guests had all moved into the living room to watch the movie. Several people were quoting along with the actors, and he grinned.

Amanda grinned. "Touch me," she whispered, just loud enough for the three of them to hear. "Touch me, touch me."

James bit his lip, eyeing their guests. Nobody was paying any attention to them. He slid his hands from her waist around to her front, pulling the bra cups down so her breasts spilled over the top.

Tony made sure his body was shielding her from any accidental voyeurs, arousal spiking as James fondled her, long fingers pulling at her nipples until they drew in tight.

"Oh God," Amanda gasped, pressing into his touch. "More."

Tony captured her lips with his own, unable to hold back from swallowing her breathless sounds. She sucked on the tip of his tongue, he bit her lip, the heat rose between them. He could feel James's hot breath as he latched onto the skin of her neck.

"I think it might be time to show James the surprise we prepared for him," Tony rasped, pulling back from the kiss.

James raised his eyebrows.

"Here?" Amanda whispered, eyes flicking to the living room in excitement.

Tony followed her gaze. Everyone was entirely focused on the movie. "Are you going to be our good girl?" he murmured, brushing her hair over her shoulder.

She practically melted in their hold. "Yes." She took James's hand and pulled it behind her, down between her cheeks.

His eyes widened at the solid, flat obstacle that met his fingers. "Sunshine, are you wearing a plug?"

She nodded, her skin flushing pink. "A new one. It's stretching me."

Tony's cock throbbed at the heat in James's eyes. "Why do you need to be stretched, darlin'?" Tony prompted her.

"After the party, I want you to fuck my ass while Tony's inside me," she said, resting her cheek on James's shoulder.

"No," James said, pulling her closer by the hand on her ass.

Tony's heart sank.

"I don't fucking care about the party. We're going upstairs right this second," James ordered. "Go on, sunshine." He lightly slapped her ass.

Amanda bit her lip and did as she was told, not even bothering to fix her bra to cover herself.

"You two are menaces," James said to Tony, a chuckle seeping into his tone. "Fuck, I almost came on the spot."

Tony raked his eyes over his best friend. "You have no idea," he drawled.

"Don't tease," James said, rolling his eyes. "Let's go."

Amanda was waiting for them on the bed, her clothing in a pile on the floor. "You took your time," she informed them. "I was wondering if I should put on my second costume and go back downstairs!"

"Plenty of time for that later," James said. "Hands and knees. Show me my surprise."

Tony shrugged out of his lab coat, dropped it onto her discard pile, and rounded the bed to get the lube and a condom while she flipped into position. "Not going to lie, I've been developing a fantasy involving these gloves and your ass, darlin'."

Amanda chuckled. "Go for it. Oh fuck, James," she groaned, dropping her head onto her forearms.

James had pulled on the plug until the widest part of it was stretching her rim. "Jesus, you guys weren't playing around with this. You're going to take me without much prep at all."

"That was the plan," Tony said, slicking up two gloved fingers, one on each hand. "Pull it out all the way... Slowly, yes, that's it." His cock throbbed at how puffy her rim looked, how stretched out she was already. "Let's test you out," he murmured, running one finger inside her.

"Oh, look at how good you are for us," James breathed. "I can't wait to be inside you."

Tony shifted, using both hands now, stretching her further.

Amanda clawed at the comforter. "Stop teasing me," she whined. "Please."

"Sure, we can head back downstairs," Tony said, pulling away.

"*No!*" she nearly sobbed. "I need you both inside me. *Please!*"

"Since she asked so nicely," James said, tearing open the condom.

"Might as well," Tony agreed calmly, as if his cock wasn't aching to be buried in her warmth. He peeled his gloves off and dropped them on the floor. "I can't bend super well," he added, sitting on the edge of the bed to show the immovability of his corset.

James chuckled. "That won't be a problem. Lie back and let Amanda do all the work."

She slid off the bed onto her knees between Tony's legs. "Lift your ass," she said.

Tony fell onto his back and pushed his hips up, letting her pull the tight black speedo down just far enough to release his cock. The wide holes of the fishnets did nothing to restrain him, digging almost painfully into his hard flesh. She pulled the waistband down, easing it over his cock, and tucked it under his balls.

"Oops," Amanda said, catching a drip before he could dribble any pre-cum onto his corset. "That's no good." She sucked the head between her lips, swirling her tongue around the weeping eye.

"I thought you wanted him in your pussy, not your mouth," James reminded her, tapping her ass with his toes. "Up."

"Right." She climbed onto Tony, plastering her body over his and sinking onto his cock with a slight angle of her hips. "God, you feel good," she mumbled into his neck. "This corset is the perfect amount of texture against my nipples."

"That's great, because you're going to be feeling it rub while I pound into you," James said, his cock slipping over the base of Tony's as he pressed into Amanda.

She gasped, her body relaxing into the stretch of two cocks within her. Hot puffs of air tickled Tony's shoulder.

He rubbed up and down her back, soothing her. "You're doing amazing for us," he murmured in her ear. "How do you feel?"

She nodded, her cheek rubbing against his. "Full. So much. *God*, James, please *move!*"

Tony clenched his jaw against the pleasure of feeling his best friend dragging against him through the thin membrane.

Amanda shuddered in his hold at the inward thrust. "Just like that," she whimpered.

"Feels fantastic," James grunted as he picked up his pace. "So good for us."

"You gonna come for us?" Tony asked, pressing open-mouthed kisses along her neck. "Gonna milk us dry?"

"Yessssss," she hissed. "Close. James, keep that angle, fuck..."

Stars exploded behind Tony's eyelids when she clamped down on him as she came, and his hips stuttered up as he emptied into her.

James followed them into ecstasy after one more pump of his cock. He slumped over them, breathing hard. "You good?" he panted.

"I feel fan-fucking-tastic," Amanda purred, stretching as much as she was able between them. "Ready to put on a corset and blow everyone's minds."

"Sunshine, their minds were already blown by you." James pulled out with a hiss.

Tony's cock twitched weakly within her at the loss of pressure.

"I'm going to go pee before I get dressed. See you down there?" She pressed a kiss to Tony's lips before getting to her feet and repeating the motion with James, leaving a smear of red lipstick across his lips.

"You won't need any help getting into your corset?" James asked.

"No, it hooks up the front," Amanda chirped, waltzing out the door completely nude.

"She remembers that there's a party downstairs, right?" Tony asked rhetorically.

James chuckled and held out a hand. "She gets off on being seen." He hauled Tony to his feet. "Need help getting that speedo back up?"

"Ugh, you have no idea how difficult it is to bend in this thing!" Tony complained, dabbing at the excess cum with a wipe. "*Please* help." He pulled up the fishnets again, wincing at the way they trapped his cock once more. He hadn't fully softened yet.

"Since you asked so nicely." James finished adjusting his own costume before helping Tony get back into his once he'd finished cleaning himself off.

"You've got a little lipstick," Tony said, indicating James's face.

James shrugged after looking in the mirror. "I'm supposed to look tousled at the end of the movie. It's sexy, right?"

Tony chuckled. "Dude, you don't have to *try* to be sexy."

"Thanks." James grinned bashfully. "Shall we?"

They crossed paths with one of Amanda's new friends on the stairs.

"Oh, you might want to wait a moment until Amanda's out of the bathroom," Tony said, putting a hand on the guy's shoulder.

"I don't mind waiting upstairs," he said.

"She's naked," James added mischievously.

The guy flushed, his eyes darting between the two of them. "I...see."

At that moment, Amanda appeared at the top of the stairs. "James, you were right. I do need some help."

The guy made an alarming choking noise, his eyes wide as he took in the half-naked woman.

"Bathroom's free, Brian," Amanda said cheerfully. "James?" She held out her corset with a pout.

James shook his head with a grin. "Menace," he whispered to Tony as he brushed past.

"You love it," Tony murmured back.

"You know it." James winked.

Tony's heart skipped a beat and his grip tightened on the railing. *I'm a mess,* he thought desperately, watching James's barely covered ass flex on his way up the stairs.

"Sorry," Brian muttered, his face red.

Tony had completely forgotten the man was standing next to him. He shrugged. "Nothing to be sorry about. Bathroom's free."

He rejoined the party, grabbing a fresh cup of water on the way. Sex noises were coming from the downstairs bathroom, and Glenn and Patty were missing from the couch. Tony chuckled softly, mentally congratulating himself on having the forethought to have easy access to condoms.

"Having a good time, handsome?" Amanda asked, wrapping her arms around his waist from behind.

"Better now that you're back down here," he replied smoothly. He turned to look at her and spilled a little of his water on the floor. "Shit, darlin'. A little warning next time!" he gasped, taking her in. "You look *fucking* hot."

Amanda smiled demurely, at odds with her breasts practically spilling out of her corset. He could definitely see the top half of her areola. "I like looking fuckable for my boys," she said, twirling on the spot.

Tony nearly swallowed his tongue. "There's not much back on those panties."

"No, there isn't." She pressed herself against his body, nuzzling into his neck. "Do you like it?"

"A little too much." He palmed one ass cheek and gave a squeeze. He met James's gaze over her shoulder. "You're trying our patience, love."

"We *just* had sex!" Amanda exclaimed playfully. "You need some recovery time."

"My cock didn't get the memo." Tony pressed his lips under her ear, making her shiver in his hold. "I can't help it."

James sandwiched her between them, his hip against Tony's hand. "We probably shouldn't disappear again so soon. You know, actually be the hosts at our party?"

Amanda giggled. "Then we should get to hosting. Doctor, our guests look hungry. Why don't you serve the meatloaf?"

Tony groaned. "Why did we decide to have a party?"

"Because we wanted to have fun with our friends," James said with a sigh.

"Don't sound so disappointed about it!" she said. "We've got all night."

"That's what I'm afraid of," Tony growled, making them chuckle.

Chapter Thirteen

Tony

He'd been home for two weeks, give or take, and happier than he could have thought was possible. Finally telling James how he really felt about him was a weight lifted off their relationship, and the three of them were the stronger for it.

He was worried about how Amanda took the transition from being the focus of both of their attention all the time. But he was working on building his communication skills, and using methods he learned at work, he finally managed to broach the subject after lunch.

"How are you doing?" he asked, pulling her down onto the couch in the living room.

"This project at work is kicking my ass," she groaned, leaning against him. "They want me to come up with ideas *all the time*. I'm so drained."

"You can delegate," Tony suggested. "Focus groups, maybe?"

"Maybe."

They were silent for a moment, Tony playing with the tips of her hair. "That's not what I meant, though," he soldiered on. "I meant with us. Are you okay with us?"

"I *love* us," she said happily. "You two are my rocks. I'm so glad I come home to the two best guys ever."

Tony frowned. "I... That's great. I love our trio too. That isn't what I meant though." He sighed, frustrated.

"Take your time," Amanda said, sinking down until she was resting her head on his lap. "James, come join us. The dishes can wait."

"I'm going to need more room than that," James teased, tapping Amanda's stomach. "Come on, sit up."

With a groan, she obeyed, letting James sit next to Tony before squeezing herself between him and the arm of the couch and throwing her legs across their laps. "Try again, Tony," she said encouragingly.

He blew out a long breath, nervously not meeting the curious gazes of his lovers. "I'm trying to ask Amanda if she's okay with the change in our relationship dynamic."

"Ohhh," she said, nodding her head. "Thank you for checking in. First of all, I want to say that I am thrilled that you two finally admitted you're in love with each other."

James pretended to be shocked. "Love?"

She poked him. "Yes, love."

"You're right." James beamed and twisted slightly to kiss Tony on the lips.

Tony meant to keep the kiss chaste, but then James let out a tiny moan and he was done for. His head spinning, his tongue darted out, begging for more than just a taste of James.

His hand rested lightly on Amanda's calf, his thumb brushing over the skin that was developing goosebumps.

"Second, it's fucking hot when you two get going." Her voice filtered into his brain, and he pulled back from James, breathing hard.

"Sorry," he whispered. "Didn't mean to get distracted."

"And third," she said, reaching out for him. "If I need to be the center of attention, I know how to ask for it, and I know you both will provide."

"Damn straight," James said roughly.

"You don't feel left out?" Tony asked, still concerned.

Amanda opened her mouth to answer, but he put a finger over her lips.

"Please, really think about this. I want you to feel included, and if there's anything I've been doing wrong, I need to know." Tony's heart was pounding, and he bit his lip. He didn't want to hurt one of his favorite people in the world.

Amanda licked the tip of his finger before taking his hand in both of hers. "Trust me, if I ever felt left out, I would say something immediately. I know that even if you two are in the middle of fucking each other, you'd pause and make space for me in some way."

James nodded. "You're right."

"I was a tiny bit disappointed that I didn't get to see the two of you together for your first time. We've done all our firsts together as the three of us. But I think it was important that it was just the two of you because you'd been hiding your attraction for so long. If I'd been there, you might have held back. You would have included me, but it needed to be you two. I saw that when you recreated it for me. It was fucking hot," she smiled, "and I'm not disappointed any longer. Do you feel left out when it's me and James?"

Tony frowned.

"Let me help you decide," James said, and cupped Amanda's head, bringing their mouths together.

The kiss quickly grew heated as Tony watched, and he got harder the longer it went on. Eventually James pulled back, placing tiny pecks on her upturned lips. She smiled a little dazedly.

"Well?"

Tony let out a rush of air. "Fuck, that was hot," he admitted.

"Do you feel left out?" James prodded.

"No." Tony shook his head for emphasis. "If I had let you know I wanted in, you would have shifted to give me room."

"Exactly," Amanda nodded.

"Now that we've settled that, I think we should take advantage of our free afternoon and finally go shopping for a new bed," James said, clapping Tony on a shoulder hard enough to throw his body forward.

They drove, arriving at the closest mattress store, and Amanda immediately flung herself on the bed nearest the door. "Nope, nope, nope!" she muttered, getting up quickly, relieved that the store was nearly vacant.

Stifling chuckles, James and Tony followed her to the next.

"What was wrong with that one?" asked Tony, grinning.

"I hate the feeling of pocket coils." She shuddered. "It's like each one is digging into my skin. Very uncomfortable."

"May I assist you?" asked an attendant, who was about their age. "My name is Kevin."

"Ohmigod *Kevin*!" Amanda squeaked, throwing herself at him in a bear hug. "I haven't seen you since graduation! How have you been?"

"Oh, hey guys," Kevin said bashfully, rubbing the back of his head. "I swear I didn't recognize you."

She gasped, putting a hand to her chest in shock. "How very dare you not recognize me! We only took every high school math class together!"

"I wasn't expecting to see you in Boston," he said. "Last I heard, you were heading to Texas."

"Been there, done that." She wiggled a little in place. "I came back two years ago and have been shacking up with these two ever since."

Kevin finally turned his attention to the two men hovering behind her. "You're still friends then?"

Tony huffed a laugh. "More than friends."

Kevin's eyebrows rose. "Really?"

Amanda nodded firmly. "Really."

"If you don't mind," James said, interrupting the reunion, "we're looking for a King, no pocket coils." He shrugged. "Other than that, we have no idea."

Kevin nodded and headed over to a terminal.

"King?" Tony asked, leaning into his boyfriend's shoulder.

"The frames generally have extra support in the middle, which we need, and I don't want to fall off when I'm rolling around with you again," James teased.

"You didn't fall off," Tony protested.

"Yet." James winked at him, making his heart flutter.

Kevin returned and led them to a corner. A giant mattress drew their attention. "This is our California King Pillow Top mattress. There are three different levels of firmness; soft, medium, and hard. Your feet won't hang over the end, like they might on a regular King. Sheets might be more difficult to come by, but there are some great online sites that I could recommend."

Amanda sank onto the mattress. "Ooh!"

Kevin grinned. "This is our softest mattress. You might want a harder one if you have any back or neck soreness when you get up in the morning."

"A harder mattress means you're less stiff in the morning?" asked Tony.

"I doubt that," teased James.

"No, that's exactly right," replied Kevin, misunderstanding the joke. "The softer the mattress, the more your body twists."

Amanda got off the bed with a sigh. "Better show us the harder ones then." She ignored the men's snickers. "I don't want to get used to this one, and then feel uncomfortable later on."

Kevin led them two beds down. "This is the hardest model."

Amanda sat and grimaced. "People actually buy this one?"

"Yes, they do," Kevin laughed. "Try lying down. You don't sleep sitting up."

Amanda lay down in the middle of the bed on her back.

"Lie as you would when you're about to fall asleep," suggested Kevin.

Amanda exchanged glances with the men standing behind him and grinned. "How do I usually fall asleep?" she purred.

James grinned and crossed to the other side of the bed before climbing in beside her. She rolled to face him. "Usually on top of me," he said, pulling her body against his.

"This doesn't feel quite right." Amanda draped her leg over his hips. She beckoned over her shoulder at Tony.

Tony climbed on the mattress behind her, making the bed rock a little. He spooned her body, wrapping an arm around her waist.

"This is really hard," Amanda said after a moment.

"No, I'm not," murmured James in her ear, making her giggle. "Yet."

"Next one," she announced.

Tony rolled off, and Amanda unwrapped herself from James. Mutely, Kevin showed them to the next mattress over. They resumed their position on the bed.

"This one feels nice," sighed Amanda, wiggling her body between the men.

Tony's arm clamped down on her waist to hold her still. "If you keep moving like that, we might give Kevin a show," he whispered.

Her breathing quickened, pupils dilating with arousal. James, who could see her face, groaned. He glanced up at Kevin, who was staring, jaw dropped, and pulled her mouth up for a deep, slow kiss.

Amanda whimpered quietly, thrusting her hips backwards against Tony's quickly hardening cock.

"You two are quite the exhibitionists, aren't you?" he groaned, trying to stay quiet.

Kevin cleared his throat, and they all glanced up at him. He had a dull red flush creeping up his neck, his eyes firmly fixed on their waists.

Amanda giggled. "Sorry, Kevin."

"You don't sound sorry," Tony whispered in her ear.

"It's okay," replied Kevin in a strangled voice. He clapped his mouth shut after speaking.

"You *sure* this is okay?" James asked cautiously.

Kevin nodded eagerly. "I wasn't expecting it, but I'm not complaining. If a family comes in though..."

"Got it," James said with a nod.

"I'd like to try the soft one now," Amanda announced, changing the subject abruptly. "But so far this one is my favourite."

Tony took a deep breath, trying to control his raging erection, before rolling away from them and standing up. He only half succeeded.

James stood up in between the medium and soft mattresses, picked Amanda up from her prone position, and tossed her onto the softer mattress.

She bounced a little with a laugh, and reached for him. Unable to resist, he crawled onto the bed, lowering his body over hers and dropping kisses all over her face before slipping his tongue inside her mouth, making her groan.

Kevin glanced at Tony, who gave a crooked half-smile.

"Excuse me," Tony winked, before walking around the bed to join his partners on the softest mattress he had ever sat on.

James pounced on him, pushing him onto his back and straddling his hips. Tony shifted his weight, rolling them over until he had the upper hand.

He grinned down at James. "How many more times can we roll on this thing before we fall off the bed?"

"Let's find out," growled James playfully, wrapping his legs around Tony's waist and pulling him down for a blinding kiss. He rolled them, taking the top position again.

Amanda squeaked and pulled herself to the top of the bed, out of their way, eyes dancing with amusement.

Without breaking the kiss, Tony flipped them again and kept rolling until they had completed a full rotation.

"Fuck," mumbled James into Tony's mouth. They broke apart, breathing heavily, muscles screaming at them to thrust against each other.

Tony snuck a glance at Kevin. He was watching them, eyes half-lidded. Tony's eyes traced the line of his shoulders, noticing their tenseness, and bit his lip, concerned that they had gone too far. Then he noticed that Kevin had a rather impressive erection himself, and relaxed. "I like the size of the California," he said casually. "But I think I prefer the medium firmness over this one. Do you agree?"

The other two chorused their agreement, and Kevin lifted his eyes to Tony's, throat working. "I'll get the paperwork for you. When you're ready, I'll be over there." He gestured to the office space in the centre of the building.

"Thank you!" Amanda chirped with a smile, and he fled.

She nudged Tony. "And you said we were the exhibitionists! Show off," she teased.

Tony grinned at her from underneath James. "I was provoked."

"Right," drawled James. He ground their pelvises together, and Tony's eyes closed with pleasure.

"Fuck, James, aren't we supposed to be calming ourselves down?" Tony said in a strangled voice.

Reluctantly, James got to his feet. Tony remained on the bed, breathing deeply as he watched his lovers calm down.

Amanda let her hungry gaze linger on the men, tracing the bulges in their jeans with her eyes. She licked her lips.

"Looking at us like that is not helping matters any, sunshine," growled James.

She grinned at him. "I'll go sign the paperwork. Delivery this weekend would be ideal, wouldn't it?"

"If they can manage it so soon," James shrugged. "Since we've been sleeping on our current mattress on the floor for the past two weeks, sooner is better. No big deal."

The men let Amanda go ahead but had a perfect view of Kevin startling when she sat across the desk from him. Tony pulled James to a stop just outside the door so they could overhear the conversation and see without being seen.

"Where is," he stopped himself, and then tried again. "Where are..." He flushed.

Amanda chuckled. "Oh, they'll be along in a moment. They needed some extra time to calm down."

Tony snickered into James's shoulder at how flustered Kevin was.

Blushing an interesting shade of crimson, he passed her the paperwork, and she scanned it quickly, making notations with a pen. "We won't need the flimsy bedframe. We're going shopping for that next. Box springs, yes. Is there the option to have a split box spring? It would make it easier to get up the stairs." At Kevin's nod, she continued. "We don't need pillows, so get rid of that. Yes, we do want delivery." She glanced up at him coyly, batting her eyelashes. "Would this Saturday be possible? We've been sleeping on our old mattress on the floor since we broke our last bed."

Kevin cleared his throat loudly and tried to speak. "I...I..." he stammered, and closed his eyes. "I'll see what I can do." He turned to his computer and tapped quickly on the keyboard. "There is space on the truck. We can get it to you by five. No guarantees on the time, though, I'm afraid."

"I understand," she nodded sympathetically. "We should be home all day, so no worries. We can move it ourselves, if that helps?"

"I'll make a note of that. It would speed things up for other deliveries if they don't have to stick around to put it in place." His fingers danced across the keyboard.

"Any chance of a discount?" she asked, smiling prettily at him.

"Uh, I'll see what I can do." Kevin swallowed hard. He lurched to his feet. "I'll go ask my manager for approval."

He walked quickly towards the half-open door in the corner of the office area and disappeared inside.

Tony tilted his head at the office door. James nodded and led the way inside, taking the seat beside Amanda. Tony leaned against the partition beside him.

"How's it going?" asked James, tucking a strand of hair behind her ear.

"We're getting it delivered on Saturday." She beamed at him happily. "We need to go shopping for a frame next. And sheets, since we only have queen size right now."

"I have some thoughts about what I want in a frame," put in Tony with a smirk. "It has to be sturdier than our last one, for sure. And I'd like it to have slats in the headboard."

Amanda grinned up at him. "Perfect for tying me up."

"And maybe me?" Tony suggested hesitantly.

A muscle jumped in James's cheek. "You'd want that?" he asked, shifting in his seat.

Tony leaned forward to drop a kiss on James's lips. "I'd love to try it."

"That sounds hot," Amanda said, eyes half-lidded. "Sold."

Kevin came back and she returned her focus to the paperwork in front of her. "If you can pay the whole thing now, we can knock three hundred off the price."

She narrowed her eyes at him as she handed over her credit card. "You're taking a hit to your commission, offering us that. Financing would be no more than two hundred. Don't cut yourself short just because we went to high school together."

Kevin blushed. "Call it an entertainment bonus," he mumbled.

James grinned. "Say 'You're welcome,' Amanda."

"But," she tried to protest.

"Say 'Thank you,' Amanda," chuckled Tony.

"Thank you, Kevin," she said, smiling up at him.

He flushed a darker shade of red. "You're welcome. I didn't expect you to notice."

James grinned. "She finished top of her class at Harvard, a Masters of Business in Marketing Analysis," he boasted proudly.

Kevin stared, and then looked at his computer again. "Sorry for under-estimating you," he mumbled. "If you could sign here, please." He handed the receipt to her.

Amanda signed quickly before standing up. "It was very nice to see you again. I hope you have a nice day." She walked around the desk to kiss him on the cheek. "Sorry for putting you on the spot like that," she said.

"No problem," he gasped. He met Tony's eyes and swallowed hard. His expression seemed a mixture of embarrassment and arousal.

Tony grinned. "Have you kept in touch with anyone else from back home? Glenn's in Boston, and regularly has parties that devolve into nudist Bacchanals," he said with a wink.

Kevin shook his head, scanning the trio to see if they were teasing him.

"Give Amanda your number and she'll pass it on to him. He's planning something big for Thanksgiving," James said. "Come on you two, it's time to look for a bed frame."

Amanda danced back over to the men after securing Kevin's number in her phone, and they took each of her hands in theirs. "Bye!" she said brightly over her shoulder.

"You are such a tease," murmured Tony, once they were outside the store. "Riling poor Kevin up like that."

"I just kissed him on the cheek for the discount, and apologized for pointing it out to him!" Amanda said, eyes wide. "You two were the ones who riled him up, rolling around on the bed." Her eyes closed, and she hummed happily. "Fuck that was hot."

James swatted her ass. "Do you want to go look for a bed frame or not? We can go straight home and re-enact it if you want."

They headed to the big box furniture store, eager to pick out just the right frame for their new mattress.

"They'll probably have limited options for a California," said James. "Don't get too attached until we can find out if it comes in the size we need."

"Did you bring the handcuffs?" Amanda asked, one eyebrow raised. "I didn't plan on being attached to any furniture until we got home."

Tony groaned at her pun and laughed. "I could use my belt to tie you down."

James tightened his grip on the steering wheel. "Can I drive without you torturing me with these mental images? We don't want to get kicked out of the store. Not everyone will be as understanding and laid back as Kevin."

Amanda flushed with desire, and Tony grinned. "Then I won't paint you a picture of Amanda lying on our new bed, wearing nothing but leather wrapped around her wrists and ankles."

"Fuck, that's gorgeous." James licked his lips. "Bed frame first, and then we're going to go home and tie her up."

There were only four bed frames for California King sized beds. The first one they looked at was really low to the ground.

"Next!" announced Amanda, wrinkling her nose.

The attendant led them to a spindly-legged bed frame.

James put one hand on the footboard and wiggled it back and forth. The whole bed shook wildly. "No way," he said.

The third was a standard blocky frame. The headboard was made up of horizontal bars. James and Tony exchanged smirks.

"This one is nice," said Amanda. "A little boring, but sturdy."

"We do have one more model," said the attendant. "It's the last one in stock, so you'd have to buy the floor model, but it's a little more unique." She led the way to a massive sleigh bed. It was made of rich mahogany wood, and there was a bar at the top and bottom of the bed.

"Ooh," gasped Amanda. "It's beautiful." She ran her fingers lightly over the footboard and gripped the bar firmly. "I love the feel of the wood. How much?"

When told the amount, Amanda frowned. "You did say that we would be getting the floor model. It's been used and bumped, and there are scratches on it from being on the floor. You want to get rid of it, don't you?"

The attendant smiled. "Let me get my manager."

After haggling with the manager, they came to an agreement on a price much lower than first suggested. The frame, too, would be delivered on Saturday.

"You drive a hard bargain," said Tony admiringly as they left the store. "I am so turned on by you right now."

Amanda grinned. "Next stop: home!"

"And you get a reward," James added. "For being so awesome today."

"Do I get to pick my reward?" Amanda chirped the question.

"Of course you can," James said magnanimously.

"I want to know why Tony doesn't like the name Anthony," she said, looking up at him as if she hadn't just punched him in the chest.

To give himself time to think, Tony opened the back door of the car and slid into the seat. He didn't miss the glance that his lovers exchanged and had to force his frown away.

James drove them home, Amanda filling the car with chatter about her project at work.

Once in the house, coats hung and shoes tucked away, Tony silently grabbed Amanda's hand and pulled her into the living room, sinking down on the couch in almost the same position they'd occupied before shopping.

"It's going to sound silly, because it was so long ago," he began, burying his forehead against her shoulder so he wouldn't have to look at his best friends.

The couch shifted as James settled in beside him and pulled Amanda's legs across his lap.

"It's not silly—" Amanda began.

"Let him talk," James interrupted her. "He knows we don't think that."

Tony squeezed his eyes shut. He didn't really know that. "I was real young, maybe four or five? My foster families didn't keep track of my birthday, and I didn't even know what day it was until I was older. I was called Anthony by all of them, but there was one man..." He let out a sigh. "If he'd physically abused me, then maybe it would make more sense. He never laid a hand on me. Just singled me out for extra duties, enough that the other kids picked on me too. Asked me to run and get things for him, clean up little messes, dust his trophies, his voice twisting my name into a little singsong call…"

Tony swallowed convulsively. "Maybe it would have progressed as I got older, I don't know. Maybe that's why the other kids hated me so much. I learned in college about how kids protect their abuser because they need to feel special. Thankfully, I was moved to another family in a nearby city after only a few months. I wonder what happened to the kids. What happened to him. I don't even remember a name to look any of them up… I feel like I failed them."

He let out a shuddering breath that echoed in the silent room.

"You were a tiny kid," James said finally. "Younger than my students by a lot. Do you think any of my kids could handle that responsibility?"

Tony shook his head with a snort. "Your kids can barely tie their shoes."

"Does that help put it into perspective? You were new to him. The abuse hadn't progressed yet, because he hadn't figured out how best to get to you. You were lucky you were rescued before it got worse." James rested his hand on the back of Tony's neck, the warmth and weight reassuring. "You got out, you'll recognize when it's happening to other kids, and you'll be able to help them the same way someone helped you."

"You think so?" Tony's voice cracked a little.

"I know so," Amanda said soothingly. She ran her hand through his hair, pushing it off his forehead. "I'm sorry for making you dig into an old wound. Thank you for telling us."

Tony hugged her tighter, feeling like a weight had been lifted from his heart. "Sorry it took so long."

"No apologies needed," James said. "There's no time limit on dealing with trauma. We are here for you whenever you want to talk, but maybe you should talk to your therapist about this. They'd know how to help you better than us."

"Yeah, okay. I'll do that."

Chapter Fourteen

Flashback: High School Reunion

Laughing and teasing each other, Tony's old teammates from high school got redressed in their formal wear.

"Thanks for talking me into this once again," Tony said, throwing an arm across Glenn's shoulders. "That was a lot of fun."

"Get dressed, you exhibitionist, you," Glenn said with a chuckle, pushing Tony away.

"I've got my underwear on!" Tony protested with a chuckle. "Am I too much man for you?"

"Dude, you're too much man for all of us," one of his teammates put in, making the rest laugh. "The only one who can handle you is James."

"Or Amanda," Glenn said teasingly.

"Perhaps. They tamed me the summer before grade seven," Tony said, pulling on his shirt and vest.

The team *ooh*'d in chorus and Tony grinned.

"What? You didn't know me. I was a feral child."

"Now *that* I believe," Glenn said. "Come on, let's head back to the ballroom."

Tony pulled his phone out as he walked, noting and reading James's message with a furrow on his brow.

In the empty hall down the left. You turned Amanda on, and we're waiting for you to join us.

They were greeted by a clamor of cheers, people gathering around them to laugh and congratulate them on a job well done.

"We had to recreate the streak from graduation," Glenn was loudly telling anyone who would listen. "It's going to be a tradition from now on!"

"They left about ten minutes ago."

"We should probably go soon if we want to catch them in the act."

Tony looked around frantically for the speakers. Carolina and several of her cronies, along with a bunch of old soccer teammates of his and James's, including Ben and Damien, were talking nearby.

"You think James is a one and done kinda guy?"

"Nah, he probably has stamina."

Tony clenched his jaw. "Hey man, I gotta go," he said to Glenn before pushing through the admiring crowd, making sure to pass by the loud group with the angriest expression he could muster. *Not too difficult, when I think about the grief Carolina has caused all of us.*

"Oh shit, Tony's looking for his girl!"

"Do you think he'll actually fight James?"

"Maybe he's looking for his guy, ever think of that?"

"No way they're gay. Didn't you see the way the two of them were dancing with her earlier?"

Tony bit the inside of his cheek to keep from smiling as he continued his angry stalk across the ballroom.

"Should we follow him?"

"Yeah, I wanna see this."

Shit, I sold it too well, Tony thought, rounding the corner into the hallway. The second he was out of sight, he burst into a sprint, hoping that his friends were far enough away that he'd get to them with plenty of time to warn them.

He turned another corner, slipping in his dress shoes on the clean floor. One last corner, and he saw James kneeling on the floor in front of Amanda, who had her dress half off and her leg over James's shoulder.

He whistled, turned on by the view, and James twisted to look at him.

"Not that this isn't the hottest thing I've seen in a long time," Tony gasped for breath, skidding to a stop in front of them, "but you two were *not* discreet enough when you left. A bunch of them, including Damien, Ben, and Carolina, were talking about it when I got back, trying to decide how long they should wait before they started to follow you." He carefully pulled a bobby pin from Amanda's hair and bent over the lock on the door next to them. "I pretended to be really angry when I came after you, and unfortunately it worked a little too well, because now they're coming to watch a fight." He took a deep breath and the scent of Amanda's arousal flooded his nose. "Fuck, Amanda, you smell amazing."

The lock clicked open and the three of them slipped inside the room. James flicked on the light before Tony locked the door behind them. He looked down at the bent out of shape bobby pin in his hand. "Uh... Sorry, darlin'." He chuckled. "I'm a little out of practice."

"I forgot you knew how to do that." Amanda plucked it from his hand and walked over to a garbage can by a desk to toss it in. "I have about five hundred of those. If my hair is a little messier than when I left, who would blame me?"

Shouts echoed on the other side of the door, followed by numerous footsteps.

Amanda giggled. "It's like the best game of hide and seek ever!" she whispered. "How long do you think we have to hide in here?" She gestured at the waiting room they were standing in.

"Dunno, but I'm certainly not complaining about the view," Tony rasped.

Amanda ran a hand over her breast and pinched the nipple. "You mean this?" She put her left foot up on a chair and lifted her skirt over her knee with her free hand, exposing her sex to their greedy eyes. "Or do you mean this view?"

Tony licked his lips. "Please, may I?" he groaned, legs shaking.

"You ask so nicely," Amanda purred, rubbing her fingers through her folds. "James was a little too enthusiastic at cleaning me up. I seem to be all messy again. Can you do something about that?"

"Fuck, yes, I can." Tony strode across the room to her, sinking to his knees so that he was eye-level with her busy hand. "Let me taste you," he breathed.

Amanda's knees wobbled.

"Hey, James, want to support our girl?" Tony asked, calling James over. He waited until James wrapped an arm around her waist before he licked over her sex, the combination of her arousal and James's saliva going straight to his cock. His tongue wiggled deep inside her for a thorough taste and then up to her clit.

He did it again when she gasped, and her hands wove into his hair, messing it up as she tugged.

Tony smiled against her body before writing his full name with his tongue over her, her hips bucking with unreleased energy. The fingers in his hair clenched tighter and he hummed encouragement. Glancing up her body, he saw that James had claimed her mouth, keeping her cries quiet. Her hips were moving frantically now, searching for release. Tony slid a finger inside her, desperate to feel her heat around him again, and she cried out, clenching around him and drawing him deeper.

He kept his mouth on her until she pulled him away by his hair.

"Fuck, Tony," Amanda gasped.

He smirked up at her and licked his lips, tasting her juices on them.

"Damn," James said breathlessly. "You are so sexy."

Tony chuckled as he got to his feet. "Thanks, Jamie." He winked.

"It's not enough, though," Amanda whined, her fingers once again dropping to her folds. "I feel so empty." She pouted at them.

It was James's turn to laugh. "You're insatiable, sunshine."

"Good thing there's two of us," Tony added, admiring her disheveled state. "How do you want to do this?"

"Against the desk," Amanda said decisively. She crossed the room to it, bent over, and flipped up her skirt. "Who's first?" she asked, wiggling back and forth.

James grinned at Tony. "Ah, I think you're going to have to guess."

"Fun!" she said. "I know you both pretty well by now. I bet I can tell just by how you enter me."

James undid his pants, gesturing for Tony to do the same. "We're ready, are you?" he asked.

"I'm dying for you," Amanda groaned.

James tested her, dipping two and then three fingers inside her. He whistled low. "You are so wet."

"All for you two," she said, pushing back against him. "Fuck me!"

"Don't worry. We will." James pulled back and nodded to Tony, who shook his head, stroking his cock slowly. James nodded and thrust deep, drawing a cry from her.

"James!" she shouted.

"How'd you know it was me?"

"I told you I know your cocks," she said.

"Well, hang onto the desk, because I'm going to fuck you until your teeth rattle."

"Sexy," Tony said, chuckling.

James pulled back and slammed into her, the desk creaking from the force.

"Oh *God* yes!" Amanda shouted.

"They're going to hear you," James commented as if on the weather, his hips pistoning inside her.

"I don't care if they hear me getting the best sex of my life," Amanda said between thrusts. "They can be as envious as they want. We're in a relationship, and— *Yes*, James, right there!" she shrieked.

"Fuck," James panted. "I don't know which is hotter, you getting off on being heard or the sounds you're making."

"Her noises," Tony said vehemently. "Always. Come on, darlin'. Make James come so I can fuck his cum back into you." He shucked the rest of his clothes, not wanting them to get covered in fluids.

"So close!" she squeaked. "That's the perfect... Oh God, everything, James. Keep that— Oh God. Oh *God*." She scratched at the wood top of the desk, her fingers curling.

James slammed into her once more and she screamed, her legs curling up, letting the desk take her weight. He clenched his jaw, "Amanda—!" and he was coming, hips making aborted twitches as he held himself deep within her. "Wow," gasped James. "You're like a vise."

Tony watched his best friend fall apart inside their girlfriend. *Fuck, I want to swallow his groans with my mouth. He's so sexy.*

"Wow is right," Amanda hummed dreamily in agreement. "I don't know how you're going to top that, Tony."

"I don't need to top it to bring you pleasure," Tony replied.

When James pulled out, Tony was there, flipping Amanda onto her back on the desk and entering her in a smooth thrust.

Her mouth opened on a silent cry, her back arching in pleasure.

Tony leaned over her and drew her nipple into his mouth, letting her get used to the new cock and how it fit her differently. "You're so sexy," he murmured, switching to the other side. He had to tug the material out of the way to get at her breast, which he teased with his tongue until it hardened. "Your body is so in tune with us."

"Shouldn't we be getting back to the dance?" asked James with a chuckle.

"You had your time, now it's mine," Tony replied without heat. He withdrew slowly, the added lubricant making the movement slippery, and then pounded in.

The wet *squelch* made him smile with amusement.

"You hear that?" he teased. "That's the sound of a well-fucked pussy."

"Damn straight," James said with a chuckle.

Amanda was soon thrashing on the desk under the onslaught of his thrusts, her hands flying to her hair and then behind her head to the edge of the desk to hang on tightly.

Tony rubbed his thumb over her clit, finding the rhythm she liked best with the ease of familiarity. Her walls tightened convulsively around his cock. "You're close, darlin'. Come for me. Let me give you my ecstasy."

Two more thrusts and she exploded, drawing him along with her into orgasm.

He folded over her, pressing his sweaty forehead to her sternum. "Damn, girl. I guess this reunion *was* a good idea."

James snorted. "Shall we go home now? Well, to our parents'," he amended.

"Oh, but I didn't get any dessert!" Amanda said with a pout.

"What do you call this?" Tony teased, gesturing at the room in general.

"An appetizer," she said saucily.

"You're really willing to head back into that ballroom containing our graduating class with sex hair and our cum dripping down your thighs—No, actually, that sounds super hot, let's do it," Tony said eagerly.

Amanda giggled lazily. "Well, I could wipe up a little. Pass me those tissues, please?"

They cleaned up and got dressed again, exchanging kisses with her sporadically.

The hallways were empty as they made their way back to the ballroom, with a quick stop at the restrooms for Amanda to pee.

"Ready?" James asked them just before they turned the last corner. "We don't owe them anything. We could just leave."

"No, I want to cause a sensation," Amanda said with a chuckle.

"Of course you do," Tony said, smirking.

"And I want dessert." Amanda reminded them. "Okay, let's do this."

James draped his arm over her shoulders, Tony wrapped his arm around her waist, and they walked casually out of the hallway into the ballroom.

The heat from Amanda's bare back burned against the sensitive skin of Tony's inner forearm. He smiled down at her as they headed towards the dessert buffet, ignoring the silence that spread through the room.

"Chocolate covered strawberry?" James asked Amanda. When she nodded, he reached for one and held it to her lips, one hand underneath to catch any drips.

Amanda hummed with pleasure as she bit into the berry.

"That sounded almost orgasmic," Tony said, almost too loudly. "Does it taste good?"

"Find out for yourself," Amanda said, flipping her hair over her shoulder as she turned to him. She pulled his mouth to hers, opening to him immediately and letting their tongues dance.

The leftover chocolate and strawberry mingled with the slightly bitter aftertaste of her come, which had transferred to her mouth via their kisses. Tony groaned, holding her against him tightly, unable to get enough of her. He pulled back slightly, breathing hard, and stared down at her dreamy expression. "Yum," he rasped.

James had spent the time filling a plate with a variety of desserts. "The baklava is delicious," he said. "Perfect balance of pistachio and honey."

"I *love* baklava!" Amanda exclaimed.

Tony rescued the plate as Amanda threw herself into James's arms, delving into his mouth.

Gasps met his ears as he unconcernedly looked over the dessert table, selecting a few favorites that James hadn't had a chance to grab. "Hey," he said, putting a hand low on Amanda's back. "Want to sit at our table to eat the desserts?"

Amanda pulled back from James and smiled. "Great idea." She took their hands and pulled them through the gaping people to their table.

Carolina stepped in front of her, smirking. "After *that* little display, I can't believe you gave *me* such a hard time this summer at camp."

Amanda wrinkled her nose. "Tony, as the person who took a law class, would you care to explain the difference between sexual assault and consensual sex?"

Tony shrugged. "I think you summed it up quite well. One is illegal, one is not."

"Now, if you'll excuse me, I have desserts to be fed," Amanda said, trying to move past Carolina.

"'To be fed?' A bit presumptuous, aren't you?" James said, chuckling.

"What? Like you wouldn't if I asked." Amanda stuck her tongue out at him playfully.

Carolina pushed her shoulder, sending Amanda stumbling back a step. "You little *slut*!" she screamed, getting in her face. "I *knew* you were fucking them both behind all our backs! I *heard* you in the room back there!"

"Did you?" Amanda asked rhetorically, a wicked grin curling her lips. "Green is really not your colour." She pulled on Tony's hand to follow behind her as she tried to walk past Carolina.

Carolina grabbed Tony's shirt and tried to kiss him. Encumbered as he was by the plate of desserts and Amanda's hand, he barely managed to turn his head away. "You're making yourself look *really* desperate," Tony said, attempting to control his anger. "I repeatedly told you at the camp that I'm not interested in you or what you're offering."

Their audience gasped audibly.

Carolina growled in his face and groped at his crotch.

Tony froze in shock. "What—?"

Smack.

Amanda slapped Carolina across the face so hard that she staggered into one of the chairs beside them.

The crowd *ooh*'d in unison as Amanda stalked forward and backed Carolina against the table. "What part of 'consent matters' did you not understand?" Amanda snarled.

"He was asking for it. He was already half hard for me." Carolina smirked, touching the red mark on her cheek that was blossoming into a perfect mirror of Amanda's hand. "Everyone knows guys are just begging to be touched all the time."

Amanda shook her head. "Where do you get your information? Porn? Because in the real world, guys only want to be touched by the people they consent to. I don't think I need to explain why he was half hard, and it had nothing to do with you."

"Do you fight all your *boyfriend's* battles for him?" Carolina sneered.

"I do when he's being forcibly touched by someone. Besides," Amanda said as she tossed her hair over her shoulder, "I'm doing this as his friend, not his girlfriend. As his friend, I'm livid on his behalf. As his girlfriend, I'm offended that you would think so little of our... What was the phrasing you used in high school?" She tapped her chin in thought. "Oh yeah. So little of the 'code of sisterhood and cheerleading' that you would try to steal my boyfriend. Not that you *could* steal him."

"He'll get bored of waiting for you eventually. You can't possibly handle two men at once!"

Amanda smirked and stepped back, returning to her place between the two men. "Maybe *you* can't. But..." Amanda took their hands again, lacing their fingers. "Well, don't we *all* look thoroughly *fucked*?" She turned away from the visibly seething woman.

"How *dare* you?" Carolina screamed over the whoops and cheers of their avid audience.

"How dare I what?" Amanda asked over her shoulder. "Walk away from you? I'm not sorry to say that you're not the center of my attention."

"You slapped me!"

"Yeah, she did," Tony interjected. "It was super hot."

"Yeah, well, I can get her charged with... with... with aggravated assault! Then you'll beg for my attention!"

Tony turned back. "Or I could press charges against you for sexual assault." He chuckled without humor. "You're shit out of luck, Carolina. Good riddance." He joined his best friends at their table, leaving behind a flurry of whispers. "Dessert is served."

"Nice, you got all my favorites!" Amanda exclaimed happily. "Feed me one?"

"It would be my utmost pleasure, my knight in shining armor," Tony said with a smile.

Chapter Fifteen

James

"Is it just me, or are these houses getting bigger?" Amanda asked as they drove down the curving road.

"They're *definitely* getting bigger," Tony piped up from the back seat. "And I know *big*," he added suggestively, making the other two chuckle.

"But you're sure we're going the right way?" James asked, leaning forwards over the steering wheel to stare up at the multi-turreted roof of the house they were driving past.

Amanda waved her phone in the air. "The address he gave us is just up ahead, right at the end of the road."

"Okay…" James said, clearly still unsure.

They passed a gate first, fortunately with the number on the wrought iron so they could confirm that it was the correct place.

The driveway was wider than the road and lined with massive trees. The house wasn't visible from the gate.

"There it is!" Amanda said excitedly, pointing at a gray building with blue shutters. It was two stories tall and had lots of windows amidst the stonework. "It's so pretty!"

Tony rested his forearms on the back of the front seats. "Doesn't that look smaller than the houses we passed?"

"It does," James said slowly. "And the driveway continues past it."

"Holy mother of God," Tony murmured when they reached the edge of the house and the rest of the property was revealed to them.

"That's a *house*?" Amanda whispered.

"When Glenn throws a party, he throws a *party*." James pulled their car into a spot next to the others.

"Look, there's a gazebo over there!" Amanda pointed.

"My parents have a gazebo," Tony said dryly. "That's a fully covered deck, and another building just beyond it."

"The view is amazing," James commented. "We can see right over the water."

"I think we can see down *to* the water, actually. Is that a dock?" Tony asked, stretching until his head hit the roof of the car. "What are we still doing in here?"

Amanda stifled a laugh. "I think we're a little intimidated. I know I am."

"You wouldn't want to live here?" James asked.

"No way. Can you imagine cleaning this place? And we're only three people, I'd never find you two!" She shook her head. "It'll be fun to stay here for the weekend though."

"Agreed." Tony slapped the back of the front seats. "Let's go before someone else drives up and we look weird just sitting out here in the car."

James popped the trunk and grabbed their bag before they headed for the double front doors of the three-story mansion.

"He says to just… Open the door and walk in," Amanda said. "I didn't quite understand why before, but if he's not sitting right beside the door, it would take him forever to keep replying to the bell."

"Here goes," James said, twisting the doorknob and pushing the door in.

It swung easily, letting them into a white marble foyer. There were several bags stashed against the twin curved staircases that led up to the second floor. A massive golden chandelier hung high over their heads from the ceiling up above.

"Whoa," Amanda said, spinning in a circle.

"Let's explore," Tony said, tossing their bag next to the others and heading for the opening between the stairs.

"Definitely," Amanda said, trotting after him.

James moved a little slower, taking it all in. The grandeur of the place was imposing. He caught up to them and their host in the kitchen, which was easily the size of the entire first floor of their house.

"Hey man," Glenn said in greeting, slapping James's upper arm. "What do you think of my parent's potential income generator?"

"Sorry, not following."

"They're considering buying this place and renting it out for big events like weddings, mitzvahs, family reunions, corporate retreats… You know, the kind of event that lots of people will come to and spend a shit-ton of money to live it up like rich people for the weekend." Glenn grinned. "As part of the buyer's agreement, we get to test it out for Thanksgiving! There's only a fifteen-page survey to complete on Sunday."

James squinted at him. "That sounds like a joke."

Glenn chuckled. "There *is* a survey, but it's two pages. My parents want to make sure they're making a good investment."

"We'd be happy to complete the survey," Amanda said with a smile.

"Wonderful." Glenn gestured at the counter. "Pick your bracelet for the weekend. Green means you're up for a good time with whoever," he waggled his eyebrows, "yellow wants to be seduced, and red is off-limits."

"Reds all around," Tony said firmly, reaching for the little plastic bands. "Based on the quantity of alcohol I see here, I get the feeling that clothing is going to become optional fairly quickly."

"Doesn't it always at my parties?" Glenn said with a grin. He elbowed James. "Are you even friends if you haven't seen each other naked?"

James shook his head. "I think you just enjoy getting naked in front of people. Have you considered stripping?"

"I don't have the moves," Glenn said mournfully. Then, brightly, he added, "What about if I got an OnlyFans account?"

"Maybe," Amanda said, tilting her head in consideration. "How's your stamina?"

Glenn wavered his hand in the air. "Could be better, if I'm being honest. Why, how long do you last?"

"I'm not usually paying attention to the time," James said dryly.

"Long enough," Tony added.

Amanda rolled her eyes. "You can always start off with extended foreplay on camera. Girls will eat that up with a spoon."

"Good point," Glenn said thoughtfully. He clapped his hands together suddenly, making James jump. "Make yourselves a drink and hang out around here. Everyone else is out on the patio. Once the rest of the group arrives, I'll give the tour and you can put your bags in your room."

"What's the sleeping situation like?" James asked as his lovers headed for the bar.

"I've assigned the people with partners to rooms that will accommodate their needs," Glenn said seriously. "You three have one of the primary suites because the bed's a king. I thought you'd appreciate the space and privacy."

"Thanks, man." James clapped Glenn on the shoulder. Then what he'd said fully sank in. "There's more than one primary suite?"

"Oh yeah." Glenn rubbed his hands together. "This place is *massive*."

"Amazing," James murmured, more to himself than his friend.

"We also have a couple of chefs for the weekend," Glenn added. "They're in the secondary kitchen—" He indicated a door to the side of the fridge, "—prepping snacks, lunch, and dinner."

"Secondary kitchen," James echoed, shocked.

"This one is apparently too fancy to get dirty, or something." Glenn shrugged. "I think it's a holdover from when the rich people didn't want to see their servants making the food."

"Then why have this kitchen at all?"

"Dunno. Maybe the housewives wanted to pretend to cook?" Glenn glanced over at the door behind James. "Welcome!"

James left Glenn to his hosting duties, joining his lovers at the far end of the living space next to the kitchen. Tony silently handed him a blue drink with a little sword stuck through a maraschino cherry. "Thanks," James said, taking a sip and looking out over the water. It was gray, reflecting the cloudy sky. It *looked* like a typical November day, but the unseasonably warm weather was anything but usual.

"You going to tell us what's bothering you?" Amanda asked.

"This place feels overwhelming," James admitted. "There are at least two primary suites. There's a secondary kitchen. Glenn said he'd hired chefs, plural, for the weekend."

"I certainly wouldn't want to cook for all those people," Tony said, nodding at the patio that was crowded with people, some they recognized and some they didn't.

James rolled his shoulders, unsettled. "No, that's true. We're here for vacation."

"That's right." Amanda patted his chest. "Relax."

Tony took a sip of his orangey drink, eyeing James. "Spit it out."

"Is this the level of grandeur you two expect?" James asked. "Want, need, whatever?"

"No way," Amanda said vehemently.

"Is that some kind of misguided patriarchy thing?" Tony asked, wrinkling his nose. "You're not our *provider* or something."

"I'm happy with our house," Amanda said. She shook her head. "Happy doesn't even *begin* to cover it. You know what I mean." She gestured with the hand holding her red drink, making it tip dangerously. "This place is grand, and it's fun to visit for a party, but as a regular thing? No way."

"The only way I can see any of us wanting to give up our house is when we have a baby," Tony said. "That front entry is pretty small for a stroller."

James stared at him, shocked that Tony had brought that up.

"What?" Tony said. "I got some first-hand experience at Adam's recently. Their front entry is shit for the stroller, and the back is somehow even worse. It really opened my eyes to accessibility needs."

Amanda played with her mini sword. "I don't disagree about that," she said slowly. "You said 'when'."

"What?" Tony repeated, confused.

"*'When* we have a baby'," James quoted softly, his heart pounding.

Tony flushed. "Oh. Well... I know we haven't really talked about that. And now's not really the time—"

"Now's a great time," James interrupted firmly. "You want that? You've been thinking about a baby?"

"Travis gave me baby fever," Tony admitted. "He was so cuddly and sweet. I never had much exposure to babies. Even back when we babysat,

I usually took care of kids old enough to play sports. What about you, darlin'? Is that something you can see in our future?"

"Yeah, I'd love to be a mom someday," Amanda said with a tiny nod. "But not soon. We all just finished our Master's and are starting out in our fields. I want to spend time with you two and settle into our life together before we add a little person into the mix. I'm sorry if that's not the answer you were looking for," she added quietly, looking down at the floor.

"Hey." Tony tipped her head up by cupping her jaw. "I can wait as long as you need. Having a baby with *you* is the goal, whenever that happens." He kissed her lightly. "I can see the positives of waiting. We're young. We have lots of time."

"What about you, James?" Amanda asked, turning her focus to him.

"I'm glad you want to wait," James said. "I'm nervous about bringing a baby with three parents into the world. How would that work? We would need to look into the legality of it."

Tony nodded. "We'd have to look into that. I'm not suggesting we start trying this weekend!"

Amanda chuckled. "Nothing like an IUD to put a damper on that," she teased. "But I don't mind practicing." She winked at them.

"That was a good talk," James said. "I appreciate you easing my fears about your expectations, and us talking about having a baby."

"I certainly wasn't *expecting* that one," Amanda put in playfully, making them groan at her pun.

"House tour!" Glenn called from the kitchen before opening the patio door and calling the outside guests.

The trio waved at some of the people they recognized from high school, but didn't want to interrupt Glenn's flow by chatting. James made a mental note to check in with Kevin, who he spotted hanging back.

The group followed him into the foyer, and he climbed a few stairs before turning and addressing them.

"Thank you all for accepting my invitation to Thanksgiving this year," Glenn began. "I'm really excited to be your host this weekend. We have lots planned on the itinerary, starting with this house tour. We'll be heading down to the private beach afterwards. The water is definitely too cold to swim in, but we can play on the sand and we'll have a tour of the coast on the yacht after lunch. The big formal dinner is tomorrow night, which I know isn't typical, but whoever said I was normal?"

"No-one!" shouted Tony, and Glenn acknowledged him with a tiny bow.

"As you can guess, this is the foyer of the house," Glenn said with a dramatic flair. "Moving over to the east wing of the house, we have an office and attached library."

He led them through the first floor, pointing out different rooms and explaining their purposes.

"Now upstairs," he said cheerfully. "We have two more floors to see, and they're pretty much all bedrooms."

"Nice!" cheered Damien.

James noted that he was wearing a green bracelet and hadn't seemed to have brought anyone. He nodded at Tony, who caught his meaning and frowned.

"No matter where you go, one of us should always be with you," James said to Amanda as people headed up the stairs, following Glenn.

She snorted. "Even the bathroom?"

Tony nodded. "Especially then."

"I can take care of myself," she said.

"I'd rather avoid you *needing* to," James said firmly. "Please."

Even then, Amanda set her jaw, a frown on her forehead. It wasn't until Tony pointed out that both Damien and Ben were wearing green bracelets that she understood.

"We want you to feel comfortable to be yourself this weekend," Tony said.

"Even if that means that you end up showing off that beautiful body of yours," James murmured in her ear, making her shiver and lean against him.

"I'm not going to say I will, but I'm not going to say I won't," she told them. "We'll see what the vibes are like first."

The last few stragglers had reached the top of the stairs, so the trio hurried after the group, peeking into several rooms along the way.

The east wing seemed to consist of a series of twin bed rooms, some with bunk beds, others squeezing three singletons into the floor space. Many of them had bags on beds, but their occupants had continued on with the tour into the west wing.

The other side of the mansion had fewer rooms with bigger beds. Whispers filtered down the line that most of these ones were not assigned, and would be first come, first claimed.

Tony snorted. "First come," he repeated, rolling his eyes. "Classic Glenn."

The assigned rooms had paper taped to the door, but James didn't know their names.

"We must be on the third floor," he said to the others. There were stairs at either end of the wings that spiralled up and down.

Once they arrived on the top floor, they saw Glenn's name on the door of a massive room that looked out over the water.

"Come on, you three!" he called to them from the other wing. "Your room is over here!"

Tony whistled. "When you go all out, you go *all out*," he said, patting Glenn on the shoulder as they entered the room.

"This bathroom is bigger than our bedroom at home!" Amanda squeaked. "Look at that shower! You could fit ten people in there, easy!"

"You asking?" Ben asked, smirking at her.

"No," Amanda replied flatly, disappearing into the bedroom, Tony at her heels.

James regarded Ben for a long moment, until the other man visibly squirmed. Then he nodded once and pushed past him to check out the bedroom.

"Even if we unpack our entire bag, I think we'd only fill the tiniest corner of this closet," Amanda said in amazement. "What are we going to do with all this space?"

"Make good use of the bed," Tony said, tugging her to him in a spin.

She shrieked with laughter when he used her momentum to toss her onto the bed, toppling over her in the next instant.

"Dude, there are still people in here," a guy that James didn't know said.

"We're still clothed," James replied with a quirk of his mouth. "You're not pinned in place. Feel free to leave if you're uncomfortable."

"I just thought you'd want to know," the guy mumbled, ducking his head.

"Everyone, this concludes the tour of the house," Glenn said from the doorway. "If you wouldn't mind changing to beach wear and meeting me on the back patio, I can continue the tour with the outdoor portion."

"How long do we have?" James asked, one eye on the bed and the pair making out.

"Not *that* long," Glenn said with a chuckle. "Not if you want the full tour, anyways. Five minutes."

"There's a lot we can do in five minutes," Tony said from the bed once James had closed the door.

"Personally, I like the idea of edging Amanda," James said, picking up on Tony's playful tone.

"Guys, come on, we're at a party!" she whined.

"All the better." James nodded. "Strip her," he ordered Tony. "She's not wearing any of that down to the beach anyways."

"Yessir," Tony said, pulling Amanda to sit up and undressing her efficiently, tossing her clothing on the floor.

"Lie back and spread your legs, hips at the edge of the bed. Tony, get ready for the beach while I eat her out, and then we'll switch." James finished getting undressed and knelt in front of her. He glanced up at her face, her chest heaving as she panted. "Remember, you're not allowed to come."

Less than five minutes later, the trio joined everyone else on the back patio. If Amanda looked a little flushed and the men smug, nobody commented.

Glenn led them over the property, starting with the massive heated pool just off the back patio, the outdoor dining area, and fire pit. Then he pointed out the cozy guest house with its own private pool and the gazebo before he led them down the stairs carved into the side of the bluff overlooking the inlet. The beach itself was privately owned and had a boathouse with a cozy seating and dining area nestled where the water came up to the cliff. On the exterior of the house, far away from the water, were several individual showers and changing rooms to clean the sand off.

"There are heated stairs inside the bluff that lead from the house up above to this one," Glenn explained, opening a hidden door in the kitchen. "It'll be useful in the winter, when guests want to be near the water but don't want to navigate the frozen stairs on the cliff. It's also easier to transport the food, as there's a trolley system next to the stairs."

"Fancy," Amanda murmured.

"Outside, we have every sort of comfort or activity I can think of. There are large loungers, which are great for families—"

"Or fucking!" Damien interjected.

"—or *cuddling*," Glenn continued. "I set up the beach volleyball net, but we have other sporting equipment in the shed in the boating area. All the safety equipment for the seadoos, canoes, and kayaks are in there as well. Please, if you're going out on the water in the smaller vehicles, wear a lifejacket. That is non-negotiable." He pinned a few people with a glare. "I will not have any preventable deaths this weekend. The yacht trip, I don't care as much if you wear a vest. It's a big boat, and as long as you're not doing something stupid, you should be fine."

The group split up, several people heading for the beach volleyball, while others got out the seadoos.

"What do you want to do?" James asked the others.

Amanda shifted in place, her thighs rubbing together, and he grinned.

"No, we can't continue what we started up at the house," he teased.

"But we can cuddle up on a lounger," Tony suggested.

"Strip volleyball!" shouted Ben from the direction of the game.

"Each time a person misses an easy ball, they lose an article of clothing!" Damien agreed.

"But it's cold!" complained one of the girls.

"I know how to warm you up afterwards," Ben said salaciously.

"A lounger sounds great," Amanda said.

"Shade or sun?" James asked, pivoting it on its pedestal.

"Sun. It's too cold for shade," she replied.

"Good call." Tony stripped off his shirt and tossed it onto the cushion before climbing on. "I wouldn't mind darkening my tan a bit."

"You're too heavy to turn this thing if you're on it," James protested.

"Or you're too weak," Tony countered. "You barely have to move it an inch. Come on, Jamie."

"This is great, James," Amanda said, stretching her arms over her head. The movement made her cropped oversized sweatshirt ride up high enough to see the swell of the undersides of her breasts, barely covered by the string bikini she was wearing.

"You're a fucking tease," Tony commented. "Get down here and let me get my hands on you."

She chuckled and crawled onto the lounger, her ass swaying from side to side.

The scrap of fabric on her lower body barely covered her ass too, James noted as he circled behind her. Today was going to be a long test of his and Tony's patience.

She threw herself beside Tony, and his hand immediately found its way under her sweatshirt.

Okay, a test of my patience, since he has none, James thought, amused. Watching them make-out was riling him up though, so he sat, back to his lovers, on the edge of the seat, and looked around at their housemates for the weekend.

Glenn was out on the water with several of his university crowd and Kevin. James was glad the other man was opening up a bit. The volleyball game was progressing nicely, several people from both high school and university having lost articles of clothing already.

Oddly enough, Carolina was by herself on one of the other lounge chairs, still bundled up in a full length sweatshirt and pants, playing on her phone.

Come to think of it, she wasn't all over Tony when we arrived, and she didn't get in Amanda's face at all. She barely said two words to us, if that, he thought.

James hadn't heard from Carolina since their disastrous interaction at their high school reunion. He wondered what had happened to change her personality so drastically in the two years since he'd last seen her.

He shook his head, banishing her from his thoughts. She didn't deserve to have any of his attention, even if it was only curiosity.

"Hey, do you two remember when our parents rented that cottage on a lake? How old were we, fourteen?"

"Hmm," Amanda hummed. "I think we were thirteen."

He twisted to look at them. "Thirteen? Really?"

Tony released the skin of her neck and propped himself up on an elbow. "It was the summer between seventh and eighth grade. I'm sure, because it wasn't the year we moved, and I started working at the sports camp the year before high school."

James nodded slowly. "That timeline makes sense."

"Come cuddle us," Amanda said, reaching out for him.

James felt his willpower crumble like a cracker under her pleading. "Yeah, be right there."

Chapter Sixteen

Flashback: Cottage Rental

"I'm excited that you rented a cottage this summer, Dad!" Amanda exclaimed, half bouncing in the back seat of the van. "We've never done this before!"

"We've talked about it with the Lavallee's for years, but the timing never worked out," he replied.

"What's different this year?" James asked. "Mom and Dad can't make it up until halfway through the week."

"We're afraid that next year, you three will be too busy with camps to hang out with your old and decrepit parents," Amanda's mom teased.

"Mom! You're not old!" Amanda gasped.

"Just decrepit," Tony's dad said with a chuckle.

"We also thought it was past time for the three families to spend quality time in the woods together," Amanda's dad said.

"Sounds ominous," Tony's mom said with a fake shiver. "Is that why you had us pack shovels?"

"That's to dig the latrine," Tony said with a straight face.

"Ewww," Amanda whined. "Da-ad, please tell me you rented a cottage with running water?"

"He'd better have," her mother said. "Why the shovels, dear?"

Tony's mom laughed. "No shovels. I was being silly."

"Of course there's running water," Amanda's dad reassured everyone. "Electricity too. Shocking, isn't it?"

Everyone groaned at the pun.

"What's first on your agenda, kids?"

"The lake," the trio chorused, and then grinned at each other.

"I got my fishing license for Massachusetts," Tony's dad said. "I can catch some fish for supper."

"And I packed several fish in the cooler just in case they're not biting in the middle of the day," his mom said, leaning over the space between the middle seats to kiss her husband's cheek. "You might want to try to fish first thing in the morning, darling."

"It's my vacation," he pouted. "I don't want to get up early."

Amanda muffled a laugh with her hand.

"Which is why I brought fish," Tony's mom chirped. "If you do catch some, I'm sure the three bottomless pits in the back seat won't complain."

The boys didn't bother hiding their laughter.

"What else do you want to do?" Amanda's mom asked from the passenger seat.

"Berry picking," Amanda said.

"Campfire tonight," Tony added. "With marshmallows, chocolate, and graham crackers."

"Canoeing," James said. "Although that might count as being part of the lake activities."

"I'll allow it," Amanda's mom said with a smile.

"Going for a jog along the trails!" Amanda shouted.

"Not so loud, dear," Tony's mom said.

"Sorry."

"We're heading onto the lake road," Amanda's dad said, slowing to a stop and putting on his blinker. "I need quiet unless someone's giving me directions."

"Got it."

The lake road was a narrow, gravel one-lane strip. Occasionally, they had to pull off onto the side to allow a car to pass in the opposite direction. There were hills so high that they couldn't see if a car was coming until they got to the top.

The three thirteen-year-olds held each other's hands tightly in the back seat and released a sigh of relief when the van finally turned onto a driveway leading up to a two-story pine cottage.

"It's perfect!" Amanda exclaimed.

"I'm glad you approve, jelly bean," her dad said.

They spilled out of the car and raced from one end of the wrap-around deck to the other to stare out over the lake.

"The dock is huge!" Tony exclaimed, pointing. "The three of us can jump off the end together no problem."

"I want to paddle out to that island," James said, pointing out to the bit of land not far away. "There's a low rise beach on this side, so it'll be easy to pull up."

"Let's get changed and head down to the beach," Amanda urged.

They ran back to the van and helped the parents unload the luggage and food into the cottage.

The main floor was open concept, with floor-to-ceiling windows facing the lake. The furniture looked well-used and comfortable, with large couches, a massive harvest table, and a wood-burning fireplace.

At the back of the house, there was a guest room, a bathroom, the kitchen, and a staircase that led up to the second story.

They grabbed their luggage and headed up the stairs, eager to peek in the rooms.

They were nearly all the same size with different bed configurations; two rooms with large beds for the adults, and one with a bunk bed: the lower a double and the upper a single.

"Race you to the lake!" Amanda cried, digging through her bag for her bathing suit and racing out the door to the bathroom.

"Hey, come on, we need to pee too!" James called after her. "It's been hours!"

"We can just piss in the lake," Tony suggested with a shrug.

"Dude." James shuddered. "Just no."

"Behind a tree?"

"That'll work."

After a full day on the lake—Tony's dad did *not* catch a fish—the trio fell into their respective beds exhausted.

"You're okay?" Amanda's mom said, leaning over the boys to stroke Amanda's hair off her face. She was in the top bunk, with the boys sharing the double below her.

"Why wouldn't I be?"

"You took a tumble off the dock and bumped your head."

"I creatively jumped in."

"Uh huh."

"I promise, I'm not dizzy or anything."

"We'll come get you if anything happens during the night," James piped up.

"I know you will." Amanda's mom kissed each of their foreheads before turning off the light and leaving the room.

Their eyes adjusted to the star-lit room slowly.

"You know, I had no idea I'd inherit two other sets of parents when I became friends with you two," Tony said quietly.

"It wasn't like that with friends in Texas?" James asked, rolling over to look at Tony's profile.

"I didn't have friends like this in Texas," Tony spat. "I had people who wanted things from me, people who thought it was cool to hang out with me because I... I don't know... Was *edgy* or something."

James snorted. "Edgy," he repeated.

"What? I'm cool," Tony protested, but they could hear the smile in his tone.

They were all silent for a moment.

"You know that we like you because you're fun to be around, right?" Amanda asked.

"It's been a year. If you had motive or pity, I would've noticed by now," Tony said dryly.

This time the silence was broken by a sniffle from the top bunk.

"Does your head hurt?" James asked instantly, sitting up and almost whacking himself on the underside of the frame.

"No," Amanda said, her voice watery.

The bed shifted, sheets rustled, and she swung herself over the side of the bed, half-falling onto James.

"These are not the kind of acrobatics your mom would approve of with a head injury," James gasped, winded by her hand landing on his sternum.

"Sorry," Amanda said, crawling in between them. "I needed to give Tony a hug."

"You couldn't take the ladder like a regular person?" Tony asked.

"When have I ever been normal?" she demanded, the top of her head hitting his chin as she threw herself at him in the dark.

James sighed. "At least get under the covers. You're pulling the sheet off me with all this moving around."

"You're okay with that?" she asked quietly.

"Why wouldn't I be? Do you kick in your sleep?"

"Not that I'm aware of." She struggled with the sheet in the dark before managing to slide under it between the two warm bodies. "I heard some people talking at the mall the other day."

"About what?" James asked when she didn't continue.

"Us. Saying that our parents should take more care to keep us separate, that it isn't right that I should be such close friends with guys." She sniffled again. "I don't understand why not. You're the best friends I could ever ask for!"

"You were there when our parents had the sex talk with us," Tony said dryly.

"Yeah, but that's not how it is with us. It's creepy that adults speculate about us like that. I didn't even recognize them." Amanda shuddered.

"Why would adults speculating about our relationship make me not want to cuddle up with you?" James asked, confused.

"It sounds silly when you put it like that," Amanda said sheepishly.

"People talking hasn't bothered me before," James said, hugging her close. "It's not going to start now."

"I was worried it might," she whispered.

"I care way more about *your* opinion and feelings than people I don't know."

"This is starting to feel like my therapy sessions," Tony groaned. "Why do we have to have healthy coping mechanisms?"

Amanda giggled and buried her face in his shoulder. "Speaking of talking like a therapist, who says that?"

Tony made a grumbling noise. "She said it a lot at my last session."

"I'd rather talk this stuff out than have it upset one of you," James said. "Let's make a promise."

"About what?" Amanda asked, twisting to look at his profile behind her.

He put his hand out. "I promise to tell you two if anything bothers me, to always consider your feelings in my actions, and be the best friend I can be."

"Wow. Deep," Tony drawled.

Amanda poked him in the ribs before putting her hand on James's. "I promise."

Tony's hand landed on top of the stack. "I'll try."

"Come on, man," James said.

"Please?" Amanda begged.

Tony sighed. "I promise."

"Love you guys," Amanda said happily, snuggling under the covers. She gave Tony another squeeze and yawned. "Night."

"Night."

Chapter Seventeen

Amanda

After a dinner that made her sleepy because she'd eaten so much good food, a bunch of the guests gathered around the fire pit.

Some people were toasting marshmallows, sitting close to the fire with their long sticks. Tony and James were taking turns at the fire pit, the other one cuddling her on a large chair.

Tony brought a gooey graham cracker sandwich back to the chair, holding it up to her mouth with his hand cupped underneath to catch any drips.

"Hot?" she asked.

"I cooked the marshmallow in the freezer," he teased.

She huffed a laugh. "Did you blow on it yet?"

"It could use a bit of blowing." Tony made an obscene gesture with his tongue in his cheek and winked at James.

"Sure thing." Amanda scooped her hair behind her head and used an elastic from her wrist to tie it back in quick, practiced twists. She leaned forward seductively and blew softly on the sugary confection before glancing up at Tony. "Like that?" she asked, her voice low.

"Yeah, darlin'. Just like that," Tony matched her tone.

She noticed a dribble of marshmallow oozing over the edge of the graham cracker and lapped it up with a little moan. "Tony, give me more," she asked, eyes dancing in amusement.

"I'll be careful not to choke you," Tony said, adjusting his hold on s'more. "Take as much as you're comfortable with."

"You two are doing a great job with the double entendre," James remarked, one hand rubbing Amanda's upper thigh. "Turning me on even though I know you're about to use teeth."

She snapped at him playfully before taking a bite of s'more, the marshmallow and melted chocolate oozing out the sides. "Oh my God," she mumbled, covering her mouth with a hand. "I think my mouth just orgasmed."

"And made a mess of my hand," Tony said with a chuckle.

"I can clean that for you," James offered.

"Let me finish first," Amanda begged.

"Of course, ladies always come first," James said, squeezing her leg.

Tony shifted in his seat. "This is a dangerous game we're playing," he said as Amanda took a bigger bite. "Are we— Are you—" He shook his head slowly.

Amanda sat up. "Is this too much PDA?" she asked quietly.

"I don't want to stop whatever this is," he reassured her. "But how far are we going with it?" His eyes flicked from hers to James. "Are we coming out? Because if you suck on my fingers in public, there's no coming back from that."

James snorted. "Because me cock-warming you in front of half these people two-and-a-half years ago doesn't count?"

"That was for a dare," Tony argued. "It's not the same thing."

"I don't need to be dared to show physical affection," James said, his eyes dark. "I want to claim you as mine in front of the world." He held Tony's gaze calmly. "But only if *you* are okay with it."

Tony swallowed hard, his throat visibly working. He tore his eyes away from his boyfriend when Amanda put her fingers lightly on his wrist.

She took the last bite delicately from him, sucking his thumb and index into her mouth, her tongue working to gather all the gooey sugar from the fingers.

"That's hot," Tony breathed, meeting her heated gaze with his own before looking back at James. "I—"

"Are you three getting started on the party games without the rest of us?" Glenn said cheerfully, walking up to them. "I thought we might start with a blindfold kiss test."

Amanda released Tony's wrist and wiped delicately at the corner of her mouth. "What would that entail?"

"One person would wear a blindfold, a selection of people line up, the blindfolded person kisses each one until they either find their partner or, if they're single, someone they like kissing."

The trio exchanged glances.

"I'm not interested in kissing other people," Amanda said at last.

"Me neither," James said.

Tony nodded.

Glenn tapped his lips in thought. "What if you don't have to kiss the person? What if you go by scent?"

"No touching from either side?" Tony asked, frowning.

"Scouts' honor," Glenn said, raising a hand.

Tony chortled. "You were never a scout!"

"No, I wasn't," Glenn agreed readily enough. "But I promise."

"I'm willing to give it a shot," Amanda said, getting to her feet. "Where's the blindfold?"

The rest of the party was filled in on the game. It was agreed that the kissing version would not be played by people wearing red bracelets, and no green bracelets would participate in the scent test. The yellow could play in either version.

Amanda let another girl tie a thick blindfold over her eyes and lead her over to the row of men.

The first guy smelled like salt water and campfire. His aftershave was minty, dulled after a day on the beach.

"Not mine," Amanda said, shaking her head, and was led to the next guy.

Familiar laundry detergent hit her nostrils, combined with a subtle deodorant scent. The natural scent of the man was more than familiar, but didn't match the deodorant. "Mine," she said confidently.

"But which one?" Glenn's voice said from behind her.

Amanda grinned. "It's Tony, but he's wearing James's shirt."

"Damn, I thought we could catch you." Glenn didn't sound disappointed.

"Do I keep going? Is James in the lineup too?"

"Yup."

"Okay."

More confidently, she moved down the group of guys. The next two, she didn't need to get close to before knowing they weren't right. James was last, and she recognized him just as quickly as she had Tony.

"You knew them both immediately!" the girl guiding her exclaimed. "How?"

"I've known them longer than anyone else," Amanda replied with a shrug. "They're as familiar to me as my parents."

James kissed her cheek. "I think you know us better."

She giggled. "You're probably right."

The guys switched their shirts back quickly, and the game moved on.

"We should shake things up a bit," Glenn said, a twinkle in his eyes. "Now we should have the girls be the ones sniffed, but the guys should be on their knees."

James chuckled. "Glenn, old buddy, are you trying to start an orgy?"

"I meant to have the guys smell their hip bones," he replied with an altogether too innocent shrug.

"Well, girls, how do you feel about strangers getting up close and personal with your—" Tony raised an eyebrow at Glenn, "—hip bones?"

"As long as the no touching rule stands, I'm fine with it," Amanda said, and everyone else agreed. "I think the kissing version is going well," she added, nodding to the other side of the patio where several people had paired off and were making out heavily.

James whistled. "Hope you brought condoms."

"I'm not new," Glenn snorted. "I know how my parties usually end up. Yours, too, for that matter. Must be something to do with pheromones."

"I don't think humans have pheromones," Tony said thoughtfully.

"Your girl picked you out of a line by scent alone." Glenn shrugged. "I'm not saying that's proof, but it's certainly something."

Tony rolled his eyes. "I'll go first this time. There's no way I'll be able to do this by scent."

Amanda was placed fourth in the line. They were instructed to stand still, feet exactly shoulder width apart, and to not make a sound.

"He should crawl so he doesn't smell anything above the waist," one of the guys said.

"Agreed."

Watching Tony crawl across the deck, James's hand gently on his neck, made her bite her lower lip so hard it nearly bled.

James smirked at her, knowing what she was thinking, and shook his head minutely.

When Tony reached the first girl, he sat back on his heels and sniffed the air. His forehead furrowed over the black fabric. "No, not this one."

The next girl got the same reaction, but the third had him cocking his head. "I don't think so? Can I come back to her later?"

"Sure thing," Glenn said.

Then he crawled to Amanda's feet. She locked her knees to stop them from trembling in want.

"Oh." Tony grinned. "Okay. I get it. This is Amanda."

"Are you sure?" Glenn asked.

"No doubt at all," Tony said, taking off the blindfold.

James chuckled. "How'd you know?"

"Because she's fucking aroused," Tony drawled. "The scent shot straight to my cock."

"Sorry if the sight of you on your knees riled me up," Amanda said, flushing.

"Not the marshmallows from earlier?" James asked.

"That too."

"Making out before dinner?" Tony added.

"Down at the beach?" James lifted a finger. "On the boat, in our room, am I forgetting anything?"

"I think you've made your point."

The girl beside Amanda fanned herself and leaned over to whisper in her ear, "I think the other guys will have an easier time after that list. It's hot how into you they are."

Amanda grinned. "Thanks."

"How do you manage to divide your attention between them? Is there ever any jealousy? Aren't you exhausted?"

Laughing a little, Amanda shook her head. "We talk a lot. If someone is feeling left out, we voice it immediately. And I think the word I would use is *sated*."

"Nice."

They rearranged themselves for the next guy, who took his time going down the whole row, his confusion growing until he finally reached the last girl. "Oh thank God, I was afraid I'd missed you!" he said in relief when he'd chosen correctly.

Amanda didn't pay much attention to the next attempt. She was last, so it was unlikely that he'd get to her. Instead, her attention kept wandering over to the other side of the patio. Something was missing. Or rather, some*one*. When the guy's turn was over, she walked over to Glenn. "Where did Carolina go?"

He frowned. "I'm not sure. I haven't seen her since my second s'more, come to think of it."

"What was she doing?"

"She was on her phone. I only remember because I thought it was unusual for her."

"She's been off all day," Amanda said slowly. "I'm going to go look for her."

"I'm coming with you," James said when she told him. "I don't like her, but I don't want you alone."

"You stay out here and have fun. You can keep an eye on the trouble-makers over there, but I have a feeling they'll leave me alone this weekend."

"The game is for *partners*," Tony said, tugging playfully on Amanda's hand.

"So?" She grinned. "You've got one partner here with you." She raised her eyebrows pointedly. "What do you say?"

Tony flushed and glanced almost bashfully at James. "Wanna play?"

"Yes," James replied instantly.

Amanda clapped her hands excitedly, distracted for the moment from her mission of finding Carolina.

Glenn seemed unsurprised by the turn of events, the other couples taking the new pair in stride.

"Proud of you," Amanda said to Tony as he tied the blindfold over his eyes.

"I haven't found him yet," he mumbled.

"You will," she said confidently. "Want me to lead you?"

"Nah, go find Carolina." He made a face. "Can't believe I said that."

"Love you." She pecked his lips before turning and letting herself through the patio doors.

Other than the expected muffled noises from the secondary kitchen, the house was silent.

She made her way to the front hall, deciding to start with the bedrooms. Just as she got there, she caught a glimpse of the front door closing.

Rushing over, she saw Carolina heading down the front steps carrying her suitcase.

"Where are you going?" Amanda blurted out.

Carolina shrieked and dropped the bag; it bounced down the rest of the stairs loudly before landing with a thud at the bottom. "You scared me!" she exclaimed, whirling to face Amanda.

"Sorry." Amanda closed the door behind her. "Why are you leaving?"

Carolina wiped at her cheeks before gesturing at her phone. "My phone died."

"I'm sure someone could lend you a charger. What kind do you need? Android?" Amanda asked, confused.

"I just need to get home."

"Why? I mean, you don't have to tell me, but I'm here if you need to talk."

Carolina snorted inelegantly. "Why do you care? You, with your perfect little life with not one but two guys who worship the ground you walk on. Where are your shadows, by the way?"

"Having fun. I care because you haven't been yourself at all this weekend. We are cheer sisters. You may not have been my favorite person, but I'm worried about you."

"You're worried about me?" Carolina stomped up the stairs to poke Amanda in the shoulder. "Where was that worry two years ago?"

Amanda frowned, confused. "Two years ago? The last time I saw you was at the high school reunion when you aggressively hit on one of my boyfriends. You were yourself at the time."

Carolina opened and closed her mouth a couple times before whirling and sitting on the porch swing. "I forgot about that," she admitted. "I'm sorry. I never really understood why you needed both of them."

"Is that a question?" Amanda asked, trying not to laugh.

"Not really." Carolina sighed heavily.

"What happened two years ago?" Amanda gingerly sat beside the other girl. She reached up, pulled the elastic out of her hair and fluffed it around her face, hoping that would help keep her warm.

Carolina was silent for a long time. "I began seeing this guy from work. He was attractive, high up in management, well-liked by everyone. The sex was phenomenal. Then I found out that he was married." She bit her lip. "I asked if he was leaving her for me, and he called me his bit on the side. Someone to scratch his urges at work. It felt like shit."

Amanda took her hand and squeezed it.

"I broke it off, but I stayed working there. I liked the job, but it was awful seeing him every day. And then—" Carolina sniffled and put a hand low on her belly. "I was too far along to do anything about it. I was pregnant at the reunion, by the way. Didn't know it yet though. He said he didn't believe it was his, that I spread my legs for anyone with a cock. I didn't have the money to take him to court for a paternity test, and at that point, I had to save every penny I could."

They watched the stars for a moment.

"I was going to give the baby up for adoption, but when she was born, they put her on my chest, and she looked up at me with her big eyes... I couldn't do it." Silent tears fell down her cheeks. "I moved back in with my parents until I finally found a place. I'm living with three other women in a similar situation to mine in a house in Boston. We're raising our kids to be like siblings. I thought I could come here and have fun like I used to, but..."

This time, the silence stretched on.

"Are you still working at the same place?" Amanda asked quietly.

"No." Carolina shook her head vehemently. "I'm with a new company, and my salary is better. They have daycare in the building, so I can bring Rosalina with me and I can nurse her on breaks. I'm doing well."

"I'm glad."

"You're not going to rub it in my face?"

"What? No!" Amanda exclaimed, shocked.

"I would have."

"I don't think you would have."

She shook her head. "I was a horrible person to you. And now I can barely go a day without crying because I miss my little girl."

"You could always come back for dinner tomorrow," Amanda suggested. "Bring her with you."

"You think this crowd would welcome a toddler?" Carolina asked incredulously.

Amanda shrugged. "Some will, some won't. You can sit with us. Tony's missing his nephew. I'm sure he'd love to meet Rosalina."

"I'll think about it."

"Please do. Even if it's not this weekend, I'd like to meet her. Get my number from Glenn, and give me a call. We'll arrange something, okay?"

Carolina threw herself at Amanda, hugging her tightly. "Thank you."

"Anytime." Amanda pulled back and stood. "You have a car?"

"Yeah."

"Drive safely. Give your little girl a hug for me."

"Okay."

Amanda waited outside until Carolina drove off, hugging her arms around herself to keep the chill of the night away, only heading in when she couldn't see the brake lights any longer.

Back on the patio, the fires were still blazing, casting flickering lights over everyone's faces.

It was hard to believe she'd just had her mind blown by Carolina's story when none of these people had any idea about what had happened.

She scanned the faces for her men, but didn't see them right away.

Glenn nodded at the chair they had occupied earlier, and she flipped her fingers in an acknowledging wave before heading over to it.

James was straddling Tony, fingers buried in his hair. Tony's hands were in the back pockets of their boyfriend's jeans, pulling him into a slow grind while they made out.

She rested her hand gently on James's shoulder, and he pulled back from the kiss, blinking up at her dazedly.

"I have a lot to tell you," Amanda said. "And I'm horny."

Tony took her hand, kissing and licking along her fingers.

"We'll go up to our room," James said, getting to his feet.

"Or we could show off?" Amanda whimpered, pinned by Tony's heated gaze.

James brushed her hair off her shoulder, molded his front to her back, and mouthed along her neck slowly. "We could do that," he murmured between kisses.

She pushed back against him, his cock hard against her ass, and her knees buckled.

He caught her with a hand at her crotch, setting her nerves on fire. His other hand skated up her body under her sweater to push her bikini up over her breasts. "I love to watch you fall apart under us, and I'm sure everyone else would get off on it too."

"Fuck, James," Tony rasped, finally releasing her fingers. He got up, cupped her head, and claimed her mouth with a deep kiss that had her dizzy in seconds. He ground against her, James's hand caught between them.

"You're going to come for us, right here on the patio, fully clothed. Everyone's going to know how much you crave us. And if you're feeling frisky tomorrow, maybe I'll bend you over and take your cunt in front of everyone. Is that what you want?"

Amanda whined against Tony's lips and nodded as best she could, arousal slicking her bikini bottoms.

Tony left her mouth and kissed down her neck.

"What do you want, sunshine? My fingers fucking into you, or Tony's tongue on your clit?" James mouthed at the shell of her ear.

"Oh God," Amanda gasped, bucking between them. "I want your cocks."

"Not here. This is all about you. I can fuck you with my fingers, is that what you need?"

"Yes, God, *yes*!" she cried, gripping James's hair with one hand and Tony's with the other.

"Good girl," James praised her, sliding his hand inside her sweatpants. He made quick work of the ties of her bikini, letting it fall loose down a pant leg.

Amanda barely felt the spandex hit her foot because her nerves were firing overtime from the two fingers James was running over her.

"You're so wet," he groaned. "You're going to come fast, aren't you?"

"I've been turned on nearly all day. You edged me and I haven't come since, remember?"

James chuckled. "I remember." He slid two fingers inside her, curling them perfectly to hit her G-spot. "Nearly had me coming untouched from how you begged to orgasm."

"More!" she moaned. "Faster, please, James!" She was mindlessly rocking into his fingers, her body searching for release.

"How do you want me?" Tony asked, gentle fingers pulling her hair out of James's face.

"Suck on me," she begged, pulling up her sweater. "I need more."

James dropped his hand from her breast to her waist, supporting her.

Tony hiked her shirt up, latching onto her nipple, alternating between flicks, gentle bites, and suckles.

"Let us hear you orgasm," James murmured. "Get everyone at this party riled up by your cries of pleasure."

She was quickly losing all thought beyond the need to come. Tony bit down, and she shouted wordlessly, arching in their hold, her walls fluttering around James's fingers as she was consumed by ecstasy.

They carefully drew out her pleasure until she was quivering from oversensitivity.

James withdrew his fingers from her pants and offered them to Tony, who sucked them into his mouth with a groan.

"Do you feel how hard you make us?" James asked her, grinding against her. "How much we need you?"

Tony released the fingers and pulled James into a messy kiss over Amanda's shoulder while she recovered her ability to stand.

"Let's go," James said at last, taking her hand and pulling her toward the house.

"Thought we were going to get a show," Glenn teased them as they passed.

"Didn't you?" Tony asked with a wink.

"Good night, kids!"

Art class was always fun in the seventh grade classroom, and even though their teacher, Mrs. Callaghan, wasn't in today, she left detailed instructions for the substitute teacher.

Desks scraped across the floor as everyone made three misshapen circles with them.

"You get ten minutes with these vases," Mrs. Rodenbo said, weaving between the desks to place a sculpted vase on the table in the center. "This is just a warm up. Use the top left corner. You only get one paper, so use the space wisely."

Tony bent over his desk alongside everyone else, focusing on the shape of the vase in front of them. It had a funny little handle facing him and a spout just barely visible on the far side. The sides were flat-ish but twisted subtly from top to bottom. He almost got overwhelmed, trying to draw too much at once, but he remembered what Mrs. Callaghan had taught them the last time she had done this exercise.

"Start with the basic shape. Is it a circle? Square? Oval? Some combination of those? Once you get that down, then you can start refining. But if you don't get the basic shape right, you'll be floundering with the details."

He took a deep breath and looked at the basic shapes again. *Round on the bottom, kinda rectangular at the top? Cylinder, maybe?* he thought to himself, slowly sketching out the shapes on his paper with a pencil. He tilted his head once he'd completed them.

"Hey, James," he hissed at his friend beside him. "Does this look right to you?" He showed his paper.

"Yeah, that looks good," James said. "I forgot about the shape thing. Good on you."

Tony glanced at his friend's paper, which had a wobbly outline of the vase. "Yours isn't too bad."

"Boys, please focus instead of whispering," Mrs. Rodenbo said from behind them. "You have three minutes left."

"Sorry."

Tony tried adding details to his sketch, like widening the opening at the top and putting the handle on, but it seemed to only make things worse. He sighed.

"That's time," the teacher said. "One more quick sketch, this time of a stuffed animal." She replaced the vase in front of them with a brown bear.

"Aww, he looks like Teddy," James said to Amanda.

"He does!" Amanda agreed, beaming back at him.

"Who?" Tony asked.

"My sleep bear," Amanda replied, leaning around James.

Tony nodded. "Right. Forgot his name."

"You still have a sleep bear?" jeered Mathias on the other side of her.

"I still have *my* sleep bear," Amanda corrected. "It was a gift from my grandfather when I was born. I would never give that away."

Mathias made a face. "How do *they* know about him? Have *they* slept with you?"

More kids were paying attention to them now.

Amanda rolled her eyes and began to sketch the bear on her paper.

Taking her cue, James and Tony did the same.

"Hey, I was talking to you!" Mathias shouted, and then squirted her in the head with his water bottle.

"That's quite enough," Mrs. Rodenbo said firmly. "Please move your desk to another circle." She handed Amanda some paper towels, but they didn't do much for her sodden sketch.

"Can I get another paper from the supply closet, please?" Amanda said, wiping her face with her dry sleeve.

"I'm afraid I don't have the key," the teacher replied.

Another group of tables required her attention at that point, and she left them.

"But I can't draw on this," Amanda said sadly.

"Put it on the back lab bench," Tony suggested. "I'll get you another paper."

He left his half-completed ovals in the shape of the stuffed bear and looked in his desk, pulling two paper clips off of previously completed work.

Heading for the supply closet in the back of the room while he straightened the clips, he glanced around the room quickly. Nobody was paying him any attention. He stuck the two clips into the lock, expertly wiggling them until he heard a click. He opened a door just far enough to be able to grab the spare paper, and then closed it again, coming face-to-face with Mrs. Rodenbo.

She raised an eyebrow. "Do you have a key, Mister Carlson?"

Tony swallowed hard. "No, ma'am."

Her second eyebrow went up and she held out her hand. When he put the bent paper clips in it, she pursed her lips. "I'm going to have to report this, you know."

"She needed a paper," he whispered.

"I was going to call the office to send me a key."

Tony hung his head. "I just wanted to help."

"I know." She sighed. "Bring the paper to your friend. You have detention at lunch today."

"Okay."

On the way home from school, Amanda apologized again. "I'm sorry I got you in trouble."

"You didn't. I got myself in trouble," Tony said, scuffing his boots through the January snow. "I knew I shouldn't have picked the lock."

"How did you even know how to do that?" she asked.

"I was taught when I was about four in one of my foster placements." Tony kicked a clump of hardened snow. "The kid who showed me said I was a natural," he added bitterly.

"It was pretty cool to see," James said. "Useful."

Tony scoffed. "The only time it's useful is for breaking rules, and then I get in shit. Mrs. Callaghan isn't going to trust me now."

The trio were silent as they crossed the street.

"And why would she?" Tony exploded once they were on the sidewalk again. "Why do my parents? Why do you two?"

"I can only speak for myself, but you've proven to have my back when I need it," James said. "You know how to pick a lock. So what? You haven't used it for nefarious purposes."

"Nefarious," Amanda repeated with a chuckle. "Sounds like a movie villain. Which you are most definitely *not*," she added quickly. "I trust you, and your lock picking skills aren't going to change that."

"Why not?"

She twisted her mouth into a frown. "Let me put it this way. When you're over at my house, I don't lock the bathroom door because I know you're not going to barge in on me. I trust you to respect me and my boundaries. I think Mrs. Callaghan and your parents will feel the same way, especially if you're up front with them about what happened today. Tell your mom as soon as you get home and have her write to Mrs. Callaghan to arrange a meeting or something."

"Tell my mom about getting in trouble?" Tony asked, shuddering. "Do I have to?"

"Dude, she probably already knows," James said, putting his arm around his friend's shoulders. "And if she doesn't, she will. Better to hear it from you."

"Want me to come with you?" Amanda asked tentatively. "It was because of me that you did it."

"No, if she's going to yell at me, I'd rather you not be there," Tony said sullenly.

"Is she in the habit of yelling at you?"

"I don't think I've ever heard her yell," James added.

"Well, no."

"I think everything will be fine," Amanda said bracingly. "Bring your homework over after and we can get started on our book reports." She gave him a sideways hug before heading up her driveway.

"See you soon," James called after her. He punched Tony lightly on the shoulder. "You too." Then he crossed the street to his house.

Heart sinking down to his toes, Tony trudged up the last few feet to his house. There was an unfamiliar car in the driveway behind theirs, and he frowned. Why was his dad home early? Had the school called him too?

Panic fluttered in his stomach. *What if someone's here to arrest me?*

He briefly considered running as far and as fast as he could, but then he caught sight of the snowman he and his friends had built his front yard last weekend. If he ran away, he'd never see them again.

That thought was too painful to bear.

He trudged up the walk to the front door and pushed it open, the warmth hitting his reddened cheeks and making them sting.

His mom came into the hall before he'd managed to get his second boot off. "I'm glad you're home. Someone's here from the DCF to check up on you." She smiled at him.

The DCF? he thought frantically. *They already know?* Aloud, he said, "Okay. Can I have a snack, please?"

"I have peanut butter apple slices waiting for you in the kitchen. Once you've washed your hands, I'll bring them into the living room."

"Thanks." He shrugged out of his jacket and hung it on the hook before grabbing his lunch box from his bag. After rinsing his containers and washing his hands, he hugged her tightly.

"What's this for?" she asked, surprise in her voice, but hugging him back.

"I got a recess detention today," he mumbled into her shoulder.

"I know, sweetheart. Did you want to talk about it?"

"I shouldn't have done it," he said.

"Then you won't do it again."

"I might," he admitted. "If there's no other way."

"Then perhaps you should get permission first?" she suggested.

Tony froze. "I can do that?"

His mom laughed. "That's usually how it works, yes. If Mrs. Callaghan or a supply teacher really needed to get into a cabinet and didn't have the key, and you offered to help them open it, they would probably say yes if they had exhausted all their other options."

"That could take *forever*!" Tony groaned.

"But it's honest."

"Ugh."

She chuckled and tapped his nose. "You are a helper, my son. You just need to figure out how to help *without* getting in trouble."

"How boring," he teased.

She ran a hand through his hair. "You are anything but boring. Shall we go meet the social worker?"

"'Kay."

He spent the entire interview on tenterhooks, worried that she'd bring up the lock picking, but she asked him questions about the move, his friends, sports, schoolwork, extracurriculars, and how he felt about each of those. At the end, she asked to see his room, and if she could talk to him alone.

While she checked out his room, she asked what he thought of his parents and brother.

Then she packed up and left.

"I'm late to do my homework at Amanda's," Tony said, coming back into the living room. "I'll be back for dinner."

"It's at six. Set an alarm on your phone, please."

"Already done." He stomped into his boots and slung his bag on his back.

"Wear a coat!" his mom shouted after him as he closed the door behind him.

But he was already running across the flattened snowy path between the two houses. He flung himself up the stairs and through the door, shutting it behind him.

He neatly arranged his boots beside James's and half-slid down the hallway to the kitchen where his friends were sitting at the table.

"Took you a while," James said, frowning slightly.

"Is everything okay?" Amanda asked.

To his utter horror and embarrassment, Tony burst into tears.

He barely heard the sound of chairs scraping the floor before he was surrounded by two tight hugs. He rubbed his eyes with the heels of his hands. "Fuck," he whispered.

"What *happened*?" Amanda asked anxiously.

"Someone from DCF was at my house. She didn't ask about the lock picking, but why was she there *today* of all days? What if she takes me away? I *can't*—" A lump in his throat prevented him from finishing his sentence and a fresh wave of tears overflowed down his cheeks.

"I think you need to talk to somebody," James said.

"I see my therapist next Wednesday," Tony said miserably.

"What about your parents?" Amanda suggested.

"Maybe."

"Want me to call them for you?"

He nodded and buried his face in James's shoulder.

"I'm going to pick your pocket now," Amanda said, grabbing his phone. "Although you could probably feel that."

Tony let out a wet, weak chuckle. "I think *James* could feel that."

"Be right back." She left the kitchen, her voice fading as she headed to the front of the house.

When she returned, his parents were with her.

"Oh, honey," his mom said. "Come here."

He hugged her.

"What happened?" his dad asked, looking to James for an explanation.

"He's afraid he'll get taken away from you," James said.

Amanda wrapped her arms around him, a worried crease on her forehead as she watched Tony.

"*Why?*" Tony's dad asked, baffled.

"Because I got in trouble," Tony explained between hiccuping sobs.

"Sweetheart," Tony's mom said, pulling back and holding his face in her hands. "Nothing, and I mean *nothing*, will take you away from us. You are our son, for better or for worse. The DCF was checking in on you to make sure the move was right for you. Remember when they came by in Austin after we first fostered you? Right before we adopted you?"

He nodded, sniffling.

"It was to make sure we were right for you, not the other way around."

"The school didn't call them?"

"No, it was just coincidental timing. They wanted to wait until after Christmas so that you were settled here. The social worker was very pleased with what we told her before you arrived home. Unless you said anything worrying, she's talking about closing your file for good."

"Really? You're my parents forever?"

"Forever." His mom was crying now too, and she wrapped him up in a hug again. "Love you, sweetheart."

"I love you too, Mom."

Part Three:

Looking to
the Future

Chapter Nineteen

Tony

It seemed later than it was; the sun was mostly set when Tony walked up his front steps whistling *Joy to the World*. He kicked the snow off his boots before opening the door.

"Honey, I'm home!" he shouted up the stairs, shedding his outdoor gear.

James appeared at the top, his phone to his ear. "Yeah, sunshine. Tony just got home. We'll get dinner ready for you."

Tony glanced at his watch. "She's running late."

"Meeting ran over time," James said, covering the microphone, and Tony nodded in understanding. "We can decorate tomorrow, don't worry about it." He laughed a bit at what she said. "Or we can decorate today. You sure you're not too tired?"

"We could take off an article of clothing for each decoration we put out," Tony said playfully, jogging up the stairs and into James's arms.

"We wouldn't get much done," James said with a chuckle. He repeated Tony's suggestion to Amanda. "But it looks like I'm overruled. You two are going to wear this old man out."

Tony snorted. "You're only a month older than me."

A scream pierced the air, quickly followed by screeching brakes and a thud that even Tony could hear.

"Amanda!" James shouted.

The heart-stopping seconds continued, the two men staring at each other in horror, holding hands tightly.

"Amanda!" he shouted again, putting the phone on speaker. "Answer me! Please!" His voice broke on the last word, and Tony's heart climbed to his throat.

"Hello?" said a voice.

"Hi! Hello! What happened?" James said frantically.

"She was hit by a car," the woman said. "Someone's calling for an ambulance. I'm Patricia. I can stay with her until they get here."

"Thank you," James said. "We'll go straight to the hospital."

"I'll ask the paramedics where they're going to take her and pass that on to you," she replied.

"It'll probably be the General," Tony whispered, nudging James toward the stairs. "We'll start heading that way."

Tony drove, because James stayed on the phone with Patricia. The paramedics arrived before they'd even left the neighborhood and confirmed the hospital. Patricia gave Amanda's phone to them after saying goodbye, and then the guys drove in tense silence to the north end of Boston.

There was a line of cars waiting to get into the parking lot, so Tony dropped James off near the emergency room before waiting impatiently in the line. At least one of them would be with her. He was tempted to abandon the car at the side of the road, but forced himself to take deep breaths. James had the situation in hand. As much as he wanted to be with her, losing their car wouldn't help anyone.

It took about fifteen minutes for him to get a parking spot, and then booked it to the hospital entrance.

"Amanda Beyer, came in on an ambulance, car accident," he gasped to the desk. "Where can I find her?"

He felt a hand on his back and looked up at James in confusion.

"They wouldn't tell me anything," he murmured. "Family only."

Tony gaped at him before turning back to the receptionist. "I'm her brother," he added between gritted teeth.

"Right this way, Mr. Beyer."

"Her boyfriend should come too," Tony added.

She shook her head. "Family only. And only one at a time. You can keep him updated until she wakes up and can have visitors."

James grabbed Tony's hand for a long moment, searching his eyes. "I'm right here," he said at last.

Tony nodded silently before turning and following the receptionist to another desk. There, he was handed off to a nurse, who pulled out a clipboard.

"She has some bruising on her hips, and a potential concussion, but overall, she's doing fine. She fell asleep, and we're monitoring her. Once she wakes up and we can check her brain for swelling, she should be good to return home."

Tony nodded, overwhelmed. "Nothing's broken?"

"Her bones are all in the right places," the nurse said with a smile. "I don't often get to say that. She was very lucky that the car slowed down as much as it did."

"Do you know what happened? I heard it over the phone."

"It must have sounded worse than it was," she said sympathetically. "The car skidded on ice when it was trying to stop. He slid right through the red light and hit your sister. She flew a few feet and hit her head on the pavement."

Tony winced. "Can I see her?"

"Of course. Come with me. You should be able to phone anyone you need to from in the room. She's hooked up to the automatic call system, so if her vitals change, we'll know right away."

Stealing himself at the door to her room, he followed a step behind the nurse, and then his attention was arrested by the sight of Amanda lying in the white hospital bed.

There were a few tubes connected to each arm, and oxygen under her nose. Her face was white, and he could see some blood caked in her hair.

"Amanda," he whispered soundlessly.

"She's doing very well, considering," the nurse said, looking at the read-out on one of the machines. "She should wake up soon."

"And then her boyfriend can come in and see her?" Tony asked.

"Is he in the waiting room?"

"Yes. He got here before me and was denied entry."

The nurse rolled her eyes. "Of course he was. They're sticklers out there. You can go get him now. Say that Nurse Penny sent you."

"Thanks." Tony took a moment to gently brush Amanda's knuckles with the tips of his fingers. "I'll be right back, darlin'," he whispered. "We're here. You're safe."

They returned home just before midnight, with an official minor concussion diagnosis, orders to take it easy, and no screens for three days.

"I'm sorry we didn't get to decorate today," Amanda said softly once they were all seated as close together on their couch as they could manage. She'd taken a shower, with Tony's help, and was dressed in comfortable pyjama shorts and sweatshirt.

"I don't care about that," James said, pulling her onto his lap.

Tony grabbed her legs and draped them over his, running his fingers over her skin, needing to touch her as much as possible.

"I liked Tony's suggestion of strip-decorating," she said, wiggling a little. "I hate that we can't do it because of this." She gestured at herself.

"It wasn't your fault." James brushed her hair over her shoulder.

"I know."

"I've been thinking," Tony blurted out, and then flushed when his lovers looked at him.

"That's not unusual," Amanda teased.

"What about?" James asked.

Tony swallowed hard. "About state laws and marriage."

Amanda clapped a hand over her mouth.

"What conclusions have you come to?" James asked, his voice quiet.

"I want to marry you. Both of you. But the state won't allow that, so while we can exchange rings and vow to be together forever, I think the two of you should have your names down on the official marriage certificate. James can't pass for your brother the way I did, and you can easily list us as co-agents for medical power of attorney to prevent either of us from being excluded in the future," he finished with a rueful grin.

"So romantic," James said with a smile.

"You want romance?" Tony rubbed his chin, trying to put his feelings into words. He took Amanda's hand in his. "When I think about my life, I can't imagine it without you. I was happy with us simply living together, being together, but tonight opened my eyes. I want the ring on my finger that matches yours. I love you," his voice cracked, "so much. Will you marry me?"

"Yes," Amanda said, tears in her eyes. "I want to throw myself at you. Damn this concussion!"

"I'll come to you, don't hurt yourself," Tony said, leaning over and brushing her lips with his.

When he sat back again, he turned to James. "You have been my best friend for the better part of my life. I have shared my soul with you and can't imagine living my life without you in it, continuing as my best friend, my lover, and my husband. I have loved you for so long that I didn't recognize it for what it was. Will you marry me?"

"Of course I will," James said, cupping the back of Tony's head and meeting him halfway.

When they pulled back, Tony felt dizzy from emotion.

"And I'll accept your suggestion about the official paperwork, but when it comes to name changes, I think we should both take on your last name. What do you think, sunshine?"

"Oh, I love that!" she exclaimed. "The three of us with the same last name!"

"Why mine?" Tony asked, surprised.

"When you were adopted, you chose to take the Carlson name. We haven't had that choice before, and I, at least, would be honored to take your last name." James cleared his throat. "I'll start the process first thing in the morning."

"And this way, even though your first name isn't on the certificate, your last name will be," Amanda said. "I'll take it after the ceremony."

"Guys," Tony said, shaking his head and smiling through his tears. "Thank you. It means a lot."

"I, umm..." James trailed off, his cheeks darkening in a blush. "I may have looked up how to change a last name as an adult while you were in California. A bit presumptuous of me, but I had hope."

"Did you really?" Tony asked, delighted. "So this wasn't completely out of left field?"

"I was going to propose at Christmas," James admitted.

"Sorry for stealing your thunder."

"No apology necessary." James turned to Amanda. "One last question. Amanda, will you marry me?"

"Absolutely!" She leaned into his chest, pressing their lips together chastely before cuddling in and meeting Tony's eyes. "If you weren't expecting to propose, does that mean you don't have a ring?"

"No," Tony replied sheepishly.

"Perfect! We can go pick them out together!"

"Once you're feeling better," James promised, kissing her temple.

"Speaking of Christmas," Tony said. "My brother's coming here this year. What do you think about having the ceremony at home with the families?"

"I think that's a great idea," James said. "I wouldn't want more than a simple ceremony anyways. It's not like we need to do much before then. Just the rings, name change, and license."

"I love it! We should tell them—Oh my God! I didn't tell my parents I was hit by a car! Did you?"

"I considered calling them while I was waiting to be let in, but I didn't want them to worry. And then I forgot," James admitted.

"Do you think they'd mind being woken up at one in the morning?"

They made an appointment with a jeweler for the coming weekend to let Amanda rest.

She was practically vibrating to get out of the house as she got in the back seat of their car. "Do you understand how boring it was with you two at work? I couldn't use the computer, play on my phone, watch TV, read, or even listen to music! Healing from a concussion has to be the most boring job in the world!"

"Is that why you made so many cookies?" Tony teased.

"That, and it's Christmas," she replied. "Oh! I forgot to tell you, James, but I finally got my grandmother's shortbread recipe from Mom. She said that since we're getting married, she can share it with you now. It has to stay in the family, afterall."

"Excellent, the plan worked," James muttered in a loud aside to Tony. "Only took a decade. We grab the recipe and take off for parts unknown."

Tony chuckled and kissed her hand. "I can't wait to eat the first one."

"I already did," she admitted. "I couldn't resist. It tasted like my childhood."

"I wonder what would make me think of my childhood," Tony mused. "Watery mac and cheese, I suppose."

"I promise to never make you watery mac and cheese," James said. "Write that down for me so I don't forget to add it to my vows."

Tony snorted. "Laying it on a little thick."

"Like cheese," Amanda said, nodding enthusiastically. "I promise to make you cookies that will remind you of Christmases spent with us for the rest of your life."

"I think I've cried enough lately," Tony said. "I'm going to lose my macho street cred."

"Nobody here but us," James said, drawing a circle in the air. "Cry if you need to."

"Or we can talk about something else?" Tony suggested. "Like what we want our rings to look like?"

"I just want them to look similar enough that people know we're all together," Amanda said.

"Agreed."

When they arrived for their appointment, the jeweler took them into a little room and showed them a wide variety of rings, but most of them were either too ostentatious or too simple.

"I like this one," Amanda said, indicating a slender band with a heart-shaped gemstone on one end. "But it's too delicate for you two."

"What if we thickened it up? And we can add a second heart on the other side, to show your bond with two people," the jeweler suggested.

"Could we use our birthstones for the gems?" James asked.

"Absolutely!" The jeweler beamed at him. "What are your birth months?"

"March," James replied.

"April," said Tony.

"May."

"Like stepping stones," the jeweler said cheerfully. "You have a choice to make for March, between aquamarine and bloodstone." She showed the two samples and placed a diamond and emerald beside them. "April and May," she explained.

"I like aquamarine better with the diamond," Amanda said, putting the two next to each other. "They're both light and airy."

"The bloodstone looks nice with the emerald," Tony said. "Why not use both? Different facets of him for each of us."

"I love that," Amanda said. "James? What do you think?"

"I agree."

"Wonderful!" the jeweler exclaimed.

She took their measurements, wrote down the details of the rings, and gave them a receipt. "The rings will be ready in two weeks," she said. "You can pick them up any time after that."

"Thank you so much!"

When they left the jewelers, Amanda pulled her phone from her pocket with confusion. "I'm glad I put this on vibrate because it rang five times while we were in there."

"Your parents?" Tony guessed.

"Work?" James asked.

Amanda's eyebrows rose. "Carolina."

"Really?"

She had told them Carolina's story and they'd hoped to see her and meet Rosalina the next night on Thanksgiving, but she hadn't turned up. She had texted Amanda once, to share her number, but that was it.

"I'll call her and see what's up," Amanda said, putting the phone on speaker and they huddled around it.

"Oh my God, you called back!" Carolina half-screamed when she answered. "Please don't hang up. I need your help!"

"What's wrong?" Amanda said.

"Can you come over? It's easier to explain in person."

"I'm with the guys. Can they come too?"

Carolina was silent for so long that Amanda thought the call had been dropped and checked her connection.

"We don't judge," James said, just loud enough for the mic to pick up. "We'll look after Rosalina while you talk to Amanda."

Carolina let out a sound somewhere between a sob and a laugh. "I'll text you my address."

The line went dead. The trio stared at each other.

"What is that all about?" Tony said at last.

"We'll find out." Amanda clicked on the address Carolina had sent her. "She's in the west end. Let's go."

The house they pulled up to was old but well-maintained. There were a couple of snowmen in the front yard, as well as a toddler slide.

Carolina answered the door, a tiny dark-haired child on her hip. "You came!" she said, surprised.

"I said I would," Amanda replied.

They took off their outdoor gear in the crowded entryway before Carolina led them into the living room.

The little girl squirmed to be let down, squeaking happily once she was on the ground. She toddled over to a short table with pieces of a train set on it and banged two of them together.

Carolina winced. "I didn't know who else to call," she said. "Nobody else from high school knows about Rosalina. I don't—" She broke off and turned away, wiping her eyes.

The two men sat down with the little girl to give the women a semblance of privacy.

"Do you need a hug?" Amanda asked.

When the other girl nodded, she held her arms open.

Carolina practically fell into them, letting her tears flow silently.

Amanda rocked her back and forth for a while until the shaking stopped. "What about the other two women you live with?"

Carolina shook her head. "They don't... We're not *friends*. I trust them to look after Rosalina if I pay them, but I can't *talk* to them."

"Okay." Amanda guided her to the couch and moved enough toys from the cushions so that they could sit down. "What's going on?"

Carolina's lower lip wobbled before she bit it. "I got a call from the DCF," she whispered, looking miserable. "They got a report that Rosalina was mistreated at home. They're coming to check on me."

"Okay," Amanda said again. "First of all, the DCF is not the bad guy. They're going to come and check on her, find that everything's fine, and close the file."

"How do you know?" Carolina started crying again. "I may not have wanted to be a mother, but she's all I have. I can't lose her!"

Amanda opened and closed her mouth a few times. "Tony?" she asked plaintively, taking Carolina's hand. "A little help?"

Tony swivelled around to face the women. "I want to reassure you that this conversation is off the record," he said to Carolina. "I'm a social worker for the DCF. I'm not the one who received your file, so this is the first time I've heard of the situation, okay?"

Carolina hiccuped and nodded.

"I also grew up in the foster system, so I'm familiar with that side of it as well," he continued. "Did you know that I was adopted?"

She shook her head.

He nodded. "Not long before we moved to Massachusetts. The DCF were involved in my case once we got here. They are not in the habit of taking kids away from their families unless there's a serious concern. Do you do drugs?"

Carolina shook her head.

"Do any of the women you live with do drugs?"

"No," Carolina said.

"That's good. Did you want me to look into the report? I can't show it to you, but I can ease your mind with what they'll be looking for."

"You can do that?" Carolina asked, eyes wide.

Tony winced. "Unofficially. Let me make a call."

"Please."

While Tony headed into the kitchen to call a co-worker he knew had a Saturday shift, he heard Amanda ask, "You said mistreated. Can you think of any reason why someone might think that?"

He shook his head and waited for the phone to stop ringing. "Hey Mallory," he said when the phone picked up. "I've got a friend..." He explained the situation.

Mallory clicked her tongue a few times while she pulled up the report and read through it. "This is a really low concern. If I had to guess, it's either a neighbor who's annoyed at living near loud children, or the mother pissed someone off and they retaliated. The report doesn't even have the name of the child, which is basic info that anyone close enough to see mistreatment should know."

Tony scoffed. "Truth. What exactly were the concerns?"

"Constant yelling, locking the child in her room, and never letting her outside."

"When will someone be by?"

"Tomorrow. The mother works during the week and the child is in daycare."

"Thanks, Mallory."

"No problem."

Tony tapped the phone against his mouth for a moment before sighing and tucking it in his pocket.

Carolina looked up, eyes hopeful, when he returned to the living room.

"I think everything will be fine," he said. "They're coming tomorrow, so you don't have to worry about work. Just be yourself, okay? Don't change how you do anything."

"That's all you can tell me?" she asked.

"Yes," he replied with a shrug. "As I said before, we don't take kids away from their parents without a very good reason, and I can tell you, from where I'm standing, there's no worry about that."

"Would you tell me if they're going to take Rosalina away from me?" Carolina asked, narrowing her eyes.

"No," he admitted. "Because there'd be a flight risk." He squatted down in front of her and took her hands. "As your friend, you are doing a great job. Do you hear me?"

Carolina nodded slowly, not looking away from his face. "Are you sure you don't want to take on the position of father?" She smiled teasingly.

Tony chuckled. "Not to Rosalina. She's a sweetie, but my heart belongs to my fiancés."

Carolina's jaw dropped. "You're engaged?"

Amanda beamed. "Since earlier this week."

"Wow." Carolina chewed her lower lip for a moment. "Do you know what my job is?"

Tony blinked at the sudden change in topic. "No."

She pointed at the portrait over the fireplace. "I'm a photographer."

Tony got up to look at it closer. It was a black and white portrait of a very pregnant Carolina wrapped tastefully in a sheer sheet. "It's stunning," he said.

"I do maternity shoots, but also boudoir photography. Do you know what that is?"

"No," Amanda said.

"I take pictures of women in lingerie in seductive poses." Carolina gained confidence as she spoke. "Every woman I've photographed has left rave reviews on my profile. They say it's given them confidence in their daily lives. If I can take photos of them that make them feel sexy, then perhaps they're sexier than they realize."

"Good for you," Tony said. "Why are you bringing this up now?"

She took a deep breath. "It's a great bachelorette party experience."

Amanda's eyes widened. "That would be fun! We were just going to keep the wedding to family, and *maybe* a few close friends. You're the first person we've told outside of family."

"I'm honored."

"We'll keep your suggestion in mind," Tony said. "I'm glad you brought it up. Do you have a card or website?"

"Yes, of course!" Carolina leapt to her feet and riffled through a drawer near the entryway. "Here!" She handed Amanda a card with her name and website, a little camera in the corner.

"Thank you. If we have a bachelorette party, I will definitely be in touch," Amanda said.

James stood and stretched. "We'll be in touch, even if it's not for the bachelorette. I won't say no to boudoir photos of you, sunshine."

Amanda beamed up at him. "Thank you. It sounds like fun."

They got ready to leave.

"Text us tomorrow after the visit, okay?" Amanda said.

"Thank you."

Chapter Twenty

Flashback:
Wedded Bliss

Tony and James watched Amanda dance with the bride and her friends. They had bonded during the bachelorette party the night before, and it was fun to watch them together, bouncing to the beat.

Adam flung himself down in the seat beside his brother and threw his arm around Tony's shoulder.

"Dude, you're soaked with sweat," Tony said, pushing halfheartedly at his brother's chest.

"That's what happens when you dance with everyone and their grandmother," Adam replied cheerfully. "You'll find out when you get married."

Tony raised his eyebrows. "When, huh?"

Adam nodded. "It's only a matter of time for you three."

"How much have you had to drink?"

"I'm drunk on love, baby brother!" Adam exclaimed. "Look at her!"

"Which 'her'?" Tony asked, stifling a laugh.

"My *wife*!" Adam shouted happily. "I have a *wife*, dude. Isn't she gorgeous?" He beamed at Sophia, who was dancing with Amanda.

"Yeah, I was there when you got married." Tony exchanged amused glances with James. "She is beautiful."

"She chose me." Adam shook his head in astonishment. "I can't believe I get to go home to her every day."

"Weren't you living together before this?" James asked.

"It's not the same." Adam shook his head slowly. "You'll see. Are you looking forward to moving in together?"

"Obviously."

"Just remember one thing," Adam said seriously. "You've been apart for four years, going to colleges across the country. You've changed a lot, and so have they. Don't assume things."

"Wise words from a twenty-seven-year-old," Tony said, amused. "You're not that much older than me."

"This is the first time you'll be living with your partners," Adam continued. "I've lived with Sophia for five years now."

"Took you a while to pop the question," Tony teased.

"Don't judge," Adam scolded. "Everyone has their own reasons for doing things in their own time, even me."

"Even you," Tony repeated playfully.

"You need to communicate your needs," Adam said.

"Is this a second thing I need to remember, or still part of the first one?" Tony asked.

"Still part of the first one," Adam said haughtily. He looked between the two men. "Communication is the most important thing in *any* relationship, even more so in your case. You have two other people to think of, not just one."

"Thanks for stating the obvious," Tony said, amused.

"I'm grateful that you finally got together, so I don't have to listen to your pining anymore."

"I'm allowed to miss my best friends while away at school," Tony said.

"How many times did you call after that party at Glenn's at the beginning of summer?" Adam asked. "'I'm so in love with her'," he said in a falsetto.

Tony snorted. "I do *not* sound like that."

"'I'm going to die living with them if I keep my affections bottled up like this'," Adam added blithely.

"I definitely did not say that," Tony said.

Adam put a finger over Tony's lips. "It was implied. Hush." He cleared his throat. "'How can I get so turned on—'"

Tony clapped his hand over his brother's mouth. "I think that's enough of pretending to imitate me."

Adam raised an eyebrow, and when Tony released him, he smirked. "I noticed that you didn't object to me calling James your partner. Is that new?"

"I get what you're implying, but the relationship between James and I is platonic. We are partners, I could never deny that, but not in the same way we are with Amanda." A knot formed in Tony's stomach as he said that.

"Partners forever," James said, resting his hand on Tony's knee. The warmth seeped through the material, setting his nerves on fire.

"Want to dance?" Tony said, standing abruptly.

"I'm still catching my breath," Adam replied. "You go on."

"Of course I'll dance with you," James said.

Tony's heart skipped a beat.

When he glanced back at his brother, Adam winked at him with a smile.

Tony might be able to fool James, but his brother knew him better than he'd realized. *Thank goodness we live on the opposite side of the country*, he thought, even as he caught himself holding back tears.

"You okay?" James asked, leaning in.

"It just hit me that my brother's moving here permanently."

James nodded sympathetically. "At least you've got us and a good phone."

Tony chuckled weakly. "I guess it'll do."

Chapter Twenty-One

James

"I can't believe you threw this together in what, a week?" James said, fiddling with the sash that proclaimed him a 'groom-to-be'.

"Two weeks," Glenn corrected. "And only because you didn't tell me sooner. Do you know how many strings I had to pull?"

"Well, we weren't expecting any of this," Tony said, shaking his head. He was wearing a matching sash.

"Then you don't know me very well," Glenn declared. "Not only do you three give me hope for true love, but I feel responsible for you getting together in the first place."

All the men in the car chuckled at that.

"What?" Glenn asked.

James's dad patted his shoulder. "It was obvious to all of us that these three were in love with each other."

"Whatever happened at your party—and I do *not* want to hear about it—may have been a catalyst, but certainly not a genesis," Amanda's dad added.

"Partying *with* the parents is certainly not the usual way of having a bachelor party," Glenn grumbled.

Adam laughed. "What do you normally do at bachelor parties?"

"I've never been to one," Glenn admitted. "But in the movies, they go to a strip club, get drunk, and talk about sex."

Tony's dad grimaced. "I'm too old for all of that."

"You're never too old for a strip club," Glenn corrected.

"If you insist. But unless my wife is stripping—"

"Dad!" Tony and Adam exclaimed, horrified.

He gave them a *look*. "In case you weren't aware of how babies were made, I have, in fact, seen your mother naked."

"I pretend that you had sex once to procreate, and you did it in the dark with a turkey baster," Adam said.

"Is that how you did it?" Tony asked his brother slyly.

"Absolutely."

"Man, you are missing out," Tony said, shaking his head.

Everyone laughed.

"Mister Carlson," Glenn began, but he was cut off.

"Call me Michael."

"Xavier," James's dad added.

"Paul," Amanda's dad supplied.

"Wait, wait," Tony said, holding up his hands. When everyone looked at him, he said, "You guys have *first names*?"

The limo nearly rocked with their laughter.

When Glenn calmed down, he tried again, "Michael," he said, "what advice would you give to the grooms?"

Michael stroked his chin as he thought, looking at first one and then the other. "There is no shame in asking for help."

Glenn opened and closed his mouth.

"What is it?" Adam asked.

"That's the perfect set-up!" Glenn exclaimed.

"Go ahead," James said with a sigh.

"In bed!" Glenn crowed, to the groans of everyone else.

"We're here," the driver announced.

"Thank you," everyone said as they piled out.

The neon sign over the door cast green light over Tony's face, highlighting his features. As if drawn to him with a magnet, James cupped his face and ran a thumb over his cheekbone.

"Everything okay?" Tony asked.

James gave himself a shake. "Yeah. Got distracted by how handsome you are."

"Aww," the men cooed, making James blush.

"I think we need to start a game," Glenn said. "Anytime one of you touches the other, you need to do a burpee."

Tony rolled his eyes. "That's hardly fair."

"Normally party games include everyone," James pointed out. "Like if someone says the word 'love' or 'groom' or something."

Glenn tapped his chin as he thought. "Alright, I need paper."

They entered the mini putt, and while Michael and Xavier signed in, Glenn grabbed a piece of paper and tore it into six pieces, writing a word on each one before handing them out to each person.

"Here's the game; you each have a word that you can't say. Only you and I know what it is. If you say it, I will dock you a point on your score.

If someone else guesses what your word is, they are immune and I will no longer dock points from them."

"What about you?" Tony asked.

"I have to keep track of you six," Glenn said haughtily. "I don't have the brain power to remember a word for myself too. I will sacrifice myself for the greater good."

"And most likely win at mini putt," Adam muttered.

Glenn grinned. "There is definitely potential for that."

"Oh, it is on," Tony said, rubbing his hands together. "You don't give a Carlson a competition without us fighting for every last point."

"May the best man win," James said, shaking Tony's hand.

"Burpee!" Glenn cheered.

"What?"

"I thought that wasn't happening!"

"No touching for the whole evening," Glenn reminded them.

Groaning, the two grooms jumped before doing a pushup.

"This is just evil," Adam said, watching them.

"I love it," Xavier said.

Glenn raised his eyebrow at James's dad and made a note on the iPad the mini putt place had given them.

"It's our turn," Paul said, spinning his club between his fingers. "Pick your ball."

James chose the lime green amongst the variety of colors.

"After each hole, there's a question about one groom or the other," Glenn said cheerfully. "If you're the first to get it right, you gain a point."

"What if the answer includes your word?" Tony asked.

"Then you'll have to get creative," Glenn replied.

The first hole was an easy one, and they all finished in less than 2 putts.

"First question," Glenn said, waiting until he had everyone's attention. "How many goals did Tony score in his first soccer game of senior year?"

"Two," James said promptly.

"Correct."

Tony stared at James. "How did you know that? I didn't even know that!"

"It might have escaped your notice, but I've been head over heels for you for a long time," James murmured, eyes dancing.

"Fuck the rules," Tony muttered, grabbing James by the neck and hauling him in for a deep kiss. When they parted, he added, "It's the number of times we touch, right?"

"Right," Glenn replied, eyes narrowing.

"I'm still touching him," Tony said, pressing their foreheads together and rubbing their noses.

"I think we may have underestimated their penchant for finding loopholes," Michael said in a loud aside to Xavier.

"Do we need to amend the rules?" Paul asked in amusement.

"We might need to, if they're going to pull this shit," Glenn said, poking Tony. "You have to let go of him at some point."

"I know." Tony claimed James's mouth one more time, both panting heavily by the time he pulled back.

They silently handed their putters to their fathers before doing the burpee required.

"You know, I don't think the punishment is enough incentive," Adam said thoughtfully as they moved on to the second hole.

"What are you suggesting?" Xavier asked.

"What if we had them lose an article of clothing?"

Glenn shook his head. "Won't work."

Michael groaned dramatically. "I did *not* need to know that."

Tony laughed and winked at James. "Glenn's the instigator. He's had the entire baseball team streak at both prom *and* our high school reunion."

"I have to admit, I'm somewhat relieved to hear that's all it is," Xavier said, eyeing his son, who grinned.

"For some reason, I'm thinking it isn't," Paul muttered. "I'm too old for this. Just, please, tell me Amanda's not involved in this."

"She's not involved in this," Tony parroted.

"That doesn't make me feel better. Why doesn't that make me feel better?" Paul asked the other two.

"Because he's lying," Michael said, narrowing his eyes at his son.

"You guys are kinky as fuck," Adam said with a whistle.

"We're in a triad relationship, what part of this *isn't* kinky?" James asked with a chuckle.

"I try not to think about that," Xavier said, the other fathers nodding in agreement.

They completed hole number two as quick as the first.

"Second question," Glenn said, rattling the papers in front of him. "When did James take his first steps?"

"At daycare," Xavier said.

"I asked when, not where," Glenn corrected.

"At seven months," Tony said. "He needed to get to Amanda because she was crying."

"Correct."

"I'd forgotten about that," Paul said. "You two were inseparable, and they put you in a different room one day. You left and got halfway down the hallway to her before anyone noticed. They watched you walk the rest of the way to her nap mat and cuddle up with her. They couldn't believe you'd done it. Seven months is really early."

"Aww," Adam said. "That's so cute!"

"Why did they move me?" James asked.

"Your usual room had one less adult that day, so they lightened the load by moving five kids to other rooms. They chose incorrectly with you," Xavier said with a smile.

"How did you know that?" Michael asked Tony.

"Mrs. Beyer told me once. They're my favorite people, and it was a cute story. Of course I remembered it."

"Random. How did that come up?" Adam asked.

Tony flushed. "We had a worksheet in grade nine French about what we remembered from our childhood. We could ask our parents if we didn't know the answer, but..." He twirled the putter between his palms, avoiding his family's gaze. "I don't have many memories from before the Carlsons, and it made Mom sad when I asked about things like when I was born. Why would I make things worse by asking about when my first steps were? She wouldn't—couldn't—know the answer. Mrs. Beyer was trying to make me feel better."

Glenn rested his hand on Tony's shoulder. "Sorry man. I didn't realize the question would bring that up."

Tony gave him a crooked smile. "How could you have known?"

"Shall we move on?" Michael said.

"Yes, of course."

James took Tony's hand behind everyone else and gave it a squeeze. "You okay?" he asked.

"Yeah." Tony grimaced. "It's tough sometimes when I remember that my early childhood wasn't as amazing as yours."

James nodded. "We're working on making the rest of your life better than you could ever imagine."

"Hey!" Glenn said, snapping his fingers at them. "Burpees!"

"I can't comfort my fiancé by holding his hand?" James asked, raising an eyebrow.

"I'll allow it, but only this once," Glenn said.

"I need more comfort than a hand can provide!" Tony exclaimed dramatically.

Adam launched himself at Tony, who caught him by instinct. "I'll comfort you, little brother!"

"Dude," Tony gasped, his biceps bulging. "A little warning!"

"Damn, what are you lifting now, man?" Glenn asked admiringly.

"Somewhere between one-sixty and two-twenty," Tony replied cheekily, dropping his brother on his feet. "Depending on the day."

"You walked right into that one," James said with a chuckle, clapping Glenn on the shoulder.

"I don't get it," Paul said.

"How much do you think James weighs?" Michael asked, amusement making his eyes twinkle.

Paul's eyes widened and he flushed. "I didn't need to know that."

"I've decided to compartmentalize," Xavier commented. "We aren't talking about our kids, but rather adults that are about to get married."

"Does that mean I can ask the next advice question?" Glenn asked excitedly.

"Go ahead." Xavier nodded.

"What advice about sex would you give to them?"

Xavier winced. "Compartmentalize," he muttered to himself. "Prep is important. Foreplay is mandatory. Use lube."

After a moment of silence, Glenn clapped slowly. "Bravo, X. I didn't think you had it in you."

James laughed. "Thanks, Dad. Those are all important to remember."

"I don't remember getting that advice before I got married," Adam mused.

"You didn't ask," Xavier replied with a grin.

"What's the difference between prep and foreplay?" Glenn asked.

Tony put a hand over his face. "You can't be serious," he moaned.

"Oh, I know this one!" Paul said cheerfully. "Foreplay is about pleasure, but prep is to get her—or, errr... him—ready for... ummm..." He floundered, blushing.

"You can say penetration," James said with a smirk.

"Or penis," Adam said.

"Cock," Tony added mischievously.

"Compartmentalize," Xavier said bracingly.

"You already know what I'm trying to say," Paul said, flustered.

"Does that make sense?" Michael asked Glenn, who was almost as red.

"Yeah, got it."

They had gone through almost all the holes by this point.

"I wasn't expecting mini putt to take such a short time," Glenn said, examining the iPad. "We've only got one hole left, and we're all within a point of each other. One last piece of advice from Paul. How would you suggest they best handle your daughter?"

Michael and Xavier began to chuckle. Paul pointed at them. "Stop."

Xavier shrugged. "I can't help it. That's where the conversation keeps going."

"I'm not going there," Paul said. "I can't compartmentalize that well." To the young men, he said, "I suggest you keep doing whatever it is that you're doing. I've never seen her so happy."

"I thought you said you weren't going to go there," Michael snickered.

"I'm not listening," Paul said, covering his ears.

Glenn chuckled. "Okay, last hole. Not sure what to do after this, though."

"We could play through again?" Adam suggested.

"What about the bowling alley next door?" Michael suggested. "It's not a strip club, but there's lots of bending and twisting involved."

Tony laughed. "You're hilarious, Dad."

"I'm glad you're finally figuring that out," Michael replied haughtily.

"Only occasionally," Adam said loudly.

"I think you don't always get the joke," Tony teased.

Adam's jaw hung open. "Rude! Dad! Did you hear that?"

"I think you're old enough to fight your own battles," Michael said calmly.

The brothers still bickering, they returned their clubs and Glenn tallied up their scores.

"If I may have everyone's attention?" Glenn waited until everyone was listening. "We had a very close game. X would have won, if he hadn't said his word first thing. Any guesses as to what that word might be?"

Everyone shook their heads.

Glenn grinned. "You all had the same word," he said with a laugh. "Love. Anyways, because of that, Paul won by one point, then X, Tony, Michael and James were tied, and Adam trailing the pack by three."

"What about you?"

"I recuse myself."

"He was last at nearly every hole," Tony mused. "I think he just doesn't want to tell us how badly he did."

Glenn returned the tablet. "I resent your implications," he said haughtily.

"Alright, man," Tony laughed, slinging an arm around his friend's shoulders. "Recuse away."

They headed over to the bowling alley next door.

"A round for everyone?" Paul said, to the enthusiasm of the group.

Once everyone had a beer in their hand, James stood up and called for attention. "I want to thank everyone here for celebrating with us tonight. There are some people in particular who need shout-outs. First, to Glenn's parents, for gifting us their enormous vacation house for the week. It was unexpected, and we greatly appreciate it."

Glenn spoke up, "My parents said that it was a small token for how you kept me in line."

Tony chuckled. "*That* was a job and a half!"

Glenn nodded. "Exactly."

"If I can continue?" James asked, and everyone quieted. "To Glenn, for organizing this at the last minute."

"I've always wanted to plan a shotgun wedding," Glenn said.

The three dads whipped around to James and Tony.

"What?" Paul said softly.

James shook his head. "Amanda's not pregnant. We rushed this so that Adam, Sophia, and the boys would be here for the wedding when they came for Christmas."

"Is *that* what that means?" Glenn asked, eyes comically wide.

Tony laughed. "You asshole. You know exactly what that means. Stop trying to give our dads heart attacks."

"I can't speak for the others, but I would be thrilled to be a grandfather," Xavier said.

"Me too," Paul said.

"Three times over," Michael added. "But get pregnant in your own time. A baby changes more than you realize."

James nodded. "I understand. We haven't started seriously discussing timing yet." He clapped his hands together. "Which brings me to you three. Thank you for loving us as your own children, even if we were born to other people. The way you blended our families because of how close we were showed us the many forms love could take. We couldn't ask for better fathers."

"Don't make me cry," Xavier said, rubbing his face. "It was such an honor to watch the three of you grow up."

James patted his father's shoulder affectionately. "Adam, thank you for getting your officiant's license for Massachusetts and agreeing to perform the ceremony. I can't imagine anyone better suited to the role."

Adam inclined his head in acknowledgement.

"And last, but certainly not least, to Tony and Amanda. She's not here, but she knows how loved she is, so I'm going to focus on Tony." James put his beer down and took Tony's hands, ignoring the muttered 'burpees' from Glenn. "Tony, from the moment I laid eyes on you, I knew you'd be awesome. You completely surpassed my expectations. We grew closer than little twelve-year-old me could have imagined, and I fell in love with you. You pushed me to be a better person, to see the world in new ways, and to see that love was limitless. Thank you for being you and for coming into our lives."

"Well, that last one was more due to my parents," Tony said thickly. He rubbed the heel of his hand over his eyes. "I didn't know we were reading our vows tonight, or I would have prepared something."

"This was kinda spontaneous," James admitted.

"Damn," Tony said, the corner of his mouth ticking up and making James's heart pound. "If you can pull that out of your ass, what are your vows like?"

"Overthought and worked to death," James said with a chuckle.

To the rest of the group, Tony said, "We worked on the thank yous to you together, so forgive me if I don't repeat them." He turned back to James. "Thank you for being there for me, for helping me break down the walls around my heart, and for confusing the *heck* out of me when I didn't understand that I'd fallen in love with you as well as Amanda."

James chuckled. "I think the only one not confused was her."

"Possibly." Tony swallowed hard. "My parents did a lot for me and I appreciate it, but I wouldn't be half the man I am today if it weren't for you. You talk about me pushing you to be better, but you did the same for me. That's why I know we work together. We lift each other up. I can't wait to see how that evolves in marriage."

"Now that the sappy love stuff is out of the way, can we bowl?" Glenn asked, breaking the silence.

"I'm too emotional for this," Xavier said, wiping under his eyes. "And I deal with death daily."

Chuckles rippled around the group.

"One more person to give advice!" Glenn said after they'd bowled the first frame. "Adam, what advice would you give to newlyweds?"

"Never go to bed angry," Adam said promptly. "Communicate like you just did. Never assume."

"Good advice, bro," Tony said, giving him a hug.

Adam held up a hand. "I'm not done. You embarrassed the hell out of me at my bachelor party, so it's only fair I return the favor."

Tony's eyes widened. "You wouldn't," he whispered.

"Make sure you scream the correct name when you orgasm," Adam finished with a flourish.

"Oh my God, I am never telling you anything ever again," Tony mumbled, covering his face with his hands while the others laughed.

"Whose name did you call, and with whom?" James asked through his chuckles. "Also, why haven't I heard about this before?"

Tony scrubbed his hands down his face. "Because I'd succeeded in blocking it out of my memory. It was your name, Jamie, and it was with a guy in second year. We obviously didn't stay together for long."

"I get it," James said, sharing a smile with Tony. "And I don't think that'll be a problem again. We're ready for tomorrow."

Chapter Twenty-Two

Flashback: Love in All Its Forms

"Beverly broke her hip," Amanda overheard her mother say on the phone when she entered the kitchen after school. "And Susan and Mary are away for at least a week each. I can try to swing by and help her, but I've got a lot of work with report cards due on Friday."

"I can do it, Mom," Amanda said.

"Hang on Ava, Amanda just came in," her mother said. She put the phone on speaker.

"Hi Mrs. Lavallee," Amanda said to the phone before turning to her mother. "I can help Beverley after school. She and her sisters have always been nice to us, and I'd love to help her out."

"Sisters?" her mother replied, a small smile on her face before giving her head a shake. "Doesn't matter. If you're willing to help, that would be great. It's going to be a lot of work, though."

"I know, but it'll only be for a week."

"Julie, what if we got the boys involved?" Ava asked, her voice distorted by the speaker.

"We should get Debra on the line. Get her opinion on this."

"The boys are coming over to study," Amanda said, opening the fridge and grabbing carrots and celery from the veggie drawer. "Should be here any minute."

"How do I do a three-way call again?" Julie muttered, poking at her phone.

"This button," Amanda said, dropping the veggies on the counter.

"Ah, thank you."

"I use it all the time," Amanda said with a chuckle.

"You would," Ava said.

"Hello?" Debra's voice came through.

Amanda's mom explained the situation and the proposed solution.

"What about their end of year exams?" Debra asked.

"We're on top of all our coursework," Amanda said. "And I'm almost done writing out all my study notes."

"What's this about study notes?" James asked, coming into the kitchen with Tony.

Everything was explained again to the boys.

"I think we can handle that," James said. "It's only for a week. And with three of us, we should be able to finish quickly."

"If we make meals on a rotating schedule, the kids can bring them over after school," Julie suggested to the other women. "We'd each only need to make two. And it's only for Beverly, so it shouldn't be too difficult."

"Agreed."

"I've got spaghetti in the slow cooker for tonight," Debra said. "I'll add extra pasta to the pot and then Tony can grab it when he's finished his chores."

"Let's go!" Amanda said eagerly.

"I'll call Beverly while you're heading over," Julie said. "To warn her," she added to the other women, who laughed.

The trio hurried to put their shoes on and head down the street. The women lived a couple doors down from Amanda and often sat on their front porch in nicer weather to talk to the kids when they were coming home from school.

They rang the doorbell and waved at the camera.

The lock whirred as it unlocked remotely, and they walked in.

Beverly tried to get up from the easy chair to greet them.

"Stay put," James said. "We're here to help, not make your life harder."

"I'll get along just fine," Beverly protested.

Amanda shook her head. "Just fine is not good enough." She looked at the boys. "I've got the dishes."

James nodded. "Where's Lavender?" he asked Beverly. "I'll take her for a walk."

"She's out back," Beverly said. "Thank you."

"Where's your vacuum?" Tony asked. When he was directed to the bathroom, he unhooked it from its charger and started it up, running it over the carpets in the main part of the house.

It took Amanda and Tony less time than James to finish their tasks, and they moved on to cleaning the bathroom.

"It looks like it's been a while since they did a thorough cleaning," Amanda whispered to Tony to avoid offending Beverly.

"I can't imagine any of those old ladies getting on their hands and knees to clean behind the toilet," Tony replied, wrinkling his nose. "It's not too bad, just really dusty."

"This is only the powder room. The main bathroom will probably be worse," Amanda said.

"Fun."

"Think how happy she'll be to have a clean house."

"I didn't say I wasn't going to do it," Tony replied.

Once they were finished, Amanda approached Beverly. "Is it alright if we clean the bedrooms and main bathroom?"

"If you insist, child. I have nothing to hide."

"Great!"

Tony got the vacuum again. This time, he opened doors to the rooms off the hallway, and Amanda hunted for the main bathroom, which was an ensuite off the biggest bedroom. She got started in the shower, the glass door covered in soap scum.

Tony joined her by the time she was cleaning the vanity, removing rust around the faucets with an old toothbrush she'd found under the sink.

"Did you notice something funny about this house?" he asked her quietly.

"They're called antiques," she teased.

He elbowed her in the ribs. "Not what I meant." He lowered his voice even further. "There's only one bedroom."

She cocked her head to the side. "I saw you cleaning the others."

He shook his head. "They don't have beds. One's a craft room that would have my mom in heaven; material and yarn in shelving on the walls, a sewing machine under the window, and a massive cutting board taking up the middle of the room."

"And the other?"

"An office slash library. There's an old Mac computer and a dot matrix printer, filing cabinets, and bookshelves full of books."

"Maybe the other bedrooms are downstairs?" Amanda suggested.

Tony pointed at the vanity she was cleaning, where three toothbrushes were lined up in a row. "Then why are their things up here?"

"I don't think they're sisters," Amanda said slowly.

Tony chuckled. "Seems unlikely."

"Susan and Mary are visiting their kids this week, though," she said. "In two different states."

"They must have met later in life," he said. "I've never heard of three people in love before."

"I think it's sweet." Amanda stretched her back. "It would be like living with your two best friends."

"Do you think the three of us will live together?" Tony asked absent-mindedly, and then flushed. "Not that we're in love."

She laughed. "I can't imagine living with anyone else."

"Me neither."

James appeared in the doorway. "Lavender's done her walk. I cleaned up the backyard too. You should swing by before school. I would, but I have swim practice every day."

"No problem," Tony said.

"We won't have to do a deep clean tomorrow, so it'll take less time," Amanda added. "And we can quiz each other on exam stuff while we walk her."

Tony pulled his vibrating phone from his back pocket. "Mom says I can come get dinner now. I'll be right back."

"I'm almost done here," Amanda said. "The toilet should be ready for a scrub."

"I've got it," James said. "You did a great job."

"Thanks!"

Amanda stripped off the cleaning gloves and placed them back where she'd found them under the sink. "We should dust tomorrow," she said, stretching. "Tony said there were bookcases in one of the smaller rooms."

"Good idea."

"I'm going to ask Beverly if she wants any yarn or something to occupy her."

Beverly did want things brought to her. "I've exhausted my attention span for movies and TV shows," she said. "There's a little table over there. Could you bring it closer to me? Excellent. A nice pile of books and some yarn would be lovely."

Amanda spent the next five minutes bringing a selection of books back and forth until Beverly had six that she said she was the most excited to read. The yarn was simpler; a bagful of navy blue yarn and a small baggie that contained crochet hooks, scissors and a yarn needle was all she wanted.

"This is going to be a sweater for Mary's grandson for Christmas," she said. "He's growing so fast, he'll be out of the one I made him last year by the time winter rolls around again."

"How old is he?"

"You three are fourteen?" When Amanda nodded, Beverly continued, "He's about a year or two older. He's packing on the muscle. Got real serious about weight lifting since January, and it's changed his whole body shape." She shook her head. "He's on the school football team and has a good chance at a scholarship in a few years if he doesn't kill himself on the field. I hope you two don't play football," she said, pinning Tony and James with glares.

"No ma'am," Tony said. "Soccer and baseball are my sports."

"I swim and play soccer," James added.

"Good for you. Much less dangerous," Beverly said.

"I brought you spaghetti for dinner," Tony said. "And Mrs. Lavallee asked if you had any preference for tomorrow."

Beverly's eyes filled with tears. "You're so kind to me."

"Hey, none of that," James said, alarmed.

"We're happy to help out," Amanda said.

Tony put the tupperware of food on the table beside her books, a fork from her kitchen beside it. "Did you need anything else? We'll come by around nine to walk Lavender again."

"If you'll just get my purse, I can pay—"

"No!" the trio exclaimed at the same time.

"If you pay us, we'll leave," Amanda said with a chuckle.

"Oh, but..."

"She's right," James said.

"It's what neighbors do," Tony added.

"Thank you," Beverly said softly.

Chapter Twenty-Three

Amanda

For the second time in a month, Amanda was arriving at the enormous house in Cape Cod. It was now owned by Glenn's parents, and they had gifted a week to them for their wedding and the Christmas holidays.

The white Christmas lights that decorated the outside of the house, combined with the dusting of snow on the roofs, made it look almost magical.

Her mother put her hand on her arm. "Are you sure this is the right place?" she asked, wonder in her voice.

"I know, right?"

The limo pulled up to the sweeping entry stairs and stopped. "We have arrived," the driver announced.

Everyone got out, but before they could head to the trunk to get their suitcases, the front door opened and Glenn came running out.

"Welcome, wedding party!" he exclaimed. "Head inside, there's warm apple cider and mulled wine on the stove. Don't mix them up." He winked at Cody, who grabbed Sophia's hand. "Carolina and Juliette are already here, and Rosalina is coloring in the family room." Juliette was a nanny that had been hired for the next couple days so that the parents wouldn't have to worry about their kids while participating in the wedding events. "Do you like to color?" he asked Cody, who buried his face in Sophia's leg without answering.

Tony chortled. "And here I thought you were good with kids."

"I *am*," Glenn muttered under his breath.

Adam picked Cody up. "He's a bit jet lagged. Don't take offense."

Glenn grinned. "Kids acclimatize in their own time. By the end of the week, he won't leave me alone."

"That's the dream," Adam said, following Sophia and Travis inside.

Tony and James had managed to unload two suitcases before Glenn got to them. "Stop that," he said. "All you have to do is tell my men whose bag is whose, and they'll bring them to the right rooms."

"Fancy," Ava said, eyeing the three helpers that had followed Glenn out of the house.

"It's a wedding," Glenn said. "It's supposed to be."

"That's ours," Amanda said when their bag was picked up.

Her mom gasped. "You can't share a room!"

"Mom," Amanda said with a chuckle. "We've seen each other naked before."

Julie waved her hands in the air. "It's bad luck to see your fiancé the morning before the wedding!"

"Seriously?" James asked.

"Isn't that a bit old-fashioned?" Tony added.

"Do you want to risk it?" Julie retorted.

"Does that mean the boys can't sleep together either?" Amanda asked.

"Yes," Ava and Debra said in chorus.

"Fuck that shit," Tony said, shocking the mothers, and crossed his arms. "I want to get a good night's sleep."

"It's one night," Julie protested. "Just grab your pyjamas and suits for tomorrow from the suitcase and you can sleep in separate rooms."

"I knew I forgot something," Tony said, snapping his fingers.

"You forgot your suit?" Debra gasped.

"No, my pyjamas."

"That's my dress," Amanda said to the man carefully lifting a garment bag out of the trunk.

"You three are sleeping in separate rooms, and that's final," Julie said firmly. "Glenn?"

He nodded sheepishly. "Yes ma'am. Amanda's in the guest house, and I put the men in the two primary suites on the third floor."

Tony perked up. "There's only two rooms up there."

"If I have to sleep in the hallway between you, I will," Julie said with a glare. "Do you think I'm bluffing?"

"I was going to offer to share a room, but if you forgot your pyjamas..." Michael said with an amused glance at his son.

"To be perfectly honest, I'm not sure if we even have pyjamas in the house," Tony admitted cheerfully.

Glenn laughed. "Stop being a shit disturber. I thought that was my job. Come on in and get warmed up. Once Carolina's finished setting up, we'll head out for the bachelor party. I want to make sure she has everything she needs first."

Rather than go inside the house with their parents, the trio walked around the house to the massive gazebo where the wedding was going to take place the next day. It had been decorated with holly, pine, and fairy lights, and there were four massive free-standing heaters in the space, making it toasty warm. The view of the water was stunning.

"We can survive one night, right?" Amanda said. "We managed four years in college."

"That was before," Tony said glumly. "That month in California was the worst sleep I've ever had, and that's saying something. I'm tempted to stay up all night just so I don't have to sleep."

James laughed. "I understand the sentiment, but you'll want to be well rested for our wedding night."

Amanda tilted her head consideringly. "You say that like sex will be different once we're married."

"I'll have a husband and a wife," James said, his voice husky. "It will be different."

"Is that how it felt when your name change came in the mail?" she asked.

Tony and James exchanged heated glances. "Well, Mister James Carlson?" Tony asked teasingly. "Was sex different with you having my name?"

James shivered slightly, even though Amanda was overheating. "Yeah, it was."

"Do the parents know about the name change yet?" Amanda asked.

"I told mine," James said. "I wanted them to understand our reasons."

"And did they?"

"Of course."

"I haven't told mine yet," Tony admitted. "I thought it would be a nice surprise when we're announced. Adam agreed."

"That's why I haven't told mine either," Amanda said. "Although I know my mom is dying to ask what we're doing."

"She's making us sleep in separate rooms, she can wait until tomorrow at eleven," Tony muttered.

"Hey! It's not just mine. Your moms were just as insistent."

"What is up with that?" James said. "The dads didn't say a word."

"Either they agreed and the moms were saying everything they wanted to, or they didn't and they didn't want to get in trouble," Amanda said.

"You know," Tony said thoughtfully, "I don't remember Adam and Sophia being separated before their wedding. Do you?"

"We left the strip club and got into the limos to head back to the hotel," James said, narrowing his eyes as he remembered. "All the couples were making out, barely keeping clothes on."

"I only remember the two of you," Amanda said. "I could barely walk, I was so turned on. I think Tony carried me into the elevator?"

"Yes, and Adam and Sophia were right behind me," James said. "They got off on the fourth floor—"

"—And we got off on the fifth," Tony continued. "It's possible the parents were lying in wait for them—"

"—but we'd have to ask," Amanda finished.

They exchanged looks, and as one, turned to the house.

"Adam!" Tony bellowed when they entered.

"Dude," Adam said, sticking a finger in his ear as he walked out of the kitchen. Travis's cries echoed down the hall.

"It's a big house," Tony said unapologetically. "Did Mom make you and Sophia separate the night before your wedding?"

Adam looked guilty. "We were supposed to," he whispered. "We told the moms that we would, but I snuck out of her room at the horrid time of five in the morning."

"That's it," Tony said, shaking his head. "You two are happily married. That superstition is bullshit. I'm sneaking out."

"Me too," James said. "We'll meet in your room, sunshine."

"Thank goodness," she sighed, relieved.

"Time to go!" Glenn announced, trailed from the kitchen by the fathers. "Say goodbye! We'll see you tomorrow morning. Anything you need, the staff will see to. They've got some rosé on ice for you ladies to help you relax before your boudoir session." He winked at Amanda.

"Have a good time," Tony said, kissing Amanda's cheek.

"Love you," James added, brushing his lips over her forehead.

Amanda stood in the empty foyer, the men's voices echoing outside until the limo door slammed shut.

She shook off her annoyance at their mothers with a heavy sigh and headed into the kitchen.

"There you are!" Carolina exclaimed, greeting her with air kisses. "We're ready to get started now. We will be using the library and adjoining office as our change room and photography studio. Nobody will be allowed in but us, and Juliette if Travis needs feeding." She nodded at Sophia. "It is a positive space. We only compliment, never criticize. Every body is beautiful and we are here to celebrate ours."

"Here here!" Ava cheered, raising her glass in the air.

"I usually take a photo of all participants together, but since you're family, I will stick to individual shots. You will each receive two professionally edited images of your choice, and the bride will have one bonus shot. Did you all want to be in the room together while I'm taking the photos, or would you rather one at a time?"

The women exchanged shy glances.

"I would feel more comfortable as a group," Sophia said first. "You said it's a positive space, and I could use the confidence."

Debra took her hand. "I am here for you."

Sophia smiled at her mother-in-law. "Thank you."

"If you could all grab your outfits from your rooms and come to the office, we can get started. I have robes for each of you while you wait for your turn." Carolina turned to one of the staff. "We'll be needing the snacks in the library, please."

"Yes, ma'am," he said with a little bow.

"By the way," Carolina said, grabbing Amanda's hand as she passed. "Thank you for everything you did with Rosalina."

"I didn't do anything."

"You were there when I needed you. I know the file was closed and everything's good, but..." She took a deep breath. "I was panicking, and you were there. Thank you."

"You're welcome."

Amanda quickly retrieved the small white bag with the lingerie she had bought for the occasion. When she returned, everyone else was waiting nervously. There was a screen in the corner for them to change behind, and a row of silk robes hanging in front of the window.

Carolina ushered the staff out of the office and closed the door behind him. "Time to get changed," she said firmly. "Any hair or make-up you want done, do it now, but it's not necessary. Natural generally shows up better on camera."

"I didn't even think of make-up," Amanda admitted.

"Not necessary." Carolina opened the door to the library. "Come on through when you're ready."

Ava gripped the lime green lace fabric she was playing with and squared her shoulders. "I'll go first." She grabbed a robe and stepped behind the screen.

"I'm not going to wait for the screen," Amanda said. "That'll take too long."

Sophia chuckled. "If you're going to change here, so will I."

They grabbed robes and moved over to two chairs, getting ready with politely averted eyes.

Amanda slipped into the soft silk lace thong and matching halter baby-doll. It was mostly sheer, not hiding anything, and she wondered what her mother was going to think of it. Before she could second-guess herself, she wrapped the robe around her body, tying the belt around her waist.

"What color are you wearing?" Sophia asked.

"White," Amanda said. "It's what I'll wear tomorrow night too."

"Not under your dress?"

"It's a halter." She showed the collar around her neck. "My dress would show it."

"Ah, I didn't think of that."

"What about you?"

"Dark purple." Sophia blushed. "It's one of Adam's favorite colors on me."

"What about you, Mom?" Amanda asked.

"I've got dark blue," she said from behind the screen. "I'm really nervous, ladies."

"It looked amazing on the hanger," Debra said encouragingly. "It'll look great on you too."

Julie stepped out, her robe tight around her body.

"I've got burgundy," Debra said, twirling the silky babydoll around her finger. "And black panties." She winked.

"Nice!" Amanda said encouragingly. "Get changed and then we're ready!"

"I think I need more wine," Julie said, grabbing the bottle on the desk and pouring a healthy amount in her glass. She drank half of it in one gulp. "I haven't been this nervous to take off my clothes since my wedding night."

Amanda choked on a laugh. "Mom!"

"This is a safe space," Sophia reminded her. "We're family, remember."

Julie hugged her. "We are, aren't we?"

"You three raised me," Amanda said to them, once Debra had returned from behind the screen. "Each of you is a mother figure to me. I'm so lucky to have three sets of parents."

"Oh, darling," Ava cooed, petting her hair. "I've always thought of you as my daughter. To gain you as one for real is a dream come true."

"We will really be sisters after tomorrow," Sophia said. "I'm so happy for you!"

"Shall we begin?" Debra asked, ushering them into the library.

Julie grabbed the bottle of wine and brought it with them. "Anyone else need a top up?"

Everyone held out their glasses except Sophia, who had water.

"A toast!" Ava said. "To women, to family, and to loving ourselves!"

"Here here!" Amanda cheered.

"Who would like to go first?" Carolina asked.

"I will," Ava said, shedding her robe to reveal the lime green cut-out bodysuit that fit her body to perfection.

Amanda whistled. "Yes, Mama!"

The other women clapped.

"Wonderful," Carolina said, leading Ava over to a large tufted cushion. "We're going for sensual, sexy, and tasteful. If you're feeling too porny in a pose, dial it back."

Ava laughed. "I'm not sure where to begin."

"Not a problem." Carolina got on her knees, perpendicular to the camera, and arched her back, hands on the cushion. "Start with this, and we'll go from there."

While Ava got into the position, Carolina returned to her camera. "Beautiful," she murmured. She showed Ava the picture, and her eyes widened.

"That's what I look like?"

"Stunning, aren't you?" Carolina asked with a grin.

"Yes!"

Julie cheered. "Get it, you sexy woman, you!"

Carolina walked Ava through pose after pose for fifteen minutes, complimenting her every step of the way. At the end, everyone clapped for Ava, and Carolina took a drink of water.

"Who's next?" she asked.

Sophia stood up. "I would like to go now, please."

"Go ahead, dear," Debra said.

Sophia nervously untied the rope around her waist, revealing a lace bra and panty set.

The other women cheered heartily.

"It looks alright?" Sophia asked hesitantly.

"Your boobs are filling that bra to perfection," Amanda said admiringly.

"That's what happens when you breastfeed," Sophia replied wryly, heading over to the cushion. She sat backwards on it, before lying back and giving the camera an eyeful of her cleavage.

"Yes!" Carolina said excitedly. "Stunning." She clicked the shutter as Sophia moved through several poses.

The office door opened, and Travis's cries preceded Juliette's appearance in the door.

"I'm so sorry," she apologized. "I just changed him, and I tried everything, but I think he wants his mom."

Sophia went to her and took the baby, who hiccuped and tried to bury his face in her chest. "It's alright. I've got him."

"If you want me to come get him later, let me know," Juliette said, heading back into the main part of the house.

"Sorry," Sophia said over Travis's whimpers.

"Don't be," Carolina said. "We can come back to you."

"Or you can continue with her," Amanda suggested. "There's something beautiful about feeding your baby, and doing it in lingerie?"

"Do you want to give that a shot?" Carolina asked.

"Sure." Sophia sat on the cushion and adjusted Travis until he latched onto her breast, suckling greedily. His tiny hand reached up, patting her collarbone. She smiled down at him and the shutter clicked.

"What do you think?" Carolina asked, showing her the picture.

Sophia visibly melted. "Oh, I love that. I've got some more ideas for poses?"

"I'm ready when you are."

After Sophia, it was Julie's turn. She turned an adorable shade of pink when she stripped off her robe.

"Go Mom!" Amanda cheered.

Ava put her fingers between her lips and whistled sharply, startling Travis.

"I'm going to need suggestions," she said shyly to Carolina.

"Why don't we start at the book ladder?" Carolina suggested. "Lean against it, back arm up higher, yes, and pop your foot... Perfect." She lifted her camera and took the picture. "There, see?"

Julie flushed. "Do you think Paul will like that?" she asked her friends.

"I think Paul would crawl on his knees to catch a glimpse of you in this," Debra said enthusiastically while gesturing at Julie. "Wear it tonight." She winked.

Julie grinned. "Maybe I will."

"Yes, Mom!" Amanda exclaimed, snapping her fingers.

Carolina helped Julie through the rest of her poses, and then Debra took the floor. She tossed her robe with a flourish to cheers from the others before taking a seat on the cushion, arching her back.

"Beautiful," Carolina said, snapping the picture.

"I don't know what else to do," Debra admitted when Carolina waited for her to move to a new position, chuckling with everyone else.

At last it was Amanda's turn. She swallowed hard, nervous all of a sudden. She'd been naked in front of dozens of people, even fucked in front of them, but she was shy to show off her lingerie in front of her moms and sister.

"Ohhhh, darling," Julie breathed once her robe was off.

"Damn, girl," Sophia said.

"Lucky boys," Debra said with a low whistle and a lift of her glass.

"It's okay then?" Amanda asked, playing with the hem of the babydoll.

"Honey, it's stunning on you," Ava reassured her. "Relax and let Carolina take pictures of you."

Carolina led her over to the center of the room. "You really do look beautiful," she murmured quietly. "Bridal. I'm envious."

"I don't mean to rub it in," Amanda said apologetically.

"You're not. Tony was never mine. I just couldn't see it. I do now. He looks at you and James like you're the only stars in his sky."

"That's a romantic notion." Amanda sank to her knees on the floor, placing her hands on her body the way Carolina directed her. "Like this?"

Carolina looked through the camera and huffed a laugh. "Pretend the camera is one of the boys. Give me your bedroom eyes."

Amanda flushed and lowered her gaze.

"Come on, girl!" Sophia encouraged her. "Remember, your guys are going to be looking at these pictures. You want them hard as rocks, don't you?"

Amanda giggled, her amusement winning over her embarrassment. "I mean, that's not normally a problem."

"It could be in the future," Ava said, taking on her 'doctor' voice. "Chances of erectile dysfunction increases with age."

"Yeah, but that doesn't have anything to do with how I look," Amanda pointed out.

"Are you going to let three middle-aged women out-sexy you?" her mother demanded. "In *that* outfit?"

Amanda scoffed. "I hope I'm half as sexy as you when I'm your age."

"Earn it. You've got this."

Funnily enough, her mother's pep talk helped get her out of her head, and she was able to imagine that James and Tony were behind the camera.

"Jesus," Carolina muttered, snapping the shutter. "I'm glad I don't have film, because it would be on fire."

Amanda bit her lip to stop the laugh, and brought her hands to her head, threading through her hair and cocking her hip.

"Great. Okay, you're going to rotate ninety degrees to keep the backdrop of the bookcases. Perfect. How's your flexibility these days?"

"Better than ever."

"Arch backward until you're lying on the ground. Take your time. I'll grab as many shots as I can, but the slower you go, the more angles I can get."

It was a challenge. Not only did she have to control her fall, when the guys usually helped her, but she had to keep her hands soft and her face seductive. Once she was flat on her back, she laughed. "I hope you got something out of that. I don't think I could do it again."

"We'll go through them together after," Carolina said. "Roll onto your stomach and arch your ass in the air. No, more than that. Up on your knees a bit. Yes, there. Good." She squatted down close to the ground. "Look over your shoulder at me. Seductive, not a death glare. Yes, that's better."

Amanda tried not to laugh at the description of the look she'd given Carolina. She wasn't sure what she'd done differently, but imagining the guys seemed to be working, so she would keep doing that.

"This pose is great, but I want the angle from the front, so please rotate again."

"Will I get to do the one that Sophia did first on the cushion?" Amanda asked as she obediently followed directions. "That was stunning. I don't have the cleavage for it, though."

"We will get to the cushion after you finish on the floor," Carolina promised. "Just a few more. Tilt your head and stretch out your arm as if you're reaching for the camera. Lovely. Okay, we can move to the cushion."

First they did Sophia's position, and then Carolina had her doing a strange wide straddle with her heels popped up. She showed her the image afterwards, and Amanda made a mental note to trust Carolina's artistic eye without question moving forward because she looked fucking hot.

After they finished her photoshoot, Carolina sent them to get dressed while she hooked up her camera and laptop to the projector in the library.

Once dressed, Sophia brought the milk-drunk Travis out to Juliette to put to bed.

"Thank you for including us tonight," Julie said, hugging Amanda.

"Of course!" she replied, confused. "I had fun, once I got over my nerves. Thanks for helping."

"I'm glad it did." Julie played with her hands. "This wasn't easy for me, to see you all grown up. But you're an adult now, and though you've been living together for two years, marriage is a huge step."

"We're thrilled to have you officially be a part of our family," Debra said.

"Sometimes I look at you and see the little girl who skinned her knee on our driveway and came running over to me with tears dripping off your cheeks," Ava said. "Do you remember that?"

Amanda shook her head.

The older woman smiled. "You were around three years old. You let me bandage your knee but only once James was holding you."

"Even when you were babies, you two were calmer when you were next to each other," Julie said. "We often would put you to sleep in the same crib for your naps, and once you were crawling, we'd come in to find you cuddled up together, even if you were placed at opposite ends."

"That's so sweet," Debra said, putting her hand to her heart. "We didn't get Tony until he was older, but we saw how he and James gravitated to each other when they had sleepovers at our house."

"Thank goodness we're all cuddlers!" Amanda said with a laugh.

"Let's go look at the pictures," Ava said, when Sophia returned.

Carolina had a blank image up when they walked in. "Anyone hungry? Need more wine?"

"I could use a little more," Debra said, and the other mothers agreed.

"We'll go in the order the pictures were taken. I'll star your favorites to narrow them down," Carolina said.

The first picture popped up on the screen and Ava's jaw dropped. "That's me!" she exclaimed. "How do I look so good?"

"Because you're damn sexy!" Debra cheered. "Xavier is a lucky man, and he'd better show his appreciation for you."

"He certainly will," Ava said with a nod.

Amanda bit back a laugh and leaned over to Sophia. "It's kinda funny to hear my moms talk about seducing my dads."

"No weirder for them to know that we're doing the same to their sons," Sophia replied with a wink.

"Our boys are good to you though, right?" Debra said, half leaning over Julie to talk to them.

"You don't have to worry about that," Sophia rushed to reassure her. "Adam is a sweetheart."

Debra shook her head. "That's not what I meant. They're *good* to you?"

Amanda couldn't hold in her laughter. "Are you asking if we're *satisfied* by them?"

Debra nodded enthusiastically. "I think I may have had a bit too much to drink," she said with a giggle, toppling into Julie's chest. "Your boobs are fantastic, Jules. I wish I had bigger ones."

"Your boobs are great too," Julie said. "You don't have to worry about wearing a bra. If I don't, they slap against each other when I turn too fast."

All the women were giggling now.

"I know what you mean," said Ava. "I look fantastic when I wear a bra, but take it off, and it's sag city."

Debra made a sad face. "But you're so nice to hug! Are yours sensitive? When Michael plays with mine, it's like: okay, move on to something that actually does something, please."

Torn between amusement, horror, and fascination, Amanda listened to the older women complain about what their husbands needed to focus more on in bed.

"So what about you?" Debra asked, turning back to the girls.

Sophia blushed. "Adam listens when I tell him where I like to be touched. He doesn't have an ego in bed."

Everyone turned to look at Amanda. "I'm satisfied," she said.

Her mother threw a pillow at her. "More detail than that!"

Amanda choked on her laughter. "How much is too much? There's never been an issue with either of them finding my erogenous zones."

"Do they fight over you?"

"Never."

"How do you decide who to have sex with first?"

Carolina coughed lightly to cover a laugh, and Amanda rolled her eyes at her. "Sometimes we play a game, other times it's just proximity." She shrugged.

"But who was your very first?"

"To give me an orgasm or to fuck me?" Amanda asked, trying to shock them.

"Both!"

"Oh dear," she muttered. "It was a wild afternoon of debauchery. I could barely remember my own name by the end of it."

Sophia grinned slyly. "But you knew theirs."

"Well yeah," Amanda grinned back at her. "I kept using them over and over and over."

"Do they have sex with each other now?"

"Absolutely. They're making up for lost time." Amanda squirmed a little in her seat as she remembered that morning. "It's so hot."

"And you don't feel left out?"

Amanda chuckled. "That is the number one question we get asked. No, I never feel left out, even when they're absorbed in each other, because I know that they'll focus all their attention on me the instant I ask. I love that they love each other as much as I love them. Watching them together is as amazing as being part of it."

"You almost make me want to try a threesome," Debra said, making Julie raise her eyebrows. "What? Like you weren't thinking it! But I don't like to share."

"It's not for everyone, and that's okay," Amanda said. Then she added mischievously, "You can always get a dildo if you want to feel what it's like."

The women gasped in unison, some giggles escaping.

Sophia admitted, "I convinced Adam to try that. It took a lot of time to get me ready to take both."

"For sure," Amanda agreed, nodding.

"I have a question," Ava said, resting her elbows on her knees. "Do you think you and James would have ended up together if Tony hadn't moved here?"

"The number two question," Amanda said with a wry twist to her lips. "I can't answer that. Tony moved here before my romantic feelings towards them both began. I didn't fall in love with them one at a time, but both together, and who we were as a trio. It took college for me to see my love for what it was and to gather my courage to approach them to give this a try." She bit her lip. "I have to be honest with you, this summer was getting rough. Tony was shutting down, and so was James. I was really worried about them and what would happen to us. When Tony went to California, they left things on a bad note. They weren't *talking* to each other. I finally got James to open up to me about his true feelings for Tony and his fears that I would be upset. When Tony came home, they finally worked through their emotions together. I don't think we'd be getting married tomorrow if they hadn't."

"Men can be stubborn," Ava said.

Debra snorted. "You have no idea."

As they had talked, Carolina had continued showing them the images.

"You know what?" Ava said. "These are all stunning, and they're not even edited yet. I want all of mine. What about you ladies?"

The others all nodded enthusiastically.

"That's settled then. We'll pay extra for the lot."

"You're an extremely talented photographer, dear," Debra said. "You not only made us feel comfortable but sexy too!"

"You *are* sexy," Carolina protested. "I just took pictures."

"Finished emptying the last box of clothes," Amanda said, tossing it at the top of the stairs on her way into the kitchen. "Why do we have so many?"

"Because there's three of us?" Tony said, raising his eyebrows.

"Yeah, but I don't plan on wearing them at home very often."

James looked up from the dish he was unwrapping. "You're wearing them now."

"Yeah, but if I strip, we won't get the kitchen unpacked. And I really want to be all moved in."

"Good incentive," Tony said. "Why don't you help fill the dishwasher. It'll make things go faster."

"Many hands make light work," Amanda said cheerfully, joining them near the sink. "What's first on your list of things to do after we get rid of the boxes?"

"Christen the couch, I think," Tony said thoughtfully. "James?"

"I'm of the mind to play through a fantasy," he said. "We've got the time."

"What kind?" Amanda asked.

"Have you ever had a fantasy that you've thought was too much or too far? What's the most depraved desire you've ever had?" he asked her.

She swallowed hard. "I don't think I can say," she whispered, blushing and averting her eyes.

"Oh God, the mental images that just flipped through my mind," Tony said, gripping the counter to stay upright. "Please tell us. What do you want to try?"

"I don't know if I'll like it, but..." Amanda sucked in a deep breath. "Being forced?"

"Forced to what?" Tony asked, confused.

"No, I get it," James said, holding his hand up to stop Tony. "You want us to pretend to be strangers and force you to have sex with us?"

"Yes?"

He chuckled. "I need more consent than that. This has the potential to be a rough scene. How far do you want to go? Knife play? Bondage? Just slapped around a little?"

Her breathing came a little quicker at each suggestion. "All of that sounds good. I'd like to try it."

"Fuck," Tony said, pupils wide with desire. "That's so hot."

"Look at me, sunshine," James ordered. When she met his gaze, he continued, "Green, yellow, red are the standard words. If I get even the faintest hint that you're not enjoying yourself and you don't use your words, the scene stops immediately, clear? I will not cut you. Blood play, unless you're on your period—" he flashed a grin, "—is not on the table. Even if I threaten it in the scene, you are safe, do you understand?"

She nodded.

"The point of this is to heighten excitement, not scare you." He rubbed his chin as he thought. "Or are you planning on fighting back or being a brat? Or are you going to put up a semblance of protest?"

"I... I'm not sure?" She chewed her lip.

"You're usually a bit of a brat when we order you around," Tony supplied helpfully.

James nodded. "I agree. We'll keep the knife out of play until you're tied up so you don't accidentally hurt yourself." He handed her a plate. "After we're done in here, you're going to go get changed into clothes that you don't mind if they're destroyed." He cupped her chin in his hand after she'd put the dish away. "Don't be a brat and put on our clothes. Use your own."

Amanda grinned. "That hadn't occurred to me."

"It might have once you got up there," he muttered.

"Actually, I have a ratty old shirt that I brought with me for yard work," Tony offered. "If you can't find one of your own, you can use it."

"The one that says 'My other ride is your mother'?" she asked with a chuckle.

"Glenn thinks he's so funny," Tony says cheerfully. "That's the one."

"I noticed it was a little threadbare when I put it away," Amanda agreed. To James, she asked, "Pants too?"

"And underthings," he said seriously. "I plan on cutting everything off your body."

She shivered.

"Good?" he asked, handing her the last plate.

"Very good," she said breathlessly.

"Go get ready. Tony and I'll finish up here and then take the boxes out to the recycling. We'll ring the doorbell and that will start the scene. What are your words?"

"Green, yellow, and red," Amanda repeated.

"If you tell us *no*, we will not listen. Only your safe words will stop us. You've asked to be forced, and we will do that until you are sobbing for mercy. Even then, we will continue until *we* are satisfied. Do you understand?"

"I understand. I want that."

"I could cut glass, I'm so hard," Tony muttered. "Fuck, Amanda."

She giggled a little. "I assume no kisses?"

"Not as such," James said, shaking his head. "I'll lay claim, but it'll be possessive, not passionate."

"Kiss now?"

"Absolutely." James pulled her into his arms and gently joined their mouths as if trying to make up for the violent scene in advance.

She clung to him, drawing his plush bottom lip between her teeth and flicking over it with her tongue.

He growled and pulled back, panting hard. "Don't test my patience, sunshine."

She smiled innocently at him. "It was just a kiss."

"It's never just a kiss with you," Tony said, spinning her to face him. "You draw us in until we forget everything else." He pressed a finger to her lips, and she licked it. He smiled before affecting a stern expression. "Don't forget your words, and we'll have fun this afternoon."

"I won't forget," she promised.

"Good." He kissed her upturned lips lightly. "Go get ready," he said, patting her ass.

She padded quickly to the stairs, turning and giving the guys a wave before she ran up to the second floor.

Tony's shirt was the obvious choice, and Amanda grabbed a pair of white cotton panties that she hated. Then she perused her bra collection. She'd gone through and gotten rid of all the stretched out and old ones before she'd moved, and she was loath to lose any of these.

The front door banged closed, letting her know that her time was short. Her heart pounded in excitement.

She decided to go bare under the shirt.

Taking her cue from Tony, she grabbed an old pair of her pyjama pants that were getting ratty along the hem and pulled them on just in time to hear the doorbell ring. She grabbed a hair elastic from the top of the dresser and hurried down the stairs while twisting her hair up into a messy bun.

At the door, she took a moment to breathe, reminding herself that they were going to pretend to be strangers. She peeked through the eyehole to see them standing on the other side of the door, arms crossed and looking bored.

"Hi, how can I help you?" she asked, pulling the door open.

"Hi yourself," Tony said, giving her a once over that made her wet. He leaned on the door frame, showing off his tattoos. "Saw the moving truck the other day, and wanted to welcome you to the neighborhood." He grinned at her, but there was something dangerous in it that made her mouth dry.

"Manners," James said, and introduced them, using their real names. "If you ever need anything, we're more than happy to offer our services."

"Actually, there's a drip under the sink that I'm worried about," Amanda said brightly. "Do you know anything about plumbing?"

"I wouldn't mind getting a closer look at your plumbing," Tony said, his tone suggestive.

"Oh, thank you!" she said breathlessly. "It's the kitchen sink. Shoes off please."

They followed her into the house, James closing and locking the door behind him. The click of the lock almost sounded ominous, but it made her insides quiver with need.

"The kitchen?" James asked, getting in her space. He moved a curl she'd missed behind her ear and she gasped at the light touch. He smirked at her, a hardness in his eyes she'd never seen before.

"Th— This way," she stammered, turning and leading them up the stairs to the main floor. She regretted not choosing short shorts, but could feel their gaze like a brand on her ass anyways.

Tony whistled when he got to the top of the stairs. "Nice place. I like the kitchen island. Very sturdy."

"I haven't had the chance to use it yet, other than to rest the boxes on," she admitted. "I look forward to rolling out cookie dough on it, though. All that space!"

"Show me this leak," James said, opening the cabinet under the sink.

She bent over and pointed to one of the connectors. "It gets wet around here whenever I turn it on," she said, proud of her word-play.

Tony coughed behind her to disguise a laugh, and she preened a little.

"I see," James said. "It could probably use a little tightening. Do you have a wrench?"

"Umm..." She couldn't remember where they'd put the tools. "I have one around here somewhere."

She headed for the cabinet near the back door, which seemed like the most logical place. She was right, and retrieved a wrench for James, who laid on his back, his head under the sink.

"Perfect, doll," he said, taking it from her. He pretended to tighten the screw. "Turn it on."

"But what if you get wet?" she asked.

"Then I'll have more to fix."

She turned the tap on and then off again before bending over. "Did that work?"

"It looks great." James got up and handed her the wrench.

"Thank you so much!" she said cheerfully. "I wasn't strong enough to get it." She returned the wrench to the toolbox, and when she turned around, James was *right there* in her face.

"Now we should discuss the matter of payment," he murmured, tracing her face with a finger.

"I can give you money," she said, eyes wide.

"Come on, that's not very neighborly," Tony drawled, coming up beside them. "We do you a favor, you do one for us."

"Like what?" Amanda asked, trying not to rub her legs together for friction. "I can make you cookies?"

"I think you know what we want," James said, his voice dark. "You're not as innocent as you're pretending."

"Your body knows what we want," Tony added with a grin and a pinch of his fingers over her nipple.

She gasped and tried to slap his hand away, but James was faster, catching her wrists up in one hand and holding them over her head.

Tony lifted her shirt, balling it up and stuffing it in her mouth. "Fucking gorgeous tits," he said, groping them. "As soon as I saw you, I knew I had to get you naked."

Amanda writhed, trying to remember that she was supposed to be getting away from them. Tony's harsh treatment was a good reminder. She managed to spit the shirt out and said, "No! Let me go!"

James chuckled harshly. "We won't be letting you go until we've had our fun with you. Every time you see us in the neighborhood, you'll remember today."

She twisted, her wrists suddenly free, and bolted from between them.

Tony caught her and pressed her face-first into the island. "We can do this the easy way or the hard way," he told her. "But we're bigger and stronger than you. You're getting fucked by both of us, whether you play along or not. So what's it going to be, angel? Are you going to cooperate?"

"No!" she cried, bucking against him.

He ground his cock against the seam of her ass. "Feel how your body gets me hot," he whispered in her ear, his hand pressing her head to the counter. "Don't you want this cock buried inside your sweet cunt?"

She breathed harshly for a second before saying, "No!"

"That's really too bad," James said, slowly taking off his belt where she could see it. "Bring her," he ordered Tony. "She's got a home gym at the front of the house. We'll give her a workout she won't soon forget."

Tony tossed her over his shoulder, keeping her immobile.

She beat at his back with her fists, but all he did was chuckle and slap her ass hard enough to sting.

"This one's feisty," he informed James upon entering the room.

"All the more fun to break," James replied. "Put her on the mat. Might as well make sure she's comfortable, since she'll be there for a while."

They chuckled darkly at that, and Tony bent to put her down.

The instant she was on her back, she flipped over and started crawling for the door.

Tony was closest, grabbing her legs and hauling her towards him. "None of that, angel. You're gonna hurt my feelings. I'm a handsome guy. You should be thrilled to be getting with me."

"Flip her over. We're going to have to pin her down somehow."

"Seems pretty flexible," Tony said. "Maybe those barbells over her ankles?"

"I like the way you're thinking," James said. "She's got a good bit of muscle on her thighs, so I'll make sure to load them up."

"No!" Amanda shrieked, trying to push Tony away.

"Maybe get her hands tied up first?" Tony said conversationally.

"Here." James tossed his belt over. It landed with a *clink* beside her head.

Using his weight to pin her body down, Tony managed to wrangle her arms over her head, tying them with the belt and linking them to the base of the home gym. He pressed on her fingertip to check for circulation and nodded when it reacted properly.

James had managed to trap her left leg and was working on her right by the time Tony released her. He cupped Amanda's face. "You'll have fun," he told her.

She shook her head, a tear escaping one eye.

He wiped it away with a thumb and brought it to his lips. He grinned. "Tastes sweet."

"We forgot something," James said once he finished weighing her down.

"What's that?" Tony asked.

"We didn't strip her first."

"Hmm." They looked down at the girl spread-eagled in front of them consideringly.

"I saw a knife set on the counter. We could cut her clothes off," Tony suggested.

"I like the way you think." James left the room.

Amanda whimpered. "Please," she whispered.

"I told you that all you had to do was cooperate," Tony told her. "Now look at what we have to do. Not that you don't look fucking hot like this. Hang on." He squatted down and yanked her shirt up again, exposing her breasts. "Fuck yeah," he breathed.

James returned at that point, a knife in his hands. "Okay doll, you know how sharp this is. No wiggling, got it? I don't want to cut more than material."

He knelt between her thighs, pressing the flat of the knife over a nipple. "It's nice and cold, isn't it?" he asked, chuckling when she tried to flinch away from it. He switched it to the other side and grinned. "Look how tight her nipples are, Tony. She's loving this."

"Hell yes," Tony said. "See, angel? We'll make it feel good for you if you don't fight us."

James rested the knife on her belly and used both hands to grope her breasts, plucking hard at the tight buds.

"Want to see her cunt, man. Stop torturing me," Tony begged.

"I never could say no to you," James said, picking up the knife. He drew the point down the seam of her pants, the threads snapping as he cut through them. He put the knife back on her stomach and gripped the pant legs, giving her no warning when he yanked and the seam gave away.

"Such cute little innocent panties," Tony cooed. "All the better to see how wet you've made them. I can see from here how soaked you are. You want this. Stop fighting us."

"Do I cut these off of you?" James asked, a hard tone to his voice.

Amanda bit her lip. "Please don't," she begged.

"That sounds like a yes to me," James chuckled. He slipped the blade along her thigh, the sharp edge away from her skin, until the waistband was completely on the knife. He pulled up hard, snapping the elastic in half. He repeated the action, emotionless, on the other side, leaving her sex covered by the scraps of her underwear. "Do you want the honors?" he asked Tony.

"I'm not going to be able to hold back once I see her," Tony warned. "You fixed her sink. Shouldn't you get first dibs?"

"You're right," James said. "Put this away, please?" He flipped the knife in the air, catching it by the flat of the blade and offering the handle to Tony.

"Please don't do this!" Amanda sobbed.

"Those cries might make Tony hard, but I prefer silence, got it?" James growled. He ripped her underwear away from her body and then stared, a grin forming on his face. "You're so fucking turned on by this, doll." He chuckled. "And here you were pretending you didn't want it." He unzipped his pants and pulled out his cock, slapping it against her clit a couple times, the wet smacks echoing in the room. "I think this pussy is going to be the best I ever had," he said, aiming true and sinking into her. "Oh fuck, you're hugging me with everything you got, doll," he gasped.

Amanda's eyes rolled back in her head. After being tossed around and edged, she'd been dying to get one of them inside her. She almost came just from penetration.

James started up a quick rhythm, hovering over her and refusing to pay any attention to her clit. "I'm going to fill you up with my cum," he muttered. "You're going to take every last drop, suck it deep inside you. And then Tony'll give you even more."

She gasped for air, the force of his thrusts knocking the breath from her lungs. "Oh God," she said, belatedly adding, "No!" at the end.

He smirked down at her. "You're not going to come this time. You're going to be a good little cum dump for me. Fuck..." His head hung down and his hips stuttered as he came. Panting heavily, he stayed within her, his cock twitching. "That was just what I needed." He claimed her mouth, biting at her lips and sweeping his tongue inside her mouth deeper than usual, exerting dominance.

Finally he got off of her, pushing back onto his knees.

"She's gushing with you," Tony said admiringly, taking James's place. He stuck his fingers inside her and scissored them open. Pearly white cum bubbled between them, overflowing down her slit and into her butt crack. "Fucking beautiful," he said, pushing his fingers in deeper and pulling out more cum. He used it to lube up his fingers as he circled around her ass.

"No!" Amanda cried, shaking her head.

"This is what I want," he growled, pressing in. "And I'm going to take it."

"Nononono," she chanted as he started thrusting his fingers inside her.

He used his other hand to scoop more cum out and dribble it down for use as lube.

"This is going to feel amazing. You're loosening up like you were meant to take cock up your ass." He raised his head, looking for his friend. "Help me flip her over. I need her ass-up."

James nodded and easily lifted the barbells that had held her legs immobile while Tony rolled on a condom.

The instant she was freed, she tried to scramble away, but she was still tied by her hands, so she didn't make it far.

"I guess she's ready," Tony chuckled darkly. He pinned her legs with his, pushing her head against the ground with one hand. He guided his cock, taking her in a relentless push. "Goddamn, her ass is like a vise," he gasped. He started pounding into her, his thighs slapping against hers on each inward thrust.

"Oh God," Amanda cried, her cheek squished against the mat. She gripped the belt around her wrists. "Tony!"

He chuckled. "Angel, you keep calling my name like that and I'll think you actually do want this."

"Nooooooo!" she moaned at the reminder that they were in a scene, her breasts rubbing against the floor with each bounce and sending shockwaves directly to the pleasure centers of her brain.

"Need to feel you properly," Tony panted, pulling all the way out and ripping the condom off, throwing it aside. He tilted her hips up, forcing an unnatural arch in her back, and plunged in, lower this time. "Fuck, your pussy is a dream."

The squelching sounds coming from their coupling filled the air.

"Wanna feel you come on my cock," he groaned, reaching underneath her and pinching above her clit.

She shattered with a cry, tears streaming down her cheeks as the pain reacted like pleasure to her overstimulated brain.

"Fuck yes," Tony grunted, slamming his hips against hers as hard as he could and holding her tight against him while he pulsed inside her.

James undid his belt from her wrists. "Thanks for the great time, doll," he said, slapping her ass once Tony had pulled out.

"Maybe we'll do this again sometime," Tony said, getting up and pressing his toes against her pussy, making her whimper. "See you around."

They left her in a heap on the ground, still shaking from the aftershocks of her orgasm.

The front door slammed shut, and she weakly pulled herself upright, tugging the shirt down over her body. The sight of the discarded condom made her shiver. Her body ached from the pounding they had given it.

She bit her lip to stop its quivering, pressing her hands over her mouth.

Tony rounded the corner. She hadn't heard him come back up the stairs. "Darlin', can I touch you?" he asked gently, squatting down beside her.

She nodded, a sob escaping her, and he tucked her body against his. "I love you," he murmured, rocking her back and forth. "Did you forget your words? Did we go too far?"

"No, I didn't forget," she whispered. "I was so turned on. You treated me so... so harshly! And I got off on it, it was perfect. Exactly what I asked for. But now I can't stop shaking and I'm crying and—" She broke off. "What's wrong with me?"

"Nothing's wrong, darlin'. This is sub drop. Remember what it was like when we tied you up and teased you until you cried earlier this summer?"

She nodded and sniffed inelegantly.

"We took care of you afterwards. A massage, lots of cuddles, a bath. We're going to do that for you again. James is upstairs getting the tub ready for you right now. Do you want me to carry you?"

"Cradle?"

"I think I'd bang your feet, head, or both," he said, making her chuckle weakly. "How about reverse piggyback?"

"I'm dripping," she said quietly.

Tony whipped his shirt off over his head. "Put that against you. It'll clean."

"How did you know I wouldn't feel comfortable taking off my shirt?"

He gave her a long look. "Darlin', you just had your choices taken away from you, your body used and abused." He held up his hand when she opened her mouth to protest. "You asked for it and enjoyed it, I know. That doesn't negate the fact that your body thinks it just went through a traumatic incident. We just need it to catch up to your brain, okay? That's what aftercare is all about. Now let's get you into the tub and I'll massage that long setting shampoo into your hair. Does that sound nice?"

"God, I love you," Amanda said, leaning against his chest.

"James needs to hear that too. He's feeling a little guilty about how forceful he was with you."

She lifted her arms and wiggled her fingers. "Carry me."

"Anytime."

Chapter Twenty-Five

Tony

"You're not supposed to be in here!"

The shrill voice of his very soon to be mother-in-law pierced through his dreams, waking him abruptly.

"Fuck tradition," he mumbled. "Adam and Sophia are fine." He cuddled Amanda closer, hand sliding up to cover her breasts.

"Out!" Julie said, yanking the covers off from the bottom of the bed. "Oh my God!" she cried, clapping a hand over her eyes. "I thought you were joking about not having pyjamas!"

Tony chuckled sleepily. "Nope."

"Go *away*, Mom," Amanda groaned.

"You need to get your hair and make-up done," Julie said, now facing the wall. "You're getting married in five hours."

"Does it really take five hours to do all that?" James asked, his voice thick with sleep. "She looks beautiful to me just the way she is."

"You *would* think that." She half turned around to glare at them, but then remembered that they were naked and faced the wall again. "Can you *please* put something on?" she asked.

"I was planning on eating a long, leisurely breakfast first," Tony teased.

"You will not!"

"In deference to your time limit, I will endeavor to hurry," he said blithely. "But I suggest you leave the room unless you want to hear it."

"*Tony Carlson!*"

"No, you're right, you should probably head back to the main house." Even with her still standing at the foot of the bed, his cock was hardening. "I'm not bluffing."

She fled, to his relief.

"You're a menace," James said, chuckling.

"So I've been told," Tony replied with half a shrug, his hand moving between Amanda's legs to trace around her clit. "You didn't mind, did you, darlin'?" he asked, biting her shoulder and dipping his fingers inside her. "Fuck, you really didn't."

She rolled her hips with a moan and hooked her leg backwards over his thigh, trying to get him deeper. "Tony?" she gasped.

"Yeah, love?"

"Want your mouth on my clit."

"I love it when you tell me what you want," he said. They maneuvered themselves with the ease of familiarity until he was between her legs, her thighs over his shoulders. His fingers speared slickly inside her, getting coated with her arousal. Tearing his eyes away from the evidence of her desire, he latched onto her clit with enthusiasm.

Her back arched and she started chanting his name, the headiest sound in the world.

James groaned, and Tony re-evaluated his ranking of sexiest sounds. Using the hand that was wet, he reached over and encircled his soon-to-be husband's cock, stroking it in the same rhythm as his tongue.

"God, Tony," James groaned, hips thrusting up into his hand. "That's it."

"Kiss me, James!" Amanda whimpered, gripping Tony's hair with one hand.

Tony watched, his eyes half-closed in bliss while they made out sloppily. He couldn't help rubbing against the bed, the friction combined with the noises of his lovers almost sending him over the edge.

"Oh God," Amanda cried, breaking the kiss and holding his head tighter to her body. "Tony, make me come." Her voice got louder, repeating his name until she quaked under him, one heel digging into his back. "Inside me," she panted. "Need you now."

Not bothering to take her legs off his shoulders, Tony knelt and hauled her body down the bed, folding her in half and burying his cock in her warmth.

"Yes!" she shouted, arching as best as she could underneath him.

"Feed me your cock," Tony ordered James, who got to his knees over her head, holding his cock down for Tony to swallow.

The lingering flavor of Amanda's arousal on James's cock nearly made him come on the spot.

It was the pinpricks of pain from her fingernails digging into his shoulders that set him off, though.

Amanda followed after he slammed into the hilt, and James took a couple more thrusts before he pulsed down Tony's throat.

"I can't imagine a better way to start our wedding day," James said, pulling Tony up and plundering his mouth with a moan.

"I could have done without the abrupt wake-up," Amanda said from below them. She hummed happily. "I'm loving this view, but I should probably have a shower and get ready for the day."

The guys parted reluctantly, placing lingering kisses everywhere they could reach.

"I guess we should head to our own rooms for showers," James said.

"Although I just ate well, I could go for some carbs with the protein," Tony teased, rubbing his stomach.

"I think I spotted danishes in the fridge last night," James said thoughtfully.

"Can you bring me one?" Amanda asked plaintively.

"I'll get Julie to bring two when she comes back," James promised, dropping a kiss on her forehead.

Tony kissed her gently while he pulled out, both of them groaning at the loss. "We need to leave, or we'll end up following you into the shower, and then your mom will be *really* pissed," he said.

"Good plan." James got off the bed and headed for the clothes they'd left in a pile the night before. "Yours," he said, tossing Tony's underwear at him.

He caught them easily, but wrinkled his nose. "I really don't feel like putting these on."

"Go commando," James said with a shrug, throwing his jeans next. They fell short, landing on the edge of the bed.

Tony sighed. "I hate doing that in jeans, but it's better than day-old underwear."

"You should've brought a change with you," Amanda said, padding past him to the bathroom.

He swatted her ass lightly, and she shrieked playfully.

"We didn't go up to our rooms first. Told the others we were coming to say goodnight to you, and then just...didn't leave." Tony grinned. "How could we, when you opened the door wearing what nature gave you?"

Amanda laughed. "Well, now you'll have to deal with it." She disappeared into the bathroom.

"Fuck this, I'm just going to walk over naked," Tony grumbled, throwing the jeans on the floor again. "If we'd just been allowed to leave our clothes here, we wouldn't have this problem."

"I actually do kinda appreciate that we'll have a shower on our own," James admitted. "I won't get distracted."

"Do I distract you, Jamie?" Tony asked, tonguing his canine as he grinned.

"You know you do, cowboy," James replied with a chuckle. He finished pulling his jeans on, leaving them unzipped. "If you're ready?"

"Yeah." He kept his underwear in his hand to use as a shield if they came across anyone, and they headed down the stairs and out of the 'little' guest house on the property.

There were several people setting up the gazebo for the wedding, not that Tony could fathom what else needed to be done to prepare it.

"Brisk," he said to James, the chilly wind off the water covering his body in goosebumps in seconds.

James chuckled. "No shit."

They picked up the pace, nearly running the last few steps to the front door of the house.

They left their boots at the door and almost made it up the stairs without being seen.

"There you two are—" Julie cut herself off. "You're going to catch your deaths! Why are you *naked*?"

"Thought we'd make the wedding a nude affair," Tony teased.

"Dude, nobody wants to see that," Adam said, coming up behind Julie. "Get your ass dressed."

"I was just about to do that," Tony retorted cheerfully.

"I don't mind," Carolina said with a whistle from the top of the stairs.

"Neither do I." Sophia came up behind her husband. "Are we talking everyone, or just the bride and grooms? Because I'll have to put my foot down about the kids. They'd be too cold."

Julie threw her hands up in the air. "Has everyone lost it but me?"

"We're joking," James said.

"Promise," Tony added. "You're too easy to tease."

"I never know when you're serious," she said.

"Generally, if he's trying to shock you, he's joking," Adam drawled, pretending to cover Sophia's eyes. He glared at his brother. "Except right now, apparently. Cold out there?" he asked with a grin.

"Quite," Tony replied gravely, making everyone laugh. "I need a hot shower ASAP."

"And Amanda would like some danishes when you go back over, please," James told Julie. He smacked Tony's ass when he passed.

"Hey, I thought we agreed to separate showers?" Tony said. "Don't tease."

"You're the one flaunting your bare ass," James growled. "Get going before I get you."

"Make me," Tony said, wiggling his hips.

Adam rolled his eyes. "Keep it in your pants until *after* the ceremony, if you can manage it, please."

"You've already delayed the bride's schedule by almost an hour," Julie exclaimed. "How are you still..." She waved a hand in their direction, blushing.

Tony laughed. "I'm sorry, have you *seen* my fiancés? How could I not?"

"Why are you still down here?" Michael and Xavier came out from the kitchen. "Let's go, boys. Up the stairs." They herded their sons all the way up to their rooms, closing the doors behind them.

Tony leaned against the wall, cheeks hurting from smiling so much, but he couldn't stop. He tossed his worn underwear on the floor and headed into the shower to warm up.

After getting clean, he combed and styled his hair, brushed his teeth, and got dressed in his gray wedding pants and white shirt. He grabbed his matching vest and slung it over his arm before trotting down the stairs to the kitchen.

James whistled when he walked in. "Damn, you look nice. What's the occasion?"

"Oh, you know," Tony said, blushing slightly. "Nothing too world-shattering." He crossed the room, dropping his vest on James's coat draped over the back of a chair on the way, and slid sideways onto his lap. "You look incredibly handsome," he murmured. "Wanna get married today?"

"I can't think of anything I'd rather do," James replied with a grin.

"Okay, you can stop flirting now," Adam said, pretending to gag.

"In front of my cornflakes!" Glenn gasped. "I clutch at my pearls!"

Tony huffed a laugh. "Fine. I'm hungry anyways." He kissed James's lips lightly, barely resisting the urge to fall under his spell, and headed for the fridge.

His mother walked in at that moment. "You two aren't supposed to see each other before the ceremony," she said.

"Don't start that again," James groaned.

"You weren't around when Julie came back from the guest house, were you?" Glenn asked her, eyes twinkling.

"No, I went to have my shower when Julie left to wake Amanda," Debra said, sliding into a seat at the table. "Why? What happened?"

"Let's just say she got an eyeful of two virile men."

James spat coffee across the table.

"Dude," Tony said, laughing. He grabbed napkins on his way back to the table and handed them to James. "Who says 'virile'?"

"You were having sex?" Debra gasped.

"Not yet," Tony said, still chuckling. "She left before that started."

"Then how did she..." Comprehension dawned across her face and she shook her head. "You three are so much more casual with your bodies than I ever was."

"You have no idea," Glenn muttered under his breath.

"What's that supposed to mean?" Adam asked.

Glenn grimaced. "Sorry, didn't mean for that to be overheard."

"Hey, we're rarely the instigators," James protested.

"You spent *hours* printing out those Truth or Dare cards two years ago," Tony added. "The entire party ended up naked that time."

"I don't want to hear any more," Debra said, shaking her head.

"*That* time?" Adam repeated, amazed. "How many times has this happened?"

"I haven't been counting," Glenn admitted.

"Adam?" Sophia burst into the kitchen, looking frazzled, a screaming Travis in her arms. "I'm sorry to break this up, but I need help. Cody is refusing to be bathed, Travis is hungry, and I haven't even started getting ready."

"I'll take care of Cody," Adam said immediately. "You should have called me earlier."

"You should have noticed the time."

He winced. "Sorry." He held a pastry up for her to bite into. She hummed while she chewed.

"I think I'm hangry," she admitted.

"Sit," Debra said, taking the pastry. "Go," she added to her son, who nodded and left swiftly. "Eat," she said to Sophia. "And then Travis can eat. He'll survive two minutes without a boob in his mouth."

"I can take him after he's eaten," Tony offered. "Then you can get ready."

"No," Debra said firmly. "You don't want anything on your suit before the pictures!"

"Do you really think I care if he spits up on me?" Tony asked incredulously. "Besides, I know how to use a burp cloth."

"Travis really does like him," Sophia said, adjusting her clothing and holding Travis to her boob. It took a moment for the baby to realize that he was finally being offered food, but once he did, he latched on and began greedily and noisily drinking.

"He's got a good set of lungs," Glenn said.

"You should've heard Cody at this age," Sophia said, relaxing in the chair. "He had this pterodactyl screech that you could hear a mile away, I swear."

"Sounds horrendous," Glenn replied. He gathered his breakfast dishes and put them on the counter. "I'm going to go get ready now. Catch you later."

"Where did Carolina go? And the dads?" Tony asked.

"And Mom?" James added.

"I believe Ava is at the guest house," Sophia said. "Carolina went over there to take some pictures of Amanda getting ready. She'll be back to take some of you two. The dads are down at the waterfront, 'fishing.'"

Debra rolled her eyes. "Keeps them out of trouble."

"What kind of trouble could they have gotten into in the half hour since I saw them last?" Tony asked.

"They want to 'help'," Debra used air quotes. "But their idea of helping was driving Julie up the wall."

James chuckled. "She's a little obsessed with this wedding going off exactly the way she envisioned, isn't she?"

"It's her only daughter getting married."

"My mom isn't as bad, and I'm her only son," James said, confused.

"It's not the same thing," Debra said, shaking her head. "Your mom sees Amanda as a daughter already, so she's being officially added to the family. I think it's an old-fashioned thing, where the daughter 'leaves' her family to be with the husband's family."

"I still don't quite get it, but..." Tony shrugged. "We're merging three families, not taking away from anyone."

Debra patted his arm. "That's my view too, dear."

"Tony, are you still offering?" Sophia asked.

"Hell yes," he said, leaping to his feet. "Let me wash my hands."

After, he took the burp cloth and half-asleep baby from her, carefully holding his head.

"You remember how to burp him?" Sophia asked.

"Yup."

"Great." She half-ran from the room.

Tony sat on the edge of a sofa and put Travis on his knee, leaning forward, holding his head with the burp cloth over his hand. "Pat, two, three, rub, two, three," he murmured softly, gently encouraging Travis to burp up any air bubbles he swallowed while drinking his milk. After the third cycle, the baby let out a loud burp that woke him up the rest of the way.

Travis bobbled his head around to look up at Tony. The baby scrunched up his face like he was going to cry, but Tony cooed at him and rubbed the baby's spine.

"That was uncomfortable, wasn't it? You feel better now, or do you have another one in there?"

The baby stared at him.

"You know what I'm saying, don't you? You remember me? We were nap buddies only a couple months ago. I'm your daddy's brother. We look nothing alike, I know."

Travis let out another burp, smaller this time.

"Good job, bud. Ready for a nap now?"

The baby continued staring at him.

"Let's give it a shot, huh?" He flipped the cloth over his shoulder and scooped Travis up, putting him chest to chest on his shoulder. He rubbed slowly down the tiny spine, once, twice, and on the third time Travis put his head down with a long sigh.

"That was a world-weary sigh, buddy. Wanna talk about it?" Tony asked, continuing the motion of his fingers. "Was it that you were hungry and mom didn't feed you right away? You know, she's a busy woman. You have an older brother who has needs too. And she has to take care of herself as well. Sometimes you just have to wait a tiny bit. I know it felt interminable, but I assure you, it was no longer than a few minutes. Your mom loves you so much and takes care of you so well. Or did you sigh so heavily because you were asleep with a boob in your mouth, which sounds like a little slice of heaven to me, and then you were suddenly woken up by a painful burp, and mom wasn't holding you anymore, which means no more food until she comes back?

"I like to think I'm a decent alternative as a nap source, but I'm afraid I can't give you any food. In about three months, you'll be eating solid food, and then you can come to me. I can't wait to sneak you things like bananas, cheese, and cucumber. Your brother loves those, and I bet you'll enjoy them too."

The slightest shift in weight indicated that Travis had fallen asleep, and Tony relaxed back into the couch, swinging his legs up onto the lounge.

"You made that look so easy," James said admiringly, coming to sit beside him.

"Travis likes the deep sound of my voice," Tony said. "That, plus the massage, puts him right to sleep. I'm glad it still works."

"How did you know when to stop?"

"When babies fall asleep, they lose all the tension in their bodies." Tony chuckled quietly. "It's a small thing, but they feel a little bit heavier once they're asleep."

"You look really good, holding a baby," James murmured.

"I really love it." Tony shifted slightly to rest his head on James's shoulder. "It's so relaxing having a baby sleep on you."

"I'll take your word for it."

"I'm sure you'll get the chance later this week."

"I won't be as good as you."

"Don't compare," Tony scolded. "You know better than that. You'll develop a different bond with Travis, as you should." He rubbed the little back once more. "You're going to be a great father. Look at who you have for role models."

"Thanks," James whispered. "And I'll have you. You're a natural."

They were still in that position when Carolina came back in, and she quickly took a photo before saying, "Sophia's on her way down the stairs, Amanda's ready, and nearly everyone's at the gazebo."

"Did we fall asleep?" Tony asked.

"I don't think so."

"Tony, you're a baby whisperer," Sophia exclaimed as she came in, wearing a purple dress with a wide black belt. "I'm just going to change him, and then we'll be ready."

"You look beautiful," Tony said.

"Thanks." She gently scooped the baby up and rested him against her neck. "Oh, I hate to do this to him when he's resting so well."

"He'll be fine. And he could probably use a new diaper. I felt warmth about two minutes ago."

"Oh good, so he's waking up a bit anyway." Sophia disappeared with the baby, leaving the grooms alone with Carolina.

"I'm nervous all of a sudden," Tony said, getting up and heading for his vest. "Why am I nervous?"

"Cold feet?" James asked carefully, following him.

"God, no!" Tony chewed his bottom lip as he thought. "I think it's that old fear of being unlovable rearing its head."

"You're worried that Amanda or I have cold feet," James summarized, pulling on his jacket.

Tony looked up from buttoning the vest. "Do you?"

"From the moment that I knew I loved you, I wanted this," James said. "I am so excited to be marrying you."

Tony blew out a breath. "Okay. That helps."

"Good."

They paused at a mirror in the front hall so Tony could fix his hair from being smushed against the couch, and then headed out to the gazebo.

The heaters were working beautifully. The instant he stepped onto the wooden structure, the cold breeze was barely a memory. The heater near where they were instructed to stand to wait was pumping so much warmth that Tony rolled up his sleeves.

He had just finished the second one when the door to the guest house opened, and a princess stepped out.

Scraping his jaw off the floor, he took in the beauty that was his bride. He and James reached out for each other at the same moment, their fingers colliding and then gripping tightly.

"She's beautiful," James breathed.

"She's ours," Tony added.

"Thank God. I think I'd lose it if she was marrying anyone else."

Tony huffed a laugh, not taking his eyes off her as she approached.

Instead of flowers, she had her hands inside a white fur muff that matched the capelet around her shoulders. Her dress, which had been reflecting the morning sun so brightly that he couldn't tell the color, turned out to be an icy blue with a sheer overlay that sparkled.

Once she was under the heaters in the gazebo, she shed the fur, revealing the strapless dress in its entirety.

She joined them, taking their hands and making their circle complete.

"You look so beautiful," James said.

"You two look very handsome," she replied.

Tony couldn't speak around the thick feeling in his throat, so he just squeezed both of their hands. *This is really happening,* he thought dazedly. *What did I do to deserve so much happiness?*

"Welcome, family, for we are one family, and friends," said Adam, standing beside them. "Welcome to the marriage ceremony of three people who have found true happiness with each other. Marriage is a step that should not be taken lightly. It is hard work, putting another person's needs above your own. In sickness and in health, richer or poorer, good times and bad, you must be there for each other." He spread his hands wide. "We, who watched you grow up, have seen you deepen that love from best friends into what you now share. You truly know each other and have proven time and again that you belong together, to the exclusion of all others. This marriage is blessed by your family." He smiled. "Tony told me that when you were younger, you made a promise to each other: to communicate, to put each other first, and to be the best friends possible. I think you have achieved that, and now you are taking the next step in cementing your foundation for the future. Please exchange your vows."

"You accepted me for who I was, when I didn't even know myself." Tony's voice cracked at the end and he took in a shaky breath. "You taught me to share, to accept myself, and to love. I am my best when I am with you, and I promise to be your husband for the rest of my life."

A choked sob came from Tony's mother. He glanced at her and she smiled at him through her tears.

"All of my best memories come from being with you." James squeezed their hands. "And all of my worst were made bearable by you being there with me. I promise to love and cherish you from this day forward as your husband."

"You have been my best friends for my entire life, or least most of it." Amanda smiled brilliantly at them, making Tony's heart stutter. "I trust you with the entirety of my heart, my soul, and my body. I promise to be your wife until I draw my very last breath."

"May I have the rings, please, Cody," Adam asked his son, who proudly toddled up to his dad carrying a cushion. Three rings were tied to it with ribbons of silver, white, and pink. "These rings are a symbol of your love for each other, the heart-shaped gemstones representing your loved ones."

He untied the white ribbon holding James's ring and gave it to Tony and Amanda. They slid it on his finger silently. Adam repeated the process with the pink ribbon holding Amanda's ring, and then the silver with Tony's.

"By whatever power may be invested in me..."

"None," snickered Tony, and everyone chuckled.

Adam glared, a small smile playing on his lips, and they subsided. "I now pronounce you husband, husband, and wife. You may kiss."

They leaned across the minimal space and brushed their lips together lightly. Tony wrapped one arm around Amanda's waist and one around James's shoulders, pulling them closer. Behind Amanda's back, James gripped Tony's arm, holding them together. The three-way kiss deepened, and Amanda whimpered softly.

Clapping drew them out of their lust-filled haze, and they broke apart, sheepishly grinning at their families.

"Congratulations," grinned Adam. "I wish you all the happiness in the world, little brother."

Tony choked up, and hugged him. "I already have it."

Adam cleared his throat, working through his emotions. "May I present Misters and Mrs. Carlson?"

"Seriously?" shouted several people at once, beaming smiles all around.

That was the cue for everyone to crowd around the newlyweds, hugging and crying happy tears.

Chapter Twenty-Six

James

Carolina took pictures of the families and the newly married trio until Amanda's stomach rumbled loudly.

James looked down at the woman in his arms with surprise. "Didn't you eat breakfast?"

His father chuckled and pointed at his watch. "It's past lunch."

"Food is ready whenever we want to eat," Glenn reminded them. "Inside, though." He shivered dramatically.

"Oh, but…" Amanda trailed off, looking disappointed.

Julie rolled her eyes. "You have the rest of your life with them. You can spend a little time with your families on Christmas Eve."

"We'll sneak away after lunch," Tony whispered to them.

"No, you will not," Julie said.

"I'm not bluffing," Tony said calmly, and she flushed, obviously remembering the conversation from earlier that morning.

Michael chuckled, eyeing his son. "I think you'd have to tie them up to keep them away from each other at this point. Let 'em blow off a little steam. They'll join us for dinner."

"Only because they'll be starving," Julie muttered.

"A reason is a reason," Ava said placatingly, ushering people into the house and leaving the newlyweds alone in the gazebo.

"I'm not that hungry," Amanda said.

"Yes, you are," James said with a chuckle when her stomach immediately protested her words.

"We'll all have more energy after eating proper food," Tony said bracingly. "Even though I'm more desperate to get that dress off you than I should be."

"It's the wife effect," James said, nodding seriously. "Knowing she's ours is going straight to our cocks."

"Not sure that's a thing," Tony said thoughtfully, eyeing Amanda. "But I'm willing to accept it."

Amanda posed against the railing. "See something you like?" she asked playfully. "Because I sure do."

James gathered her into his arms, pressing kisses over her face. "So glad you didn't wear makeup," he murmured. "Stop procrastinating. Food, and then we can have sex as newlyweds for the first time."

"Okay," she said breathlessly.

"You aren't actually procrastinating, are you?" Tony asked as they headed for the main house. "Are you okay with this?"

"Okay with what?" she asked, confused.

"Having sex after lunch."

"I've been trying to convince you to have sex *before* lunch," she said with a laugh.

"Oh good," he said, exaggerating his relief.

When they walked into the dining room, everyone stood and applauded them.

"What's this for?" James asked, pulling out a chair for Amanda.

"It's standard to greet the newlyweds with congratulations," Debra said.

"I thought that was the next morning," Tony said, passing a platter of bacon to James. "You know, after consummation?"

"I think it depends, historically," Michael said.

"You mean you haven't yet?" Glenn demanded. "You were out there alone for five whole minutes!"

James exchanged amused grins with Tony before saying, "If you think five minutes is enough, I feel sorry for your partners." He took the eggs from Amanda and served himself.

Glenn's jaw dropped. "Such disrespect. And in my house!"

Paul patted his shoulder. "It's okay. Not everyone has stamina."

Everyone laughed at the shock on Glenn's face.

"I can't believe you said that," Glenn said once he recovered, shaking his head with a chuckle. "How did my joke get turned around on me?"

James speared a bite of food. "Five minutes," he said, popping his fork in his mouth, and everyone laughed again.

They ate as quickly as they could without inhaling their food. Amanda pushed her chair back first. "I would say I hate to eat and run, but that would be a lie. See you later!"

Tony was out of his chair and after her in a flash, his fork clattering to his plate.

James patted the corners of his mouth delicately with his napkin. "Good afternoon," he said. "I have an appointment with my spouses."

"Yeah you do!" Glenn cheered.

James couldn't stop grinning as he followed his lovers' footprints to the guest house.

They hadn't even made it past the entry. Tony still had one boot on, standing between Amanda's legs as she sat on the half-wall separating the entry from the main living space. The skirt of her dress was hiked up between them and his hand was buried underneath it.

"It didn't take me that long to follow you, did it?" James asked incredulously.

"Must have been the boots," Tony mumbled against her lips. "Get in here, husband."

His knees weak, James walked around to the main living space and hugged Amanda's back to his chest. He kissed across her shoulders, brushing her hair aside to get at the back of her neck.

Tony traced her collarbones with his tongue before brushing his lips over the pulse point in her neck on his way up to claim her mouth. "Fuck, you taste amazing, wife," he murmured.

She moaned in reply, her hips rolling.

James couldn't wait, yanking up the yards of material to join Tony's hand in playing with her. "Where are your panties, sunshine?" he asked, smiling against her bare shoulder.

"In Tony's pocket," she whimpered. "I want to be naked while you're still dressed," she begged.

James tilted her head back and drew her into a deep kiss, her mouth dragging him under her spell until he could barely breathe. "That's hot." He drew down the zipper at the back of her dress, pressing kisses to the skin it revealed, which wasn't much. "What's this?" he asked, amused, as his lips met the hard boning of her corset.

She didn't answer, not that he expected her to, and he continued to pull the zipper down her back, eyes feasting on the delicate icy blue fabric that matched her dress.

"It has to go over my head," she murmured, dazed.

They helped her down and Tony kicked off his boot. As one, they pulled the dress over her head.

"Oh my God," groaned James. "Love, you look gorgeous."

Two bright spots of color appeared high on Tony's cheekbones. "I don't think I've ever been this turned on," he breathed.

Amanda stood between them, clad in a lacy pale blue corset and nothing else. The corset pushed her breasts up, and barely covered her nipples. "You've seen me in less," she teased.

"Not as our wife," murmured James. "It feels different. It's more."

Tony let go of the dress, letting it swish into a pile on the couch, and ran his fingers over the tops of her breasts. Her breath quickened, and he slid his hands underneath the edge to pull them out of the cup. His eyes, heavy-lidded, gazed at first one, and then the other, before his mouth descended to hotly swirl over her left nipple. His fingers massaged the other, while he brought her body closer to his with his free hand on her ass. She gasped, and he raised his head to kiss her, their tongues tangling together.

Watching them take pleasure from each other was making James as hard as a rock, his pants constraining almost painfully. His fingers stroked down the laces at the back of her corset until they reached the knot at the base of her spine. He untied it quickly, his fingers shaking but still obeying his commands. Slowly, he loosened the laces, working his fingers underneath the sides of the corset and pulling them away from her body. The motions were soothing but only served to rile him up more.

Groaning, Tony released her mouth. "God, I want you," he panted.

"Arms up," murmured James before she could reply, and he lifted the corset over her head, letting it fall on top of her dress.

Finally, she was bare between them.

"And now?" asked James, his voice rough with desire.

"I want to watch you make out on the bed. Can you stay clothed, please?" Amanda asked. "I have lingerie that I want to put on for you."

"Do you care who is on top?" asked Tony, shrugging out of his vest as fast as possible and reaching for James.

"Fight for the power," she grinned.

James groaned and pulled Tony to him, grinding their cocks together. Their mouths met, hard and bruising, as they fought for dominance. "I want to fuck you into the mattress," he breathed into Tony's mouth. "I want you inside me. Why can't I have both?"

Tony chuckled, gripping James's ass. "We've got our whole lives ahead of us. We'll get to it."

"First one to the bed gets to be on top."

Tony ran for the bedroom, James hot on his heels and passing him on the stairs. At the door, James grabbed him and pulled him into another heart-stopping kiss, backing Tony up until they hit the bed.

Tony surprised him with a burst of strength, flipping them and pushing James down onto the mattress. Their mouths only separated for a moment. Tony quickly pounced upon James, one leg between his as their mouths crashed together again. Their hips ground against each other, James's hands pressing Tony's ass down as he arched his back to gain more friction. They gasped into each other's mouths.

Lifting James higher up onto the bed, one hand behind his back, Tony surged his body against him.

Flipping them over, James ran one hand down Tony's body and gripped his thigh, hiking it over his ass. "God, I want you to be naked," he moaned, rolling his hips.

The bed dipped as Amanda crawled onto it beside them. "I want you to pay attention to me now," she murmured. "Keep your clothes on. You look so sexy."

Growling, James detached himself from Tony, knelt, and grabbed her arm, hauling her to him roughly. She gasped in surprise as her body made contact with his; soft curves pressed against hard muscle.

"Bridal lingerie," said Tony, whistling. "You're a vision."

James pulled back to look at her, the sheer fabric hiding nothing from them. "Damn, how did we get so lucky," he murmured, running a thumb over her nipple until it beaded. "So responsive to our touch."

Tony tugged the knot at the base of her neck until the front sagged open, latching onto the exposed breast with teeth and tongue.

"Oh God," Amanda gasped, writhing against them.

"I have an idea," Tony said, getting off the bed. "Be right back."

James busied himself stripping her skimpy little thong off her body, and then pressing hot kisses to her mouth until he was dizzy with them.

Tony came back and settled on the bed beside them, running a hand over her body from breast to pussy. "How are your handstands, Amanda? Do you think you could hold the position while we eat you out?" he asked wickedly.

"I don't know, but I really, really want to try."

"We'll hold you up," grinned James.

She arched backwards in his arms, putting her hands on the bed, and then saying, from her upside-down position, "I think an elbow-stand might be more stable." She adjusted and paused. "You should probably either get out of my way or help me."

"Just a moment, love," breathed James. "I want to admire your flexibility." She was on her knees and elbows, face-up, her back arched, her breasts pressing into the air and her hips level with his. He ran his hands up her thighs to her ass. "Ready?" At her word, he lifted her gently, and her legs unfolded from underneath her into the splits, her wet folds level with his chest.

"That was hot," murmured Tony. He slipped one hand into the ice bucket that he had placed on the foot of the bed, and offered a small piece of ice to James to suck on. James grinned and accepted the sliver. Tony moved to the front of Amanda and ran his fingers lightly over her body. "Your body looks even better upside-down in person, love," he said, referencing the video that had been made without her permission back in high school. "Did I tell you how often I fantasized about your breasts after watching that damned video? Every fucking night. Almost as often as I would try to imagine what your pussy looked like." He bent his head and licked a wet line across her folds. She shuddered and wobbled, prompting his hands to join James's at her hips, supporting her. His tongue dipped inside her, and then swirled around her clit, making her gasp and moan.

James, the ice melted, joined him in his feast, copying his movements and dipping his tongue inside her before circling around her clit, his cold tongue tangling with Tony's. The instant his tongue hit her flesh, she whimpered and cried out.

"What?" she gasped, surprised at the temperature difference.

They chuckled, and James reached for another ice cube, bigger this time. He put it directly on top of her folds, and then pushed it towards Tony with his tongue. They played with it for a while, pushing it back and forth across her, suckling her around the cold, wet cube as it melted against her heat.

The temperature difference, combined with their talented teasing, made sure that her orgasm came slowly. Amanda's arms and thighs were shaking. Tony nibbled on the hood of her clit, and she cried out, the sensations becoming too much as she shattered between them.

Quickly, James sucked the ice cube, now a sliver, into his mouth, and Tony lapped the leftover fluid from her body.

They gently lowered her body onto the bed, and she looked up at them hovering over her. "God, you guys are fantastic at that," she whimpered.

They grinned proudly.

"Strip, please," she ordered. "I want to suck on your cocks. Give you a taste of the ice cold torture you gave to me."

They scrambled off the bed on opposite sides and removed their clothes in record time.

Amanda moved to the foot of the bed as they stripped, beside the ice bucket, and popped an ice cube in her mouth, sucking on it with relish. "Whenever you're ready, please lie on the bed beside each other," she said around her mouthful.

Tony immediately climbed onto the bed. James fell over, trying to get his second sock off. They all laughed, and Tony helped him remove the offending garment before the men lay down side by side.

Spitting the ice cube into her hand, Amanda draped herself along their adjoining legs. She ran the ice cube over Tony's lower abdomen, purposefully avoiding his twitching cock, and then traced James's hip bones with the quickly melting cube. She popped it back in her mouth again before it melted into a puddle, and then enveloped James's cock in her mouth.

He writhed on the bed, straining not to move his hips as she sucked him deep.

She released him with a pop, and then sat up to slip a new ice cube into her mouth. She spat it into her hand as soon as she laid down again, treating Tony's cock to a hot/cold mouth.

"Fuuuuuuuck!" He dragged the word out, hands clenching the pillow over his head in an effort to keep still.

The hand holding the ice cube was not idle, and she rubbed it over James's throbbing erection in time to the bobbing of her head. She slipped the ice cube in her mouth again as she switched her position, and then James was in her mouth and Tony in her hand.

It was exquisite torture; alternating between the warmth of her mouth, getting harder than he thought imaginable. Once he could barely stand it, she switched to ice cold, and blood drained from his cock, softening but still full of desire.

Both men were panting as she teased them.

"Fuck, Amanda," whimpered Tony as she swallowed him again. "I want to be inside you."

She popped back up and gave him a wink. "You were just inside me."

James barked a laugh that turned into a groan when she focused her attention on him. "Yes, Amanda, let us fuck you."

Tony sat up and moved her off his leg. "I think it's time we took matters into our own hands, Jamie." When all James could do was grunt his assent, Tony smirked and picked Amanda up, turning her to face him.

"I love being manhandled by you," she said. "It makes me feel so delicate and petite."

"I hate to break it to you," chuckled James. "But you are neither."

"I think she's saying that she likes our muscles, and that we can throw her around," teased Tony. "Hold onto my shoulders, darlin'."

Amanda wrapped her arms around his neck, and he scooped her up under her knees, spreading her legs wide around his waist.

After liberally applying lube, James moved in close behind her and impaled her slowly, feeling her take every inch of his cock.

Her head fell back on his shoulder as he pumped into her slowly. He coated his fingers with his saliva, and then ran them over her clit. "What are you thinking, sunshine? Together in your pussy, me in your ass, or Tony fucking me into you?"

"Can I be selfish and ask to be in the middle this first time?" she asked. "I want you to stretch my pussy for both of you, please."

"You ask so nicely," Tony said, nuzzling her neck. "I love stretching you open."

James took one of her legs from him, and Tony's fingers stroked around his cock, testing her ability to take him by sliding a finger inside along with the cock already inside her. "Darlin', you're so turned on, this is going to be easy."

"Are you ready for him?" James asked her, kissing her temple.

"Please," she whimpered. "Want you both."

He slid mostly out of her and aligned Tony's cock with his own. "God, you two always feel so fucking amazing," he growled as he pushed them both inside of her.

Tony panted hard as they filled her. "Feels so good to be together like this."

Once they were fully seated in her, they gripped each other's forearms under Amanda's knees, raising her body up until they were barely inside her, and then lowering her slowly.

"Oh God," Amanda moaned. "Please, faster!"

They picked up the pace, slamming her body down onto theirs, rocking their hips into her on the down stroke.

"This feels so fucking good," groaned Tony. "I'm going to come."

"Me too," gasped Amanda. "Oh my God, Tony, James, I'm so close!"

"Not yet," growled James, his brow furrowed in concentration. "Hold on."

"I can't, James, I can't," she panted. Her eyes closed. "I have to come. Too much! Oh my God!"

The men slid deep inside her one last time, and her muscles clamped down on them as her release hit her. James gasped in unison with Tony as his orgasm washed over him, feeling her walls milk him as intimately as the pulsing of Tony's cock. They sagged against each other, still supporting Amanda, eyes meeting over her shoulder. Without speaking, James leaned in and dragged his lips weakly against Tony's, desperate for the added connection.

"Holy fuck," breathed Tony, breaking the kiss and pressing their foreheads together. "I don't think I can move."

James chuckled quietly. "I sure as hell can't stay like this. Just a second…" He shifted his arms back from holding Amanda up and slid his softening penis out of her, before lifting her off of Tony, lying her on the bed between them.

James moved the bucket off the bed, impressed that it hadn't toppled off. "You should go pee," he whispered to her.

"My legs are overcooked noodles," she whined, reaching for him. "Carry me?"

Tony snorted. "Can't blame you."

James helped her into the bathroom and leaned against the counter while she sat on the toilet.

She stripped off the lingerie from around her waist and dropped it on the floor. "You're right, it does feel different when you're married."

His heart warmed at the thought. "I can't believe we're finally at this point. The three of us together just makes sense."

They crawled back on the bed, and Amanda curled her sated body in between them.

"I love you, my wife and my husband." Tony grinned foolishly as he said the words. "I'm never going to get tired of calling you that."

"I love you too, my husband and my wife." James kissed Amanda's forehead and blew a kiss over her to Tony, reaching out for his hand.

"Words cannot express how much I love you, my husbands." She smiled dreamily at them. "I can't wait to see what happens next."

Chapter Twenty-Seven

Flashback: A Christmas Carol

"'Twas the Night before Christmas, and all through the house, not a creature was stirring, not even a mouse…"

"But none of our houses even have mice!" Tony interrupted Amanda.

"That's really not the point," she said around a giggle. "Everyone was asleep."

"There was a mouse in the Grinch movie we watched today, too," continued Tony. "And that wasn't even a pet mouse. It was scavenging for food."

"I still can't believe you'd never seen *How the Grinch Stole Christmas* before today," marveled James. He leaned forward so he could see Tony around Amanda. "Or heard this story before."

Tony flushed. "I have heard this story before. A long time ago, when I was really little. But Christmas wasn't exactly celebrated in the foster homes I was in."

There was an awkward pause.

"Sorry," apologized James. "I forget sometimes that you didn't grow up next door to us."

"We can't all have happy childhood memories," sneered Tony.

Another pause.

Amanda continued reading aloud from the book on her lap, but her hand reached out beside her and lay palm up on the floor between her and Tony. He glared at it for a page before giving in and resting his hand on it. She squeezed it gently, and he sighed.

"Sorry James," he said, interrupting Amanda again. "Christmas doesn't exactly have the best memories for me."

"It's okay," replied James, his teeth flashing in a quick smile. "We'll make new ones."

"What sort of memories are you thinking?" asked Tony, curious.

"How about we start by finishing the story?" teased Amanda.

At the nods of the two boys, she continued.

"...Merry Christmas to all, and to all a good night!" Amanda closed the book.

"That was cute," mused Tony. "I liked it, but I think *A Christmas Carol* is more interesting. Ghosts make every story better."

The twelve-year-olds all chuckled.

"What are we going to do to make new memories with Tony?" asked Amanda. "Caroling?"

"We did that last weekend," complained Tony. "It's only fun once a year."

"True," Amanda hummed in thought. "Make paper decorations?"

"I got it!" exclaimed James. "We'll put on *A Christmas Carol* for our parents!"

"The movie?" questioned Amanda. "That's not exactly a memory-maker, James."

"No, no! As a play!" James swept the other two up in his enthusiasm. "We can each be a character or two, and act it all out!"

"I don't know if I'll be able to memorize all the lines by tonight. It's Christmas Eve morning!" Amanda's eyes were wide.

"We'll just wing it, say approximate lines, and fudge the rest." James's rebuttal came out entirely too gleeful. He rubbed his hands together, eyes sparkling. "Who wants to be Scrooge?"

It was agreed that Tony would play Scrooge, James would be Bob Cratchit, Jacob Marley, and the Ghost of the Past, and Amanda would take on the parts of Belle, Mrs. Cratchit, and the Ghosts of the Present and Future. Amanda's toy bear would be making his debut as Tiny Tim, as the three agreed that Tim was necessary to the story, but they didn't have enough people to play him, too.

"We can leave out the parts at the counting house, and focus on when the three Ghosts visit Scrooge that night. Four Ghosts, I suppose, if you count Marley!" Tony was getting excited. "We can have Scrooge complain about Cratchit under his breath, and that gives enough backstory."

Everyone nodded enthusiastically.

Amanda grinned. "And we can make the chains of Marley out of construction paper!"

Tony and James groaned half-heartedly.

"Well, your suggestion of making paper decorations had to be included somehow!" laughed James.

The parents all loved the play, and the kids bowed to a standing ovation.

"I'm so impressed that you pulled this off in only a day!"

"Bravo!"

"Tony should win an Oscar!"

"Amanda made a great creepy Future Ghost, a much better choice than trying to be intimidating."

"James really captured Marley's spirit!"

"Da-ad!" groaned James. "That was a terrible pun!"

Everyone laughed.

The parents helped put the living room back to normal.

As Amanda came down from her room, she noticed that Tony wasn't in the living room with the rest.

"Where did Tony go?" she asked.

"I thought he helped you carry the costumes back upstairs," replied James.

"No." Amanda frowned.

"I saw him head towards the kitchen," Adam said. "Thought maybe he went to get more snacks or some water."

The pre-teens exchanged glances and silently left the party to hunt for their friend.

He wasn't in the kitchen.

"Patio," James said, looking through the back door.

Amanda looked down at her knit dress and leggings and made a face. "If we go get our coats, the parents will get suspicious."

"I hope he knows how much we love him," James said, sliding the door open for them to slip out into the cold December air.

She ran across the stone to the large suspended bed and leapt onto it, crawling the rest of the way to where Tony was huddled under the blanket. He held open one side for her, and she curled into him.

James followed more sedately, joining him on the other side.

They stared out over Amanda's snow-covered backyard for so long that her nose turned pink with cold. She turned to bury it in Tony's shoulder.

He took in a shuddering breath. "I've never done anything like that before."

There didn't seem to be anything to say to that.

"Do you know how long it took me to hug my mom?" he asked, changing the subject.

Amanda lifted her head. "I don't understand the question."

"When the Carlsons fostered me. Do you know how long I waited before I hugged her?"

"No."

"Not until *months* after they adopted me." Tony buried his face in his knees. "She cried," he said, his voice cracking. "I didn't know how to hug someone. I watched Adam, but he didn't do it often enough for me to understand why he did it when he did. But then she bought me a book. I liked to do the Sudoku in the paper on Saturdays, and I guess she noticed. She gave me the book and said I could do them whenever I wanted, I didn't have to wait for Saturday, and I hugged her."

"I'm sorry," Amanda said.

He shook his head, still pressed against his knees. "You two are so affectionate. It almost hurt, how often you wanted to hug. This summer, sometimes I'd go home after hanging out, and I'd be shaking because I'd gotten more hugs in a day than I had up until that point. I told my therapist about it, and she said that I was something called 'touch-starved' and 'overstimulated'. She was sure you would understand if I needed a break.

But—" He sniffed. "I like the way I feel warm when you hug me. Even when I'm shaking, I don't want you to stop hugging me ever."

"Never ever," Amanda said, ignoring the tears streaming down her cheeks and wrapping her arms around his chest.

"Don't cry," Tony said, finally lifting his head and revealing red-rimmed eyes. "If you cry, I'll cry." He hugged her back, tucking her head under his chin.

"I can't help it. I keep thinking about baby Tony not getting hugs, and—" Her voice squeaked out at the end.

James joined in the cuddle, holding them both. "We'll more than make up for it now."

Tony let out a shaky breath. "What I was trying to say was that I'm glad I have you two as friends. Today was a lot of fun. I'd never been in a play before. And the best part was getting to be with you all day."

"Being with you is the most fun ever," Amanda said thickly. "I love you."

"Love?" Tony asked, surprised.

"Love," James repeated firmly. "Not like, you know, romance. More like how you love your parents. I would do anything for you that would make you happy. I want to be around you. Best friend love."

Tony rubbed his chest over his heart. "I don't know much about love," he said quietly. "But if that's what you mean, then me too, I guess."

Amanda squeezed him tighter for a second. "We'll be with you to show you every step of the way."

"Thanks for making this my best Christmas ever," Tony said, resting his head on hers again.

"We've got so many more ahead of us," James said.

Chapter Twenty-Eight

Amanda

Amanda woke slowly on Christmas morning, warmth from her husbands on either side of her, and sighed happily.

"You're awake?" Tony whispered behind her.

She hummed and tipped her head back a bit to see him. "Merry Christmas," she said, keeping her voice quiet to not wake James. "How long have you been up?"

"Since the sun," Tony replied.

"Why?"

"Thinking."

"Uh oh."

He huffed a laugh, kissing her shoulder. "Come on, let's go downstairs to talk," he suggested.

"'Kay." She pressed a kiss to James's chest before following Tony off the bed and down the stairs to the kitchen. "He's going to wake up soon," she said. "He always does when he gets cold."

"Speaking of cold," Tony said, running the back of his hand over her breast. "Did you want to get dressed first?"

"Pfft, no," she scoffed. "I'm sure you can think of a way to keep me warm."

Tony chuckled, shaking his head as he scooped coffee into the filter. "Many ideas come to mind."

"Well, when you decide on one, let me know." She pressed her body against his side, resting her head on his shoulder to watch his motions.

He closed the machine and pressed the button, the hiss of the water boiling filling the kitchen.

"Why'd you wait until I woke up before coming downstairs?" Amanda asked.

He turned to face her, hugging her tightly. "I wanted the company, not the coffee."

"Ah." She leaned against his chest, her arms loosely draped around his waist.

"I was thinking."

"So you said upstairs. How scared do I need to be?" she teased.

He lightly tapped her ass, making her jump against him. "Brat," he said affectionately. "I was thinking about our first Christmas together. Do you remember the play we put on for the families?"

"Of course. You were such a good Scrooge."

"Thanks." He grew quiet again, the sizzle of the coffee hitting the pot loud in the silence. "Do you remember our conversation out in the backyard afterwards?"

"You told us you had been touch-starved your whole life and didn't know how to hug," she said softly.

"I think I've had some good teachers on that subject."

"Your hugs are awesome," she agreed readily.

"You told me you loved me for the first time that night," Tony said, petting her hair.

"I did."

"You don't know what that meant to me."

The coffee burbled, startling them. He let go of her and grabbed two mugs, filling them while she grabbed cream from the fridge. She added the appropriate amount to each while he scooped out sugar and then stirred the liquid.

They carried their mugs to the couch, placing them on coasters on the end table to cool.

"Wanna be inside you," Tony whispered, tugging her hand.

"I want that too," she said, letting him pull her down to straddle his lap. "You've been hard since I woke up, but I didn't want to push."

Amanda rose up so he could notch his cock at her opening, and then slid down his length.

"So warm," he hissed, throwing his head back against the cushions, his hands gripping her hips to keep her seated. He took a couple deep breaths, collecting himself. "Where were we?"

"Something about telling you that you were loved."

"Right. Love. It was such a foreign concept to me." He took a breath. "In my world, everything had a cost. When I met you, I kept waiting for the other shoe to drop, for you to demand something of me that I didn't want to give. That happened more often than I could count. And then you said that, and so casually! I could hardly believe my ears. I couldn't even say the word without it getting stuck in my throat. I think that's what really started my healing. To have the two of you choose to love me like that... To say it so easily..." He nudged his nose against hers. "It really was the greatest gift."

"I wish I'd realized sooner how much you needed to hear it," Amanda said. "I knew I loved you, in my childish way, back in the summer."

Tony chuckled. "Probably for the best. You would have terrified me. I could barely handle the hugging!"

"And look at you now," she said admiringly.

"Not only am I hugging my *wife*, but she's cockwarming me!" Tony said with exaggerated shock.

Amanda giggled. "Who would have guessed?"

"I'm glad we figured our shit out."

Movement on the stairs drew her attention. "Merry Christmas!" she greeted James. "Were we too loud?"

"Smelled coffee," he groaned, rubbing his face. "Cold without you." He ambled over behind the couch, grabbed Tony's mug and took a sip. "Good coffee," he murmured. "You can carry on," he added, raising an eyebrow at them.

"We were just talking," Amanda said.

"Cozy. Can I get in on this little chat?"

"Sure!" She looked down between her legs. "Position?"

James ran a hand through Tony's hair. "Do you want to sit on me?"

He tipped his head back and grinned. "You mean on your cock?"

"Obviously." James rolled his eyes.

"Yeah, I'd love that."

"I can go get the lube," Amanda offered, moving to get up. "I could use a little if we're planning on adding friction."

"Hard to believe," Tony murmured teasingly.

"No, you stay. I tossed it somewhere last night," James said, leaning down and kissing her upturned lips. "Wish me luck."

"If you're not back in five minutes, we'll come help," Tony promised.

"If I'm not back in two minutes, we're using olive oil," James said before heading back up the stairs.

"Have you given any thought to where you want to go for our honeymoon?" Tony asked, running the back of his hand over her shoulder.

"A nudist resort?" she said with a chuckle. "I know we put money aside for a honeymoon rather than buying Christmas presents, but honestly? I'd rather stay at home, order in, and have sex for a week straight."

"The point of a honeymoon is to go somewhere together and see new sights while whetting our appetites for each other," Tony said with a shake of his head. "Even *I* know that. A stay-cation is cute, but I want to show you two off."

"We'd have to pick somewhere that wouldn't get upset about our relationship."

"I'm sure we can find out when we go home. Would you rather Europe or the Caribbean?"

"I can see positives for either one," she said thoughtfully. "The castles in Scotland, France, or Germany would be awesome. But the Caribbean has beaches and ruins. I think we should wait until after we research before we set our hearts on a place."

James thundered down the stairs again.

"Are we raiding the kitchen or were you successful?" Tony asked.

James tossed him the bottle of lube, which Tony caught easily. "Successful. Let's get you prepped."

Tony made a face. "I'm not going to be able to hear that world without thinking of Paul trying to explain what it means."

Amanda stared at him. "My *dad*? What on *Earth* did you get up to at your bachelor party?"

"Glenn," Tony said, as if that explained everything.

"Ah," she replied, because it did.

They changed positions, him pressing her down into the cushions.

"I am never going to get over getting to be with you like this," James said, kneeling behind Tony. "Tell me if I hurt you."

"Obvi— Oh fuck that feels good," Tony groaned, his eyes closing in bliss.

Amanda ran her hands along his body, tracing his tattoos with delicate fingers while he panted and moaned above her.

"I love how you always look like you're about to fall apart just from being stretched open," she murmured. "Both of you."

"He's really good at it," they said at the same time, and then chuckled.

"I know," Amanda agreed readily. "It's super hot to watch your face react to his touch."

"Goddamn it James, I'm ready," Tony groaned. "If you keep hitting my prostate like that, this is going to be over before it starts."

James chuckled. "Sorry." The tear of the plastic from a condom met her ears. "Ready?"

"Yeah. Facing forward or backward?" Tony asked, pulling out of her slowly.

"Would I fit between you if it's forward?" Amanda asked, already missing his warmth within her.

Her husbands exchanged glances. "I'd like to try," James said.

"We can rearrange if it doesn't work," Tony agreed, straddling James and taking him down to the hilt. "Fuck, you feel good."

"I think that's my line." James used the lube to slick up Tony's cock. "Come here, sunshine."

"Where are my legs going to go?" she asked, moving slowly.

"Squat. You'll fit just fine, darlin'," Tony said.

They balanced her as she stood on the couch and straddled them both, facing Tony.

"I could eat you out like this," he mused.

"Later," James replied, amused. "We do have a time limit."

Amanda glanced at the clock on the mantel. "It's only eight."

"Sit on my cock now." Tony growled the order.

"Yes sir," she said with a giggle.

"Naughty little brat. Do you deserve coal in your stocking?"

"No, Santa's elves punish me themselves," she said, dropping down and taking Tony inside her again.

"Sexy," James said. "Do they use peppermint sticks as canes?"

"How did you know?" she gasped playfully.

"I think I could come just from sitting here like this," Tony said shakily. "I..."

Amanda cupped his face in her hands. "This is what it feels like to be surrounded by love."

Tony nodded. "Yeah." He gulped. "I know I don't say it as often as you two do, but I love you both. I may have played Scrooge in that play when we were kids, but I felt like the Grinch, my heart growing three sizes when I moved into your lives." Tears filled his eyes, and he blinked rapidly.

Amanda kissed his eyelids, wiping away the tears that overflowed.

"Oh fuck," he groaned.

She felt him pulsing within her. "Did you just come?"

He nodded sheepishly.

"You're such a softie. How did anyone ever think otherwise?"

"I'm a tough guy," Tony grumbled.

"You're not, and I'm glad of it," Amanda said, pressing a thumb over his lips. "Make me come with your fingers, please."

He reached between them, rubbing across her clit until she came with a cry.

"Now it's James's turn," she said once she could breathe.

"I'm good," he said.

"I didn't feel you come," Tony countered, raising an eyebrow.

"I don't need to come," James protested.

Amanda and Tony exchanged looks. He helped her stand, and then she did the same to him. Tony removed the condom, and they both knelt at James's feet, licking and sucking down the sides of his cock as if they had choreographed it.

"I... Oh God, Tony," James groaned when Tony reached underneath him with one hand, sliding down the couch cushion to grant better access. "Yes, fuck, Amanda, your mouth!"

"Use me," she gasped, pulling off him and scooping her hair out of the way with one hand.

James took over, holding her hair back with gentle hands that gripped her head. He slid her slowly down his cock, getting her used to the motion before he picked up the pace. "Fuck," he muttered. "Fuckfuckfuck." He breathed hard for a few more strokes. "Want to come inside you," he groaned, pulling her up until she could swing a leg over him and guide his cock inside her. "You're dripping with our husband's cum," he told her. "This messy pussy belongs to us. Tell us."

"This messy pussy belongs to you both," she panted as she bounced on top of him. "Come in me, James. I need it."

"Damn right you do," James grunted. "Yes, Tony! God, Amanda."

His cock pulsed inside her, gushing his release. He sagged back on the couch, all tension gone from his body.

She leaned forward, hugging him. "I love you," she whispered.

"Love you too."

"Our coffee got cold," Tony pouted, making her chuckle.

"Microwave it," she suggested, getting shakily to her feet and heading for the stairs.

"Then we should head over to the big house," James said drowsily.

"I'll make you a coffee too," Tony said, going to the kitchen.

"Thanks."

Amanda got dressed in red patterned leggings and a fluffy white sweater before trotting back downstairs. "I'm going to go get breakfast at the house. Come along when you're ready."

Tony kissed her gently in passing, carrying James's mug to him. "Your coffee's on the counter, darlin'."

"Oh, thank you."

It didn't cool much on the quick trip between houses. She let herself into the foyer and followed the happy shrieks to the living room with a Christmas tree set up at one wall. Adam and Sophia and the boys were the only ones in the room.

"I'm surprised to see you before noon," Sophia said. "Merry Christmas!"

"We got up early," Amanda said, sitting beside her and hugging her. "How did the boys sleep?"

"Like logs. Adam was the one up with the sun."

"Just like his brother," Amanda said with a grin.

"You're practically glowing this morning."

"I'm *married*."

"You are," Adam replied, amused. "And how is married life treating you?"

"Like a dream," she replied with a happy sigh.

Sophia covered a laugh with a hand. "I can tell. Your parents are in the living room off the kitchen." She shook her head in amazement. "This house is massive. Your friend is quite generous."

"He might be spoiled, but he isn't rotten," Amanda said. "And yes, he is generous."

"He left an envelope for you three in the kitchen last night before he left," Adam said.

"Really? That's sweet. I thought we said our goodbyes. Must have something to do with leaving instructions." She blew a kiss to Cody, who was zooming a toy plane around the room, and headed for the kitchen.

Her husbands were already there, making plates of food from the hot plates on the counter.

"Mmm, waffles," Amanda said. "And bacon."

"Already got those for you."

"Amazing." Leaving her plate in the capable hands of her husbands, she followed the low rumble of voices to the living room. "Merry Christmas!" she announced to the parents. She gave hugs around the room. "Going to eat breakfast now." She kissed her mom on the cheek.

"How are you feeling?" Julie asked.

Amanda beamed at her. "Loved."

"I'll say," Debra muttered under her breath.

Dancing back into the kitchen, Amanda took the seat beside James and dug into her food. "What's that?" she asked Tony, indicating the letter in his hand.

"Tickets," he said. "From Glenn."

"Sorry, what?"

"Well, the promise of tickets," Tony clarified. "Anywhere we want to go, up to ten grand, and the leftover money goes to us too. So we can have a dream honeymoon." He put the letter down. "Wow."

"Wow indeed," Amanda said, momentarily forgetting she had food on her fork. "We don't deserve him."

"It's from his parents, mostly."

"Why couldn't they be here for the wedding?"

"They were coming home from India on a late-night flight. Glenn picked them up at the airport and then drove them home for their family Christmas." Tony cut a bite of pancake. "I'm glad my parents aren't jet-setting all over the world."

"Unca! Unca-unca-unca," Cody screamed, racing into the kitchen and throwing himself at Tony's leg.

Adam followed more sedately. "You're up," he said in mild surprise. "And clothed," he added with a smirk.

"Yeah, I was allowed to have my clothes where I slept," Tony said dryly. "Heya Cody." He picked him up and put him on his knee. "Did you get that plane for Christmas?"

"Me fie plane!" Cody chirped excitedly.

"You *flew the plane*?" Tony asked, eyes wide. "Must have been low on pilots."

Cody nodded vigorously, making the adults laugh.

"He got to see the cockpit," Adam explained. "The co-pilot let him sit in his chair, and even push a button."

"Wow. I've never done that," Tony said. "Lucky you." He squeezed his nephew.

"We're actually on the way upstairs for a b-a-t-h," Adam said.

"R-k-c-f-p!" Cody shouted.

"He knows a few letters of the alphabet, and knows we're spelling things, but he hasn't quite caught on yet," Adam said with a chuckle. He picked up the toddler and flipped him upside down. "Astronaut flight!"

"Ass-not fie!" Cody screamed delightedly as they left the room.

"Oh my God, I think my ovaries just exploded," Amanda murmured.

"He's pretty cute," Tony agreed.

Sophia interrupted them next, carrying Travis. "Oh shoot, I just missed Adam, didn't I?" she asked.

"What do you need?" James put his fork down.

Sophia bit her lip. "I need to use the toilet."

"I've got him."

"You sure?" Tony asked.

"Yeah. I'm done eating, and you're here in case he freaks out."

"*Thank* you." Sophia passed the squirming infant to James and dashed out of the room.

"All I know about babies is that you should hold their head," James said, one hand hovering behind Travis's head. "But he's not resting and he's looking around."

"Oh, yeah, he's got a super strong neck," Tony said helpfully. "You're doing the right thing."

"Okay." James relaxed onto the chair a bit. "This isn't as scary as I thought it was going to be. Hey Travis. I'm your Uncle James."

The baby gave him a wide, gummy smile.

"Oh my God," Amanda murmured.

"What?" Tony asked.

"I want one."

Tony nodded. "Baby fever hits hard and fast, doesn't it?"

"We can discuss it after we get back from our honeymoon," James said. "We've got all the time in the world."

Acknowledgements

Thank you to my beta, Dani, for all your encouragement.
Thank you to my husband for continuously telling me that I'm doing a
good job and tightening up the beginnings of my chapters.
Thank you to Geneva for believing in me and my book(s).

www.ingramcontent.com/pod-product-compliance
Lightning Source LLC
Chambersburg PA
CBHW031207310726
48969CB00001B/248